A
DARKNESS
BLACK

TAMSEN SCHULTZ

*everafter*ROMANCE

EverAfter Romance
A Division of Diversion Publishing Corp.
443 Park Avenue South, Suite 1008
New York, New York 10016
www.EverAfterRomance.com

Cover Design by Sian Foulkes
Edited by Julie Molinari

For more information, email info@everafterromance.com

First EverAfter Romance edition April 2017.
Print ISBN: 978-1-63576-040-8

To my former teammates—Susan, Cate, Sheree, Melissa, Reid, and Clare. My four years of working with you wouldn't have been the same without your intelligence, humor, friendship, and yes, the hashtags #howwillIeverbeabletotopthisdedicationnexttime?

CHAPTER ONE

CALEB FORRESTER SCANNED HIS SURROUNDINGS. There were too many kids. They were everywhere. His chest tightened as a baby crawled between its father's feet. He opened his mouth, about to call out a warning, then stopped himself. He shouldn't—doing so would bring attention to him—but if the man wasn't careful, god only knew what could happen to the infant. Fortunately, the man reached down, scooped the baby up, and walked off.

Caleb let out a small sigh of relief then tried to loosen the constricting collar around his neck. The material of the black outfit he wore seemed to trap his body heat and reflect it back onto him in waves. His feet, confined in unfamiliar shoes, ached. He couldn't remember the last time he'd felt so uncomfortable—a sobering thought, especially considering he was there willingly.

"You're gonna dance with me, right, Uncle Caleb?" Emma Hathaway said, interrupting his thoughts from her perch on his lap.

He glanced down at the curly haired four year old dressed in a puffy dress and shiny shoes and found her big brown eyes watching him. He wasn't her uncle, not by blood, and Caleb rather suspected that Emma's mom, his friend Jesse Baker Hathaway, had given him the moniker just to make him sweat.

"Of course I am, sweet pea," he replied.

Tucked into a corner farthest away from all the action, he eyed the dance floor. He should be in South America or somewhere in North Africa or the Middle East. How he had come to be wearing a custom tuxedo at a decadent reception in the quaint little village of Windsor on a chilly fall evening waiting to dance with tiny little person, was lost on him.

Only it wasn't. Not really. Caleb watched a couple move into his line of sight—his younger sister Kit in the arms of Garret Cantona. Caleb had been to Windsor more times in the past year and a half than he had in the several years preceding put together. And it was all because of Kit. The strained and tumultuous relationship they'd had for years was a relationship he was now trying his best to rebuild.

As the music played, Kit slid her palms from Garret's chest to behind his neck then tilted her head up. Garret smiled and obligingly leaned down and brushed a kiss across her lips. Caleb looked away. He may be much closer to his sister now than he had been since they were kids but that didn't mean he had to sit there and watch his best friend kiss her. He had to draw the line somewhere, he thought as he turned his gaze back to the little girl who sat upon his knee.

"When, Uncle Caleb?" Emma pressed as she played with one of his jacket buttons.

"When this song ends, peanut." It was a slow one; a song that had many couples swaying—Kit and Garret, and Emma's parents, among them.

But not the bride and groom. Caleb swung his eyes over to where Drew and Carly Carmichael stood. Carly looked stunning in her gown, and Drew, with his fingers laced through hers, did not look the least bit interested in letting go of her. Smart man.

When he had first met Drew, Caleb hadn't taken kindly to the fact that the CIA agent had involved Kit in the trafficking of intelligence. Then, when Caleb's and Kit's two worlds had collided in a spectacular mess eighteen months ago, Drew had been caught in the middle. But despite that less than auspicious beginning, somehow, all these months later, Caleb now found himself with Drew as a friend. And during his frequent visits to Kit, Caleb had become, if not friends, then at least friendly, with most of Kit's social circle, including Carly. All of which explained his attendance at Windsor's wedding of the year.

Again, he tugged at his collar—god, he hated tuxedos. He thought about untying the bow tie altogether but as he glanced around at the well-dressed guests and his gaze landed again on a smiling Carly and Drew, the phrase "suck it up buttercup" came to mind. There were more important things to think about—like the happiness of his friends—than his minor discomfort.

Caleb let out a small sigh of resignation but then a baby howled and his heart leapt into his throat. His eyes jumped in the general direction of the sound and he started scanning the crowd to locate the specific source.

"That's just Charley," Emma said.

"Charley? Matty and Dash's baby, right?" Using a four-year-old for intel was a new low for him.

Emma nodded. "And he has a sister, too. Daphne."

"What about those two?" he asked with a nod to two little boys chasing a balloon.

"That's TJ and his cousin, Andrew. They're Carly's new family."

Caleb wasn't exactly sure what "new family" meant, but when he saw the boys run smack into the arms of two women, it made sense. Dani Fuller and Sam Carmichael pulled the boys onto their laps, laughing as they both proceeded to tickle their sons. TJ and Andrew seemed pleased with the tickle attack for approximately two seconds; then they both clambered off their respective mother's laps and dashed off. Caleb had met Dani at around the same time he'd met Drew. He knew she'd been an agent at the CIA too, but had left the agency several years earlier. Sam, her twin sister, was married to Drew's brother Jason. Carly's new family.

Caleb turned his eyes away from all the family. His stomach churned and he felt his pulse kick up. There were too many people, too much family, too much *love*.

And just having that thought made him feel like an asshole.

He didn't have anything against love, but having been more or less a loner for the past decade and a half, being relaxed in social situations, being comfortable with the casual intimacy of family and love, wasn't one of his strongest skills. But he did like seeing his sister happy, and as she came back into view—still in Garret's arms—it was quite clear that she was.

He smiled at the sight as he felt Emma tug at his bow tie.

"Is it crooked?" he asked, looking down at her.

"No," she said, bending it back and peering at the knot. "I just want to see how it's tied. My daddy wore the other kind of tie and my bows don't look like this."

Caleb smiled again. Emma liked to figure things out. She was a little like her brother James, a math and science savant who was currently out on the dance floor with his girlfriend.

"What's James's girlfriend's name?" he asked.

"Chelsea. She's nice, but I don't see her as much anymore since she went to college." Emma stumbled a bit over the word "college."

"That happens."

"Did you go to college?"

No, he thought. He'd had an education of a completely different kind. He'd spent his time and money teaching himself how to navigate the dirtiest, scummiest, least ethical people and places on the planet in an effort to destroy an empire his own father had built. It had been a far cry from the hallowed ivory towers his ancestors had graced.

"Let's go dance," he said as the song changed to something more upbeat, but not so upbeat that he wouldn't know what to do with his feet.

Dropping her question with a squeal, Emma slid from his lap and caught his hand in hers.

Her fingers and palm felt so tiny in his and, in a rush, memories of a different time, of a different child, sucked the breath from his lungs. He nearly yanked his hand back and made for the exit, but Emma turned and smiled at him.

He forced himself to breathe. He didn't have the right to pull away from her. He didn't have the right to hurt her feelings by breaking his promise to her. He knew that. He believed it. Still, his heart raced and his mind began to spiral down into a deep, dark place.

A place where children died. A place too black with sorrow to even allow the light of mourning in. A place where parents buried their babies and silently went crazy from the pain.

"Uncle Caleb?"

He looked down. They'd come to a stop on the dance floor. He couldn't dance. He couldn't do it. He had no right to celebrate.

"Caleb?"

At the sound of Garret's voice, Caleb's eyes came up. As his former partner in the world of black ops and covert assignments, Garret Cantona was about the only person who could understand the crippling impact of a memory.

"Are you okay?" Kit asked from within Garret's embrace.

Well, maybe Garret wasn't the only one. Looking into his sister's eyes, Caleb took a deep breath, inhaling her strength. She'd been through hell and still managed to love. Still managed to laugh. Still managed to dance.

He nodded. "It was just a moment, I'll be fine." Both Garret and Kit eyed him, but when Emma tugged on his hand, he turned his attention to the sprite. Moment by moment, he willed his feet to move. Thirty seconds later, he was dancing with Emma, truly dancing—spinning her around and making a promise to himself to always be her favorite uncle.

Not wanting to break his promise, he let her convince him to escort her around the floor for another two songs. And when a slower song came on, he swung her up into his arms and swayed to the music, to her unending delight.

David and Jesse smiled as he slid by them with their daughter in his arms. As he twirled her around, he caught sight of Vivi DeMarco and her husband Ian, dancing together with their son Jeffery. His eyes took in the swell of her belly, and even though his breath hitched slightly at the thought of another baby being brought into this world, he made a mental note to ask Kit when her friend was due with her second child.

Garret tapped Caleb on the shoulder. "May I cut in?"

"I don't know, peanut, what do you think?" Caleb asked, drawing his head back to look at Emma.

She looked at Garret, then at Caleb, then back again at Garret. "Is Kit going to dance with Uncle Caleb if I dance with you? I don't want him to feel left out."

"Yes, Kit is going to dance with her brother," Kit said, stepping around Garret as Caleb handed Emma over to him. The little girl grinned, obviously pleased to have two dance partners vying for her attention.

"He's not going to be nearly as fun as me, Emma, so you know where to find me when you get bored," Caleb said as he took his sister's hand in his.

"Ha!" Garret said as he gripped Emma and orchestrated a dramatic three-spin move away from them.

"I didn't see him twirl you like that," Caleb teased as his sister's hand came up to rest on his shoulder and they began moving to the music.

"Because he knows I'd probably get sick on him if he did."

Caleb's eyes shot to his sister's. She wasn't one to get motion sickness and so the most obvious reason for her to be feeling nauseated was...

"You should see your face," she said with a laugh. "But no, I'm not pregnant if that's what you were wondering. Just getting over a little touch of the flu."

Garret and Kit had been together for over a year and a half and had never mentioned marriage or kids, at least not to him. Knowing how happy they were, he hadn't given it much thought, but seeing so many kids there that night, along with so many other happy couples, he wondered.

"Do you want kids?" he asked, not sure he really wanted to know the answer. She was still his little sister and he just hadn't ever thought of her as having kids of her own.

Kit shrugged. "Probably not, but we'll see. We have so many

friends with kids that we certainly aren't lacking for babies to spoil or kids to act as surrogate aunt and uncle to."

Caleb wasn't quite sure what to say. Kids, and whether people had them, wanted them or didn't, was one of those topics he preferred to avoid discussing. Because whatever he said always felt like the wrong thing.

"What about you?" she asked.

A sharp pain lanced through him.

"I'm not even in a relationship," he managed to say.

She tilted her head and studied him. "I didn't mean *now*, it was a general question."

He shook his head. The thought wasn't one he could let himself contemplate. Not here. Not now. Not with so many families surrounding him and memories knocking at the door waiting to be let in.

Eyes the same golden color of his looked back at him. Caleb was about to make a stupid comment to deflect the tension coiling in his body when Kit abruptly stepped away. "I'm feeling a bit tired. Do you mind if I sit the rest of this one out?"

He wasn't sure if she was truly tired or had sensed his growing discomfort, but he nodded and led her to a seat. "Can I get you anything to drink? Some water or tea?" he asked.

She shook her head. "Why don't you go outside and have a look at the moon. It's full tonight and should be rising on the horizon about now."

He hesitated.

She smiled and squeezed his hand. "Go, Caleb. Go get some fresh air and let me know if I'm going to have to finagle Garret's jacket from him when we leave. It was starting to get chilly when we arrived for the reception. You can let me know if the temperature has dropped much more."

He knew she was bullshitting him then. She'd never have to finagle anything from Garret, ever. Despite the continued weirdness of having his sister and his former partner living together, he was grateful that Kit was with a good man.

He nodded and made his way toward the exit. The wedding reception was being held in a refurbished barn on the grounds of an upscale bed and breakfast. It was a huge building with exposed beams, rough-hewn wood, and long distances between exits. When he found one, Caleb stepped out into the cold night air and onto a large flagstone patio. He imagined that for warmer weather events, the big rolling doors to his right could be opened to allow guests to flow freely between the inside and outside settings.

As it was, on that cool evening, he was the only one out there. He looked up at the sky and saw the first evening stars twinkling dimly in the dusk. The moon hung over a darkened hillside, bright and unapologetic. Not quite full, but close.

Behind him, he heard the strains of music coming from the barn, along with the constant murmur of conversation punctuated by the laughter of one or another of the many guests. He hadn't been to too many weddings in his life, but even he knew that this one was something special. It wasn't flashy but had all the casual comforts money could buy, and he knew Carly and Drew had been more interested in creating an atmosphere that let them celebrate *with* their friends and family rather than one that placed them at the center of all the attention and festivities.

Not five minutes of quiet had passed when Caleb heard a door open and close behind him and he didn't need to look to know who had followed him out.

"Everything okay?" Jesse asked as she slid an arm through his.

"Yes, everything is fine."

"Liar," she countered, but didn't press further.

Jesse was like that. Of all of Kit's friends, she was the only one who had never been intimidated by him and she'd been the first of them to claim him as a friend. She was also the one he now counted on to look past his lies, forcing him to ask questions and confront his own doubts. He didn't always like it—hell, he rarely liked it—but she was also the only one who ever seemed to have any answers for him. She wrapped them up in questions and gave them to him, like little gifts, for him to unwrap when he was ready.

But tonight, he wasn't ready. And she seemed to sense that.

"I never thought I'd see the day when you wore a tux," she said, leaning into him a bit.

"I never thought I'd see the day when you came up to my chin. What are you wearing, six-inch heels?"

She bumped him with her hip. "Be nice," she said with laughter in her voice. "And it's not my heels, it's my hair. My hairdresser went a little overboard today."

He chuckled. Jesse Baker Hathaway claimed to be five-foot-two, but he'd swear she was five-foot-one if she was an inch.

"Emma seems to be doing well," he said.

"Mmm hmm," she nodded. "She is. It's been a little rough this fall though, since James hasn't been around as much. He's been so busy with school and then, when he does have free time, he tends to go visit Chelsea at college. Emma misses him a lot, and it's been much quieter at home, but she's getting used to being more or less the only child."

"I'm sure that will be very tough for her. Being the only child."

Again, she bumped him with her hip. "Stop," she said, laughing quietly in the night. "She's not totally spoiled."

"Not totally, no," he answered. "At least not until I come to town."

"Or send ridiculous gifts. Really, the four-foot stuffed pumpkin was a bit much."

"Just getting you back for having her call me Uncle Caleb."

"You love it."

He kind of did, so he said nothing. The silence of the night seeped into his bones, as did the cold. He turned to look at Jesse to make sure she had a coat on.

"You should have something warmer," he said, eyeing the wrap she wore around her shoulders.

She shook her head. "I'm fine," she paused. "How are you, really, Caleb?"

"I'm fine," he mimicked her.

She sighed and he knew she was about to say more, but in that moment his phone buzzed in his pocket with a text message.

She rolled her eyes and shook her head, as he reached for the device.

"Gee sorry, I have to get this." He held his phone out, waving it in front of her with an unrepentant grin. But then he saw a name flash on the screen and his grin died.

"Caleb?"

He hit the ignore button and slid his phone back into his pocket.

"Who was that?"

"No one." He was aware of the slight tremble of his hand in his pocket as he answered Jesse.

"I saw the name," Jesse said. "Who is Catherine?"

He was about to say "no one" again when his phone vibrated. He heard it. Jesse heard it.

"Aren't you going to answer it?"

"Drop it."

"Oh, hell no," she answered with a knowing laugh. "Wrong answer, Caleb. In more ways than one, that was the wrong answer, and you know it."

He did know it. Jesse had raised two boys, dealt with the loss of a less than stellar husband, and was no shrinking violet. He hadn't thought about his command before he'd issued it. Had he done that, he would have realized that, of all the things he could have said to Jesse, telling her to drop it was the exact wrong one.

He exhaled. "It's nothing, Jesse. Please."

The "please" gave her pause and for about three seconds he held out hope that she would let it go.

"Caleb, I don't know who Catherine is, but I can feel the tension in your body now." She gave his arm, the one she still had hers looped through, a gentle nudge to prove her point. "Only someone who means something to you would cause that kind of reaction."

And that was where she left it. With a little something for him to think about. A question posed as a comment. Because she was right, there were very few people who would cause him to react the way he had. So, what did Catherine mean to him?

"She's Tommy's widow," he said softly.

Her quick inhale gave him some satisfaction. Tommy was someone he didn't talk about. Caleb would like to say he didn't ever talk about him, but that clearly wasn't the case. There was one person who knew. Unfortunately, she was standing right beside him.

"Maybe it's time," she said.

He turned his head and looked down at her green eyes.

She didn't blink or back down. "I'll leave you to it," she said as if it were a forgone conclusion he would do the right thing.

Behind him, he heard the sounds of the reception grow louder and then quieter again as Jesse opened and closed the door to the barn. His phone buzzed again. His fingers curled around the device in his pocket. It was warm from being close to his body, the edges sleek and sharp.

It vibrated in his hand.

He made his way to a bench at the edge of the patio and pulled it from his pocket as he sat with his back to the reception.

"Caleb?" the message read.

The second message said, "Is this the right number?"

He stared at the phone for a long moment, his fingers feeling clumsy and uncoordinated.

"Hi Cate," he typed back. "Yes, it's the right number."

"Thank god," came the immediate reply. Then, after a moment, "Are you anywhere near the eastern seaboard? The north part?"

His eyes lifted. The bucolic Hudson Valley spread out before him. It was too dark to see the colors of the leaves but he knew, in the light of day, fall was still making its statement there in the Northeast.

"Yes," he typed back. Then he waited. And waited.

"Cate?"

"Never mind," she replied. "Sorry to have bothered you. I'm glad you're stateside."

Never mind?

"Cate."

He could all but hear her sigh.

"Honestly, Caleb, I'm sorry. It's nothing, just me being paranoid. Give me a call sometime and we'll catch up."

Dismissed. Only it didn't work that way.

"What's going on?" he wrote. "Where are you?"

Nothing came back.

"I swear to god, Cate, I can track your phone if I need to."

"Nice to know you haven't changed. I'm in New Hampshire. Working a job."

"And?"

She paused again before answering. "It's weird. Something strange is going on but it could just be the people I'm working for."

"Strange enough that you texted me after five years?"

"I'm not the only one with a phone." No hesitation there. He let out a deep breath.

"Where are you?"

"New Hampshire," she wrote again.

"Where in New Hampshire? Specifically," he added.

"I'm managing a family reunion at The Washington House. It's a private home not far from the resort."

Caleb ran a hand over the back of his neck and turned his attention to the stars. He wasn't one to really believe in heaven and all that, but he wondered what Tommy would be thinking right now—that Caleb should go to her, or stay the hell away?

Behind him, he heard the shriek of one of the many kids attending the reception. A shriek of laughter and love.

He rubbed his chest then returned his clumsy fingers to the screen of his phone, typing, "I'll be there in six hours." Then he shut the device off and slid it back into his pocket, not wanting her to give him any excuses to back out.

• • •

Catherine Thomson stared at her phone for a good long while. She'd texted Caleb back, telling him not to come, but had received nothing in response. She shouldn't have contacted him in the first place.

Standing in the kitchen of the carriage house that had been converted into a large three-bedroom guesthouse, she listened to her daughter in the bathtub upstairs. Elise was singing a song with her nanny, Jana.

Cate stepped outside onto the small front porch and shut the door quietly behind her. The chill of the night seeped through her lightweight sweater and jeans, but she paid it no mind. Reluctantly, her gaze went to the small building about five-hundred feet to her left. Looking at it wouldn't conjure Caleb, but she could feel his presence already occupying the empty space.

For a fleeting moment, she regretted not having housed any of the five staff members in the renovated ice house, but it hadn't made sense to put one or two in the one-bedroom guest quarters while leaving the rest in the main house. So all five were housed on the third floor of The Washington House, like servants of days gone by. And the former ice house was vacant.

It wouldn't be for long.

The thought of Caleb Forrester being so close caused her stomach to tighten and she had to will herself to breathe slowly. It had been five years since she'd seen him. Five years since . . .

Abruptly, Cate switched her focus across the driveway to the back of the main house. Warm light glowed from the windows of the grand dame of a building. Some locals called it a castle, some an eyesore, but there was no denying that The Washington House wasn't content to be obscure.

Originally built in the late 1800s as the hunting lodge of a prominent Boston family—though calling it a "lodge" was akin to calling the houses of Newport "cottages"—the four-story white stone home boasted sixteen bedrooms, twenty bathrooms, three billiard rooms, two parlors, two bars, servants' quarters, and much more. It was the perfect location for the Whatley family reunion, an event Cate had been organizing every year for nearly a decade.

Only this year it was different.

Her eyes traveled over the windows at the back of the main house. There were sixteen people inside, twenty-one if she included her staff, some of whom were serving dinner just then.

She glanced at her watch. Caleb would be there in less than five and a half hours.

It was a good thing.

It was a good thing, she told herself. Because she was fairly certain someone inside that house was going to be murdered.

CHAPTER 2

CATE ROLLED OVER AND RETRIEVED her vibrating phone from the bedside table. Instead of waiting for Caleb in her own room, she'd lain down beside her daughter and had, apparently, fallen asleep.

Bringing her phone to life, she blinked at the sudden light.

"I think I'm here," read his text.

Smiling, she ran her fingers through her hair, pushing it out of her face, then swung her feet down to the floor. The Washington House had no signs, no grand entry announcing what lay up the drive. There was just a humble, though large, wrought iron gate that remained open night and day.

"Can you see the main house?" she texted back as she headed downstairs. Pausing in the small foyer, she pulled a pair of fuzzy boots on over her leggings then began rummaging amongst the coat hooks for a quilted flannel shirt to cover the tank top she'd fallen asleep in.

Her phone lit up. "I can see a house. Big. Looks like maybe Teddy Roosevelt should be in residence. If he were Dracula."

That brought out a chuckle from her as she tugged a knit cap over her long hair.

"That's the one," she replied. "Keep to the right around the house. Pull up in the back and you'll see me."

As Cate silently exited the carriage house and made her way toward to the ice house, the casualness of the phrase "you'll see me" hit her. The headlights of his car came into view, flashing across her as he made the turn around the back of the house then landing back on the driveway. Her stomach tightened and her heart rate picked up.

Her mind flashed to memories of the last time she'd seen him and how they'd been together then—barely able to meet each other's glances. Even if the reason she'd asked for his help now wasn't so serious, there would be nothing casual about seeing Caleb again.

She tugged her knit cap down farther then crossed her arms over her chest as she stood on the porch of the ice house and watched Caleb park. The night was cold, much colder than the nights had been even a week earlier, but that was, she supposed, how it was this time of year in New England.

She glanced up at the back of the main house as Caleb rummaged for something in his Range Rover. At nearly one o'clock in the morning, the huge house was dark—no smoke coming from the chimneys, no light pouring from the libraries or games room. She scanned the windows of the second level, the floor where the Whatley family lay asleep. There was a dim light visible around the edge of the curtains in Nikki and Sasha's room, a nightlight for the young girls. Edith and Michael hadn't yet decided it was too cold; their window was cracked open to let the night air, or perhaps sounds, in. The house looked to be in deep slumber, as it should.

She dropped her eyes back to the vehicle and found Caleb, carrying a large duffel bag, taking his first strides toward her. Her gaze tracked his movements as he approached. The set of his shoulders, the pace of his gait—it was all so familiar that, for a brief moment, she felt a wave of safety, of giddy happiness, wash through her. But then, when he stopped before her, she looked into his golden eyes and, like someone coming home after a long absence, she wondered if she would be welcome again.

"Caleb," she said, unable to take her eyes from his. He had never been an easy man to read, not even when she'd known him well. And now, well, now his face revealed nothing but shadows.

He hesitated, then bent to place a kiss on her cheek. "Cate."

She cleared her throat and rubbed her hands down her arms. "Let's go inside," she said, turning toward the front door of the ice house. Shaped much like a cross, it was a decent-sized building and as she opened the door and gestured Caleb in, a gentle caress of warm air hit her. "I turned the heat on and had the bed made up once I knew you were coming. I also had the staff bring a few things over for the kitchen," she added.

She followed Caleb in, shutting the door behind them, then came to stand beside him where he'd paused. The actual ice hole was far beneath where they now stood, but back in the day, when parties came up to hunt and fish, blocks were brought up from below and stored at ground level for easy access. Four former storage areas formed the large cross that now made up the current guest suite, a single living space that comfortably accommodated two guests.

A small but well-equipped kitchen with a round table for four sat immediately to their right, its large double-paned window facing the back of the main house. A bedroom area hosting a king-size bed and two side tables lay in one of the arms of the cross. Opposite the sleeping area was a bathroom that was set far enough back into its own arm that a fireplace, anchored against an internal wall, created a small sitting area with two cozy-looking upholstered chairs. The far end of the cross, opposite the kitchen, held a dresser along one of its long walls, a large window in its back wall, and a door leading onto a back porch in its third.

Caleb walked to the sleeping area and dropped his bag by the bed. When he turned to face her, he was finally visible in the light cast by the bedside lamp she'd turned on earlier.

"Here you go," she said, holding out the ice house keys.

Again, he hesitated, then came forward and let her drop them into his hand. She turned toward the kitchen as he shoved the keys into his pocket. A moment later, he was standing beside her, shoulder to shoulder, looking out the window toward the main house.

"What's going on, Cate?"

In the warmth of the room, she slid the cap off her head and held it in her hands. The hat was a funny little thing, something Elise had picked out for her the year before, when they'd been in

Aspen for a few weeks. Elise had said she'd liked it because the grassy green color matched Cate's eyes. It didn't matter that it also had a red dinosaur-like ridge that ran from the top to the bottom and red, almost-flower-shaped weird little ears poking out the top. Elise had liked the color.

"You know I've been doing this job for a long time," she said.

"I know. You started right after I met you. What was that, fifteen, sixteen years ago?"

She didn't want to go back that far, back to the girl she'd been when she'd first met Caleb and Tommy. "I've been managing the reunions of this family, the Whatley family, each year for nine years," she continued. "This is the third time it's been here at The Washington House."

"What is this place?" he asked with nod out the window toward the building that loomed before them.

"It was a hunting lodge for a prominent Boston family when it was built. Now it's a boutique bed and breakfast, but this month it's rented out exclusively for the Whatley family," she said, knowing that eventually Caleb would want more detail.

"Rich?" he asked.

She inclined her head. "Very."

"And?"

She rolled the fabric of one of the cap's flower-ears in her fingers.

"You contacted me after five years of radio silence, Cate. What's going on?"

She turned her head and looked at him. "You could have contacted me too."

He held her gaze for a long moment then turned back toward the main house. "You said in your text that you thought you were being paranoid. About what?"

She should have known he wouldn't react to her comment. A small, childish part of her had wanted to provoke him, and whether he saw that and chose not to indulge her or had just decided not to discuss that elephant in the room, she had to admit, she was a bit grateful. It was too late, the day had been too long, and there were too many other questions she wanted to ask him.

"I think somebody is trying to kill one of the Whatleys," she said, voicing her worry for the first time.

To his credit, Caleb didn't turn any disbelieving eyes on her. He simply studied the house instead. After several moments of silence, he asked, "What makes you say that?"

Cate took a deep breath. "Two days ago, some of the family members were out for a ride, we have a stable full of horses here," she said, waving in the general direction of the stables, not that he'd know that. "Anyway, two of them came across a thick wire that had been strung between two trees across the trail."

"Was anyone hurt?"

She shook her head. "Edith's horse had lost a shoe, so she and Michael were walking, leading their horses when they discovered it."

"Michael and Edith?"

"Michael is a Whatley. Edith is his girlfriend," she answered.

"Where there any others out that day?"

She nodded but as Caleb's gaze was still fixed on the house, she doubted he'd seen. "Yes, but because it was a beautiful day to be outside, the other three members of the party had opted to take the longer way back on a different trail."

"That was lucky."

"Yes," she said into the quiet night. It was. If any member of that party had been galloping along that trail and hit that wire . . .

"Do you still have the wire?"

"Yes, it's in the barn. Do you want me to bring it to you tomorrow?"

"Yes, please. Is there anything else?"

She took another deep breath and exhaled. "Nothing con-crete. But I've been working with this family for nine years and something feels, I don't know, *off* this time. I've been hearing lots of arguing behind closed doors and there's this tension between nearly all of them that I've never noticed before—except for Dixie, Nikki, and Sasha; they seem fine."

"Dixie, Nikki, and Sasha?"

"Nikki and Sasha are Sabrina and Dominque's daughters. They are nine and eleven. Dixie is the youngest of the cousins. She's a bit of a free spirit."

"How many family members are here?"

"Sixteen now. The Italian cousins are coming next weekend, that will add three more."

Caleb placed his hands on the counter and leaned forward, as if to get a better look at the huge house. She studied his profile as he stared, caught up in his own thoughts. The first time she'd ever seen him, he been turned with his profile to her. Tommy had taken her to a dive bar in Key West to meet his best friend. When they'd walked in, Caleb had been sipping a beer, staring out at the ocean. He'd been young—hell, they'd all been young—but he'd been so taciturn, so serious. Later that night, she'd asked Tommy how and why Caleb had gotten into the business, but not even Tommy had known. All he could say was that Caleb hadn't come from the military as he had, which was, in itself, unusual. She had wondered more than a few times over the course of her friendship with Caleb what it was that had brought him into the world of black ops and covert assignments, but she'd never asked.

After all these years, after everything she knew about him, there was still so much she didn't.

Pushing away from the counter, Cate headed to a cabinet, grabbed a glass, and filled it with water. Caleb spared her a glance, but turned his attention back to the main house.

"Do you think I'm crazy?" she asked. The thought had crossed her mind. Maybe she was overreacting; maybe the wire was nothing but an accident.

Caleb shook his head. "No, I think if you think something is going on, it probably is."

She exhaled a long breath. She hadn't realized how much she'd wanted him to believe her. Not because she was happy about what it would mean if she were right, but because, she now understood, she'd very badly needed someone to believe her, to trust her.

"Do you have background checks on the family? And staff?" he asked, his eyes still fixed on the larger house.

"On the staff, yes, but not the family. I do have files on the family members' personalities—their likes, dislikes, those sorts of things."

He studied the house a moment longer then turned toward her and crossed his arms across his chest. "Bring them to me tomorrow?"

She nodded. "I have a staff meeting at six thirty tomorrow morning. It should take about forty-five minutes. Elise doesn't usually wake up until about eight fifteen or eight thirty, so I'll bring everything over after the staff meeting. We can talk, figure out what to do, and then go from there?"

"Who's Elise?"

Cate's head drew back at the question. Elise was her world; it hadn't occurred to her that Caleb wouldn't know about her. But then again, how would he?

"She's . . ." Cate paused and cleared her throat. "Elise is my daughter. She's four. I was three weeks pregnant when Tommy died. I didn't realize for another month or so . . ." She let her voice trail off as she watched the color drain slowly from Caleb's face.

"You have a daughter?" His voice was nearly a whisper.

Comprehending the shock he must have been feeling, she gave a shaky bob of her head.

"Tommy has another daughter?"

She nodded again, but glanced away at his oblique reference to her first daughter with Tommy. Brooke had been the little girl Caleb had known. She'd been everything to Tommy and had always thought of Caleb as her second father, or more like the best uncle a girl could have. And then Brooke was gone, and then Tommy was gone too. Cate knew with searing exactitude how much she'd lost that year, but for the first time, it occurred to her that she wasn't the only one who had lost nearly everything.

"Yes, he does," she answered, meeting Caleb's gaze. "She has his eyes and is quick as a whip. Though her sense of humor seems to come more from me."

"She's already sarcastic at four?"

"You wouldn't think it was possible, but yes," she said with a small roll of her eyes. Elise often surprised her too. "She's a rather serious child, though." Unlike Brooke, who took after Tommy and loved to be the life of the party, was left unsaid.

"Will you let me meet her?"

The phrasing of the question caught her off guard, as if she might need to protect Elise from Caleb. She had no idea where his doubt could have stemmed from. Never, not for a single moment, would she have thought to deny Caleb the chance to meet Elise.

"Of course."

Caleb's shoulders seemed to relax a bit.

Still confused by his question, but acknowledging that it was nearing two o'clock in the morning and that she may not be at her sharpest, she let it go. "I'll come by at a little after seven," she said, moving toward the door and placing her hand on the doorknob.

Caleb's eyes tracked her movements, but he only inclined his head in response.

"Sleep well, and if you need anything, let me know in the morning."

Again, he nodded.

A beat passed then she opened the door and stepped out. She was about to say good night when the doubt she had heard in his voice tugged at her. She turned back to face him.

"Thank you, Caleb. Thank you for coming when I needed you." Rather than wait for a response, she mumbled a rapid "good night" and pulled the door shut behind her.

The dark of the night was punctuated with only the sound of her feet crunching on the gravel as she made her way back to the carriage house. Until she heard the front door of the ice house open behind her. She glanced back, pausing as Caleb stepped out onto the small porch.

And then she smiled, knowing he'd come out to make sure she made it back to her lodging safely. She gave him a quick, small wave then resumed the walk back to her own bed, with Caleb watching over her the entire way.

• • •

In the muted light of the morning, Caleb, standing at the kitchen window as his coffee percolated beside him, caught a flash of movement to his right. Turning his head, he spotted Cate making her way across the drive toward the main house, presumably for the six thirty staff meeting she'd mentioned. She was wearing the same green hat—the one with the weird ears—she'd worn the night before but instead of the leggings, flannel shirt, and booties she'd greeted him in, she wore black, heeled boots, jeans, and a white down vest over a dark green, long sleeved shirt. She strode the distance without so much as a glance in his direction, and when the house swallowed her from sight, his eyes lingered for a moment, perhaps waiting to see if the behemoth might spit her back out again. When it didn't, he poured himself a cup of coffee, grabbed his laptop, and made his way to the small round table.

Bringing the device to life and logging onto The Washington House network, he ran a public search of the Whatley family. Thousands of results appeared instantly, but rather than cull through them, he found his eyes, and attention, drifting back toward the front window.

Given his past with Cate, he knew there was nowhere else he could be at that moment; he needed, and wanted, to be there helping her. But echoes of the last time he'd seen her refused to silence themselves and the clawing, angry guilt didn't leave much room in his mind for anything else. He knew he needed to make those voices stop—those voices that told him everything that had happened had been his fault—if he was going to be of any use to her. Only he didn't know how.

He glanced at the clock and thought about going for a run,

but she'd be back to talk with him in less than forty minutes. Not enough time to run off his demons, shower, and change. With an inward curse he forced himself to focus as he turned back to his laptop and the quagmire that was the Whatley family.

The first Douglas Whatley had started the family business by inventing a machine that shaped metals used by the auto manufacturers just prior to World War II. During the war, it was found to be an invaluable asset in building ships and airplanes as well, and the dynasty had started from there. In the mid-seventies, the enterprise, which had expanded into manufacturing all sorts of tangible goods, was taken over by Douglas Whatley's eldest son, Douglas the Second. *That* Douglas ran the business through the insanely profitable years of the eighties and nineties, but when the downturn of the early 2000s hit, he handed the business over to the current head of the family, Douglas Whatley the Third.

By all accounts, Douglas the Third had learned well from his forefathers. He made smart investments, even smarter cutbacks, and managed to bring his company through the recession intact. While it wasn't growing at quite the same rate as it had in the eighties and nineties, it was growing and producing consistently strong financial results.

Caleb saved a few articles to his hard drive then rose to pour himself another cup of coffee. Deciding food might help him stay focused, he glanced in the fridge and noted that Cate had had it stocked with many of his favorite staples—eggs, milk, some greens, yogurt, and cheese. He had no doubt that when he looked through the cupboards, he'd find bread, cereal, and fruit, as well. He decided that could wait though and instead, he opened the drawer in the fridge labelled "meat." Sure enough, there it was, a container of cooked rice and a round of linguiça sausage. He stared at the two items, feeling his heart thudding in his chest. How many mornings had she made her Hawaiian breakfast for Tommy and him? How many times had he teased her, saying that her cooking was the only reason he and Tommy had made it through whatever hell had just come back from?

He slammed the drawer shut just as a knock came at the front door. He closed the fridge and leaned against its cool stainless steel; the touch of it against his heated skin bringing him back to his current time and place. With one deep breath, he stepped away from the memories and toward the front door.

"Cate," he said, moving aside to let her in.

"Did you sleep well?" she asked, moving straight toward the table where his computer sat.

"Well enough. Coffee?"

"Please," she said as she dropped a file on the table, unzipped her vest, and pulled off her hat. Her long red hair was pulled up into a sleek ponytail, but the pull of the hat had created all sorts of static and loose strands were sticking straight out or clinging to her face. She ran her hand over her head in an attempt to tame them as he handed her a mug.

"Still like it black?" he asked.

"Yes, thank you," she answered, smoothing a hand over her hair one more time. It wasn't completely static-free when she slid her vest off and sat beside him, but it wasn't clinging to her face and neck quite as much.

"What's this?" he asked, sliding the folder toward him.

"The background checks on the seven staff members, not including me. There are three from my company and four that work for The Washington House. All but two are staying in the house—the groundskeeper has a small apartment behind the equipment shed and the barn manager has one on the second floor of the barn. The company keeps tabs on its own employees but we also run checks on any local staff before bringing guests to the location. Information on the Whatley family is in there too."

"Do you think the staff have anything to do with it?" he asked, opting to get her opinion before he read the files.

She took a sip of her coffee and, though her eyes were fixed in his direction, he knew she wasn't really focused on him.

"I don't know," she sighed. "At this point, I'm not entirely convinced there's an 'it' at all."

He could tell the moment her green eyes refocused on him.

Years ago, Cate had shown him photos of her grandmother on her father's side. A stunning Japanese actress who had married a US soldier during WW II and then moved to Hawaii with him, her face and eyes had been the most expressive Caleb had ever seen—and he'd only seen them in photos.

Cate had inherited those eyes, altered through the generations of mixed marriages, but the breadth of expression was the same. Even when she wanted to, Cate couldn't hide her emotions. Right now, it was clear she was doubting herself.

"You *are* convinced, Cate. You know something is going on. Maybe you don't want to admit it, but your gut is telling you that something is off."

"What if my gut is wrong?"

Caleb shrugged. He didn't have any proof yet, but he knew Cate was an intuitive person. She had been a champion surfer before she'd met and married Tommy and there was no way she could have been successful at either endeavor—the sport or the marriage—without good, strong intuition.

"If you're wrong, the worst case scenario is that you and I have a chance to catch up. Maybe I can even meet Elise . . ."

For the moment, the fact that he didn't doubt her seemed to be enough. She smiled and answered his original question. "Do I think the staff is involved? No, I don't. Like I said, our company employees are thoroughly vetted and regularly monitored. To my knowledge, the only ones that have ever had any contact with anyone from the Whatley family are the two that have worked their family reunions with me before. As for the local staff, again, I would be hard pressed to think that they had anything to do with it. All four of them have been with The Washington House for years. It would seem odd if one of them suddenly wanted to kill one of the Whatleys. Well, not really odd, I suppose." She paused, her brow furrowed in thought. "I guess what I'm trying to say is that if one of the local staff members had wanted to kill someone from the Whatley family, they would have left a lot to chance."

"How so?"

"Well, no one here even knew the family was coming until two days before they all arrived. They knew that the house had been rented out for a private party, of course, but not for whom. It's part of the protocol my company has in place—the less lead time a location has, the less likely there will be any leaks. Especially if we're dealing with celebrities."

"And there was no change in staff after you informed them of who would be staying here?"

Cate shook her head.

Given this information, he had to agree with her that it was unlikely someone from The Washington House was involved. Still, to be on the safe side, he'd investigate each of them.

"What about your staff?" he asked.

Again, she shook her head. "Like I said, two of them, Greg and Margaret, have worked this reunion with me for the past five years. Unless something egregious happened at one of the prior reunions that would have caused one of them to want to take action during this reunion, I would have a hard time believing that either are involved. Not to mention, Margaret has been with the company for ages, a lot longer than I have. I suppose everyone is capable of murder in some circumstance, but I have a hard time imagining her capable of anything cold-blooded."

Caleb thumbed through the files as she spoke. Margaret Brown was a sixty-two year old woman who was the head chef. She'd worked all over the world for various events hosted by the company Cate worked for. She had two grandchildren and was planning to retire soon. Again, he agreed with Cate's assessment.

"What about the other one? Your third staff member?"

"Christine is fairly new to the company. I don't know her all that well."

Caleb glanced at the file. Christine Jefferson was a Texas-born twenty-seven-year-old who'd gone to a prominent university in the northeast on a scholarship and graduated with honors, receiving her degree in tourism and hospitality. Not exactly the profile of the type of person who'd murder a guest while working for one of the most prestigious event planning companies in the US.

"And the family?" he asked as he pulled out a substantial stack of papers held together with a black binder clip.

"It's a big family. Much bigger than just the people coming here this month. Not everyone comes to the reunions."

"Why not?"

Cate shrugged. "Time, interest, those sorts of things. The cousins still make enough off of their dividends that they don't really have to work, but many, I'd say most, still do. Getting a month off from work can be difficult, and even if they manage it, they don't always want to spend what little vacation they get with extended family. Especially if their extended family isn't always the nicest or most interesting."

"You said 'cousins,' how many are there?"

Cate reached over and took the first few sheets of paper from the family files. "These are the siblings. You'll hear two groups referred to while you're here: the siblings and the cousins. Even though there are second cousins in the mix too, when we refer to the 'cousins,' we generally mean the grandchildren of the first Douglas Whatley, the Whatley who started the company before WWII. The first Douglas Whatley, long since deceased, had eight kids; of those eight *siblings*, five are still alive, but only two, Agnes and Edward, are here this month. Isabell Whatley, one of Agnes and Edward's younger sisters, passed away several years ago, but her widower, Sebastian Brandt, came to the reunion with their two children." As she spoke, she pointed out smaller stacks of paper containing information about the two siblings and the sibling-in-law in attendance.

He glanced down at the mini dossiers. Agnes was eighty-five years old, had never married, had no children, and had never worked. Edward was eighty-two, had lost his wife two years prior, and had been a history professor at a college in Maine for his entire career. He'd never had children either. Sebastian, widower of Isabell

Whatley, had also been a professor, but of literature at a university in Massachusetts.

"Okay, so those are the three siblings. You said there were sixteen people in the house, with three more to come. So the remaining thirteen must be the cousins?"

"Yes, and second cousins. But if we just call them all 'cousins,' this is who we have." She arranged the files in front of him.

He had glanced up as she'd spoken and noticed that she'd finished her coffee. "More coffee? I can put another pot on," he offered. He remembered that, much like his sister, Cate preferred tea, but he also knew that because *he* preferred coffee, it was unlikely that she'd stocked any tea in his kitchen here.

She looked up from the papers and gave a small laugh. "That was already my second cup today. I ran out of tea this morning."

"Water? Juice?"

She shook her head. "No, thanks, I'll just have something when I have breakfast with Elise and our nanny, Jana."

Realizing that she'd probably want to get back to her daughter sooner rather than later, Caleb returned his attention to the documents.

"Michael Tarantola Whatley and his brother Anthony Tarantola Whatley," she continued, pointing to two files. "Michael is a bit of a playboy, or rather he *was*. Of all the cousins, he was the one who always seemed to be living the high life—fast cars, faster planes, good whiskey—with the best of everything, he was always the life of the party. That said, he seems to be calming down now that he's reached his late forties. He has his girlfriend, Edith Barnard, here with him. They've been together for about two years."

"And does he work?"

"Yes, he does. He still has a kind of magnetism that draws the other cousins to him and he's definitely still the life of the party, but he seems more focused on his job these days. I know he was recently promoted to a vice president role, despite the fact that Douglas the Third, the current head of the family enterprises, started him out pretty low on the totem pole just a few years ago."

Caleb let his eyes wander over the top page of the dossier on Michael Whatley then, after setting it aside, picked up another. "What about Anthony? And what's with the matching middle names?"

Cate let out a small laugh. "Michael and Anthony's father is Jed Whatley, the youngest of the siblings. He's still alive but rarely, if ever, attends these family reunions. Jed married a woman by the name of Alessandra Marie Tarantola. From the name, I'm sure you can guess she's Italian. Old Boston Italian family, if you get what I mean."

"Mafia?"

Cate gave a reluctant nod. "No one has ever said as much, but it's been alluded to. Both of the boys carry her family's name, though it's interesting that Michael, the younger son, was named after her father, and not Anthony, the eldest. You may hear one of the cousins call him Michael 'Mikey-Son.' It's what Jed and Alessandra always call him to distinguish him from his grandfather and some of the cousins picked up on it."

"And is Jed busy with Tarantola family business? Is that why he doesn't attend the reunions?"

"I don't actually know," Cate said, turning her eyes down to the files of Michael and Anthony. "I've met him twice and he's very charming, very distinguished, and not at all forthcoming. I didn't find I wanted to pry too much."

Caleb's lips tipped into a small smile. Smart girl. "Okay, so back to Anthony."

"Anthony is married, has been for years, but his wife isn't here. He works with Douglas running the Whatley family business. He's been doing one thing or another for them since shortly after finishing college."

"Any ties to his mother's family? Any chance the wire could have something to do with the Tarantola side of the family?"

Cate pursed her lips in thought before answering. "It's not a world I'm at all familiar with, so I wouldn't even hazard a guess. Although I will say that Anthony seems pretty committed to the

Whatley dynasty and that, until recently, Michael seemed not at all committed to anything, so I'm not sure if either would have had time for the other half of their family."

Caleb noted Cate's hesitancy, but made a mental note to look into the Tarantola family—those kinds of ties weren't so easily cast off. Pushing aside the files on the two brothers, he rose and began pacing the room. He didn't need to study the documents as she talked, he could do that later. "Who else?"

"Isiah Whatley and his wife, Livia, are here. He's Sabrina's brother and, as I mentioned last night, Sabrina is here with her wife and their two daughters."

"Do they get long?"

"Who? The cousins with their respective spouses, or the brother and sister?"

"Yes," he answered.

She smiled at that. "Sabrina and Isiah seem close, although Sabrina is estranged from their father, Jonathan Whatley, who doesn't approve of her being gay."

"Nice," Caleb said.

"Yes, he's a charming man. Sabrina and Dominique have always had a good relationship as far as I could tell, but they *are* one of the couples I've heard fighting behind closed doors."

"What do they do?"

"Sabrina was a teacher, but she's been at home with the girls for the past few years. Dominique is an attorney. She has a big case right now, so she's spending a lot of time either working or driving to and from Boston for meetings."

Caleb pondered that for a moment. "Was Sabrina out riding the day you found the wire? You mentioned three other people besides Michael and Edith."

"She was," Cate said. "Along with Erica Brandt and Dixie."

Spouses were usually the first suspects, for good reason. If Sabrina was the target, Dominique would need to be looked at closely. He was jumping the gun with that line of thinking though.

He'd have to know all the players before he could even begin to guess who the target or perpetrators might be.

"Erica and Dixie?"

"Cousins. Dixie is here with her boyfriend. She's the only daughter of Trip Whatley, another one of the siblings. As I mentioned last night, she's a bit of a free spirit.

"Erica Brandt is here with her brother, Mark. They're the children of Sebastian, whom I mentioned earlier. Erica is an artist and Mark owns his own tech company, though what it does, I don't really know."

Caleb paused in his pacing and now stood with his hands resting on the back of the chair he'd vacated. "What about the family patriarch. Douglas the Third? These reunions seem like a pretty big production for him to just not attend." The question had been bothering him since he'd realized Cate hadn't included a dossier of the man in the documents she'd shared with him.

Cate bobbed her head. "They are a big production, and they cost the family quite a bit of money, but Douglas never comes and I don't know why. I've heard the cousins say that he used to attend when his own father, Douglas the Second, was still alive. That was before my time, though, so I can't really say if his father's death had anything to do with why he stopped coming, or if there was some other reason."

"Have you ever met him?" Caleb asked, straightening away from the chair.

"Not in person, just over the phone."

"And how does he seem to you?"

Cate frowned. "What do you mean?"

"Has he ever said anything about his cousins? Or about taking over the family business when so many of his aunts and uncles are still alive? Did he discuss anything personal?"

"No, actually. He's never talked about any of those things," Cate said after a moment. "I wouldn't expect him to discuss anything personal, but now that you ask, I realize that not once, in the dozens, maybe even hundreds of calls I've had with him over the years, has he mentioned even one of his cousins by name. He's efficient and decisive and not at all rude. Just very businesslike."

For a moment, Caleb let his mind ponder the question of what kind of man Douglas the Third was and why he never mentioned his family members by name. It didn't take long for a number of reasons to pop into his mind—security and animosity being two of them. But it wasn't either of those reasons that settled uncomfortably in Caleb's stomach. Perhaps he and Douglas the Third had something in common. Perhaps being "someone like him," meant a man who hid from himself by hiding from his connections.

Not wanting to explore that aspect of his own personality, even tangentially through Douglas Whatley, Caleb sat back down, gathered the documents Cate had already discussed, and set them to the side. "So that's all sixteen that are here," he said. "Thirteen cousins, including second cousins Nikki and Sasha, and three siblings. I assume the three that are coming next weekend are the Italian cousins?" he asked, tapping the remaining files.

Cate nodded. "Francesca, Nico, and Alex Gianni. Their mother, Anna Whatley, was Isabelle's twin. She married an Italian, Silvio Gianni, and together they run several family businesses in Italy, including several wineries in Tuscany and Umbria."

"Anna and Silvio aren't coming?"

"No," Cate shook her head. "They don't travel much these days. Not because they can't, they just seem to prefer their country house in Tuscany to pretty much anywhere else."

Having been to Tuscany and knowing what a beautiful landscape it was, it didn't surprise Caleb that a couple that had likely traveled the world would choose that quiet countryside.

"So that's it," Cate said, leaning back in her chair, rolling her empty mug between her hands.

It was a start, Caleb thought. He had a few calls to make and more reading to do, but what Cate had given him would be a good start.

"How do you want to play this? My presence here?" he asked.

Cate dropped her eyes to her mug, took a breath, then returned her gaze to his. "I was thinking we could tell everyone that my company is buying your company and you're debating whether to sell wholesale or to stay involved."

"So, I'm here to see how you guys run things?"

"It sounded like a good story to me."

He weighed the pros and cons for a moment. "It is a good story. Will the staff question it? Or is there a chance any of them would call corporate and hear a different story?"

Cate started to shake her head then stopped. "I don't think they'll doubt the story, but as for what they might hear from our corporate office, well, I called my boss last night and told him that I'd reached out to you and why. He knew Tommy and remembered Tommy and me mentioning you a few times over the years. He's worried about what's been going on here, too, so he's onboard with the plan and agrees that it's probably best to keep the real reason you're here a secret, for the time being."

Cate's simple statement gave Caleb pause. In the real world, it made sense that she and Tommy would have spoken about him— people talked about their friends all the time. Normal people. He'd never talked about Cate or Tommy to anyone other than Jesse. Not even Garret, who had *known* Tommy. No, after Tommy's death, Caleb and Garret had never spoken of him, or Cate, again. Garret had tried to bring their late friend up a time or two, but Caleb had never allowed it, never reopened that particular wound in front of him.

"Good thinking," he managed to say to Cate, glancing at the clock. "You probably want to get back to Elise?"

Cate followed his gaze and nodded as she stood. "Elise is horse crazy and I promised her I would take her for a walk in the woods on one of the ponies this afternoon. She rides, I lead," Cate clarified with a smile as she rinsed her mug in the sink. "But I think we'll do that in the late afternoon. Do you want a house tour after the family has brunch? At around two?"

Mentally, Caleb went through what he wanted to get done before meeting the family; six hours would give him plenty of time. "Yes, that sounds good. If you need anything between now and then, I'll be here—I'll probably go for a run, but other than that, I'll be here," he amended.

Cate nodded but didn't leave. Instead, she leaned against the counter with her hands behind her back. "Where were you when I called, Caleb?"

"Pardon me?"

"You arrived here so fast after I called. For years, you were never stateside for more than a few days at a time. It just seems unusual that not only would I catch you when you were in the States, but also just a few hours' drive away."

He hesitated. She wasn't asking for state secrets, but he knew that if he answered honestly, she'd hear more than just the words— he'd be giving her a glimpse, perhaps an invitation, into his life. An invitation he, selfishly, wasn't sure he was ready to offer up just yet.

Disappointment flashed in her eyes as she pushed away from the counter. "Never mind, forget I asked. I'll come by at two," she said, retrieving her hat and vest from the back of the chair she'd been sitting in. "If you need to find me before then, I'll be at the carriage house next door," she continued, gesturing toward the building he'd watched her walk to the night before with the hand that was holding the green hat. "Or Margaret will know where I am."

She was closing the door behind her when he stopped her.

"Cate?"

She paused then turned toward him. "Yes?"

"I, uh, I was at a wedding. A friend of mine got married on Saturday, near where my sister lives. I was staying with her and we were at the reception when you called."

She blinked.

He figured she'd heard about his sister from Tommy, but he'd never mentioned Kit to Cate directly. He had also never mentioned any other friends to her, probably because, with the exception of Tommy and Cate, and then Garret, he hadn't really had any, until recently. But he hadn't liked the hurt he'd seen in her eyes when he'd first hesitated to answer, and if she could be strong enough to ask an honest question, he owed it to her to try and be the same, regardless of whether or not he was ready to open up that part of his life to her.

"Um, wow. Well, I'm sorry I pulled you away," she managed to say.

He felt a small smile tug at his lips. He knew she meant it, but also knew that she was still processing what he'd just said, what he'd implied about how different his life was now.

"It's not a problem. I'll go back to Windsor when we're done here. I'll see Kit and Garret then."

"Garret? The same Garret that worked with you? And Tommy?"

"Yeah, he kind of fell in love with my sister and left the business. He works security for the UN now, and they live in Windsor. It's a small town in the Hudson Valley, about five hours from here."

"Near Tanglewood, right?" she asked.

He nodded.

"I've run a few events in that area. It's beautiful."

Again, he nodded.

"I, um, well, I'm glad you'll get to see her when this is taken care of." She turned and left, shutting the door behind her.

Caleb didn't harbor any illusions that Cate would drop the subject. He'd opened a door for her, issued an invitation into his life, and she wasn't the type not to respond.

Then again, as the memory of Tommy's funeral came rushing over him like a stampede of bulls, maybe not. Maybe she didn't actually want to know anything about him. Maybe she didn't want to hear how his life had changed in the past few years. Maybe she didn't want to hear that, for the first time in a very long time, he was starting to think that maybe, just maybe, there was a place for him in this world that didn't involve death.

Maybe she wouldn't want to know any of that. Maybe he couldn't really blame her.

CHAPTER 3

CALEB DIDN'T WAIT TO GO for a run. He had planned to make his calls before heading out, but after Cate left, after he'd left a part of himself open to a woman who had every reason to hate him, he found that he couldn't sit still long enough to make a phone call.

The Cate he used to know would have taken the little truth he'd offered and treated it kindly, not only because he was Tommy's best friend, but because he was her friend too. But that had ended long ago. Five years ago, to be precise.

Tommy had died and it had been Caleb's fault. For that, Cate had every reason to hate him. But he knew her well enough to know that she didn't *actually* hate him. When Cate disliked someone, it was complete. She didn't call, she didn't text, she simply cut that person from her life. Obviously, she hadn't done that to him. So, while he was fairly comfortable accepting that she didn't truly hate him, there was a big gap between "not hating" and the type of friendship they'd once shared. And an even greater gap between that type of friendship and the friendships he'd just begun to allow himself back in Windsor.

What Cate would do with the information he'd shared, he hadn't a clue. All he could do was brace himself for her response, and to do that, he needed to calm his mind and body. Thirty minutes after she'd left, he found himself running through the woods a few miles from the houses trying to do just that. He'd simply stepped off his back porch and picked a trail. If needed, the GPS he'd grabbed on his way out would help him get back, but with his uncanny sense of direction, he wasn't worried about getting lost. All he really wanted to focus on, to do, was to run far and fast.

As his feet pounded the damp trail littered with fallen leaves, he pushed himself harder and harder. He focused on the feel of his feet hitting the ground, the reverberations traveling up his legs, the jarring of his hips. He sucked in air as the sound of his heartbeat drowned out the memories of that last assignment with Tommy, of Tommy begging to come along, of Tommy going down.

But no run could ever drown out his other memories of Tommy: the incoherent sounds his best friend had made followed by the gut-wrenching sobs and the angry entreaties to both God and the devil. Caleb had held his friend through it all, he'd taken Tommy's angry lashings and tried, impossibly, to absorb some of his pain. Eventually, a hollow, hopeless silence had filled the room as Tommy began to accept what Caleb had told him, as he began to accept that Brooke, his nine-year-old daughter, had been struck and killed by a drunk driver on her way to school.

They'd been in South Africa when the call came in. At around four p.m. local time, Caleb, Garret, and Tommy had been gearing up to head out. Tommy, intent on unknotting his bootlaces, had tossed Caleb his cell when it rang. Caleb hadn't thought anything of it when he'd seen the number of their CIA contact flash up on the screen and to this day, he didn't understand why he hadn't sensed that something was wrong. Intellectually, he knew it was a stupid thing to dwell on; how could he have known what was coming? But when your world collapses, it's hard to accept that it can happen so quickly, with no warning at all.

Thirty minutes before Caleb had answered that call with a cheery "Hello?" Brooke Thomson had been declared dead. Cate, who had been sedated by the time they got the call, was able to give a nurse the number of Tommy's CIA liaison before she'd slipped into darkness. The doctor had called their contact and their contact had called them. Then Caleb had delivered the news to Tommy.

Tommy hadn't believed him at first. Then he'd come at Caleb like a raging beast, looking for someone to blame. Garret had tried to stop him, but Caleb hadn't. Caleb had let Tommy hit him, whale on him, beat him, until there wasn't anything left. Then his friend, his mentor, had collapsed, sobbing onto the floor.

Caleb barely remembered how they got back to the US or through the funeral, but the memories of his friend fighting then mourning the death of his daughter were ones that no run, no level of exhaustion, could ever exorcise.

Finally, after running for nearly an hour, Caleb gave up. He came to a stop, sucking in air as he tried to slow his heart rate. Resting his back against a tree, he slid down to the ground and let his head fall back. Whether it was sweat or tears tracking down his face, he didn't want to know.

Because his memories weren't done with him yet.

Nine months after Brooke's death, Tommy had begged Caleb to let him come on an assignment in Russia. Caleb had balked at the idea, believing that Tommy should stay home with Cate but eventually, he'd let himself be convinced.

Two weeks later, Tommy was dead. And everything Cate had had was gone.

Caleb rubbed his palms over his eyes then looked up through the trees again. The branches had lost most of their leaves and the sun filtering through those that remained created soft beams of light that danced on the ground around him. As his heart rate slowed, he became aware of the subtle scents of earth and decay, as well as the quiet noises made by the birds and small animals as they prepared for the winter to come. In the spring, those same animals would emerge and begin searching for mates and provisions, while the trees leafed out once again to shade the forest floor.

Caleb closed his eyes and let the soft sunshine warm his face. There was nothing he could do to change the past—not what had happened to Brooke, not what had happened to Tommy, and not what he'd said to Cate earlier. Whatever came next, he'd deal with, because that's what he always did. In the meantime, the least he could do was help Cate find out just what was going on in the Whatley family.

• • •

"We'll be ready at four," Jana said as Cate pulled on her vest. She was headed back over to Caleb's after overseeing brunch and checking in with the family members. She'd stopped in to say hi to her daughter, only to find her napping after having taken a long hike with Jana followed by a big lunch.

"Perfect, thanks," Cate said. "They'll have a helmet at the barn, so jeans and her boots should be fine."

"And a jacket," Jana added.

Cate smiled. "And a jacket." Elise hated jackets, even when it was twenty degrees outside. It wasn't nearly that cold now, but it would be chilly enough in the woods, especially by four when the sun was already setting. Elise wouldn't be happy with the short ride, but it was all Cate could manage that day. Hopefully, she'd be able to get her daughter out for a longer ride in the next day or so.

As she closed the door behind her and started toward the ice house, she thought about what Caleb had said to her that morning. Never before had he talked about his sister, and not in a million years would she have guessed that he'd been at a wedding when she'd called. It wasn't as though she hadn't ever asked about his life—they'd been friends, good friends, for years. But whenever she had, he'd always evaded and, after a while, she'd gotten the message. Then, as the years went on and they had shared experiences to talk about, his past came up less and less.

And, of course, there had been Brooke. Caleb had spent so much time with the three of them, especially once Tommy more or less quit the business, that Brooke had come to consider Caleb her uncle, and the two had become very close. With Brooke around, they had never lacked for thing to talk about.

As she sidestepped a small puddle created by a short rainstorm a few hours earlier, Cate wondered if Caleb's life, his relationship with his sister, had started to change recently or if it had started even before Brooke had been killed. Had she just never bothered to ask? She didn't know and felt like a shitty friend because of it.

The five years of silence between the two of them suddenly felt longer, bigger. After Tommy died and she discovered she was pregnant, she'd been too shocked to do anything, let alone reach out to Caleb, a man who reminded her so much of her dead husband. However, looking back on it as she approached his door now, she knew that a part of her had just assumed that Caleb would reach out to her, that he would be there for her. And when he hadn't, she'd been hurt. And because she'd been hurt, she'd stayed away.

But the expression on Caleb's face when he'd found out about Elise had shown her something else. It had reminded her that when Brooke died, and then Tommy, she hadn't been the only one who had experienced those losses. She shouldn't have waited for Caleb to come to her; they had been friends, friends who had needed each other. Friends who, in their own suffering, had let each other slip away.

She knew the saying: hindsight is twenty-twenty, and with the perspective of time, she found herself somewhat ashamed of her behavior. Thankfully, Caleb had given her an opportunity this morning, an invitation back into his life. She didn't expect their friendship to pick up exactly where it had left off, but thinking back, she thought that was probably a good thing.

"Come in," Caleb said, opening the door suddenly, before she'd even knocked. "I saw you through the kitchen window," he added.

She stepped into the room and immediately noticed a slight dampness in the air that carried a sharp, clean scent. Grinning, she said, "I suppose the body wash and shampoo they have here is a bit, what's the word I'm looking for?"

One side of his mouth ticked up. "Scented?"

She laughed. Caleb, like Tommy, had always preferred unscented soaps and shampoos. A force of habit, she supposed, from their days of covert assignments. It wouldn't do to be given away by the scent of body wash, no matter how gender neutral.

"Sorry, I can have Greg, pick up some other stuff for you when he runs into town tomorrow," she offered.

Caleb walked toward the bed, where he sat down to put on his shoes. "Don't worry about it," he said, tying the laces. "I assume I'll just smell like everyone else around here. I'm planning to run into town tomorrow anyway, so if I need anything, I can pick it up myself." He finished with his shoes and stood up. Wearing black slacks and a white button-down shirt, he would fit right in with her staff. Still, it took her a moment to pull her eyes away. Other than Brooke and Tommy's funerals, she'd never seen him wear anything but t-shirts and jeans or cargo shorts.

"You'll fit right in with that outfit," she said.

"I figured as much," he said as he opened the front door and gestured her through. "I saw one of your staff members leaving the main house this afternoon and he was wearing pretty much the same thing." He closed and locked the door behind her.

He followed her as they crossed the driveway and headed toward the back entrance to the main house's kitchen. "What are we going to see?" he asked.

She glanced over her shoulder, then stopped and turned toward him. He came to an abrupt halt only a second before walking into her. She recognized the look on his face; he was already five steps ahead of her and just making small talk. "You've already seen a plan of the house, haven't you?" she asked

"Yes."

She narrowed her eyes and wondered how on earth he'd found plans of the house in less than twelve hours. Then again, that was why she'd called him, wasn't it? To help her figure things out.

"What do you want to see?" she asked.

He crossed his arms over his chest as his eyes traveled to the house behind her. "What I really want to see are the guests' rooms, but I don't think that's going to happen today, is it?"

She shook her head. "No, some of the family members have gone into town, but most are still here. There is some talk of a family outing on Friday. If that moves ahead, everyone will be attending and you'll have some time, but until then, there are bound to be people in and out of their rooms at all times, so we'll have to play it by ear."

She could tell from the set of his jaw that, though this news wasn't unexpected, it wasn't what he'd been hoping to hear. She watched his golden eyes scan the windows of the upper floors, as if seeking alternate ways in. That this was the way his mind worked wasn't new to her, but the thought that popped into her head was.

"Does your sister have the same eyes as you?" The question had just come out and, as the eyes in question snapped down on hers, she wondered for a fleeting moment if maybe what she'd thought she'd heard from him that morning was just something she'd made up. Maybe he really didn't want her asking about his life.

Then a small smile touched his lips and his eyes went back to the house. "She does, actually," he said. "She looks more like our mom, but we have the same eyes."

She was about to ask if that meant he resembled their dad, but before she had the chance, he gestured toward the house. "Let's go."

Complying with the implicit order, she turned back toward the house and led him to the large kitchen that sat on the lower north corner of the house. Margaret glanced up from her late lunch when they entered, and Greg and Christine, standing at the sink washing and drying dishes, both turned to look at them over their shoulders.

"Hi Catherine, would you like any lunch?" Margaret asked.

Cate shook her head. "No, thank you. Everyone, this is Caleb Forrester. Corp sent him here to see how we run our family events. He'll be shadowing me for the rest of the reunion and may ask to do the same with you at some point during his stay here. Caleb, this is Margaret, our amazing chef, and Christine and Greg, my right and left hands, so to speak," she said, making the introductions.

Margaret shook Caleb's hand, but Christine and Greg were elbow deep in soap and dish towels, so they both just nodded in his direction.

"He's been briefed on all our protocols as well as the general schedule of the house," Cate continued. "If he has any questions,

I hope you'll extend him every courtesy." It wasn't a request, but her staff would know that. All three voiced their agreement at the same time.

"Where is everyone?" she asked.

"Agnes and Sabrina were going to play a game of chess, Dominique is probably with them," Greg started. "Erica and Mark took their dad for a drive, and Isiah and Livia went into town for some spa something-or-other Livia wanted."

"Anthony said something about some business calls he had to make and Michael and Edith retired for a *nap*," Christine picked up the thread. "Dixie and Luke took Sasha and Nikki for a ride, and Edward was going to read in his room."

Cate nodded. Most everyone would be out of the way for her tour of the main parts of the house with Caleb. "Thank you, all for your work this morning. And Margaret, that was an exceptional job on the brunch. Even Agnes was complimentary." Cate's comment solicited a laugh from Margaret while Greg and Christine made sarcastic "whoop" noises and rolled their eyes.

"Agnes is a dear old lady whose compliments are often wrapped in barbed wire, if you know what I mean," Margaret said to Caleb.

Cate saw Caleb smile at the description, but she could tell from the way his eyes darted around the room that he was focused on memorizing the entire kitchen while only paying minimal attention to the shop talk.

"Ready?" she asked him.

His eyes lingered on the window that faced the woods, then he nodded. "Yes," he said, shoving his hands into his pockets. "It was nice to meet you all," he added.

They had just left the kitchen and were heading toward the middle section of the house when they overheard Greg's voice back in the kitchen saying, "I'd be more than happy to extend him any courtesy he'd like."

"I don't think anything you have could extend far enough to tempt him," Christine countered.

Greg said something in return, but Cate and Caleb had

moved far enough away that it was nothing more than an indistinct mumble.

"Sorry about that. I'll speak to him," Cate said as they entered the dining room.

"Don't bother," Caleb shrugged. "Margaret called you Catherine. Does everyone call you Catherine?"

Cate stopped at the head of a table that was currently stretched to seat twenty. It was the formal dining room where they held dinners and Sunday brunches. Breakfasts and lunches were usually held in the smaller, more intimate morning room, which sat at the front of the house.

"Yes. You're the only person who's ever called me Cate."

Caleb had been taking in the ornate room, but when he heard her what she'd said, his gaze bounced down to hers. "I'm the only one who calls you Cate?"

She nodded.

"I thought Tommy called you Cate?"

She shook her head. "He called me Catherine or Cat."

He opened his mouth to say something, then paused.

What he'd initially intended to say, she wasn't sure, but she was pretty sure it wasn't what finally came out of his mouth.

"Well, I guess I'll have to be careful and remember to call you Catherine."

The name sounded strange coming from him. She couldn't remember him using her full name even once, but she understood why he would need to now. "I suppose so," she responded. "Now, shall we start the tour?"

She led him through the formal dining room, into the lounge, and then to one of the game rooms. They toured the south wing of the house that held a library and billiard room before coming back toward the center of the building and seeing the main foyer.

They mounted the main center-hall staircase and Cate was about to direct him back toward the north wing of the house when they heard voices from the second-floor library that doubled as a bit of a family space.

"I'm not saying you have to dress like Doris Day, Sabrina, but a dress every now and then would show off your figure."

"That's Agnes," Cate said to Caleb over her shoulder. "Do you want to meet some of the family members?"

In response to a nod from him, she proceeded to knock on the door, already slightly ajar, then poked her head inside. "Hello Agnes, Sabrina, Dominique," she said, pushing the door open farther and gesturing for him to follow her into the room.

"Well, hello, dear," Agnes said from her spot at the chess table.

Cate glanced down and noted that Agnes was winning. She wondered if Sabrina, who sat opposite the older woman, was letting her. Playing with Agnes was certainly a double-edged sword: if Sabrina won, her aunt would surely grumble about what an unattractive trait aggressiveness was in a woman, but if Sabrina lost, the old woman would be just as happy to point out her failure.

Agnes glanced at Caleb then let her eyes linger. "Who's this?"

"Agnes, Sabrina, Dominique, this is Caleb Forrester. He's from the corporate office and he'll be shadowing me for the rest of the gathering," Cate said.

"Lucky girl," Agnes said, openly admiring Caleb.

Cate bit her lip to hide her smile.

"Agnes," Sabrina admonished.

"Let her ogle, then maybe she'll stop commenting on your appearance," Dominique interjected from her spot at a table several feet away. It was clear from the books, notepads, and open laptop surrounding her that she was working.

Looking chagrinned, Sabrina turned to Cate and Caleb. "Welcome to the Whatley family."

Caleb offered a small smile in return.

"He'll never do, dear," Agnes said.

"I beg your pardon, Agnes?" Cate asked.

"He'll make all the husbands nervous."

Cate cast a glance at Caleb, who seemed to be only half-listening to the conversation as his eyes wandered around the room. "Why would he do that?"

"Back in my day, they would have called him 'swoon worthy,' but I think in today's terminology they'd say he's panty-melting hot. The husbands won't have it."

"Agnes!" Sabrina admonished.

Caleb was looking at Agnes now. His face was carefully neutral, but Cate could see amusement in his eyes.

"Where on earth did you learn that phrase, Agnes?" Dominique asked, with a mixture of curiosity and horror.

Agnes shrugged. "I'm on the Facebook."

"I apologize for my aunt," Sabrina said.

"Not possible," Dominique said, returning to her work.

"Dom," Sabrina said.

"For the past forty minutes, she's been harassing you about your clothing, your hair, your lack of make-up, your lack of *husband*. I'm not sure why you'd want to apologize for her," Dominique shot back without even bothering to raise her eyes.

"Sorry," Sabrina mouthed in their general direction, but she made no attempt to argue with her wife.

"It was the same for you, mind you, Catherine," Agnes said.

Cate took a deep breath. "What was the same, Agnes?"

"That first time you came to one of the reunions," Agnes said, as if Cate were part of the family. "I said you'd never do, you'd make the wives nervous."

"And there's never been a problem, has there? We're very clear that we're here to do a job, Agnes. That's all," Cate replied.

"Well, there was the incident with Michael that first year," Agnes said as she turned back to the chess game.

Cate glanced at Caleb. He was watching her, waiting for her response. "That was nothing, Agnes, and you know it."

"I agree," Dominique piped in. "Not that you aren't lovely, Catherine, but Michael hits on everyone with boobs."

Cate silently agreed, but said nothing. "Well, it was lovely to see you ladies. I'm going to finish giving Caleb a tour of the house. If you need anything, Margaret is in the kitchen and the others are around as well."

The three women mumbled their good-byes and Cate and Caleb headed toward the north wing. She planned to take him through that part of the house, take the old servants' staircase to the third floor, then come down the servants' staircase in the south wing to the show him the remaining guest rooms.

As they toured, she pointed out the rooms and named their current occupants, promising to get him a list of who was staying where when they returned to the ice house. When they climbed to the third floor and headed down the long hall that ran the length of the house—with guest rooms off either side—they ran into Lucy and Annie, the two Washington House staff members, who were getting ready to meet up with Christine and Greg to start the afternoon rounds of the rooms. Cate introduced them to Caleb and, though both were clearly curious about him, neither woman said anything other than hello.

They had just hit the foyer on the ground floor when Anthony Whatley, dressed in hiking boots and a hunter-green wax jacket came striding in the front door. When his eyes strayed to Caleb, he paused in front of them at the base of the staircase.

"Everything okay, Catherine?" he asked.

Cate had always found Anthony to be one of the more consistently pleasant members of the family. On occasion, he and his brother, Michael, egged each other on to make some stupid comment or another, and she'd heard him, maybe a half a dozen times, get fed up with Agnes's opinions, but he'd always been nice to Cate and respectful of the staff.

"Yes, everything is fine, thank you. Anthony, this is Caleb Forrester. My company is in the process of buying his, so he's spending some time with us before he decides whether to join up himself or take an early retirement."

"Early retirement, no question," Anthony said, holding out his hand.

"I don't know, no rest for the weary and all," Caleb responded, shaking the man's hand.

"Or the wicked," Anthony added.

"Maybe that too," Caleb agreed.

No doubt Anthony had been referring to himself with his last the statement, if only in jest. But Cate's heart had stuttered slightly at the weariness she'd heard in Caleb's response; she knew all too well that he had first-hand knowledge of the fact that the wicked did indeed, not rest.

"Well, good luck with the decision," Anthony said with a smile. "For what it's worth, the company has always done a great job for our family."

"Thank you," Cate said as Anthony headed up the main staircase to the guest rooms.

"He's here alone, right?" Caleb asked as they made their way through the front door and out onto a large veranda that spanned much of the front of the house.

They descended the steps leading to an expansive lawn. "Yes, he often comes alone. His wife runs her own company and can't get away as easily."

"Catherine," a young voice called from their right.

Cate knew who it was, but took a few seconds to spot Nikki Martin rushing toward them, her gangly eleven-year-old frame out of sync with the clarity of her voice.

"Hi, Nikki, how are you?" Catherine asked once the young girl was within speaking distance.

Nikki grinned. "I'm good. Dixie and Luke took me and Sasha for a ride, and guess what we saw?"

Cate shook her head and shrugged. "I don't know, a fox?"

Nikki shook her head and her brown braid went flying. "No, we saw a nine-point buck! He was huge and beautiful." Nikki's big brown eyes widened as if to emphasize the animal's size.

"He was a stunner," Dixie Whatley said, joining them on the lawn along with Luke, her boyfriend, and Sasha who was being carried on Luke's shoulders. Cate was glad that whatever tension she'd sensed between the girls' mothers at least the girls were having a good time with their relatives.

"Dixie, Luke, girls, this is Caleb Forrester. He'll be here

shadowing our work for the duration of the reunion," Cate said, making the introductions. Caleb stepped forward to shake hands with everyone, even the girls, then stepped back to stand beside her. "So, it was a good ride this afternoon?" Cate asked.

The girls nodded vigorously then, catching sight of a wild rabbit, took off across the lawn. "Stay where I can see you," Dixie called out before turning back to Cate and Caleb. "It was a lovely ride. After that little shower late this morning the conditions were perfect—the air was clear, but the ground wasn't too soft—and, of course, the buck was quite a sight." As she spoke, her blonde hair, which was baby-fine and wildly curly, escaped its tie and sprang out around her face.

"It didn't hurt that it's hard to have a bad time when the girls are around," Luke added. "I'm a geriatric physician so, other than Dixie, I spend most of my time with people over seventy. My patients are great and all, but it's fun to be around so much energy," he added as an aside to Caleb.

Caleb inclined his head but said nothing.

"So, what's on the agenda for the rest of your afternoon?" Cate asked.

Dixie kept her eyes on the girls across the lawn and tried to tug her hair back into submission as she answered. "Luke wanted to go hunting, but Mark suggested waiting until the morning for that. He said he'd take us out and show us the blinds."

"Deer season?" Caleb asked.

Luke shook his head. "Pretty much *everything-but-deer* season. Unless we want to hunt with a bow and arrow. No, we'll probably look for pheasant, but without dogs to roust them we'll likely just end up sitting in the forest for a few hours."

Dixie grinned and bumped her hip against Luke's. "I can think of worse ways to spend the morning."

"Well, whatever you end up doing, let us know if we can bring you anything. Warm blankets, coffee, you know, pretty much anything you could ask for we can at least try to find for you. Except a pheasant. You'll be on your own with that one," Cate said with a smile. The fact was, they could probably wrestle up some dogs to roust the pheasants, but she was pretty sure that wasn't the real purpose of the outing anyway. Dixie liked things most of her cousins didn't. Taking a blanket and a thermos of coffee out to a blind and communing with nature—and her boyfriend—for a few hours was right up her alley.

"Of course, thank you," Dixie said. Then, after calling to the girls and waving them inside, she and Luke excused themselves, saying they needed to deliver the girls back to their parents in time for a little rest before dinner.

They stood in silence, watching the group disappear into the house, but when Cate began walking toward the south side of the house, Caleb asked her about Dixie. "She's the youngest of the cousins, right?"

Since he'd originally arrived by driving around the north side of the house, she wanted him to see the other half. She also wanted to take him by the barn, introduce him to Mirielle, the barn manager, and pick up the wire they'd unwound from the tree a few days earlier. "She is. Her dad, Trip, had her late in life, I think he was fifty, or close to it, when she was born."

"And Luke?"

Cate chuckled. "Dixie takes after her dad; she's not really one to be tied down. She comes to the reunion with someone different every year. One year it was a sculptor, the next year a poet, another year a cowboy. I mean a *real* cowboy, the kind with six thousand acres and herd of cattle bigger than most towns in New Hampshire. Luke is the latest. Seems like a nice enough guy, he's decent to the staff, but I don't expect to see him again after this month."

"So you don't think he's capable of killing someone?"

Cate shrugged as they rounded the corner of the house and the barn came into view. "I don't like to think anyone here would actually kill someone, but I can't say for certain if Luke is capable or not. I don't know him very well, not like I know most of the others. For all I know, he could have a raging temper. Although I doubt it," she added.

"Why's that?"

"Because I *do* know Dixie. She's flighty and not particularly interested in forming lasting relationships, and I don't see her staying with someone who'd give her any sort of trouble. It wouldn't be worth her time."

"It doesn't always work that way," Caleb pointed out as they came to a stop a few feet short of the open barn door.

Cate bit her lower lip. She knew the truth of his statement more than he could know. "I know, and you're right, which is why I said I couldn't really comment on him. Do I *think* Dixie would be with someone who would hurt her or someone else? No. But I don't really have much to go on," she conceded.

"Catherine?"

They dropped the conversation as Mirielle stepped out of one of the stalls. The older woman hung up the horse's halter, gave the chestnut a good rub on his nose, then came toward them, her brown-gray ponytail peeking out from underneath her ball cap.

Cate made the same introduction she'd made to everyone else over the past ninety minutes, then mentioned that she was hoping to take Elise for a short ride at four. There was nothing Mirielle liked better than to foster a love of horses, so she immediately excused herself, offering to get Pansy, one of the larger ponies, ready for the ride. Under normal circumstances, Cate would have insisted that she and Elise do it, but given that the evening light was running short *and* she wanted to get the wire to Caleb without raising suspicion, she conceded.

The minute Mirielle was gone, Cate led Caleb into the tack room, opened one of the large cupboards meant to hold a saddle and other gear, and pulled out a length of thick wire. It curled around her wrist and arm as she handed it over to Caleb.

He eyed it before grabbing a nearby plastic bag. Flipping the bag inside out, he used it to take the wire from her then slid the bag over the coil, sealing it inside. "Fingerprints," he said.

"I know, I thought of that later. My prints will already be all over it. I was so intent on getting it down that, at the time, it didn't dawn on me that I should have worn gloves or something."

Caleb shrugged. "This kind of material isn't the best for prints anyway, so I'm guessing you didn't do too much damage. I'll dust it and see what I can find, but I'll probably end up sending it out for testing."

"Testing?"

"To string a wire tight enough to cause injury takes a bit of strength and some wrangling. It's possible that whoever strung it up might have nicked their hand or wrist on the sharper ends."

"And left DNA," she finished. She should have thought of that too, before she'd left it hanging in the cabinet.

"Again, not very likely, but always worth a look."

She eyed the wire, hoping it would end up telling them something, but before she could ask Caleb the odds that it would, they heard the sound of hooves clattering into the barn. "I'll go offer to help Mirielle," Cate said, picking up a box of brushes. Assisting the barn manager wasn't an unusual undertaking for Cate, but her motivation was less selfless this afternoon as it would also distract the Mirielle while Caleb left carrying the reel of wire. Not surprisingly, he understood and gave a smile of thanks.

Not two minutes later, as she and Mirielle brushed out Pansy's tail, Cate caught a fleeting glimpse of Caleb as he exited the barn. She paused as he disappeared, then wondered what he planned to do that evening. She hadn't asked him what he'd thought or what he wanted to do next. She'd brought him into this and, even though she knew that if something was going on she wasn't the best person to figure it out, she found she didn't like leaving it all to Caleb. She didn't like not knowing what he was thinking or what he planned to do next.

She glanced at her watch. A walk with Elise from four to five, dinner prep, and an evening staff meeting would keep her out until about nine. After that, she wasn't going to let Caleb go at this alone.

He was going to get a visitor.

• • •

Caleb glanced up from the documents spread across the table when he heard a knock at the front door. He knew who it was, but still, he hesitated. It wasn't that he didn't trust Cate or want her to be part of his investigation, it was just that, in his mind, she was still Tommy's widow, and that meant that *Tommy* wouldn't have wanted her involved.

"I have an extra key," she called from the other side of the door. "Really, the knock was just a courtesy."

Caleb couldn't help but chuckle. "Then let yourself in," he called back.

She did and, holding up the key as if it were a prize, turned and locked the door behind her. "How was the rest of your day?" she asked, joining him at the table.

Caleb eyed the papers scattered around the table and made to clear a space for her.

"Don't bother. I'll just sit down and then you can take me through everything. Although," she said, picking up a dirty dish containing the remnants of the omelet he'd made himself for dinner. "I think I'll go ahead and get rid of this."

"I wasn't expecting company."

She waved him off and deposited the dish in the sink. "Coffee?"

He shook his head. "I was just debating whether or not to have a beer."

"Even better." She opened the fridge and pulled out two bottles. Returning to the table, she handed one to him. "I'm sorry you didn't get to meet Elise today. She and Jana had a big morning then she fell asleep. I had to wake her up for her ride this afternoon."

Caleb shrugged. "It's fine."

"No, it's not, not really," she said, taking a sip of her beer as she picked up one of the pages.

He thought she might say something more but she didn't. "Those are just some notes I took based on your files," he said.

"It looks like more than just notes," she countered, arching an eyebrow as she held the page up.

"I was trying to create a visual for how everyone is related."

"Hmm." She took another sip. "You certainly did that." Setting the page back down on the table in front of her, she looked at the intricate diagram he'd crafted which indicated who was related to whom and how. There were so many names and interconnecting lines that the image resembled a spider web.

"What are these?" she asked, pointing to a series of numbered questions.

"Those are questions I had about those particular relationships," he said, pointing to lines that connected the questions to their corresponding relationships in the illustration. "There wasn't enough room to write the questions on the diagram, so I numbered them."

Her green eyes flitted to his for a moment, then dropped back down to the page. She read one of the questions. "How did they meet?"

"Dixie and Luke," he spoke. "It's a question I'll want to know the answer to. Along with whether or not he would benefit from her death or the death of anyone else in the family."

"Do you think Dixie is the target?" she asked as she set her beer down and moved another sheet of paper in front of her.

Caleb shook his head. "I don't know. At this point, we don't know anything other than that a wire was strung up that could have seriously injured or killed someone, and I know she was one of the people out on horseback that day."

"So that's who you are starting with? As the list of potential victims?"

"Yes, I am. The barn seems pretty much available to anyone at any time, and since we haven't really had a chance to talk about the family members' schedules, I figured the group that went out that day is probably as good a place to start as any. I'm not discounting everyone else though," he added.

"It's weird, isn't it?" she asked.

"What?"

"Starting with a list of potential victims? Don't you usually start with a list of potential suspects?"

Caleb shifted in his seat. "Sometimes, finding the victims is the only way we can find the perpetrator," he said, then wondered who the "we" was that he was referring to. Tommy was gone and Garret had left the business. The term "we" was a bit illusory for him at this point.

She studied him for a moment, then abruptly turned her attention back to the table and picked up her beer. "That's quite a drawing of the house, too," she said, pointing out the schematic he'd drawn. He had pulled the plans from an online site, studied them, and then, after his tour that afternoon, drawn in which guest was staying in which room.

"It will be better when I can get into the guest rooms, but it will do for now."

She paused and picked at the label on her bottle before speaking. "I know you said last night that I was probably right about something going on, but after today, what do you think? Do you think I'm crazy? Or do you think someone in there really is in danger? And if so, how are we going to stop it?"

For the first time since she'd handed him a beer, he took a sip. Leaning back in his chair, he gave Cate a good, long look. Her hair was still pulled back into a sleek ponytail and, as he'd always remembered, she wore very little makeup—with her fair skin and dark lashes and eyebrows, she didn't really need any. But it wasn't her physical appearance that he studied now, in fact, he wasn't altogether sure he was studying her at all, perhaps more his memories than anything else.

She had never come to him with questions before, not questions like these, anyway. Of course, that made sense. If she'd had any doubts before, she would have gone to Tommy, her husband. And while she and Caleb had always been close, that closeness had been founded on both of their relationships with Tommy; neither had ever felt any need or, to be honest, likely had any interest, in sharing anything as intimate as a personal doubt.

"Do you ever surf anymore?" he asked.

She blinked a few times. "Not often, maybe a few times a year."

"Do you miss it?"

Slowly she nodded, as if hesitating to admit it. "Sometimes. I miss the freedom and power I felt when I was out on a wave. I miss the way the board felt under my feet when I was on a good ride. I miss the way it made me *feel*. I'm not sure I actually miss *it*, though, if that makes any sense?"

With the exception of an ill-conceived attempt to learn while at Garret's place in Mexico one year, Caleb had never surfed. In a way, though, he understood exactly what she was saying. His job used to make him feel those things. He went into the business because he was angry and wanting revenge and, over time, it had become something he loved. And while he still liked what he did, he found that, when he wasn't doing it, when he was visiting his sister or just having down time, it wasn't the actual *work* he missed, but the way it had made him feel. Useful. Competent. *Good.*

He took a long draw on his beer. After a moment, he said. "It does make sense. But let me ask you this, how did you pick which wave to ride?"

She lifted a shoulder. "I don't know. I suppose there's probably a scientific process that someone could go through to map the perfect wave, but for me, it was always something I felt. Like it was calling to me or like I was *meant* to ride it. I know that sounds crazy, but that's just the way it was."

"It doesn't sound crazy at all. The reason I brought it up is because whatever it was inside you that told you which waves to ride is the same thing inside you that's telling you something is wrong in that house."

She gave a little derisive snort. "I surfed for *years*. I developed an intuition for what waves would suit my style. This," she said, gesturing with her bottle toward the house, "this is way outside my realm of expertise."

Caleb shrugged. He wasn't going to argue with her, even though he disagreed. In his experience, if people had strong intuition, it wasn't usually limited to a single circumstance but rather it adapted to the circumstance presented to it. In Cate's case, surfing had been the activity her intuition adapted to. Now that she was no longer riding that circuit, it made sense to him that her gut would turn to whatever she put her attention to next—in this case, her job. "I disagree, but even if you don't believe in yourself yet, I do, so we should just take it from there."

She opened to her mouth to say something, closed it, then finally spoke. "Okay, just how do you propose to do that?"

"I've ordered background checks on all adult members of the family, which should start coming in tomorrow. In the meantime, I want to know more about these arguments you're hearing, because, just based on what I read, there are lots of motives for murder existing in that house."

"Motives? What motives?"

He leaned toward her and the picture he'd drawn of the relationships. "Agnes," he said, pointing to the name.

"Yes, what about her?"

"No kids, no spouse, and she doesn't strike me as the kind of woman who'd give everything to charity out of the goodness of her heart, so where does her money go when she dies?"

Cate looked up at him then returned her focus to the diagram. "Isiah?"

"I'm betting he has an inheritance coming to him from his father that I'm sure has, in turn, been willed to his wife, Livia, in the event of his own death. Given the holdings of the family, I'm guessing it's a sizable chunk of cash."

"Jonathan, Isiah and Sabrina's father, is still alive; couldn't he change his will so that if Isiah died before Livia, Livia would get nothing?"

"He could. And in that case, who would most likely get everything?" he asked, pointing to Sabrina's name with raised eyebrows.

"Okay, so money is a big motivator, which gives pretty much everyone in the family some sort of motive. But that motive has always been there. Why would it become so overwhelming all of a sudden that someone would be willing to kill for it?"

Caleb sat back in his chair, raised his beer, and took a sip. "That's a good question, and one we won't know the answer to until I get the background checks. Maybe Isiah's business is floundering, or Dixie's dad is about to cut her off because she does nothing but flit around and spend his money," he tossed out.

Cate didn't doubt that money could be a strong motivator, but she wasn't going to settle on it until she knew more. "What else?"

"Love is the other biggie when it comes to murder. Maybe Livia is having an affair or Luke is obsessed with Dixie and doesn't ever want to let her go."

"I get your point," Cate cut him off. "Pretty much, if you put a bunch of people in a house together, there are going to be countless reasons why one of them might want to kill another."

"Pretty much, yeah," he agreed.

"And we won't really know more until those reports come in?"

Caleb nodded.

"Where will they be coming from?"

"A friend who owns a private security firm—not far from here, actually. I talked to him today and his team is going to run everything—all the names—through their systems and get back to me tomorrow."

Cate smiled. "Wow, that's twice in less than twenty-four hours that I've heard you mention a friend. Throw in the mention of your sister, and I'm starting to wonder what the hell has happened to you in the past five years."

Caleb's body stilled. "I don't know what you mean."

Cate's smiled dimmed and she cocked her head. "I'm not sure how that could have possibly offended you, but, clearly, it did."

"No, it didn't," he said, sitting forward and gather up his papers.

"Yes, it did." She put a hand on his arm.

He looked at her hand laying there, her fair skin against his black sweater. She wore no jewelry, none at all.

He took a deep breath. "I'm sorry, Cate. You didn't offend me, it's just that . . ."

"Yes?"

"These past five years haven't been the best."

Again, she cocked her head. "I wonder."

"How can you wonder? Tommy dying, it was, well . . ."

"I'm well aware of what it was like after Tommy died, Caleb. You're right, it was no picnic. If that's what you thought my comment implied, I'm sorry. That wasn't what I meant at all. I know you didn't go out and just forget about him so that you could start a new and better life. I *know* that. But what I also think is that your life probably *has* changed in the past five years; it would be weird if it *hadn't*. To be honest, I'd worry about you even more if that were the case."

"You don't need to worry about me at all."

"I think maybe I do. At least maybe more than I have been. That's not what I wanted to say, though. What I meant by my comment was that I'm *pleased* to hear that your life is changing, and in a good way. I like the idea of you having friends and I *really* like the idea of you spending more time with your sister. Those are good things, Caleb. Things I know Tommy would be happy to hear about too."

Caleb allowed her words to sink in for a moment, then abruptly rose from his seat and resumed gathering his papers. It was not Cate's responsibility to make him feel better about being alive. She'd had enough shit dumped on her; he didn't need to add yet one more thing, or person, to her list of things to take care of.

"He would be happy about it, I agree," he said. "He'd like Kit. You would too. Maybe when this is over, you can meet her, but in the meantime, we have a victim to find." He held up the papers he'd collected so far. "Maybe we can put these away for the night and you can spend a few minutes telling me about the arguments you've overheard?"

Her hand still lay on the table where it had fallen when he'd pulled his arm away. After a considered moment, she nodded. "Here, let me help you," she said, as she too gathered papers.

CHAPTER 4

CALEB STOOD IN LINE AT a big box store holding a printer, a ream of paper, and a pack of ink cartridges he was about to purchase. He'd had to drive farther than he'd wanted to in order to get a printer that worked for him, but he hadn't minded so much. He'd spent some of the time talking to Jay about the background checks that were being finalized and the rest of the time thinking about what Cate had said about all the arguments she'd been hearing. Between the money, the strained marriages, and the tense familial bonds, he was amazed the Whatleys hadn't all killed each other already.

Of course, with that realization came another. He was no longer as confident in his initial plan to start with the five riders who'd been out on the day the wire had been found—Dixie, Erica, Sabrina, Michael, and Edith. Well, to be fair, he still thought those five family members were a good place to start, but he'd heard from Jay that nearly every member of the family rode, sometimes even Agnes, and Cate had confirmed that there wasn't any set schedule detailing who was to go riding when. Given those two pieces of information, and the fact that the Whatley family would have given Agatha Christie a run for her money when it came to the sheer number of possible motives, he was rethinking his approach.

He also acknowledged that, by focusing on the five riders, he had implicitly assumed there was a single intended victim that they would need to identify who would then lead them to the killer. It was a logical assumption, but he'd forgotten, if only momentarily, that murder wasn't a particularly logical endeavor. The Whatley family was wealthy and powerful, and it was entirely possible that the target was *the family* itself. In that case, any victim would do.

He considered this option as the line inched forward a few feet. As cold as it sounded, he'd much rather find a single intended victim. He didn't like the idea of someone targeting the family as a whole because then he'd have to deal with someone whose primary motive was to inflict pain on a group of people, rather than just one. It was messier and there was more room for collateral damage. And Cate and Elise were right in the middle of it.

He felt a familiar sense of urgency as he finally dropped his items on the counter to pay. He needed to get things moving, figure things out. After signing for his purchases, he quickly made his way back to his Range Rover. He had one more stop to make, then he was pretty sure he could hole up at The Washington House for a few weeks without having to leave again. He hoped that would be enough time.

• • •

Cate watched from a second floor window of the main house as Caleb's SUV pulled back into his spot near the ice house. She was in the middle of helping Christine change out all the flowers in the house, so she couldn't go down to greet him, but as she arranged the most recent vase, she watched him carry a large box up to his front door.

"What do you think?" Christine asked.

Cate swiveled her head to examine the arrangement Christine had been working on, but found her employee looking out the window as well.

Cate frowned. "About?"

"About whether Caleb will join the company."

Cate watched Christine's eyes track Caleb as he exited the ice house and retrieved another package from his car.

"If he does, he'll most likely be situated at headquarters,"

Cate said, wondering if maybe Christine was hoping to work with him more.

"That would be a shame," Christine replied with a grin. "I wouldn't mind having him for a boss, if you know what I mean," she added with a wink and a laugh.

Cate smiled but felt a very sharp "no" echo through her body at Christine's suggestive tone.

Surprised at the strength of her own reaction, Cate turned back to the flowers she'd been arranging. She found a moment of calm, but when her eyes darted back to Christine, who was still looking out the window, Cate felt an uncomfortable surge of possessiveness wash through her. Caleb was *her* friend, he was a part of *her* life.

At the suddenness of that demanding, petulant thought, Cate physically staggered back a step—away from the window, away from Christine. She'd never been one to be possessive or jealous, and she hadn't a clue where that sentiment had come from. Not only did it not make sense to her, she knew it was completely unreasonable. There was no reason why she should want to quell Christine's obvious interest. And if Caleb was actually changing, developing friendships and other relationships, he deserved to have her support and encouragement. Considering the friend he'd been to her since the moment she'd entered Tommy's life, she knew she owned him no less.

But still…as she regained her composure she acknowledged that, even though they hadn't been a part of each other's lives for the past five years, he was still a part of her life, a part of her private life that she very much wanted to keep separate from her work and from those with whom she worked. She acknowledged to herself that her undeniable desire to protect her relationship with Caleb was at odds with her behavior of the past five years. Perhaps some-day she'd try to figure out why she'd let so many years pass without reaching out to him, but today wasn't that day.

"Have you seen Sebastian today?" Cate asked, changing the subject even as her eyes traveled back to Caleb outside. He was now pulling a garment bag and a small shopping bag from the back of his SUV.

"Yes, this morning at breakfast, and then again this afternoon. He found a few books in the library he was interested in. Last I saw, Erica and Mark were getting him situated in front of the fire in the downstairs library."

Sebastian Brandt was one of the quieter members of the family, perhaps because he'd only married into the clan. Then again, he and his children, Erica and Mark, tended to keep to themselves during the reunions, spending most of their time together as a threesome.

"And what about Erica and Mark? They mentioned something about hunting down some elusive potter Erica likes who lives in the area. Did they need any help with that?"

Christine shook her head. "Mark had some business to do this morning, then they decided to go for a hike after lunch, instead."

Cate relied on Christine for many things, but something she could always count on her to know was where everyone was at any given moment—or if not precisely where they were, what their plans might be.

It was long dark by the time Cate had finished the daily tasks and made it back to her cottage that evening. The sun set early this time of year, and it hadn't helped that a storm front had moved in as well, darkening the sky long before five p.m., when the sun usually disappeared behind the mountains to the west.

As she walked past Caleb's suite, headed to her own, she thought back to that afternoon and wondered what had been in the packages he'd unloaded from his car. She'd stop by and find out, but not until later. First, she wanted to have dinner with Elise and Jana then get Elise to bed. After that, she'd head over. At the thought of tucking Elise into bed, Cate realized that another day had gone by without an opportunity for Caleb to meet her daughter. She hoped he didn't think she was trying to avoid the introduction. She wasn't; she very much wanted them to meet. She'd even told Elise about him and the fact that he was staying next door, but between her job and all of the activities Jana had planned to keep

Elise busy, the timing hadn't been right. Tomorrow. Tomorrow she'd make it happen.

As it turned out, no one had to wait that long. Cate had just changed into a sweater and a pair of leggings when a knock sounded at her front door. Her staff would have texted or called before coming over, so she knew who it was going to be before even answering the door.

"I'll get it," she called as she jogged down the stairs, only to find that she was too late.

Elise was standing at the door, staring up at Caleb, and he down at her.

"You must be Elise?" he said.

Cate came up behind her daughter and placed a hand on her shoulder.

Elise nodded. "You're Caleb. You were friends with Brooke," she said, her brown curls bobbing.

"I was," Caleb said. "And with your father too."

"There's pictures of you in our house. Our real house, not this house," she said.

At that, Caleb's eyes came up to Cate's.

"We have a lot of pictures in our house," Cate said softly. "It's important to me that we remember the people we love, both those still with us and those not."

Caleb held her gaze then dropped his back to Elise. "I have something for you," he said, holding out a gift bag.

It said a lot to Cate that Elise didn't hesitate to take it from him. She was a rather solemn child who liked to know the rules; her tendency, at least to date, was to seek her mom's approval before doing most things, such as accepting a gift from someone she'd more or less just met.

"Elise, why don't you take that into the kitchen so we can let Caleb come inside?" Cate said.

Without a word, Elise darted past her and into the small eat-in-kitchen area where she promptly placed the large bag on its side on the table. Cate motioned Caleb inside and, as he passed by her, he handed her a small bag of her own.

"What's this?" she asked, shutting the door behind him.

"Just something I saw in town that I thought you'd appreciate." He followed her over to where her daughter sat at the table. With her hands tucked under her thighs and her feet swinging under the chair, Elise waited patiently to be told she could open her gift.

"Go ahead, Elise," Cate said.

Before the words were fully out of her mother's mouth, Elise began gently removing the brightly colored tissue paper from the bag. A few seconds later, she pulled out a white stuffed horse which looked to be about half her own height.

"Mama, it's a horse!" Elise all but squealed as she hugged the huge animal to her chest.

"I can see that," Cate replied, eyeing Caleb as he watched Elise bury her face in the soft fur. "How did you know she liked horses so much?"

Caleb's eyes came back to hers and he frowned. "Yesterday, when you were telling me you were going to take her for a ride, you said she loved horses. A friend of mine, one of the ones who got married the other day, is a major horse person. She always says that people are either born horse crazy or they're not, and if they are, they'll never change. I figured that, from what you said, Elise might have that particular affliction."

"Ooh, she's so soft mama. Feel," Elise said, holding the toy up for her mother to inspect.

Caleb's attention turned back to Elise. "I have a friend who rides a lot of horses, but one of her very favorites was a horse named Athena that she had when she a young girl. Athena was a big white mare that my friend Carly rode in a lot of shows, and she always says Athena was one of her best friends." He reached out and stroked the toy's fur. "This horse reminded me of Athena and I thought everyone could use a friend like her," Caleb said to Elise.

At Elise's solemn, and agreeable nod, Cate suspected that

Caleb's assumption about Elise was correct—only a horse-crazy person would think it completely logical to have a horse as a best friend.

"Mama, can I go show Jana?" Elise asked, springing from her seat, holding her new Athena around the belly.

Cate nodded, "But knock softly when you go upstairs. She might be on the phone, and if she is, don't interrupt her."

"Jana is your nanny, right?" Caleb asked as Elise bounded up the stairs, taking pains to make sure Athena didn't touch the ground.

"Not my personal nanny, she actually works for the same company I do and, since providing childcare is a service we offer to our guests and we have several nannies on staff, I made it a part of my contract that I get a nanny when I'm on-site at a job. Jana is Elise's favorite."

"What will you do when Elise starts school next year? Will you still bring her with you?" he asked as he leaned back against the kitchen counter and crossed his arms and ankles.

How many times had she seen him stand like that in her own kitchen? She smiled knowing that at least some things never changed. "I don't know. I haven't really decided yet. I have two more big trips on the books, one in March to Italy and another to the Caribbean in May but I know I'll have to decide what to do after those. Now what's this?" she said lifting the bag he'd brought her and diverting the subject away from a topic she wasn't ready to think about yet—not because of anything Caleb said, but because her life was going to change when Elise started school and she truly just wasn't sure what she would do then. When Brooke had started school, it had been Tommy who had quit working, for the most part, to stay home with their daughter. As a single parent, she didn't have that luxury.

"Oh, my favorite tea," she said, the sight of the familiar tin chasing away thoughts of the future. "Where did you find it?" she asked, opening the top and inhaling the delicate scent.

"In a coffee shop outside of town. I stopped in to grab a quick bite to eat and saw it there. I remembered you saying you were out, so I picked some up for you. I know you were going to ask Greg to get some next time he was in town, so you may have more than you need now—"

Cate shook her head, "No, Greg went into town yesterday and couldn't find any, so this is great. Can I make you a cup?" she asked as Elise came clomping back down the stairs with Athena in one hand and her other holding onto Jana, pulling her down the stairs with her.

Jana was smiling at them both, obviously indulging Elise in whatever story Elise was telling her. Cate noted that Jana's short, dark hair, streaked with gray, was still wet, and she hoped her daughter hadn't interrupted the woman's shower.

Caleb straightened off the counter as Elise and Jana came to a stop in front of them.

"Jana, this is Caleb. He brought me Athena, who's named after a show horse his friend used to ride," Elise announced.

Jana reached out to shake Caleb's hand. "I think Bunny might get displaced in Elise's bed tonight," she said.

"Bunny?" Caleb asked.

"Her stuffed lion," Cate replied.

"You have a stuffed lion named Bunny?" Caleb asked, looking down at Elise.

Elise smiled. "Yes, and now I have a horse named after a goddess."

Caleb blinked. "You know who Athena is?"

Elise's big eyes regarded him before she answered. "Yes," she drew out the word, as if it was obvious *everyone* knew about Athena. "I have a book. I'm just learning to read, but Mama reads to me all the time. So does Jana."

"And tales of Greek and Roman gods and goddess are a favorite. In fact, she has more than one book," Cate said. She wasn't altogether sure where her daughter's fascination with the ancient cultures came from, but she'd much rather read about them than some children's book over and over again.

"Hmm," Caleb said. "Interesting."

Cate laughed. Apparently, he wasn't so sure what to make of it either. "We were just getting ready for dinner, would you like to join us?" she offered.

Caleb glanced down at his watch then shook his head. "No, thank you. I have some things I need to go over," he said, his eyes lingering on hers for a moment.

"Shall I come over after I get Elise to bed?" she asked.

"I know you want to have dinner here, Catherine," Jana said. "But if you have work to do, I'm always happy to take Elise for the rest of the night."

Cate glanced at her daughter, who'd taken her new toy into the sitting area to show it pictures of its namesake in one of the books they'd just mentioned. "Would you mind?" Cate asked, glancing back at Jana.

Jana shook her head. "Of course not. You've had some late nights lately. If it will help you get through some stuff and hit the hay at a reasonable hour, I'm more than happy to help out. I'll give her a bath and then we'll curl up in front the fire, read a little, and she'll be out like a light in no time."

"Thank you, Jana," Cate said. "I appreciate it."

"No problem, and Caleb, it was nice to meet you," Jana said before moving off to join Elise.

"You don't need to come over," Caleb said, moving toward the door.

"I do," Cate said. "I brought you into this and I want to help in any way I can. Besides, despite all their eccentricities, I care about the Whatley family."

Caleb studied her then nodded. "Come over when you can. I've been receiving background checks all day. I went out and bought a printer this afternoon, after spending the morning with your staff. I have a lot of information that you can help me sort through."

Cate agreed, then opened the door. "Are you sure you're okay for dinner? I could bring you something," she offered.

"Thanks," he said, stepping through the door out into the cold, damp night. "I've got it covered."

Cate thought about pressing him. She wasn't sure what kind of food he had on hand, and while they'd stocked his kitchen decently, she knew that whatever he had wouldn't compare to the meal she knew Jana had pulled together. But in the end, she just nodded. Caleb was a big boy, if he wanted share her food, he would have said so.

"I'll see you in about an hour," she said.

"Have a good dinner."

"Thank you!" Elise's voice called from the sitting area making Caleb smile.

"You're welcome," he called back. "I'll see you in a bit," he added to Cate, then turned and headed into the night.

Cate shut the door and returned the kitchen. "He brought you your favorite tea," Jana said, holding up the tin.

Cate recognized the curious and amused glint in Jana's eyes. "He's a friend," she said, moving to get some plates out for dinner.

Jana put the tin down. "Good, I'm glad," she said, reaching into the cupboard for some glasses. "Friends are good to have, Catherine."

● ● ●

Caleb picked up a piece of paper from the table and pretended to study it. There was no doubt the information coming in from Jay was a worthy read, but he'd already read most of it. Now he was just trying to find a way to kill time until Cate showed up—preferably a way that kept his thoughts from turning too much toward his earlier meeting with Elise. From the moment she'd opened the door and stared up at him he had felt the past clawing at him to come back for a visit, or maybe even to stay. She had Tommy's eyes.

With a small stack of papers in hand, he stood and moved toward the back window. Staring out into the darkened woods behind his room, he allowed himself to crack open the door to the past, if just a tiny bit.

Russia. The summer had been a hot one, the kind where the nights, barely cooler than the days, offered no respite. Caleb, Tommy, and Garret were ripe with sweat, running on about two hours of sleep over past seventy-two hours, and hungrier than any of them could remember being. But none of them had wanted to give up.

They'd been contracted by a nameless western government agency to bring down an up and coming member of a particular drug cartel that had been flooding Europe with heroin of rather dubious quality. Well, he and Garret had been contracted, Tommy had begged to come along. Even though Caleb had had doubts as to whether or not a mission away from Cate was the right place for Tommy to be so soon after the loss of his daughter, he hadn't been capable of denying his friend's request.

A week after the contract was signed, they found themselves in the hills several hours north of St. Petersburg tracking a man of twenty-three. A man responsible for the deaths of at least twenty-five people, including the son of a high-ranking French intelligence officer. Tainted heroin was a particularly nasty habit.

Only once they'd arrived and started tracking the man's movements they discovered that drugs weren't his only trade. Vlad the Bad as they had started somewhat jokingly calling him, was into kids—buying, selling, using, tossing away.

Over the years, and with Tommy's mentorship, Caleb had learned to curb most of his reactionary tendencies, but when he'd seen the kids, something had triggered in him, something he didn't have to look too deep to find, and he'd made a promise to himself that Vlad the Bad wasn't going to live to see twenty-four. Itching for a fight himself, Tommy had encouraged Caleb.

Two days later Vlad was dead. So was Tommy.

"Caleb?"

Caleb spun around to find Cate in the doorway. She held

up her hands in a placating gesture even as she frowned at him. "Everything okay? I knocked, but you didn't answer."

He took a few breaths to calm his heartbeat. "Everything is fine," he said, shoving his memories back into the dark closet where they belonged. "You're going to have to keep Elise away from the rest of the guests for the remainder of the reunion. If she tells them you have pictures of me in your house, people will get suspicious, at the very least."

Cate shut the door behind her and came toward him, removing the down vest she wore over her sweater as she walked to where he'd spread his documents at the table.

"Or I could tell them that you've been in the business a long time and were a friend of my husband's and one of the people who convinced me to try this kind of job when I left the surfing circuit. That you were not just a friend but a mentor too," she countered.

He was well aware that the tension in his body wasn't her fault and so he took a few seconds to breathe and intentionally let it go. When he felt his mind was no longer torn between five years earlier and tonight, he gave a curt nod and even managed a small smile.

"Or that, that would work too," he said, joining her at the table and handing her the stack of papers he'd been holding. They were a bit wrinkled from his grip, but if she noticed, she didn't say anything.

"What's this?" she asked instead.

"The background check on Mark Brandt."

He saw the question in her eyes, but after a beat, she dropped her gaze to the papers she held.

As she thumbed through them, he moved to turn on the gas fireplace. He preferred a wood fire, but considering The Washington House's typical clientele, he supposed he was probably in the minority. The facility catered to those who desired luxury and ease; lugging firewood and patiently fanning flames didn't exactly fit that bill.

"Can I get you a drink?" he asked as she sat down, still reading the file.

"There's a bottle of port in the cabinet above the fridge. I had Lucy put it in here when I knew you were coming."

Caleb felt a smile tug at his lips. Port had always been something he and Cate had enjoyed. Tommy had made fun of them, calling it a pansy, upper-class drink—especially when poured into the proper glass—but Cate had thought it paired well with the dark chocolate cookies the guys often brought her when they traveled through Europe. And Caleb had agreed. The three of them had spent many nights relaxing on the porch, Cate and Caleb eating cookies with port in hand and Tommy nursing a beer, the only alcohol he ever drank.

"Mark Brandt's technology company is being investigated for securities fraud?"

"It is, but read on," Caleb said, pulling the bottle down, along with the two small glasses that had been placed beside it.

"And several members of his engineering team are being investigated for distributing child pornography?"

He heard the disbelief in her voice and so felt no need to confirm.

"Mark wouldn't have anything to do with that," she said firmly.

He joined her at the table, placing a glass in front of her as well as a fork and a plate containing a small piece of chocolate torte that he'd picked up at the coffee shop where he'd found her tea. She was the only person who knew of his penchant for rich chocolate. When he was on a job, he often went without anything edible for days and, so that he didn't miss it, he didn't typically indulge when he was off work. However, when he'd seen the torte sitting all alone on the counter that afternoon, it had practically begged him to bring it home.

Without skipping a beat, she picked up the fork and took a bite. The second her lips closed around the chocolate a look of surprise flashed across her face. Then she closed her eyes and savored the decadence. "Oh my god, that's good," she said when she'd finished. Her eyes had popped open and she was looking at him as if he'd just discovered Atlantis.

Caleb chuckled.

"I could spend days extoling the virtues of this torte, but back to this," she pointed to the paper with her fork. "I'm telling you, he wouldn't. Besides, if there was even a whiff of that predilection in his character, either Sabrina or Dominique would have sensed it. Those two may be having their own problems, but there is no way they'd bring their girls within a mile of someone they even suspected of such behavior."

Caleb disagreed; he knew firsthand just how easily some people could deceive others. For a true sociopath, it was effortless. He wasn't going to argue with her, though.

"You may be right. Jay's team dug up the investigation, but they're still working to get the names of the engineers involved in distributing the child pornography. Mark owns the company and is far enough removed that he may not have had any idea what was going on in his engineering team."

She held his gaze then let it fall to the table. "Even if he was part of it, how does that relate to what might be going on here? Would it give him motive to murder someone?" She paused, her eyes drifting over the report. "Then again, I imagine if someone knew their child had been involved, that would definitely be a good motive to make *him* an intended victim. Oh god—"

"Do I think Sasha and Nikki were involved and either Sabrina or Dominique knows?" he finished her sentence. She gave a halting nod.

"You said they'd be likely to sense it. I'm not sure it's always that easy, so, yes, I think it's a possibility that *if* Mark was involved in the pornography and *if* Sasha and/or Nikki were involved, it would make him a possible intended victim. What I have a hard time believing, though, is that, if either Sabrina or Dominique wanted to kill him, they would do it here."

"You mean, if they were angry enough to kill him for it, why would they bring the girls here and keep them in his vicinity?"

"Exactly. People do a lot of things in order to keep up appearances, but putting your kids in danger while you try to eliminate that source of danger doesn't seem like something two smart people would do. Especially not when they pretty much have access to Mark whenever they want, given that he lives near them in Boston."

"I sense a 'but' in there," Cate said, then sipped her port.

Caleb slid another stack of papers over to her. "Erica Brandt, Mark's sister, has been trying to have kids for years. She isn't married but has tried in vitro seven times and is now on a waiting list to adopt. She desperately wants a child."

Cate scanned the background check on Mark's sister. "You think that if Erica found out, she might want to kill him?"

"It's possible. Again, if he's even part of it. She could see him as denigrating something that means everything to her, violating it. I've seen people want to kill for less."

Cate tapped the sheets as she scanned. He couldn't tell what she was thinking, but he was relieved that she was talking this through with him and, after her initial reaction to the information about Mark, keeping her mind open to the possibilities. Then again, Cate had never been one to turn away from something because it wasn't what she wanted to hear. He suspected it was part of what made her the champion surfer she was; she might question, she might doubt, but it didn't stop her from *doing*.

"What else?" she asked.

"More?"

"Yes," she said, gesturing toward the documents in front of her. "You have a lot here, but what else have you found?"

He put his glass down, sat forward, and selected two more sets of papers for her.

"I'm fairly sure both Livia and Dominique are having an affair. Not with each other," he clarified, "and Luke Gilbert's medical practice is being sued by two different families for malpractice."

Again, Cate took a few minutes to thumb through the pages as she continued to work away at her torte. "I get why Livia and Dominique could be either the intended victim or perpetrator if they are having affairs, but what about Luke? He just seems too outside the family to be either."

"I tended to agree, until I saw the name of a woman who died recently under his practice's care," Caleb said, reaching over to flip one of the stacks open to a certain page. When he found it, he pointed to a name.

"Eunice Mayberry,"

"Survived by," Caleb prompted.

Cate scanned the list, "Her brother, her two daughters, her son, and her daughter-in-law, Monica Martin." She looked up.

"Dominique's sister," he said.

Cate blinked. "That's a coincidence."

Caleb let out a small chuckle.

"Are you one of those people who always says they don't believe in coincidence? They say that all the time on TV," Cate said.

Caleb shook his head. "No, I'm not. I think coincidences happen all the time, and that's why I want to dig into this further. We have one tenuous connection and a lot of questions."

"Such as?" she said.

"Luke's practice is being sued, but who was the attending physician? Was it Luke or one of his partners? Are Dominique and her sister close? Would Dominique even know about the lawsuit? Like I said, lots of questions."

Cate paused in thought then slid the papers back toward him as she picked up her glass and twirled it in her fingers. "Anything else?"

"Yes, quite a bit. Anthony's bank account received a sudden influx of cash recently that has piqued my curiosity. His brother, Michael, was involved in a trekking accident three years ago in which one of his friends died. Then there's Edith Barnard's involvement in a car accident several years ago that left a woman dead."

"What about Agnes, Edward, and Sebastian?" Cate asked, a touch of macabre humor in her voice at the sheer number of skeletons the background checks had turned up.

Caleb's lips twitched, but he didn't quite grin. "I've run their background checks too, but for now I'm concentrating on people I think would be strong enough to string that wire between the two trees. I know it's possible that any of the older three could have done it, it's not *that* hard, but I have a hard time seeing any of the senior siblings choosing that particular method if they did, indeed, want to kill someone."

Cate shook her head. "Agnes has the fortitude, but since she can't walk farther than a half mile at any given time, I'm inclined to agree with you. Edward does go for walks nearly every day but probably wouldn't want to stop reading his scripture long enough to hike all the way out there, and as for Sebastian, even if he could have made it out there, he'd end up lost. That man is the epitome of the absent-minded professor."

Caleb chuckled as he rose from his seat. Picking up their empty plates, he gestured toward her empty glass. "Another?"

She stared at her glass for a moment, seeming to contemplate something, then nodded. He felt her eyes on him as he placed their plates in the sink. He even heard her take a few breaths, as if she was going to speak, but she didn't.

"So that's it for now," he said, rejoining her at the table. "Tomorrow, I'll spend more time at the house, talk to the staff, maybe 'run into' a few of the family members and strike up conversation, that kind of thing. I'd like to search the guest rooms, but I'll wait until you give me the go ahead to do that. In the meantime, I'm going to have Jay keep digging on some of the things we just discussed."

Her eyes dropped down to her port glass again.

"What?" he asked.

Her eyes shot back up. "What?" she responded.

He exhaled. "You obviously want to say something to me."

She held his gaze then turned away and took a sip of her drink. "Thank you for the stuffed animal and the tea today."

"You're welcome." He knew that wasn't what she'd really wanted to say, so he waited her out.

Finally, she lifted her gaze back to his.

"That friend you mentioned, the one who rides? Who is she?"

Caleb wasn't altogether surprised by the question and he recognized that Cate's natural curiosity was more of a tentative step toward bridging the gap of years between them than a specific interest in his friend. "Her name is Carly Drummond—or actually Carmichael, now. It was her wedding I was attending Saturday night when I got your text. She married Drew Carmichael, someone I met through my sister. "

Cate took another sip of her drink then twirled the glass between her fingers by its stem. The fireplace's fan dropped down a speed and the room was suddenly much quieter. "It's strange, nice, but strange, to hear you talk about your sister and your friends. You never did before."

It was his turn to take a moment before answering. "That's because, back then, I didn't really have any. I mean, I had you and Tommy for friends, and, eventually, Garret. I'd always had my sister, but she and I weren't close, not then anyway. Other than that . . ."

"What changed?" she asked, her voice quiet in the warm room. "Was it because of Tommy?"

Caleb couldn't help but cross his arms and look away. She wanted to know if Tommy's death had woken him up, if losing his closest friend had made him realize how important people could be in his life. He wished he could say yes, that perhaps something good had come out of Tommy's death, but he didn't want to lie to her. If anything, he'd withdrawn even more after they'd lost Tommy and Cate had retreated from his life, but he didn't want to tell her that, either.

"No," he said, shaking his head. "About a year and a half ago, my sister was in some trouble. Some very unpleasant people came after her. It forced us into close quarters and there were," he paused, not wanting to say too much as a great deal of the story wasn't his to tell. "There were a lot of things we needed to clear up between us. A lot of misunderstandings, mostly on my part. I'd fucked things up with her in ways even I didn't understand."

"But you cleared those things up?"

Caleb bobbed his head slowly. "Yes," he drew out. "But it has taken time. She was hurt, badly, partly due to things I had done. Those things don't just go away."

"So you try to spend time with her now."

Caleb nodded. "I do. We both work at it." He pulled out his phone and brought it to life. After a few seconds, he passed it over to her. "That's us, with Garret, at the wedding on Saturday."

Cate smiled as she studied the photo. "Garret looks happy. I never got to know him very well, but he sure looks happy here."

"He is, they both are."

"Your sister is beautiful, and you're right, you do have the same eyes."

Caleb gave a brotherly snort. "She was all legs and bones growing up, but yes, she's grown into a beautiful woman."

"Who's this?" Cate asked, turning the phone's screen toward him. She'd obviously decided to swipe through the images.

"That's Emma, she's Jesse and David's daughter. She's about Elise's age."

"Jesse and David?"

He reached for the phone and swiped through a few more pictures before finding one of Jesse, David, and Emma along with Miranda, David's daughter, and James and Matt, Jesse's sons.

"Wow," Cate said once she'd taken the phone back.

He wasn't sure whether her comment was directed at the size of the extended Baker-Hathaway clan or simply the fact that he had pictures of friends on his phone; either way, it made him smile. Even though he was still a bit nervous about showing Cate this side of his life, this *new* side of his life, he kind of liked the look of pleased disbelief in her eyes. It was almost as if maybe, if even for a little while, she'd forgotten what he'd done. "Here, let me show you a few more," he said.

CHAPTER 5

"Mrs. Whatley," Caleb said, coming to a stop just inside the door of the downstairs library the next day. "We haven't met yet. I'm Caleb Forrester. I'm working with Catherine's company for the next few weeks."

"Mr. Forrester," Livia Whatley replied, looking up from her book. "I've heard about you from Agnes."

Caleb let out a quiet chuckle at the amusement dancing in Livia's eyes. "I didn't realize anyone was in here. I can come back another time, but while I'm here, is there anything I can get you?" He had, of course, known exactly who would be in the room.

"No, I'm fine thank you. And please, there's no need to postpone whatever it was that you were going to do in here on my account. As long as it doesn't involve a sledgehammer, it won't disturb me."

Caleb smiled in response then turned his back to her in order to survey the books on the shelves. If asked, he would tell her that he was checking the layout of the books, ensuring that the ones the guests might find most interesting were easily accessible. In reality, he was killing time. From what he'd been able to garner from Livia Whatley's background file, she spent as little time with the rest of the Whatley clan as possible. Which meant that she was probably a bit starved for conversation.

Four minutes later, she didn't disappoint. "What are you looking for? I know the library quite well by now, perhaps I can help."

He shook his head and told her his fabricated reason for being there.

"Dear god, is that the kind of stuff you all have to do for us?" she asked, unfolding her legs from her chair. Caleb thought she might rise and join him, but instead she used her feet to pull the ottoman closer then propped them up on top of it.

"It's one of the many things the company does to make sure our clients are well taken care of."

"Well, if the rest of your clients are like this lot, it must be a thankless job." She set her book down across her lap, signaling to him that she was more interested in conversation than reading.

"It has its pros and cons," he said.

She laughed softly. Livia Whatley had a soft, throaty voice with hints of a southern accent.

"That's very diplomatic of you, Mr. Forrester."

Over his shoulder, he flashed her a quick grin then went back to the books. "Call me Caleb, please."

"Caleb, then," she said, then paused. "Do you actually *like* this job? I understand you own your own company and have a chance to get out of the business altogether."

He turned to face her. Leaning against the bookshelves, he put his hands in his pockets. "I am selling my company and debating whether or not to join up with the new company or simply part ways. I like working, but it's possible that I just like working for myself." Strategically, he hadn't answered her question as to whether or not he liked *this* job, wanting to leave it open for interpretation, wanting to give her something to be curious about and engage with him about.

She cocked her head. Livia Whatley was an attractive woman. If she was having an affair, he had no problem believing that there would be many interested parties. Her blonde hair, which was cut short and had a slight curl to it, curved around her high cheekbones in an effortless look that could have taken an hour or thirty seconds to achieve—Caleb wouldn't know. Her clear blue eyes assessed him and her nails, painted a delicate pink, tapped on her book.

"My husband runs his own pharmaceuticals business. Over

the years, he tried a few things out with Michael and Anthony, his cousins, but it's hard to be in business when only one partner has any sense of responsibility."

"Your husband, I take it?"

She smiled at his assumption, at his mention of her husband, and the warmth from her smile planted the first seeds of doubt about his initial assessment of her. "Yes, Isiah takes his responsibilities very seriously. Not that he's a fuddy-duddy, but he believes in being a good man, in being a good role model for our children, in being a good husband."

That those were things that Michael and Anthony did not believe in was implied.

"You have children?" he asked. He knew the answer, but his objective was to keep her talking.

She smiled. "Yes, a son and a daughter. Max just started college this fall and Lilly is a junior in high school."

"Do you have family staying with your daughter while you're up here?"

Livia made a face. "Yes, my parents. It's great for Lilly to have the time with her grandparents, and my parents adore it, but they're getting older and I wish we didn't have to ask them to spend four weeks with our teenage daughter. A week here or there would be fine, and Lilly is never challenging, it's just tiring for them. They've already raised three kids, they don't need to raise mine."

"And there's no chance Lilly could come with you?"

Livia laughed. "No, and I wouldn't want her to either. *I* don't even like being here."

Caleb feigned appropriate surprise. "It's a beautiful setting. Fall in New England is hard to beat."

Livia inclined her head. "It is lovely, I would agree with that. We live in North Carolina and, while I love it there and it's my home, I do agree that there's nothing like the colors up here this time of year."

"I hear a 'but' in there," he said in his most charming tone.

He wasn't all that used to charming information from people, but he *had* done it before.

Livia lifted a shoulder, causing her blue sweater to shift off her shoulder a bit. As she pulled it back into place, she spoke. "The family never really welcomed me. When Isiah and I got married, we were both very young; he was twenty-two and I was twenty-one. I came from a modest background, not impoverished by any means, but nowhere near the league of the Whatley family. My father-in-law, Jonathan, has never approved of me."

Livia paused and futzed with the corner of her book. "He's barely worked a day in his life, was simply lucky enough to have been born into money. Yet he looked down on me, and my parents too—two people who worked hard, lived honest lives, and raised three good children. His elitism created a chasm we are mostly happy to each stay on either side of."

"And yet, you're here," Caleb said.

She gave him a sad smile. "Yes, I'm here because my husband believes family is part of his responsibility, and because I want to support him. However, I don't need to subject my kids to the same kind of disapproval from this family that I've had to deal with."

"And do they? Disapprove?"

Livia wagged her head. "I get along well enough with Sabrina, my sister-in-law, and her wife, Dominique—although Dominique is sometimes a bit too intense for me. And I love Dixie. The siblings, meaning Agnes and Edward, would never go against their brother, so they're barely tolerable. For the most part, I try to use my time with the Whatley family to catch up on my 'me time.' I read, nap, go to the spa, that sort of thing. Isiah and I also try to get away, just the two of us, as often as we can without appearing rude."

Again, Caleb was struck by the incongruity of her words with his initial assessment of her. She didn't speak of her husband in a way that led him to believe she was unfaithful to him.

He pushed off the shelves. "Well, more power to you. If there is anything I can do to help you enjoy your 'me time,' please let me know. I will mention that I found a nice little coffee shop outside of town the other day. It transforms into a wine bar in the evenings and they serve an amazing chocolate torte. I know Margaret makes some mean desserts, but if you're interested in a little late-night date time with your husband, I'd highly recommend it."

She turned a bright smile on him. "That sounds wonderful, perhaps we'll check it out tomorrow."

He nodded and made his way toward the door. "You know where to find me if you want the name."

"Thank you, Caleb."

He lifted his hand in a small wave as he exited the room. He'd have to revisit his assumptions about her, which meant revisiting her background files and figuring out why she had so many credit card expenses at hotels and inns all over North Carolina.

He was paused in the foyer, contemplating Livia when he heard footsteps approaching from his right. He turned to find Agnes coming toward him. Aided by a cane, she took steps that were sure, if not entirely steady.

"Ms. Whatley," he said when she came near.

"Mr. Forrester." She gave him a curt nod. "I was about to select a new book."

"Mrs. Livia Whatley is enjoying a book in the library as well. Can I give you any assistance?"

The corners of the woman's mouth pinched; the fact he noticed her grimace through her already quite wrinkled visage spoke volumes about Agnes's opinion of her nephew's wife. "Do you play chess, young man?" she demanded, apparently abandoning her quest for a book solely based on the fact that it would bring her into the vicinity of Livia. Caleb felt a sudden kinship with Isiah's wife, or at least a significant amount of sympathy for her and what she must put up with from the Whatley family.

"I do," he replied.

"Then come join me upstairs. No one else is about so you'll have to do, provided you let me win." She turned and started moving toward the stairs. He took two steps and caught up with her. When he offered her his arm, she glared up at him, gave a snort of what he thought was disgust, then took it anyway.

"Not many young men have such manners these days. Your mother must have raised you right," she grumbled as they started up the steps.

"My mother died when I was a teenager, ma'am." It was the truth, but he'd said it more to shock her than for any other reason. He got the sense that she was a woman who, appearances to the contrary, liked to be shocked.

"Well, that's a good thing, then. No mother would want to see her son grow up to be such a kiss ass."

Caleb bit back a laugh. Out of the corner of his eye he caught a glimpse of Cate hovering in the shadows by the stairs shooting him an apologetic look. He just shrugged a shoulder and winked in her direction before turning his attention back to Agnes.

"Can't go anywhere without *her* popping up," Agnes was saying, clearly in the middle of a thought.

"I beg your pardon?"

"Livia, that *woman*. She's an upstart, you know. Set her sights on Isiah when they were little more than children. He was definitely the goose that laid the golden egg for her."

"I was under the impression that she worked while her husband went to graduate school and when he was first getting into business for himself," Caleb said, knowing he shouldn't divulge much more about how much he knew about all of them.

Agnes paused and glared at him. "It was an investment, young man, and don't go thinking it was anything else. Got her claws into him early and made him feel so grateful and obligated that once he inherits from his father he'll never let her go."

Caleb thought Agnes's view of the world was a bit outdated if she thought someone prone to leave would stay out of guilt alone, but he said nothing. Knowing it would fall on deaf ears, he also opted not to point out that it was more likely than not that, after more than twenty years of marriage, Isiah and Livia stayed together because they *wanted to.*

They reached the top of the stairs and made their way into the library. He deposited Agnes in a seat in front of the chessboard, then offered to get her something to drink. Unsurprisingly, she demanded a glass of whiskey.

He set a full tumbler in front of her as he slid into a seat across from her. "I understand your father started the business," he said, making the first move.

"Hmm," she nodded, studying the board. "Just after the war. The Great War," she added, after moving her piece. "It's been in Whatley hands ever since."

"Douglas Whatley the Third runs it now," he commented rather than asked. "Does he ever come to the reunions?" He knew from Cate that the patriarch didn't attend, but he wanted to hear from Agnes why that might be.

"Why do you ask?" Her sharp eyes narrowed on him.

He held her gaze then shrugged and turned his attention back to the board. "Just curious," he said, making a move. He'd already figured out her strategy; losing to it without it seeming intentional was going to be the hard part. The good news for him was that it wasn't likely to be a long game.

His response, or the way he'd said it, must have appeased her and she turned her attention back to the board and answered. "He stopped coming when he took over, after his father died. His responsibility is to the family and he can only fulfill that by ensuring the company remains successful."

Caleb wondered if it ever occurred to Agnes that the company was also responsible for employing over thirty thousand people—something that might weigh heavier on a leader than any freeloading relatives. "I assume the business will stay in the family once he retires?"

Agnes gave a snort. "Yes, it will stay in the family. Or it will until Michael runs it into the ground, so help us all. God willing, I'll be dead long before that happens."

"Michael?" Again, Caleb kept his voice casual and his eyes focused on the board. "I thought Anthony was the one poised to take over." He knew from his files that Anthony had been working with Douglas for the past fifteen years and Michael had only recently joined the family endeavors.

Agnes shot him a shrewd look. "Anthony has worked with Douglas for many years, but Mikey-son is the heir apparent. He's not the next in line, of course, but he's the one Douglas seems to have set his sights on. Only god and Douglas know why, though."

"Not a fan, I take it," he said moving a piece into a position that, if she gave the move half a thought, she'd be able to figure out how to take.

"Not a fan," she repeated. "Michael's brains are well below his belt and always have been—or if not there then focused on where the next party is. What Douglas is thinking, I haven't a clue, but, like I said, I'll be well and dead when the company goes down the drain under Michael's leadership."

Caleb watched her study the board. He let out a quiet sigh when she failed to take the opening he'd left for her. Losing this game was going to be harder than he'd thought.

"No one else is willing to step up to the plate, so to speak?" This time, his attention on the board wasn't faked. He really did have to focus on orchestrating her victory.

"Oh, plenty are willing. Anthony, of course. And one of the Italian twins, I can never remember which, is always talking about moving to America. At least one of them would have some business sense," she said, sitting back and taking a sip of her drink.

He glanced at her as he debated which piece to move. "What about Sabrina or Dixie?" he asked, moving a piece directly into her line of attack.

Agnes scoffed. "Sabrina can barely keep her own house in order, she'd never have enough sense to run a business, and her father would never stand for it. He wouldn't stand for either of his children being the public face of the company. As for Dixie, well, let's just say she takes after her father: smart as a whip but couldn't care less about anything other than living like a common gypsy."

Caleb didn't think there was such a thing as a "common gypsy," but after meeting Dixie, he understood what Agnes meant—Dixie was the kind of person everyone would love, even as she let the company crumble around them. As for Sabrina and Isiah's father, based on what Cate had told him, Caleb would guess that Jonathon Whatley's issues with his children stemmed from their respective spouses, one being an upstart and both being women.

Watching as Agnes finally took an opening he'd left her in the game, his thoughts strayed to Sabrina and Isiah and he wondered about their relationship. They both seemed to be disappointments to their father, had they possibly bonded over that? Or had they been driven apart instead, each seeking to put the other down in an effort to curry their father's favor?

"You're awfully quiet over there, Mr. Forrester."

"It appears you've put me in checkmate, Ms. Whatley."

Her eyes shot down to the board then narrowed on him. "Rather, you put yourself in checkmate, didn't you?"

Her comment didn't require a response, so he just held her gaze.

She smiled at him. "If you can lose this effectively, I look forward to playing you when you're playing to win."

Erica Brandt entered the room, cutting off his reply. He flashed Agnes a grin and rose from his seat.

Erica paused just inside the doorway. Her eyes moved from him to the chess table and back. "She's a hustler, Mr. Forrester. She'll lose to you three times in a row, then win the next game in three moves."

Agnes straightened in her seat. "Nonsense, girl. I'll have you know, I just beat Mr. Forrester on our first game."

"Because you harassed him into losing to you?" Erica asked, moving toward the table where she stopped to study the positions of the pieces.

"I did no such thing."

"Yes, you did, ma'am," Caleb countered.

Agnes glared at him. "Only because I wanted to see your real skill. Next time, we'll have a proper game," she shot back.

"If there is a next time," Erica said, picking up Agnes's half-full tumbler. "And you do not need *this* in the middle of the day."

"I'm eighty-five, I can do whatever I want in the middle of the day. Besides, I go to bed at seven, three o'clock is practically evening for me."

Caleb had to agree with Agnes on that one.

"It's a horrible vice anyway. Erica, throw it out," came another voice from the doorway.

Caleb swiveled his head to find the one member of the family he hadn't yet met. "I'm Caleb Forrester," he said, striding toward the elderly man. "You must be Edward Whatley."

Edward, Agnes's brother, eyed him, then, after a moment's hesitation, took Caleb's proffered hand.

"Oh, don't be a prig, Edward," Agnes said. "He's not diseased. Although I imagine he's quite a sinner," she added with the same taunting twinkle in her eye that Caleb recognized from interactions with his own sister. Agnes was goading her brother.

"Mr. Forrester has joined the staff for the remainder of the reunion, Edward," Erica said, her voice placating.

"I should think if he's part of the staff, he should be doing things that the staff do and not lounging about like a guest," Edward said with a huff.

"He came in to play chess with Agnes," Erica explained, shooting Caleb an apologetic look.

"And now he has to go run some errands and do some staff-like things," Caleb said with a smile. "Ladies, Mr. Whatley." He acknowledged each of them with a glance, then turned and left the room. He had no desire to stick around in the middle of that conversation, though he did loiter in the hall for a moment to overhear what they might say in his absence. He was disappointed when the conversation quickly turned to the weather and the upcoming storm due later than night.

"How did it go?" Cate's voice carried softly in the hall and Caleb looked up to see her walking toward him carrying a few tumblers and a decanter on a tray. She was dressed like the rest of the staff—black slacks and a white button-down shirt—but also wore a dark green cardigan to ward off the chill in the house.

"I lost a game of chess," he said as they headed down the stairs together.

"Agnes?"

Caleb smiled. "She conned me."

Cate gave him a sideways glance as they made their way into the kitchen. "Doesn't surprise me. Agnes Whatley likes nothing more than to be contrary. Learn anything other than that?"

Cate set the tray down by the sink and started placing the empty items on the counter. They were alone in the room, but Caleb leaned his backside against the counter so he could keep an eye on the door as they spoke.

"I changed my mind about Livia having an affair and I know why she stays in the background now. The family hasn't been very nice to her, well, at least the siblings haven't. Her father-in-law, Jonathon, sounds like a real winner. According to Agnes, he's perennially disappointed in his children and would prefer that they stay hidden away, presumably so as not to shame him. I also learned that Anthony, Michael, and Isiah did some work together years ago, but no longer do, and that, according to Livia, Isiah is the responsible one. I found that interesting because Agnes said Michael is the heir apparent, even though, in her opinion, his brains are in his pants and the company would be better off with Anthony or one of the Italian twins, though she couldn't remember which one."

"Wow. All that in what, forty-five minutes?" Cate handed him one of the tumblers she'd just washed.

He glanced around, grabbed a tea towel and began drying. "Livia is bored. I was a neutral party to talk to. Agnes sees me as someone of no consequence, so it doesn't matter what she says to me."

Cate handed him another tumbler. "What makes you think Livia isn't having an affair?"

"Because it's obvious she loves her husband."

Cate paused, her hands covered in soap, and stared at him.

"What?" he asked.

"Do you believe that?"

"Believe that she loves her husband? Yes. I did just say that."

"No cynicism, no scoffing in disbelief . . ."

Caleb narrowed his eyes. "What are you getting at?"

Cate continued to stare at him for another moment, then smiled and went back to washing. "So you believe in love?"

He frowned and took another glass. "Of course. If I believe in hate, why wouldn't I believe in love?"

Cate shrugged. "I don't know. I agree with you, it's just not something we've ever talked about and I guess I assumed you were like Tommy."

Caleb drew back. "What does that mean? Tommy loved you."

Cate waved a soapy hand, dismissing his defense. "He did. I know. But he certainly never talked about it. It just *was*. Sometimes it felt like he was almost ashamed of it, as if loving me was a weakness that, as long as we didn't talk about it he could pretend didn't exist."

Caleb crossed his arms over his chest, preparing to defend his friend, but then he realized that he had never actually heard Tommy talk about loving Cate and Brooke. He'd loved them, of that Caleb was certain, and, more importantly, Cate was too. But she was right, Tommy had never mentioned love.

Shrugging, Caleb said, "I don't know what Tommy thought on the subject, but I've seen plenty of good and bad things come from all kinds of emotions, including love."

Cate handed him the decanter then turned to wipe down the tray. "Me, too," she said. "It just surprised me to hear you acknowledge it. So, if all kinds of things can come from love, or hate, what do you think of Livia now?" she asked, bringing the subject back around to the Whatley family.

"I don't think she's having an affair," he repeated.

"So then, not likely she'd be out to kill her husband for his money?"

Caleb shook his head.

"But if you thought she was having an affair before, maybe her husband does too," Cate suggested as she reached up into a cupboard for a bottle of whiskey.

"It's possible, but I won't hazard an opinion on that until I see them together."

"You think you'll be able to tell?"

He watched her pour some of the amber liquid into the crystal decanter. "I've been around a lot of men in love lately. Yes, I think I'll be able to tell whether or not Isiah Whatley loves his wife."

She glanced up at him and grinned. "You sound a bit disgruntled."

"I guess that's what happens when you're still a bachelor in your late thirties. But since one of them loves my sister, I've learned to deal with it."

She laughed softly and recorked the bottle. "So what now?" she asked, turning to face him.

"It'll seem strange if I spend too much time in the house chatting up the family, so I thought I would take a hike out to where the wire was found."

She nodded. "I can give you directions. The trails around here are well marked as long as you stay on the main ones. Speaking of the wire, what are you doing with it?"

"When I was in town yesterday, I sent it to a friend who works in an evidence lab. I'm not overly hopeful that she'll find anything, but if anyone can, she can."

Cate regarded him for a moment then gestured toward the door with her head. "I wanted to go check on Elise. Afterward, I'll show you the trailhead then come back and finish taking care of this," she said, waving her hand toward the crystal.

"Sounds good," he replied, setting down the glass he'd been drying.

When they left the main house, he veered off to the ice house to change while Cate headed to the carriage house to check on Elise.

When he knocked at their door about ten minutes later, Elise opened it holding her new stuffed toy. "Last night I dreamt Athena and me were riding in the woods," she said without preamble.

"Was it a good ride?" Caleb asked, kneeling down to her level.

She bobbed her head. "We walked and walked and came across a gnome and an old airplane."

"In the woods?"

Again, she nodded. "It had vines growing all over it."

"That must have been weird. What did Athena do?"

"Athena said it was time to take a bath," Cate interjected as she came up behind Elise.

When she looked up to make a face at her mom, Elise's curls to bobbed and swayed. "I don't wanna," she grumbled.

"You love baths and, whether you want one or not, you definitely need one. You were out rolling in leaves this morning and still have pieces in your hair." Cate began picking through her daughter's hair pulling out stray leaves.

Caleb rose from his crouch as he watched the interaction between the two.

"Tonight, mama," Elise insisted.

"You promised Jana you would clean up without fuss if she let you go hog wild in those leaves."

At that, Elise's little face scrunched up as she refrained from arguing.

While it didn't surprise Caleb that Elise would take after her father in the belief that a promise made was a promise kept, it did surprise him that she was following in his footsteps at the mature age of four. Her struggle was written so plainly on her face: argue and break a promise, or do something she didn't want to do. Cate flashed him a knowing smile; she recognized the "Tommy trait" too.

"Why don't I take her for a ride and then she can clean up?" Caleb knew, even as he made the offer, that he should have asked Cate first, but he was hard pressed to feel bad about it. Clearly, Elise was horse crazy. He was already going for a walk. He could easily lead her while she rode, and by the time they got back, it would be close to dinnertime, a perfect time to clean up. "Assuming it's okay with you, of course, and that Mirielle doesn't mind, I can lead her pony while I walk," he said to Cate, trying his hardest to not smile as he watched Elise, who was now bouncing on her feet and subtly trying to get her mom to agree without being whiney.

The look Cate shot him threw him back in time; it was the same one she'd given him when he had done things like taken Brooke to get ice cream an hour before dinner or let her stay up past her bedtime to watch movies when he'd babysat.

"You are a softy, Mr. Forrester," Cate said, a smile tugging at her lips.

"Jesse may have said the same thing a time or two," he replied with an unrepentant grin.

Cate shook her head and turned her attention back to her daughter. "Why don't you come to the barn with us to see if Mirielle says it's okay? If she does, Caleb will tack up Pansy while you come back and get changed."

Elise let out a tiny squeal and spun on her heels before darting back into the house. "I just gotta put Athena on the couch!"

"Do you know what you're doing?" Cate asked.

Caleb shrugged. "I've been around enough horses, we'll be fine."

"That's not exactly what I'm talking about. Hold on," she said, heading back inside.

He heard her telling Jana their plan and few moments later she was back, with Elise at her side.

"Go on," Cate said to her daughter. "Go ahead and wait for us at the barn."

At that, Elise took off at a loopy gait toward the horses.

"Are you sure you're ready to spend an hour to an hour and half as her sole source of entertainment?" Cate asked as they followed.

"She'll be riding, that's entertainment."

"I'm just saying, she'll talk your ear off. And it won't be happy chatter, like Brooke's was."

"Of course it won't be like spending time with Brooke, Elise is a different kid. A different person." He hadn't intended them to, but his words reflected the pain he still felt about Brooke and even he could hear the harsh edge to his tone.

He felt Cate's gaze on him, but then she let it drop to the path and said, "Yes, she is."

They continued in silence for a minute longer. As they neared the barn and began to hear Elise and Mirielle's voices, Caleb put a hand out and stopped Cate. "Look, Cate. I'm sorry. I didn't mean to snap—"

"It's my fault, Caleb," Cate cut him off. "I shouldn't have assumed you'd think she was like Brooke. I know you better than that. The truth is, though, I heard it so much in the first three years of her life: people who knew Brooke constantly commenting on how different they were. I guess I'm a little defensive. I don't know if you know this, but we moved about a year ago, and it was mostly because I didn't want Elise growing up in Brooke's shadow. Like you said, they're different people. They each deserve to be loved because of who they are, not judged for who they aren't."

Caleb nodded and in that moment, when the light breeze lifted some of the strands of hair framing Cate's face and she watched him with her pale green eyes, he realized that they'd never actually comforted each other after Brooke had died. Both she and Tommy had gone into deep dark places and he hadn't known how to reach either of them. When Brooke had been around, there had been plenty of hugs between them all, even him and Tommy, as well as casual touches, offers of help, and genuinely warm friendship. But since Brooke died, and then Tommy, Caleb realized he hadn't once hugged the woman standing before him—a woman who had, at one time, been one of his only friends.

"Mama," Elise called as she came walking briskly from the barn with Mirielle following behind her. "Mama, Mirielle said I can take Pansy for a ride."

Cate held his gaze then dropped it to her daughter with a smile. "Great, fun. Now why don't you skedaddle back to the carriage house and put on some jeans and your boots? Caleb and I will help Mirielle get Pansy ready."

Elise grinned back at her mother then, much to his surprise, threw her arms around his waist and gave him a quick, fierce hug before taking off.

"You sure you're okay with this?" Cate asked Mirielle, who laughed.

"It's fine. It's actually good. With the storm coming tonight, we probably won't be able to get the horses out for another day or so, so it will be good for her to stretch her legs today. I assume you're good with horses, Mr. Forrester?"

"Caleb, please," he said as the three of them started toward the barn. "I'm not a professional by any means, but, yes, I do know my way around horses."

"So you've ridden then?" Mirielle asked as she reached the stall housing the large, black pony.

"I've done my share of trail and pack riding, through mountains, deserts, that kind of thing, and I played polo when I was kid," he said, handing Mirielle Pansy's halter that he'd unhooked from the door.

"You played polo?" Cate asked.

While he hadn't forgotten she was there, he had forgotten there was so much about his life that she had no idea about. Things he was only beginning to acknowledge himself now that he and Kit were determined to wade through the quagmire of their upbringing.

"I did," he said, reaching for the leadline attached to the halter Mirielle had just clipped on Pansy. "Until I was about eighteen. Nothing big, mind you, mostly for things like charity events." It had all been a part of the wealthy, happy façade his family had portrayed. Not that the wealth had been a façade, that part had been very real, but the rest of it—his father dressing Caleb and Kit up, toting them to events, trotting them about as if he were a proud, caring, doting father—well, all that had been a thin veneer hiding a man Caleb still had a hard time believing was his father.

"Why don't you show me where the brushes are and her tack and everything?" he said to Mirielle.

"I can help with this," Cate offered after a beat.

He was under no illusions that she was digesting the information he'd dropped. "I've got this," he said. "Why don't you go check on Elise?"

Again, Cate hesitated, but then nodded and turned to leave.

"Polo?" Mirielle asked as she began to curry the horse. "You don't meet many polo riders anymore. Not outside Florida anyway."

"A lifetime ago," Caleb said, picking up one of the pony's hooves to pick it clean. Pansy was obliging and seemed to enjoy being attended to by two people. "Anything I should know about her?" he asked, moving to another foot.

"She's a pony. She's not going to spook or do anything stupid, which is why I always put green riders on her, but she may decide today is the day she refuses to pass by some particular tree, or leaf, or rock, or whatever."

Caleb chuckled. Carly had a pony she was working with at her new farm. He'd heard her complain about the same disposition in Popover; one day he'd jump everything she put in front of his face and the next he'd decide he wasn't going to leave his stall.

"So, distract and persuade?" Caleb asked, finishing up the last hoof.

"Yes, and it helps if you take some carrots or sugar cubes with you. You'll always be able to distract her with food."

Caleb glanced at the well-rounded horse and didn't doubt it.

"Ready?" Elise came into the barn walking as fast as she could manage without breaking into a run, which Caleb was sure she'd been told not to do in the barn.

"We just have to throw her saddle and bridle on," Mirielle answered.

"I can't reach them," Elise said, coming to a stop in front of Caleb with Cate trailing behind her. "I can buckle the girth once Mirielle puts the saddle on, but everything else is too high."

"Mirielle was just telling me about Pansy," he said to Cate, then he turned back to the barn manager as she reappeared carrying a saddle, saddle pad, and bridle. "Do many of the family members ride her?"

"No, most of them are exceptional riders. Even though Sasha and Nikki are young, they've been riding a long time," Mirielle replied.

"And I suppose Luke would be too big for her, even if he were a beginner?" he asked, taking the saddle pad from her and placing it on Pansy's back.

"He is too big for her, and even he's not a beginner, not really. He's pretty new to English but has ridden a lot of western."

"That's kind of unusual, isn't it? Having so many people here that are experienced riders?" he asked. He was fishing and, judging by the little smile Cate gave him, she approved of his approach.

"It is, but thankfully all of them don't usually want to be out at the same time, or even on the same days. If they did, we'd have a hard time accommodating them. In fact, I think the only ones who don't ride are Agnes, Edward, and Sebastian. Agnes and Edward grew up riding, of course, but neither has an interest in tempting fate at their age."

"Understandable," he said as Mirielle held the girth for Elise, who immediately went to work securing the saddle. "And do they have favorites they each like to ride? Like Elise obviously does," he added with a smile and a wink at the young girl.

"Dixie likes Mira, the petite bay at the end of the barn and Nikki likes Pooka, Pansy's pasture mate, but other than that, they are a surprisingly easygoing family. When it comes to the horses, anyway."

Caleb caught Mirielle's qualification and made a note to himself to check back with her at some point. Like the rest of the staff, she had no doubt seen and overheard things that the family wasn't even aware of.

"Do you know where you're going today?" Mirielle asked.

"He's going to take the Black Bear trail," Cate said.

Mirielle glanced at him quickly, then went back to checking

Elise's work. After tightening the girth, she turned to the little girl and asked, "Why don't you go get your helmet?"

Once Elise was out of earshot, the barn manager looked at Caleb. "That's a nice long loop. Are you sure you're up for a five-mile walk?"

He could tell by the flash in her eyes that she wasn't asking about the distance, but rather whether or not he wanted to trek it with a four-year-old on a lead line.

"I think we'll be okay, right Pansy?" he said, giving the mare's neck a good rub. In response, she leaned into him, making him chuckle. "She's going to do that during the whole walk, isn't she? Try to rub against me?"

"She's very affectionate," Mirielle confirmed, giving the horse a pat just behind the saddle. "You ready, squirt?" she asked Elise, who'd just returned with her helmet.

The child nodded vigorously, her curls bobbing. Mirielle slipped the halter over the bridle, clipped it into place, and handed Caleb the lead line.

Five minutes later, they were on their way, following a trail Cate had pointed out. He glanced at his watch as they headed into the forest. Cate had told him that the spot where the wire had been found was about three miles in. There weren't any distance markers on the trail, but she'd also mentioned that the two trees stood exactly opposite each other on either side of the trail, that both trees had deer blinds in them about thirty feet up, and that if he and Elise hit the Mountain Elk Trail, they would have passed the spot by about a quarter of a mile.

As they made their way deeper into the forest, Elise babbled away about this and that. If he had harbored any thoughts about Elise being a "replacement" for Brooke—which he hadn't—they would have been shattered within the first five minutes of their walk. While Brooke often chatted about her dolls and the kids in her neighborhood, Elise's chatter focused more on things she'd recently learned, either through books or talking to people. She asked a lot of questions about plants that he couldn't answer, which appeared to make her doubt whether or not he qualified as a real adult, since he clearly wasn't as smart as her mom. But he did feel that he'd passed a test when he was able to tell her why the leaves changed colors in the fall.

She was just telling him which leaf color was her favorite—the bright burnt orange—when they came to the place where the wire had been strung. The location had been easier to identify than Caleb had anticipated. The scarring from the wires had left dark slashes against the pale gray trunks and, although he did, he hadn't needed to confirm the location of the two blinds to know he was in the right spot. Pausing for a moment under the guise of catching his breath, he studied the indentations the wire's tension had caused in the trees. Based on their depth, Caleb guessed that the wire had been extremely taut, the better to inflict damage. With that thought, he was grateful that, even though Cate hadn't paused to think about fingerprints, she *had* unwound the entire wire from the tree when she'd taken it down, rather than cut it. With the entire length of wire intact, his friend Dr. Vivienne DeMarco, or Vivi as everyone called her, would have a much better chance of obtaining any DNA that might have been left on the sharp ends that had been twisted to hold it in place.

He glanced down at his watch. He'd sent Vivi the wire by overnight mail; by the time he returned to his room, she would have had it nearly twenty-four hours. More than enough time for the certifiable genius to figure out if she would be able to get anything useful from it. He'd text her when they got back and ask her to call him after she put Jeffery, her son, to bed.

"What are you looking at?" Elise asked. To his surprise, she'd been quietly watching him as he'd studied the trees and let his mind wander. At the questioning look in her big brown eyes, he hesitated. He'd never answer truthfully, of course, but he acknowledged that perhaps he shouldn't have brought her out there with him in the first place. She seemed to be an extraordinarily observant child; he wasn't sure he would be able to mislead her.

He cleared his throat and looked back at the trees. The

indentations lay well over Elise's head and there was no doubt that whoever had strung the wire had intended for it to hit someone tall or someone riding a tall horse.

"Your mom mentioned that someone had wrapped some tight wires around these two trees," he said, pointing to them and figuring that honesty—well, partial honesty, anyway—was probably the best route. "I wanted to come out and make sure the damage wasn't too bad."

Elise glanced up, her eyes darting from one tree to the other. He could almost see Tommy's DNA in her as she assessed the situation. "Will they be all right?" she asked, her gaze falling to his.

Feeling almost like it was Tommy who'd asked him that question, he nodded slowly.

As she cocked her head to the side, some of her curls fell from under her helmet. "Why would someone string wire between the trees? It's not long enough to be a zip line. I rode on one of those once. With my mom, in Costa Rica."

Caleb smiled at the image. He could see Cate, with Elise riding koala-bear-style, zipping across the jungle. With parents like hers, Elise wasn't going to be a stranger to adrenaline.

"You're right," he said, stepping around the back of one of the trees to see if whoever had been there had left any evidence. So much time had passed that he didn't expect to find anything, but he had to pursue all possibilities. "It is too short for a zip line, but maybe someone wanted to hang something from it."

Finding nothing but a makeshift ladder of wood pieces nailed to the tree trunk which led up to the hunting blind, he crossed the path to the other tree. As he stepped farther from Elise and Pansy, the leadline slid through his fingers a bit. Looking behind the second tree, he spotted a few broken branches and the same type of ladder leading to the identical blind Cate had mentioned, but not much more. He considered the possibility of coming back with an evidence collection kit, but as the thought formed, Pansy tossed her head and the leadline slipped completely out of his hand.

Reason and logic fled when he felt the tip of the rope slide out of his grip and heard it drop onto the dampened earth less than two feet from where he stood. In the three seconds it took for him to lunge for the line that kept him connected to Elise, images of Pansy taking off, of her pulling a pony stunt and gleefully dumping Elise somewhere before galloping back to the stable, flew through his brain. And the image of Elise's body lying crumpled on a trail littered with her favorite bright burnt-orange leaves seized his body. He took one giant step, his foot stamping on the line just as fast as his heart rate had kicked up. He reached for the rope and curled his fingers around it even as he continued to move toward Elise, wanting to be there to catch her should Pansy decide to bolt.

He was beside the pony in no time, his hands now gripping the reins as well as the lead, but those few moments had felt like eons. With the adrenaline coursing through his system, it took a few seconds for him to realize that Pansy had remained standing calmly and Elise still sat with her hands lying casually across the front of the saddle, loosely holding the reins.

"Are you okay?" he asked, his heart hammering in his throat.

Elise frowned at him. "Of course I'm okay. Pansy wouldn't hurt me."

Caleb took a few deep breaths. Elise watched him, her brows furrowed. He dragged his eyes away from her and looked down at Pansy. He was standing so close to the pony's head that he had to step away to see her expression. When he did, he could swear he saw her roll an eye at him.

Neither horse nor rider had moved an inch, but in the seconds he'd lost control of the leadline and had imagined Elise's life slipping away, he had felt that breathtaking weight of loss. Again.

Elise and Pansy watched him as if they were in agreement that he might not be the sharpest tool in the shed.

"We should get back," he said, abruptly pulling Pansy's lead-line in the direction they'd come. The pony tossed her head in protest of being manhandled without warning, but then obediently turned and followed.

The journey back was a little quieter than the one out. He

didn't know if Elise sensed his discomfort, but suspected she did—mostly because it was sitting on him like a wet, wool blanket. He had panicked. There was no way to deny it. And he was not a man who panicked. Except, apparently, when he loses control of a docile pony for a few seconds.

Caleb turned back to look at his charge. Elise sat peacefully, observing the shadowed forest around her, completely unfazed by the trauma he had just experienced. He grimaced and switched his attention back to the trail, thinking that the least she could do was show a little gratitude—he *had* just saved her from certain death, after all.

Since she didn't seem inclined to oblige him, he directed his thoughts to what he had seen in the forest, which hadn't been much. Whoever had strung the wire had needed strength, but, realistically, anyone who worked out or was even moderately strong would fit that bill. The fact that it had been strung relatively high didn't give him much to go on either, as the ladders nailed into the trees would have provided easy access. He went over everything he'd seen one more time as they made their way home, hoping that maybe he'd missed something that he could go back and collect as evidence.

Darkness was falling when they arrived back at the barn and, other than his own impressions of the scene, he had nothing more to go on than what he had when he'd left. Mirielle met them at the door and the three of them untacked Pansy together. Four carrots and lots of cuddles later, Elise closed the pony's stall door and she and Caleb made their way back toward the carriage house. When they arrived, she gave him another big hug, asked when they could go again—a question he said she'd have to ask her mother—and then disappeared into the house. He said good-bye to Jana and, as he made his way toward the ice house, called Vivi.

"It's Caleb," he said when she answered.

"Ah, yes. It seems mystery always surrounds you, doesn't it?" she replied. Of all of Kit's friends, Vivi had been the least quick to embrace Caleb as he came back into Kit's life. Vivi's comments harkened back to the years he had come and gone from Kit's life with little to no explanation. At the time, he'd thought it was the right thing to do, but only recently, when the chips had been down and Kit's life in danger, had he realized, had Kit *made* him realize, just how wrong he'd been then.

He trusted Vivi implicitly, along with her husband, Ian, a man with whom Caleb had worked prior to his retirement from the Rangers, but trust and friendship didn't always go hand in hand.

"What do you want to know?" he asked, knowing that complete honesty was the best route to take with Vivi, even if it didn't come naturally to him. He held in a sigh, thinking about the things he did for his sister. And for someone he could trust with evidence.

"I know you're in New Hampshire, based on the return address on the package you sent me, but what are you doing and what's going on?" she asked.

He veered away from his room, deciding to scout the grounds as he sketched out the truth for her, though he referred to Cate as simply an old friend who needed a hand rather than mention Tommy and that particular past. He knew Vivi wouldn't miss the fact that he was being somewhat vague about who exactly Cate was; after all, Vivi was not only a medical examiner and top consultant at the FBI and the NY state evidence lab, but also a trained forensic psychologist. While no one was dead *yet*, Vivi's psychology background was never really in the 'background,' and she had an uncanny way of reading people and situations. Thankfully, she also had a tremendous amount of tact, and he trusted that, at least for now, she'd let questions about Cate drop.

"Interesting, that puts a different spin on things, doesn't it—preventing a murder rather than investigating one?" she asked when he'd finished his description of the situation

"I imagine your investigations often prevent murders," he countered.

He could all but see her shrug. "We do our best," she replied. "Now, let's talk about what you sent me."

And, for the next ten minutes or so, they did. He learned

about the tensile strength of the particular wire, its composition, and where it was manufactured. Unfortunately, he also learned that it was available in most hardware stores, including the four closest to The Washington House, and that there was no DNA or even fingerprints, other than a few partials that aligned with what Cate would have left when she removed it.

"Any good news?" he asked, pausing at the edge of the woods on the south side of the main house. His gaze went to the lawn that stretched several acres in front of him; lit with lamps, it was a pool of light in the dusk that was quickly fading into night.

"There wasn't any DNA, but there was a tiny piece of leather on one of the ends."

"Like a piece that might have snagged if someone had been wearing gloves when they strung it up?"

"Exactly. What's interesting about it is that the leather, and it's a tiny sample, isn't cow skin but lambskin."

"Lambskin? Isn't that kind of old fashioned?" he asked, turning back toward the ice house. As he walked, he kept his attention on the main house, noting which lights were on in which rooms as the occupants prepared for dinner.

"It's less common now, that's for sure, but not so uncommon as to be able to narrow down a pool of suspects, unless only one person has such a pair, of course. When I did some research, I found that most modern lambskin gloves are made for women. Now, I'll be the first to say that my sample set was limited to a few online retailers and then a few manufacturers, but it was a trend I thought I would mention."

"But you still wouldn't rule out a man?" he asked

"Not a chance," she said. "Knowing lambskin tends to favor women might give me a place to start if I needed direction, but I would only let it guide me, not determine the path."

"And could you tell the age of the leather? Not the lamb itself, but the age of the glove?"

"I could run a few more tests to narrow it down, but I would say relatively new. Between three and five years old."

He wasn't sure what that bit of information would get him, but he'd rather have it than not and said so.

"So, what's your next step?" Vivi asked.

"I'm still establishing possible motives and victims. I have background checks from Jay and am working on getting to know the family."

"Will you be sending me more evidence?"

He hesitated, wondering if maybe he'd overstepped the bounds by sending her the wire. He could have sent it to Jay, or asked Jay for another lab to send it to. But the truth was he knew Vivi was one of the best in the country, *plus* she was one of Kit's good friends. In the back of his mind, he also acknowledged something he'd never admit to anyone, that maybe, by working with Vivi, he was hoping to finally win her over.

He ran a hand over his face and through his hair. "Probably, if you don't mind? I'll pay for the services, of course," he added.

A beat of silence passed before she answered. "Of course I don't mind."

For a split second, he considered asking about her hesitation, and also why she wasn't as willing as Kit's other friends were to accept him, the way she had apparently accepted Drew Carmichael and David Hathaway. Then he heard a door shut and turned to see Cate coming out of the main house. He took a step forward and the movement caught her attention. She paused to wait for him.

"Thanks, Vivi," he said, instead of voicing his thoughts.

Again, a beat of silence. "You're welcome. And Caleb?"

"Yeah?" he asked, approaching Cate.

"Don't ever hesitate to reach out to me," Vivi responded then abruptly hung up.

Not quite sure what to make of her parting words, he paused and stared down at his phone, as if the device itself were responsible for the surprising comment. Did she mean it as a friend, or strictly professionally? Did she mean anytime, or only when he needed something specific?

"Everything okay?" Cate asked, coming toward him.

He frowned, then slid his phone into his pocket and gestured toward their cabins with his head. "Yes, I was just on the phone with the person I sent the wire to," he said, then filled her in on his conversation with Vivi as they walked. The scent of chimney smoke from The Washington House's fireplaces lingered in the air and the clattering sounds of Margaret and staff preparing dinner, muted through the stone and glass of the building, echoed around them. The temperature had dropped several degrees; he guessed they'd see frost in the morning.

"And Elise? How was Elise?" she asked as they reached the ice house.

"She was great, very well behaved. Chatty, but well behaved."

That earned him a smile, but as he reached for his keys, a twinge of uncertainty grabbed hold of him. He assumed that Cate would want to get home to Elise, but she stood there as if she might want him to invite her in. "Uh, do you want to come it for a bit before you head back to your place for dinner?"

She smiled at him, a little too brightly. "I'd love to. I'd also love a beer," she said, linking her arm in his like she used to as he turned to open the door. "I miss adult conversation. I know, I work with adults, but since I'm their manager, it's not the same."

No, he didn't suppose it was. He flicked on a few lights as they entered and his eyes scanned the room. He didn't have anything in particular that he wanted to hide from Cate, it was a force of habit more than anything else. She slipped off her jacket and he hung it with his on a wall peg as she went to the fridge, grabbed two bottles of beer, and popped the tops. He began tidying the table to give them a place to sit.

"Let's sit there instead," Cate said, using one of the bottles to gesture toward the two chairs in front of the fireplace. Taking her cue, he flicked on the gas fire as she slipped her feet from her shoes and curled up in one of the chairs. Taking a beer from her, he sat in the other chair and, after a moment, slipped his own shoes off, though he wasn't flexible enough to tuck his legs underneath himself as she had.

They sat in silence for a few moments, which was ironic given Cate's stated reason for wanting to come inside, but he figured she was probably seeking adult company more than just conversation. She sat across from him, an elbow propped on the arm of the chair and her chin propped in the palm of her hand. The light of the flames reflected on her face, a constant dance of dark and light.

"Where do you live now?" he asked, suddenly realizing he had no idea. He still pictured her in the home where he'd spent so much time, even though she'd told him she'd moved.

She turned her face and the firelight lit up her hair, the wisps that had come loose over the day reflecting like gold. "We moved to a neighborhood outside of Miami. It's not far from the beach and fairly close to company headquarters."

"You don't need to be in the office, do you?"

She shook her head. "No, but like I said the other day, I wanted to move. I didn't want Elise to grow up in Brooke's shadow and I had to pick somewhere. It's a good area with good schools, and if I ever want to get out of this part of the business," she said with a wave toward the main house, "I figured it would be good to be close to the main offices."

"But . . ." he said, because he heard one.

She made a face at him. "Do you have any idea how hard it is to be close to the beach and not have any good surfing? I know it sounds crazy," she said with a small laugh, "but it's so *strange* to me. The beaches themselves are gorgeous, but I guess," she paused and her eyes dropped. She took a long sip of her beer then her eyes came back up to his. "I guess part of the reason I picked that neighborhood was because it was close to the beach. I thought it might make me feel closer to home, to that sense of freedom and power I was talking about the other day. Only the beaches near me, well, they *are* beautiful, and, I'm not exactly sure what I'm trying to say, but, I guess I realized that what was beautiful to me growing up wasn't so much . . ." Her voice trailed off.

"It wasn't so much the sand and the water, but the rawness of the power the ocean could unleash," he said.

Slowly, she nodded. "What is beautiful to me is being somewhere where I feel connected and a part of something bigger. I may be an inconsequential part of something bigger, but there's something humble and graceful about that too."

"And the beaches in Florida?"

She lifted a shoulder. "The expanse of the ocean is humbling, but I don't feel as connected to it as I have to other places. It's a nice place to live, but isn't home. What about you? Where do you live these days?"

It was his turn to look toward to the fire and take his time in answering. The oddity of having this conversation with Cate did not escape him. For nearly ten years, she and Tommy had known just about everything he ever let anyone know about him. Now, she didn't even know where he lived. That shadowy feeling of isolation that he sometimes felt when he watched Kit and Garret together, that feeling that maybe he was missing out on something important by living such a solitary life, washed over him.

He shifted in his seat and ran a hand through his hair. "I don't really live anywhere, in particular. I still travel a lot for work, but less now than I used to. When I'm not traveling, though, I try to stay with Kit in Windsor."

"You like it there, don't you?"

No one had ever asked that question and he paused to give it some thought. Every one of the friends he'd made in Windsor, with the exception of Garret and, to an extent, Ian, he'd met through Kit. And since his sister lived there, whether he actually liked it was, he assumed, either a given or irrelevant.

But as he thought about it, he realized that he actually did like Windsor. A lot. He turned his eyes back to Cate, whose green eyes were watching him. "I do," he said.

"And what do you like about it?" Her voice seemed quieter, softer than it had moments before. Or perhaps that was just his imagination.

He looked away. "It's a beautiful area. The land itself reminds me a bit of where I grew up, except that the winters are much colder, of course."

"And the people?"

"There are a lot of good people. Kit and Garret, of course, and an old colleague, Ian MacAllister. He used to be a Ranger and Tommy and I worked with him occasionally; he lives in Windsor with his wife, Vivienne DeMarco."

"Is Vivienne the same woman as Vivi? The one you sent the wire to?"

"Yes, the very same," he said on a sigh.

"You don't sound too enamored of her."

Caleb wagged his head and told her a bit about Vivi's background and obvious reluctance to embrace him the way some of the others had. Cate took a sip of her drink then laughed at his impression of Vivi's arched-eyebrow look, an expression she seemed to give him a lot.

"Yes, it's hard to believe that your incredible charm and wit haven't won her over," Cate said, still chuckling.

"Hey, I have charm and wit," he said defensively. They both knew he was lying.

"You do have *something*, Caleb Forrester," she said, setting her empty bottle on the side table and rising from her seat. "What it is exactly, I'm not entirely sure. If she has half the intelligence you say she has, though, she'll figure it out sooner or later. In the meantime, rest easy knowing that most of us already love you," she said with a smile. Then she leaned over and brushed a kiss against his cheek. She smelled like vanilla and spice. "And we, or I should say *I*, appreciate everything you are doing to help."

"Just doing my job, ma'am," he managed to reply. No one was as easy about showing affection with him as Cate. She'd always been that way: touching, hugging, and, yes, even kissing—on the cheek, of course—all the time.

"But you're not doing *your job*. You're doing me a favor. And to thank you for that, the least I can do is bring you some dinner tonight. I'm going to go eat with Elise while Margaret and the staff are getting dinner ready for the family, then I'll pop over to the main house, grab some food from the kitchen, and bring it back. She's making one of your favorites tonight: slow roasted pork with rosemary sauce and potatoes."

His stomach actually growled as she said it. Growing up in the south, pork had been a staple and when Tommy had met Cate, she'd introduced them both to all the Hawaiian ways to prepare the meat. Pork was, and always would be, one of his favorites.

She smiled at the expression on his face and took it as the acceptance it was. "I'll come back at around seven thirty?"

"Sounds good. And, by the way," he said as she moved toward the door. "I *did* charm Agnes today. I *can* be charming," he pointed out.

With her hand on the doorknob, Cate turned back and laughed. "Agnes is like a snake, no one charms her unless she *deems it worthy of* being charmed by them, but I will grant you that you *have* charmed my daughter."

"I bribed your daughter with a pony ride. That's different."

"Charm, bribery—from you it's all the same thing," she said, her laughter continuing after she'd shut the door behind her.

Unbidden, a smile tugged at his lips.

CHAPTER 6

CATE LEANED AGAINST THE KITCHEN counter, drummed her fingers against her lips, and thought about what she'd just overheard: Sabrina and Isiah fighting about money. In whispered voices, of course, as they made their way to the dining room, but fighting nonetheless. She hadn't caught enough of the conversation to understand what it was about specifically, but had heard the terms "net worth," "my share," and "protect it at all costs."

She had no idea what any of it meant, but, all the same, she'd tell Caleb when she saw him in a few minutes. Her gaze flitted to Margaret, who was just now making up the plate for her to take to the ice house.

The movement of Cate's fingers on her lips changed from a drumming motion to a gentle touch. She didn't know what had possessed her to kiss Caleb's cheek earlier. His skin had been warm from the fire and he'd smelled of the fall forest— subtly clean and crisp. Of course, she'd done stuff like that all the time before. He'd always seemed so far away, even when he was with her and Tommy and Brooke, that she'd often tried to bring him in to their circle, into the present, through touch. Tommy hadn't cared much for it, but since she hadn't cared much for Tommy's reaction, she hadn't stopped. Until she'd stopped seeing Caleb altogether.

Once again, she was struck by how much and how little things could change in five years. She'd been nervous about seeing him; it had been such a long time and, with the deaths of Brooke and Tommy hanging over them, she hadn't been sure what it would be like for them to meet again. But even though he had changed in many ways, as had she, in some ways they'd slipped not quite back into a routine, but back into a kind of comfort with each other. They still had a lot to learn about what each of them had been doing during their years apart, but since he'd come back into her life just a few days earlier, a little piece of herself, a piece of her heart, that she hadn't acknowledged had been missing was beginning to return to her.

"Here you go," Margaret said, bringing Cate out of her reverie. The chef stood before her with a plate covered in tin foil. Even though Cate had already eaten dinner, her stomach still stirred at the rich scent of savory pork with rosemary gravy.

"Mmm, smells wonderful, Margaret. Thank you," she said, taking the plate. She considered the idea that wine might go better with the meal than beer, but she'd have to go back to the carriage house to grab a bottle and didn't want to make that trip before heading to Caleb's.

"And here," Christine said, reading her mind and tucking a bottle of Montepulciano under Cate's arm.

Despite having just had the same idea, Cate raised her brows at her employee. Christine was supposed to have been returning unopened bottles from the family dinner back down to the cellar, not bringing one up for her. "This isn't a dinner date," Cate said.

"Of course it's not, dear," Margaret said. "But that wine was selected to go with this dish, and it would be a shame if they weren't enjoyed together. Now, go on with you."

As she was ushered out, Cate thanked Margaret, ignored Christine's grin, and quickly escaped the kitchen, which had suddenly become much too warm.

Caleb opened the ice house door for her before she'd even knocked and, stepping back for her to enter, reached for the plate of food.

"Wine too," she said as she entered the kitchen. "Compliments of Margaret and Christine."

He set the plate down and took the bottle from her. "It's a nice one, I'm guessing too nice for staff, unless your company treats you all very, very well." Caleb opened a drawer looking for a wine opener.

"I think my staff is under the impression that this is more than a "working" dinner. I corrected them, of course, but still."

"Here," Caleb said. "But only if you'll join me." He stood, holding a corkscrew out to her with a look in his eye that she couldn't quite place—a challenge, maybe? Or perhaps a bit of defensiveness? She studied him, trying to understand what she saw, but when it was clear that he wasn't going to reveal anything more, she accepted that all she could do was pretend she didn't see anything at all and go on as if they were just two friends sharing a drink. Because, of course, they were, and there was no reason to think that her comment about the staff would, or should, elicit any reaction from either of them.

"But only one glass," she said, taking the corkscrew.

A bottle and some port later, she was stretched out on the floor in front of the fire laughing as he described the first time he'd ever taken his sister fishing. He'd been twelve and Kit had been seven and he'd been concerned about gutting and cleaning the fish in front of her, afraid she might protest and then do something like refuse to ever eat fish again. Turned out he'd been wrong, very wrong. When he'd hesitated, Kit had taken the knife and done the job herself, having apparently watched a few fishing shows on television in preparation for the trip with her big brother.

"I should have known then that she was tougher than she looked," he said, chuckling at the memory. He sat on one of the chairs by the fireplace, his feet stretched out in from of him, half a glass of port twirling in his hand. She knew it was the alcohol, or mostly the alcohol, that had him in such a relaxed state, but she was enjoying seeing him this way—laughing, talking about his family, *comfortable*.

"You never talked about her before, or your life before joining up with Tommy. I like hearing it," she said, both curious and cautious about how introducing Tommy's name might change the lighthearted tone the evening had slipped into. It hadn't started out that way. They'd started by discussing the Whatley family and who might have it in for whom. She'd updated him on the conversation she'd overheard between Sabrina and Isiah, he'd made a few notes, and then he'd taken her through the additional background information he'd received that afternoon. They were no closer to finding either the potential victim or killer, but she knew more about the Whatley family than she had ever wanted to.

Once all the information had been shared, the discussion had moved slowly toward other topics. They'd started with Elise, then moved onto jobs, and now, his family and childhood. Bringing up Tommy's name was a risk, but Cate had to know that she and Caleb were headed back onto solid ground. She had to know that the tough topics of Tommy and Brooke wouldn't force a wedge between them again. Perhaps it was too soon to test, but if nothing else, she needed Caleb to know that she had no interest in shying away from those two names, those two people who had played such important roles in both their lives.

At her question, his eyes had dropped to the glass he still twirled. She realized that she wasn't breathing, then forced a few measured breaths as she waited for him to answer.

"We were really close as kids," he started. "But when I was twenty, I found out what a monster our father really was. I couldn't stick around and pretend everything was fine. I had to find a way to stop him. So I left."

"And you left Kit," she said, her voice soft.

He looked up sharply and she saw there in his eyes what she'd only ever seen twice before—pain so intense he was almost breathless. "I did," he said. "When I left, I thought he kept his professional interests away from the home front. In the twenty years I lived there, I never had so much as a hint of the kind of man he was. I thought Kit would be safe."

"She wasn't?"

He shook his head and turned away. "But that's her story to tell. As for me, I stopped talking about my family because I was too ashamed to be the son of a man like him, and it was too hard to imagine hiding what I knew from Kit. So I didn't talk *about* him, and I didn't talk *to* her. I just went along with my life as if I were the only person in it." He stared at his glass for a moment then downed the rest of his port. "I was a coward is what I was. I wasn't strong, I wasn't stoic, I wasn't doing what was best for *anyone*. I was just taking the easy way by not talking about, or even acknowledging, the ugliness that I hid."

"And Kit?"

A small smile touched his lips. "Like I said, I should have known she was tougher than she looked. She went through hell and came out much healthier, much stronger than I did. She took the beatings and got right back up. Me? I turned away from everyone and everything. Buried myself in work and hid from my past."

"But not with us? Not with me and Tommy and Brooke." But the moment she said it, Cate knew it wasn't true. Tommy hadn't ever been the kind of person who would reflect or think deeply about anything. He was tactical and practical and incredibly strategic. If she had ever taken it upon herself to ask him why he loved her, she knew he would have just shrugged and said, "Because I do." And he *had* loved her; she knew that. But sometimes it was important to know why.

She recognized that Caleb was asking himself those types of questions now, but back when he'd been with Tommy, when Tommy had been his mentor, Tommy would never have encouraged that type of thinking. And because he wouldn't have encouraged it, she knew he'd never truly known Caleb—at least not the Caleb she was seeing now.

"I think Brooke was the anchor for all of us," he said. "I know what she meant to you and Tommy, and you're right, I was a different person when I was with her. It was impossible not to be giving and loving and full of laughter when I was with her."

Cate felt the familiar tears form whenever she thought about her first daughter, but she didn't hide them or wish them away. This was the first time in a long time that she was with someone who'd truly known Brooke. There was something freeing in that, something she wanted to hold onto, because Caleb would understand. He would understand that she could both love and miss Brooke and love and cherish Elise. He would understand that, in having another daughter, she hadn't forgotten or tried to replace her first. She'd just been blessed with the opportunity to share her life with another child, and he would hope—he would demand—that she do it without the guilt that so many well-wishers assumed she must feel. With Caleb, she could have both girls fully in her life, even though one was now gone.

"She was a little spitfire, wasn't she?" Cate said.

Caleb smiled, gazing into the fire. "That's one way of putting it."

Cate chuckled and wiped a tear from her eye. "What about me? Why did you never talk to me?"

Caleb's eyes came down to meet hers. "At the risk of sounding cliché, it was me, not you. Back then, I wasn't in a place to have real friends. I loved all of you like family, hell, you *were* my family, but if I couldn't face my own family history myself, I sure as hell wasn't going to share it with anyone else. I still don't talk about it much, but when Kit and I had our little wake-up call a few years ago, she taught me that real bravery isn't keeping everyone away and standing alone, it's knowing you can get hurt and letting people in anyway. It's been a slow process to learn that, but I'm trying. I'm trying because I love my sister, and I'm trying because she wants me to. Maybe a little part of me still wants to be the big brother she used to look up to too. But back then, back when you, Tommy, and I were the three musketeers dancing to Brooke's tune? Honestly, I don't think I could have had the conversation we've been having tonight. It just wasn't in me then."

Cate knew she'd spend some time mulling over what he'd said, but she had a sneaking suspicion he wasn't the only one who wouldn't have been able to have the kind of conversation they'd just had. The deaths of Brooke and Tommy had certainly changed her, as had Elise's birth, and she found that, while she appreciated many of the same things she'd always enjoyed, she was much more grounded in what was important to her now, grounded in a way she hadn't been when she'd last seen Caleb. Then, life had been something that was happening *to* her rather something she'd had a say in.

She started to tell him that he wasn't alone when her cell phone beeped in her pocket. She pulled out the device and, with a dramatic sigh and roll of her eyes, silently read a message from Greg telling her that the main house was locked up for the night and if she wanted to return the plates, she'd need her key to get into the kitchen. It was his coy way of telling her that he could see the lights still on in the ice house.

"There a problem?" Caleb asked.

"No," she replied. And there wasn't, but she shouldn't give the staff any reason to talk. She brought her legs out from underneath her and rose. Standing in front of the fire, she stretched her arms over her head and swayed side to side, extending the muscles along her back. "What's the plan for tomorrow?" she asked.

When Caleb didn't immediately answer, she swung her gaze to him. He was still relaxing in the chair with one hand lying across his abdomen and the other draped over the arm of the chair, loosely holding the empty port glass. Only the reflection of the fire in his eyes showed an intensity that didn't align with his posture.

"Caleb?" She glanced over her right shoulder to see what he might have caught his attention and saw only the window, its curtains drawn back. "Is everything okay?" she asked, hoping to god or anyone who was listening that he wouldn't say he saw something outside the window.

His eyes snapped to hers. "Yes, everything is fine. Tomorrow, I'm going to head into Boston to talk to a few folks about Sabrina and Dominique. I may be back late. In fact, I'll definitely be back late, because I also want to pop by Jay's facility in Maine and run a few things by him. At this point, all we, or all *I* can do is dig, while keeping my eyes, ears, and mind open. I'll need you to do the same, not the digging but the eyes and ears part."

She frowned at his change of tone but his expression didn't

invite question. "Of course. What time will you be back? Should I bring you dinner again?"

"No. No, thank you."

Abruptly he stood and walked over to where he'd hung her jacket. His message couldn't have been clearer. She slid the garment on and then ten seconds later she was on her way back to the carriage house while he stood on his porch watching her. Whatever bee had gotten into his bonnet didn't prevent him from doing what he'd always done: look out for the people he cared about. When she reached her own porch, she turned and waved. He waved back, but didn't go back inside. She waited a heartbeat then took a deep breath and stepped into her residence, closing the door on him and his thoughts.

• • •

In the dark of the late night, Caleb heard Cate's front door close, and though he had to strain to hear it, he heard the lock slide into place too. He shoved his hands into his pockets, leaned back against the cold wood of the ice house and thought about what a fucker he was. So much so, he felt sick to his stomach.

His stomach.

When Cate had stood and stretched in front of the fire just moments earlier, her shirt had ridden up the tiniest bit, enough to give him a glimpse of her bare skin just above the waistband of her jeans. Enough to overwhelm him with the impulse to slide his hands across her waist and feel her skin against his. He had wanted to pull her toward him and place is lips on her belly, right above her zipper. He had wanted to feel her muscles contract in anticipation. He'd wanted a hell of lot more than that, but now, just as he had before, he stopped his mind from going and further. Taking a few deep breaths of the cold October air and closing his eyes, he tried to conjure Tommy's image in order to cool the heat that had come with the unexpected onslaught of desire. *Tommy's widow*, he thought over and over. *Tommy's widow*. The voice in his head was almost loud enough to drown out the memory of that sudden rush. Almost.

Taking another deep breath, he pushed off the wall and stepped off the porch toward the main house. Forcing his eyes to travel the length of building, he noted several things: the dim light glowing from the window of Sasha and Nikki's room, the fact that Michael and Edith must have finally decided it was too cold to sleep with the window open, and the flickering of a television in Edward's room.

All else seemed quiet and still.

Except the maelstrom of desire that tiny glimpse of her skin seemed to have unleashed in him. This time, he didn't so much take a deep breath as sigh. Not bothering to adjust his pants, he made his way back inside, brushed his teeth, shucked off all his clothes, and slid into bed. He knew one way to ensure a good night's sleep; his hand came up and wrapped around himself. The pressure felt welcome, needed. But when a vision of Cate came into his mind, he abruptly let go. Turning over onto his stomach, he pushed his hands under his pillow. He'd be damned if he was going to pleasure himself while thinking of his best friend's widow. He may be a bastard, but he wasn't that low.

Burying his head in the pillow, he tried to will himself to sleep, thankful that the next day he wouldn't have to see her, look her in the eye, and try to hide every thought he'd just had.

• • •

Cate danced from foot to foot in the freezing near-dawn hour as she waited for Caleb to answer his door. She hadn't planned to be out so early, or expected to be outside for more than the few moments it took to get from the carriage house to the main house, and she hadn't exactly dressed appropriately for the near freezing temperature.

When Caleb's door flew open and she sucked in a surprised breath, she was thankful that her staff had allowed her at least enough time to throw a few clothes on. Apparently, she hadn't extended the same courtesy to Caleb while banging on his door; he stood before her in the doorway with nothing but a throw blanket hanging low on his hips, the edges held together by his tight grip.

She blinked at him, her jaw falling open.

Grabbing her arm, he yanked her inside and slammed the door shut. She caught the sweatshirt he picked up and threw at her as he stalked through his room, swiping a pair of pants off the floor on his way to the bathroom. Two minutes later, he reappeared—still shirtless, but wearing the pants.

"Put the sweatshirt on, Cate, you're freezing," he said as he knelt with his back to her, rummaging around for something in his bag.

Cate glanced down at her tank top, the same one she'd been sleeping in when Greg had texted her less than ten minutes earlier. Thanks to the cold, there was no doubt about whether or not she was wearing a bra. Quickly, she pulled the sweatshirt on.

Her head had just come through the top when Caleb turned back around, pulling a t-shirt down over his bare chest. She knew there were probably all sorts of things wrong with ogling her dead husband's best friend, but damn if Caleb wasn't ogle-worthy.

"What's wrong?' he asked, sitting down on the rumpled bed to put on his socks. It was just like him to be getting ready to go, to help her, before he even knew what the problem was.

"A snake," she said, snuggling into the sweatshirt.

He glanced up. "A snake?"

She nodded.

He reached for one of his boots. "They don't normally have snakes this time of year in New Hampshire, do they?"

She wrapped her arms around her chest. "It was a copperhead, Caleb."

He glanced up again at her pronouncement. The way his eyes searched her face, she thought he might expect her to say "just kidding!" But when she didn't he turned back to his boot and laces as she continued. "This time of year, snakes are usually in hibernation. But copperheads are rare enough as it is around here, and then to be found inside a house? Thankfully no one was hurt, but the odds on something like this happening have got to be astronomical." She let the implications of her statement hang, unspoken, in the air as he swiveled his gaze toward the windows that faced the main house.

"Do you know where it is?"

She smiled for the first time that morning, smiled at the fact that he didn't question whether or not he *should* take care of it, he just assumed that he *would*. "Yes," she replied. "Christine is from Texas and apparently snakes are pretty common there—one more reason, in addition to the heat and tornados, for me to avoid that state."

Caleb quirked a brow at her train of thought.

"Anyway," she continued, "when she came across it in the hall this morning, she killed it. She was returning some clean fireplace tools to the library and used the small shovel to, well, I think she stunned it first, then, well . . ."

"Does anyone else know?" He tugged a sweater on over his t-shirt then headed toward the front door.

As she followed him, she replied. "No one of the family. Christine was smart enough to get it cleaned up before anyone woke up. She took care of it, woke Greg up, and then Greg called me. I went over to confirm everything and then came here."

"You should have stopped by on your way over." Caleb shut and locked the door behind them.

As the cold air assaulted her, she appreciated the sweatshirt all the more. "I didn't know it was a poisonous snake until I talked to Christine. All Greg had told me was that there was a snake and I should come over. Christine was the one who pointed out that not only was it poisonous, but also very rare in this area."

"Which is when you came to get me."

"Exactly," she said, opening the main house's kitchen door. The sudden warmth of the room made her flush, but she wasn't about to give up the sweatshirt. "I figured it was too much of a coincidence, given why I asked you to come here."

"Where was it found?"

She ushered him into the large pantry where Christine and Greg stood, a bloody pillowcase at Christine's feet. "I found it slithering along the second floor hall in the south wing," Christine replied, not sounding at all put out by having just come face to face with a copperhead.

Cate didn't really have an issue with snakes, but had she come across one gliding toward her in the hall, she was pretty sure she wouldn't have been quite as graceful about it as Christine.

"And have you looked to make sure there aren't any more?" Caleb asked.

Christine and Greg glanced at each other. "We did," Greg said. "But just a cursory search. Christine said this type of snake is so rare in this area that the odds of winning the lottery would be higher than finding another one. Of course, if we found one snake, maybe there could be others, whether they're the same type or not."

Caleb seemed to approve of this assessment and gave a sharp jerk of his head. "How long until family members usually get up?"

"About half an hour," Christine answered.

"Okay," Caleb said. "Let's all do a walk-through. Can we get anyone else to join us?"

"Mirielle will be up," Cate said.

"And I can get Mark, Anne, and Lucy," Christine volunteered.

"Margaret?" Caleb asked.

Greg gave an emphatic shake of his head. "She *hates* snakes, loathes them something fierce."

"And she has a scream that could wake the next county," Cate added.

"Okay, no Margaret then," Caleb confirmed. "Christine and Greg, can you organize an inside search? Mirielle, Cate, and I will search the perimeter to see if we can find any gaps or holes where it could have come into the house."

Caleb hadn't even realized he'd called her Cate in front of her staff. She hazarded a glance at Greg, the one most likely to notice, but his attention was already focused on Christine and laying out a systematic plan for searching the house.

With a twinge of relief, she started to follow Caleb who had headed back toward the kitchen door. She was nearly there when she heard Greg say, "Nice sweatshirt, *Cate*," and then Christine giggle. She knew they were teasing, so she didn't turn around, raising her hand and giving them the finger instead. Their laughter followed her out of the room.

"What was that about?" Caleb asked when she joined him outside.

"Nothing."

A fleeting frown touched his lips, but he said nothing more, just turned toward the barn with Cate following behind. "Do you need anything warmer to wear while we're outside?"

"No, I'm good." With Caleb's sweatshirt plus her leggings and fuzzy boots, she was actually reasonably comfortable.

He glanced back over his shoulder and his gaze lingered on hers. "Hold on," he said, motioning for her to stop. They were by the ice house and she watched as he made quick trip inside. When he came back out, he carried a black fleece hat and scarf. He promptly pulled the hat over her head and wrapped the scarf around her bare neck. She mumbled a thank you but he'd already started marching toward the barn.

"Mirielle," Cate called as they entered.

"Up here," came a voice from the hayloft. "Just a second."

A few seconds later, the barn manager joined them and Cate filled her in. As expected, Mirielle readily agreed to help, arming them each with barn tool of some sort to ward off any snakes they might come across. Based on what Christine had said about the rarity of the creature, Cate didn't think the chances that they'd actually find any more were high, but she had to admit that carrying a big shovel made her feel a bit better about the situation.

They spent the next twenty minutes examining the periphery

of the house, checking doors and windows to make sure they were properly closed, and looking for any way a snake might have been able to make its way into the house. The groundskeeper, Mark, joined them about halfway through, and though the work was quick, it wasn't satisfactory. They found no smoking gun. Even though Cate hadn't anticipated finding one, she'd rather hoped they would.

By the time they returned to the kitchen, Margaret had coffee going and some breakfast items laid out. Caleb stepped to the side to talk to Mark, no doubt to get a better idea of the local flora and fauna—and reptile population—so she headed to the counter, poured herself some coffee, and picked up a cinnamon scone. The first bite was melting in her mouth when the indoor search crew returned.

It was clear from the combination of relief and concern on their faces that they hadn't found any more deadly animals either and, after making that pronouncement, they proceeded to do the same thing as Cate: eat and drink.

Caleb joined her at the spread a moment later and reached for a scone.

"You don't want that one," she said.

His hand stopped mid-grab and he raised an eyebrow at her.

"It looks like chocolate chip, but it's raisin."

He pulled his hand back as if he'd been burned, making her laugh. He hated raisins.

"Those are lemon and those are cinnamon, my favorite," she said pointing to the other two varieties. "Did Mark have anything to add?"

"Not much more than what Christine already told us," he said, taking a cinnamon scone and pouring himself some coffee. "He said there are two types of poisonous snakes in New Hampshire, the copperheads, which are rare and found more often in Massachusetts, if they are found at all, and the timber rattler. Apparently, we're lucky it wasn't a timber rattler."

"Why's that?" she asked as he took a sip of his coffee.

"They are an endangered species and killing them is illegal."

"There's the silver lining, then."

Caleb glanced at her wry expression and one side of his mouth tilted into a smile. "Can we talk for a minute?"

Cate murmured an "of course" and followed him back outside, stuffing the black hat and scarf under her arm as they stepped into the cold. Caleb kept walking toward the ice house so she followed.

"I still want to head into Boston this morning and then over to see Jay. Before I do that, I want to confirm who sleeps in the south wing and I'd like you to check my notes."

A few minutes later, he handed her a folder and excused himself to take a quick shower. She sat down to take a look at the list, ignoring the little bit of wily disappointment she felt when she saw him grab a set of clean clothes to take into the bathroom with him.

Michael and Edith, Sasha and Nikki, and Edward were in the three south wing guest rooms along the back of the house; Sabrina and Dominique, Isiah and Livia, and Dixie and Luke were staying in the three guest rooms facing the front lawn. When Francesca, one of the Italian cousins, arrived in a few days, she would also be put in the south wing, but for now, Caleb's list appeared complete.

She could still hear the shower running so, rather than do nothing, she started a small pot of coffee thinking that he could take some with him on his drive. She considered making him his favorite breakfast, but decided against it. While she knew the rice and meat dish would be appreciated, it was time-consuming to make and she thought he'd appreciate the time on the road more.

"Everything all right?" he asked, stepping out of the bathroom. His hair was still wet, but he was fully dressed, with the exception of his bare feet. The steam from the bathroom floated through the house bringing with it the familiar scent of the orange-and-olive scented products provided by The Washington House along with a touch of something else, maybe a little bit of aftershave.

"Yes, it's fine. Well, relatively speaking it's fine, given that it's likely we just had a second attempt on someone's life. I made some coffee for you to take with you." She glanced at the pot, then let out a self-deprecating laugh. "God, we're like some bad version of a couple from the fifties: 'Here dear, let me make you coffee and breakfast so you can go out do all the dangerous stuff while I take care of things on the home front.'" She gave him a dramatic eye roll.

Caleb chuckled as he leaned down to tie his boots. "Except, what I'm doing isn't exactly dangerous and what you're doing is *your* job."

She made a face. "I know, but it still feels wrong. I feel like I should be doing more to help figure this out. Like I called you in to help and, really, what I've done is just dump it in your lap."

Caleb said nothing as he joined her in the kitchen area, located a travel coffee mug, then poured some coffee into it. She'd started the conversation as a joke because, well, the roles they'd taken on *did* feel a little old fashioned. Only somehow it had moved quickly onto truly uncomfortable terrain. She hadn't reached out to him for five years, and when she had, it was because she'd needed something from him. What kind of friend did that make her?

"Cate?"

She switched her gaze from the window to Caleb.

"If I'd needed help organizing an event or learning to surf, I could have called you and the tables would have been turned. Except that, since I know nothing about either of those situations, I would have been less than useless, whereas you know this family well. No one can be, and no one should try to be, good at everything. That's what friends and partners and, if we're lucky, family do for us. They balance us, give us a different perspective, and, when needed, provide us with a different set of skills. Don't downplay what you do for a living just because it's not what I do."

Hearing him defend her made her feel even worse and she couldn't fight the tears gathering in her eyes. "I should have called you before, Caleb. I shouldn't have waited until I needed your skills. I should have called because you were my friend, because I was your friend, and because we were both in a lot of pain."

Caleb studied her for a moment, then reached out and brushed a tear from her cheek before pulling her into a hug. She wrapped her arms around his waist and buried her face against his chest. It felt so bittersweet. His familiarity, strength, and willingness to be there with her felt so right, while the fact that she had denied them both this comfort for so long made her feel lower than low. Intellectually, she knew he could have called too, but she was only in the position to control her own actions and, being there now, with his arms wrapped around her and his cheek resting against her hair, she knew she'd acted less than admirably

"I'm glad you called, Cate. I'm glad I'm here. Not just because I can help you with this situation, but because it was time. It was time for us to try being friends again. I don't know what would have happened if we'd stayed in touch, but I've changed a lot in the past few years and I can see that you have too. I think maybe we both needed time to make those changes before we could be here together again."

"You're just trying to make me feel better," she said with a smile she knew he could feel against his chest. She felt his answering response on the top of her head. "Maybe, but maybe I'm right too."

While she thought he might be right, it was a lot to digest and not something she wanted to agree to in the moment. With a final squeeze, she stepped back.

He let her go, but brushed away a lingering tear before bending down to give her a kiss on her forehead. "Are you going to be okay?"

She nodded. "I'll be fine. Your list is complete, by the way." She gestured to the folder she'd placed on the table. "You think the target is one of the people in the south wing?"

"I'm not sure," he said, moving to gather his belongings, including the folder, then sliding them into his black backpack. "But, like with the wire you found, we have to start somewhere. Later, Jay and I will dig a little deeper into the guests who were out riding that day and the ones staying in the south wing. We won't exclude everyone else, but it's a place to start."

"And what can we do here?" she asked as he slipped a jacket on and scanned the room one last time.

"You can keep doing what you're doing. Keep your eyes and ears open. If you have an opportunity to get one of the family members talking, take it."

She followed him out the door and he turned to lock it. "How many of your staff know about the wire?"

"All of them, I imagine. By now, anyway. Word travels fast when you live and work together the way we do."

He put his backpack in the back seat of his car, shut the door, then turned to examine the main house, studying it like he might have to take a quiz on it later. "One weird thing, like the wire, might get noticed but not really commented on. But in the case of this snake situation, which is unusual in more than ways than one, I'm guessing your staff could start thinking that something isn't right."

Cate had to admit that she hadn't gotten that far in her line of thinking. *She* knew something was awry, but hadn't thought about what might happen if her staff began to notice. She'd made contingency plans to deal with them if she and Caleb *confirmed* that something was off, but she hadn't contemplated what to do about her staff during this period when there might be questions and chatter but no ready answers.

"Yes," she nodded slowly, "they'll notice. Especially Greg and Christine."

"And Greg seems prone to gossip."

Cate tilted her head from side to side. "He is, but only amongst the staff. He wouldn't discuss anything with the family." She paused and followed Caleb's gaze to the house. She'd need to figure out what to say to her staff. To do that, she needed some nourishment. "I'll figure it out. I'll go eat breakfast with Elise, then work it out. Everything is easier when I'm not hungry," she said with a lopsided smile, knowing Caleb would remember how out of sorts she got when she needed to eat.

"Let me know? So I can toe the line when I'm back tomorrow."

"You're not coming back until tomorrow?"

"I'll be back tonight," he said opening the driver's door to his Range Rover. "But late enough that I won't see you or anyone else here until tomorrow."

Cate rested her hand on the door handle as he climbed in. "I'll give you a call and let you know. Drive safely," she added as she closed the door.

He gave her a salute and, as his car disappeared around the bend in the driveway, she turned her attention back the main house. She had no idea what she was going to say to her staff, but this wasn't the first time she'd been in a situation where she didn't know what the hell she was doing. In fact, she had a pretty good track record of figuring things out as she went along. Of course, she'd never just "figured things out" with someone's life potentially on the line. But there was a first time for everything.

CHAPTER 7

THE EARLY DAWN LIGHT HADN'T yet made its appearance through the back window of Caleb's room. Cracking an eye open, he glanced at the clock, then, reaching over, he found what he sought and used the remote to turn the fireplace on. From underneath his layer of blankets he watched the flames jump to life behind the glass and admitted to himself that maybe there was something to a gas fireplace after all. It didn't have quite the same ambiance as a wood-burning one, but it did win on convenience.

When the fireplace's fan kicked in and took the chill from the room, he rose, dressed, and started a pot of coffee before throwing together some scrambled eggs and toast. He'd go for a run in a bit, but first, he wanted to go through the notes he'd taken in Boston the day before, as well as the additional information Jay had provided him when he'd stopped by in Portland. He'd spent the three-hour drive back to The Washington House mulling over everything he'd learned, trying to find, or make, connections. But he knew he worked better visually, so he planned to spread it all out on the table and piece the data together this morning.

An hour and three cups of coffee later, he stared down at his work. While he had never doubted Cate's original intuition, when they'd found the snake the day before, the situation had escalated from a potential problem to a more pressing reality. Frustratingly, he saw motives, many of them, as well as several potential victims, but he didn't have enough information to narrow anything down.

About a week had passed between the two incidents, and there was a little over two weeks to go before the family reunion ended.

If the killer's plan was to have the job done before the end of the family's month at The Washington House, Caleb knew that he, or she, would be stepping up their game in the coming weeks.

He studied his work one last time, then gathered it all together and tucked it out of the way before dumping his dishes into the sink and changing into his running clothes. A long run in these early morning hours should help clear his mind. After that, he planned to spend the rest of the day in the house, *conveniently* running into as many family members as possible.

As his feet pounded down the trail and the sun hinted at making an appearance, he let his mind turn over what he'd learned in Boston from his contact, Oliver Potts. The secretary of both the state and local bar associations, Oliver knew nearly every lawyer in Massachusetts. Between his professional connections and those of his family, whose roots stretched back over two hundred years to include janitors and senators and everyone in between, he more or less had his finger on the pulse of Boston. He knew pretty much everything, and anything he didn't already know, he could easily find out.

However, Oliver hadn't needed to do any digging into Dominique; she was already well known to him. And, according to Oliver, Sabrina had every cause to be uneasy in her relationship—her wife *was* having an affair. Or perhaps *affairs* would be more accurate, or would it? Caleb pondered this as he turned past the spot where he'd stopped with Elise and Pansy, the spot where the wire had been strung. Dominique had taken to visiting certain types of pleasure houses. Nothing too extreme, but definitely edgy enough, and varied enough, to explore different types of sexuality.

Caleb wasn't about to pass judgment on the marriage. Perhaps Sabrina knew about Dominique's actions and condoned them. One thing he'd learned in his life was that you never knew what went on behind closed doors. So while the discovery of Dominique's activities was interesting and definitely something he'd keep filed away, on its own it wasn't conclusive of anything.

Turning back toward the houses, Caleb wished he'd worn

a hat. The brisk morning, which had brought frost with it, was making his ears burn. The cold on his face felt fine, but, damn, his ears burned. Grinning at his own whining, knowing Tommy and Garret would have given him hell over such a minor complaint, he pushed on, turning his mind to what he'd learned from Jay.

The family of the young man who'd died on the hiking expedition with Michael didn't believe the incident had been an accident. Immediately after it had happened, they'd pressed for a full investigation—or as full as they could get, working with a foreign government—and had even hired private detectives, but nothing had been found to counter the original story that it had simply been a terrible accident. Caleb wondered if the young man's family still held a grudge against Michael. It bore investigating more thoroughly, given that two of the deceased man's brothers lived in North Conway, less than an hour away from The Washington House.

"Caleb!"

He slowed to a walk and scanned the area as he hit the back driveway then saw Elise on the porch of the carriage house in her nightclothes. Holding Athena.

"Elise, honey, it's freezing out here. You need to go back inside," he said, walking toward her. His eyes darted behind her small body, wondering if Cate was going to step out too, then realized she was probably at the staff meeting she ran each morning. Which also meant that, for some reason, Elise was up much earlier than usual.

"Come with me," she said. "I learned something yesterday and I've been waiting to show you." She held out her hand and he took it.

He knew she wasn't Brooke, but it was hard not to think of that other little girl he'd known so well. That other little girl who had held his hand so many times, dragging him around parks, her home, and her back yard. Everywhere she went, it seemed her small hand had been pulling him along. But even as he remembered Brooke, Elise's presence was no less diminished. Her hand was smaller, *she* was smaller, and rather than pulling him, she stayed beside him. Even though the distance from the porch to living room was short, she leaned into him more than once, as if to let him know that, even though she was small, she was still fully present.

After allowing him to say hi to Jana, who explained that Elise had been waiting to tell him what she'd learned since the day before, Elise seated him on the floor in the living area and went off in search of a book. As she moved around the room, searching for what she wanted to show him, she touched him regularly—a hand on his shoulder as she rummaged in a pile of books on the coffee table, a touch on his knee to let him know she was going to look under the couch. Like her mother, physically connecting with people seemed to be a natural part of her personality. Elise might be more somber than Brooke had been, but it was apparent that once she'd decided that she liked someone, she wasn't at all shy. He nearly laughed out loud when, after finding the book she'd been looking for, she plopped down in his lap without hesitation, opened it to a particular page, and pointed an image of Athena out to him.

• • •

Cate paused outside the door to her lodging, hearing her daughter's laughter inside.

"No, silly, you tickled me. It doesn't count," Elise said.

"I don't know what you're talking about, squirt. I didn't tickle you. I didn't even touch you." Caleb's denial was followed by a warm chuckle.

"Your *toes*, Caleb. You tickled me with your toes!"

"Well, I don't know about that, but do you want to try again? I have to get at least forty in, how many have I done?"

"Twenty-two," Elise answered promptly.

"So eighteen left. Do you think you can get through eighteen without losing your balance?"

"Yes!"

"Well, I admire your optimism, since we haven't made it past eight yet, but let's give it a try."

There was a pause during which Cate heard the two of them shifting around, then Caleb spoke again. "Okay, ready?"

"Ready."

"Here we go. One . . . and . . . two . . . and . . . three . . . and . . ."

Cate opened the door. Elise was posed, superman-style, on Caleb's stockinged feet as he lay on his back, hoisting her into the air with his legs on each count. Her daughter's tiny hands were wrapped tightly around Caleb's outstretched fingers to make sure she didn't fall.

"Look, Mommy, I'm helping Caleb exercise!" Elise said with a grin as soon as she caught sight of her mom. Then she giggled, lost her balance, and fell, though Celeb's hold on her made it more of a gentle descent that ended with her rolling on the floor laughing. "That was awful, Caleb!" Elise managed to say between fits of giggles. "We only made it to five!"

Caleb rolled to a sitting position. "Five is better than nothing, kid," he replied, putting on his shoes. As he rose to stand up, he grabbed Elise and draped her tiny body over his arm like a jacket. She was still laughing, but going along with whatever Caleb might have planned.

"Good morning, Cate," he said.

"Morning, Caleb. I see you've roped Elise into helping you. I have to say, I'm surprised to see her up so early." Her daughter giggled and Caleb's arm flexed as he continued to hold her.

"Yes, well, I 'have a way with young ladies,' or so I've been told. Also, she had something she'd been waiting to tell me. *And* I believe there is some sort of expedition in the works. It's been an exciting morning all around. More to the point, though, I did learn something new today. Care to hear what that might be?"

"I'll simply expire if you don't tell me in the next five seconds," Cate said, grinning.

"Mommy, what's *expire* mean?" Elise asked, raising her head in an attempt to see her mom.

"I just learned how ticklish your daughter is," Caleb said, ignoring Elise's question as he attacked her side.

Elise squealed with laughter and squirmed in Caleb's arms. Cate watched as the two wrestled into a tickling match that lasted approximately three minutes before Caleb called uncle. Elise was still in her pajamas, her face flushed, and her hair a mess, but Cate thought she looked happier than she'd seen her in a while. Apparently, Caleb had found her playful side.

"You ready for our morning jaunt?" Jana asked, jogging down the stairs. "Oh, hi Cate, I didn't know you were back. Caleb said he'd keep an eye on Elise while I showered and made a few phone calls. I hope you don't mind?"

Cate shook her head. "Of course I don't mind. Caleb mentioned an expedition. Where are you headed today?"

"There's a petting farm Elise and I discovered the other day while we were out running errands. It's only open Thursday through Sunday, so I promised Elise we'd visit as soon as it opened."

"Sounds great," Cate said moving to check the coffee pot. "Want some?" she asked Caleb, lifting the nearly full pot in question.

He shook his head, but joined her in the kitchen, Elise trailing beside him.

"Elise, honey, why don't you go upstairs with Jana and get ready? And I expect to see pictures of goats when you get back. Lots of goats," she said, running a hand through her daughter's curls.

"Sheep mama; sheep are better than goats."

"You can love the sheep, I'll stick with goats. Now, go on with you. I'll stay here for a bit so I'll be able to say good-bye before you leave."

Elise nodded and started to dart out of the room, then paused. "Are you going to be here when I'm done getting ready too?" she asked Caleb.

He shook his head. "Probably not. I need to go get ready for the rest of the day myself, but maybe, if it's okay with your mom, we can pop into town this afternoon and try some of that maple soft serve ice cream I'm seeing all over the place."

Elise's eyes got big with anticipated pleasure and turned toward Cate, who smiled and said, "If you're good today and Caleb doesn't get too busy with work, it's fine with me."

Elise let out a squeal, darted forth to hug both them, then turned and ran upstairs. Excusing herself to go help Elise, Jana followed, leaving Cate and Caleb alone in the kitchen.

"Goats?" he said, his arms crossing over his chest as he leaned against the counter. He wore running shorts and she watched the muscles in his legs flex as he crossed his ankles as well.

She lifted a shoulder and smiled. "I like goats, especially the little ones. I have a friend who has one she takes for walks and he's ridiculously cute." She watched a small smile touch his lips then poured herself a cup. "How did your day go yesterday?" she asked.

He tilted his head back and forth a few times. "Interesting. I have a few things I want to update you on."

"Go for it."

He shook his head. "I need to shower. Why don't you hang out with Elise while I clean up? When she leaves, you can come to my place and I can walk you through what I learned."

Cate briefly considered whether she could time her arrival for right after he'd finished showering but before he was fully dressed. She wouldn't mind another glimpse of what she had seen the other day. Although, she had to admit, while Caleb's build was definitely easy on the eyes, it was the way he *moved*—efficient, confident, and with a purpose—that made him so much more interesting to her than he should have been, considering who he was.

She cleared her throat and glanced away. "Perfect. Maybe half an hour?"

He agreed then called a good-bye up to Elise and Jana and headed back to his place.

Through the kitchen window, Cate watched him stride across the gravel and thought about how much she should *not* be thinking of him showering. For one thing, they were just getting their friendship back on track. And then there was the fact that she'd been married to Tommy, a man Caleb had idolized. No doubt, any attraction Caleb sensed coming from her would make him extremely uncomfortable. Of course, she wasn't all that comfortable with her own thoughts either.

She needed to pull herself together and be grateful that he was back in her life at all, be grateful that, even though they weren't quite as comfortable with each other as they used to be, they were getting there. Because, now that Caleb was in her life again, she didn't ever want him to not be a part of it. And letting herself ogle, or even consider him as anything other than a friend would be a sure way to make him flee. He would never betray Tommy—and that's exactly how Caleb would see anything more than a friendship between them—and he'd end up hating himself, and her.

So, while she might sneak an admiring glance now and then, from here on out, she would focus only on being grateful for, and protective of, their friendship.

• • •

Caleb sat at the small table in his room and rearranged his notes. For the third time. The new information he'd collected in Boston and Maine was a lot to think about, and he wasn't sure in what order he should walk Cate through it. Reshuffling his notes one more time, he glanced down at the stack unhappily. Feeling decidedly disgruntled with his own indecision, he set them down then stood up and moved away from the table so he would stop second-guessing himself.

After putting a pot of coffee on, he listened to it percolate and brew while he stood at the window and studied the main house. It was well awake now. Breakfast was over and the guests were likely preparing for the day. He'd have to ask Cate what she knew of their plans. He really wanted to get into the guest rooms, but he'd have to wait for the right moment to do that.

Out of the corner of his eye, movement caught his attention. Cate, Elise, and Jana emerged from the carriage house. Cate helped Elise get settled into the car, closed her door, then waved the two off before she turned and looked in his direction. She stilled for a moment then seemed to take a deep breath before she began walking in his direction. Like most days, she wore a winter vest, a scarf, and the funny green dinosaur hat she'd been wearing when he'd first arrived. Despite the fact that she no longer surfed, she looked like the athlete she'd been—not particularly tall, but lean, with long legs that brought her toward him with a purposeful stride.

He opened the door before she knocked, ushering her inside. Even though her time outside had been short, the cool air had turned her cheeks rosy, making her green eyes stand out even more than usual.

"Elise and Jana off okay?" he asked, shutting the door behind her.

"Yes," she said, removing her hat and scarf. "Elise was abnormally speedy getting ready. That petting farm definitely caught her interest."

"Coffee?"

She eyed the pot for a moment then nodded.

He took her scarf and hat and hung them on the hooks by the door then poured them each a mug of coffee. "Have a seat." He placed her coffee in front of her and, though she reached for it, he could see her attention already piqued by the papers.

"Is all that new information?" she asked, gesturing with her head toward documents.

"It is, but it's not as much as you would think. There's a lot of detail, but there are really only three main things that I want to get your thoughts on." He took a seat beside her, picked up a set of documents, and handed them over.

She glanced at them and frowned. "Michael is being sued in a civil court?"

"He is, but I imagine this family is a target for lots of suits.

The interesting thing about this case is that he's being sued by the family of the man who was killed during that trek a few years back."

She thumbed through the pages a bit more, then landed on the names and pictures he knew she'd find.

"Do they look familiar?" he asked.

She raised her eyes to him before dropping them back to the images. She studied them for a moment longer then shook her head. "No, they don't. These are the brothers of the man who was killed?"

Caleb nodded.

"And they live forty-five minutes away from here?"

"I asked Jay to dig into them a little more."

"They don't look familiar to me, but do you want me to ask the staff about them?"

"If you can come up with a plausible reason for asking other than because we think someone is out to murder someone else."

Cate gave a huff of a laugh. "I'm remarkably good at lying when I need to. Give me a little while and I'll think of something."

Her comment gave him pause. What did she ever have to lie about? Surely he would have known if she'd ever lied to him. Wouldn't he? "That would be great," he said, taking the notes she held and dismissing his own questions as he handed her the report on Dominique's activity. "And then there's this."

She perused the document. "Oh, wow. I wouldn't have seen that coming, but now that it's staring me in the face, it kind of makes sense." Then her brows furrowed at her own comment. "Does what I just said make any sense at all?"

He chuckled. "It does, yes, and I agree. Again, I just found out about it yesterday from my contact in Boston, so I have Jay looking into the specific clubs she frequents to see if any of the other patrons or staff pop up anywhere else in this investigation."

"I think whenever I see her now, I'm going to picture her clad in leather holding a whip. I'm sure what I think I know about the world of sexual fetishes is nothing but stereotypes, but I have to admit, she probably looks pretty damned good in dominatrix gear."

Again, he laughed and had to agree. In just his short interaction with Dominique, he'd gotten the impression that she would take easily to ordering others about. Then again, she ordered people about every day, so it was possible that when she went to the clubs she played a more submissive role. Either way, he felt the need to talk to Vivi about the psychology of it all. Not that he thought an interest in the fetish world made a person a killer; he just wanted to understand the psychology behind it so that he could better understand Dominique.

"But there's more, isn't there?" Cate asked, interrupting his train of thought. She pointed to another set of papers.

"Ah, yes, this little bit of information." He picked the papers up himself and reread the top page. "Did you know that Edward Whatley had a daughter?"

Cate frowned and shook her head. "No, I know he lost his wife about four years ago. She was a lovely woman, but I had no idea they had children."

Caleb wagged his head. "Well, they didn't have children in the traditional sense. They fostered children, several of them, over the years, but Summer Granger was the only one they adopted." He handed her a photo of a ten-year-old-girl with long blonde hair draping over one shoulder and brown eyes shining bright as she smiled big for her school photo.

As Cate traced a finger along the girl's image, Caleb regretted that they'd have to talk about the death of someone's child—even though Summer hadn't been a child when she'd been killed.

"She looks very sweet," Cate said.

Caleb agreed but he knew how, over the years, things had changed for Summer and he carried on with sharing what he'd learned. "She came to live with Edward and his wife when she was nine and they adopted her when she was eleven. She did well in school and college then moved to New York City to become a stage actress. She was working at an art gallery there to pay the bills when she was killed."

"How was she killed?" she asked, raising her eyes to his.

"She was hit by a car."

He watched the color drain from Cate's face at the memories his statement conjured. After a moment, her eyes dropped back to the photo. "That's terrible. Of course, any kind of death like that is terrible, whether it's from a car or something else, but what does it have to do with what's going in here?"

He slid the police report over. "Look at the name of the person who was driving the car that hit her."

Cate's gaze held his for a moment then dropped to the document. Her eyes widened when she read the name, then raised back up to look at him. "Edith Barnard? Michael's girlfriend?"

CHAPTER 8

FOR THE FIRST TIME, CALEB joined the staff in the kitchen for lunch. The conversation was lively, mainly led by Greg, whose somewhat acerbic wit was just edgy enough to make the others chuckle, but not so much as to be inappropriate in the client setting.

Caleb made a point of sitting next to Christine—Cate had told him that, of all her staff, she was the one most likely to know the plans of each of the family members. Sure enough, not fifteen minutes into the meal, he learned that Michael and Edith were planning a ride in the afternoon with Sasha and Nikki; Dominique was back in Boston while Sabrina, Isiah, and Livia were planning to head into town for a little shopping; Sebastian Brandt hadn't been feeling well, so he and his two children, Erica and Mark, were going to rest for the afternoon; and Anthony and Agnes had plans to play cards and backgammon while drinking whiskey—the last bit being information Christine supplemented herself and had not been specifically mentioned by either party involved. The only people whose plans she wasn't aware of were Dixie and Luke, but she grinned and gave Caleb a wink as she stated that they'd probably spend the afternoon in their room, adding that they tended to do that, more so than any other couple attending the reunion.

With that wealth of information filed away, Caleb helped with the dishes then went in search of Agnes and Anthony under the pretense of checking to make sure the whiskey and port decanters had been refilled. Knowing that the entire family had finally agreed to a family outing the following day, something Cate had told him about that morning, had made him feel less antsy. He'd be able to get into the guest rooms and have a leisurely look then.

"Ah, there he is," Agnes said when he entered the upstairs library.

"Ms. Whatley. Mr. Whatley."

"Anthony, please," Agnes's nephew said. Agnes herself said nothing, but gave him an imperious nod when he replaced a near-empty port decanter with a full one.

"Can I get either one of you a drink?" Caleb offered.

"Yes, that," Agnes said, pointing to the whiskey.

"Agnes," Anthony cautioned.

"Oh, do stop being a ninny, Anthony. Caleb knows better than to listen to you, anyway. And I certainly won't."

Anthony rolled his eyes, "Charming, Agnes. As always."

"Being charming takes too much effort at my age," she retorted.

"Are you enjoying your stay?" Caleb asked both of the family members as he placed a glass in front of Agnes.

"Yes, I always like here," Anthony answered. "There is plenty to do, but if you don't want to do anything, this," he made a general gesture to the room, "is a pretty nice place to spend an afternoon."

Agnes tsk'd. "You always were an obliging boy. Too obliging, I might add, so don't take it as a compliment."

"I wouldn't dream of it, Aunt."

"It's too cold here," Agnes continued. "If we're going to have these blasted events in October, they should be somewhere warm."

"My understanding is that the board votes on the location," Caleb said.

"And bunch of clap-jawed mooners they are, too," she said with a *hmmph*.

"I have no idea what that even means," Anthony said, raising his eyes to Caleb and offering a silent apology for his aunt, something Caleb thought the cousins seemed to do a lot.

"Other than changing the weather, is there anything we can

do for you?" Caleb asked politely. "Have you been happy with the staff?"

"Everything is great, Mr. Forrester, honestly," Anthony said.

"Please, call me Caleb."

"Yes, do call him Caleb. 'Mr. Forrester' sounds much too respectable."

"Agnes!"

"Well, he's not," Agnes said with a dismissive wave in Caleb's direction. "I know he looks the part now, but it's in his eyes. He's up to something."

"I'm sorry for my aunt." Anthony apologized aloud this time, with a discouraged shake of his head.

Caleb offered a smile. "I've always found that respectability is in the eye of the beholder. Regardless of whether or not I am respectable, it's much more fun to let people think I'm not."

"See? There you have it. A rogue," Agnes said, pointing her finger at her nephew. "He's well aware of society's conventions, but he's only going to abide by the ones he chooses."

The woman was hitting a little too close to the truth, but Caleb doubted she knew it, so he smiled once again. "Perhaps, but perhaps not. In the meantime, I trust you're familiar with all of our staff and won't hesitate to ask if you ever need anything."

"Yes, of course, we know the staff of the agency very well by now," Anthony said.

"And that of the house? They are always available to help too," Caleb said.

"The two cleaning girls are new this year, but Mirielle and Mark have been here for a while, so, yes, we know them quite well. All in all, I think we're well set and we know you all are here to help if needed," Anthony answered.

"Great," Caleb replied. "And if you ever see anyone on the grounds who is not a guest or a member of the staff, would you please let us know? This house is for your exclusive use and we don't want any stragglers interrupting that. It hasn't been an issue, but Catherine mentioned that some tourists were lingering by the gates when she came back from town yesterday. Harmless, of course—they were just wondering what was hidden behind the gates and up the long driveway—but we'd hate for any of them to bother you."

It wasn't a foolproof plan, but Caleb wanted to offer an opening for either Anthony or Agnes to mention if they'd seen anyone unfamiliar on the property. Based on Cate's conversations with the staff, none of them had seen the two brothers of the man killed on Michael's hike, but the truth was, the family members were out and about more than the staff and would be more likely to run into anyone wandering the grounds.

"Thank you, we appreciate that," Anthony said. When neither the aunt nor nephew said more, Caleb left them to their game. He took his time wandering the upstairs hall, hoping to run into another member of the family. He had stopped to consider a particular portrait hanging in the hall when Erica Brandt came out of her room and headed down the hall toward him. Her step faltered when she saw him standing there, but then she smiled and continued in his direction.

"Ms. Brandt," Caleb said, extending his hand. "We haven't been formally introduced but I'm Caleb Forrester." They'd been in the same room together the day he'd 'lost' the chess game to Agnes, but no one had made the introduction.

"Yes, of course. Dixie and Agnes were talking about you at dinner the other night," she said. The bob of her head making her wild hair sway, along with the earrings she wore that hung down almost to her shoulders.

"How is your father? I hear he's resting today?"

She nodded again and her earrings jangled. When she turned to look back toward her father's room, her long, flowing skirt swirled around her. Caleb had heard that she was an artist and, whether she was or wasn't, she certainly lived up to the stereotypically bohemian image of one.

"He's doing well. He loves this particular reunion location.

Why, I'm not sure, since it's not all that different than where he lives in Massachusetts, but he does."

"Perhaps it's the company," Caleb replied, wanting to encourage her to continue making the small talk she seemed to be offering.

She smiled more broadly. "Perhaps. We see each other often— my dad, my brother, and I—but it's true, these reunions sort of let us be together without the mess of everything else in our lives. There's no work, no kids, not even any cleaning up to do. It's rather lovely to have the time together."

"It is nice that your schedules allows you to do this. All of you," Caleb said with a gesture encompassing all the rooms.

"Well, Dad's retired and I'm an artist, so our schedules aren't complicated. Mark is an engineer who runs his own company, so he checks in a few times a day, but it's pretty stable and he has good people in place that allow him this time." She waved in the directions of the stairs, "I was just on my way to the downstairs library, would you care to accompany me?"

He saw a hint of interest creep into her eyes, but he couldn't quite tell if it was attraction or just simple curiosity. Either way, he wanted to make use of the opportunity she'd presented, so he motioned her on and stepped in beside her as she passed.

"I understand the family is much bigger than those who are here now, but still, I'm surprised so many could take the time. Not everyone can be the master of his or her own schedule like you," he said.

Erica inclined her head as they descended the stairs. "That's true, but Isiah is too loyal to the family not to come, though, I have to admit that with the way the siblings—that's how we refer to all the aunts and uncles—have treated his wife, Livia, I wonder why she even bothers. As to Anthony and Michael, well, they're like two peas in a pod. Or," she paused fleetingly at the foot of the stairs. "They used to be like two peas in a pod."

"And now?" Caleb asked, opening the library door.

"Now, well, Anthony was always the voice of reason, always the one keeping his younger brother out of trouble, but Michael doesn't really seem to need that anymore. I think Michael has finally come into his own and Anthony's not quite sure what to do with that. Navigating that change in their relationship has led to some interesting interactions between the two, but they are close. Always have been. It's nice they can both be here."

"Dominique seems to have a hard time getting away." Caleb followed her into the library and made a pretense of checking all the decanters and glasses.

Erica snorted as she turned her back to him and started looking at book titles. "I think Dominique *chooses* to have a hard time getting away. Don't get me wrong, I like her, but she and Sabrina are having issues right now and I've been wondering why they even bothered to come. No, actually, I know why they came. Sabrina thinks the girls, Sasha and Nikki, should know their family. So she pulls them out of school every year and brings them along. She homeschools them while they are here, of course, but still . . ."

"That must be stressful, trying to manage time with your family, homeschooling your two daughters, and navigating a troubled relationship."

Caleb saw the back of Erica's hair sway as she shrugged. "Yes, but that's Sabrina for you. Everything is fine; everything is *always* fine. Listen to me," she said with a small laugh as she turned around halfway to face him. "I must sound like I hate my family. I don't, really. For the most part, they are good people. Some more interesting than others, sure, but good people. The siblings are sometimes hard to take in long doses, since they love to harp about tradition and always think their way of doing things is the right and proper way, but the cousins are mostly good people."

"Your mother was one of the siblings, right?" Caleb picked up a decanter that was three-quarters empty, figuring he would take it back to the kitchen.

"Yes," she said, turning back to the books. "She and Aunt Anna were twins. Anna lives in Italy, but her kids will be here in a few days. My mom, Anna, and Trip, Dixie's father, were the outliers in the family, to an extent. The three of them were born quite close together, bunched up in the middle of the eight kids with three older siblings and two younger. The older ones were older by quite a few years, and the younger ones were younger by about the same. So my mom, Anna, and Trip formed a little band of three and are—or I should say *were*, since my mother passed away seven years ago— definitely different than the rest of them."

Caleb mulled her insight over a bit. He could see a little threesome of kids buddying up together, pushed aside by their older siblings and not having any interest in their younger ones. He didn't think the trio had anything to do with what was currently happening at The Washington House, as none of them were even present, but he wondered if the family dynamic had filtered through into the lives of the next generation. If it had, *that* might have something to do with what was going on. It was definitely something to add to his list of things to think about.

"Well, it sounds like a colorful family," he said, pushing off the windowsill he'd been leaning against.

Erica laughed. "Yes, not as colorful as you'd think, but within our own ranks, we have our fair share of stories," she said, turning to face him completely. The inviting expression in her eyes made it clear she wouldn't mind if he stayed and probed some more.

"Well, maybe someday you'll tell me more. In the meantime," he said, holding up the decanter, "it's back to work for me."

She was too gracious to show any disappointment and inclined her head instead. "It was nice to meet you."

"You too, Ms. Brandt." As he made his way out the door, he heard her tell him to call her Erica, but he pretended that he hadn't. He had no interest in being on a first name basis with anyone in the family, even if they all took it upon themselves to call him by his.

As he made his way to the kitchen, he mentally recounted everything Erica had said, then began to plan the rest of his afternoon. He'd already "bumped into" most of the guests still in the main house, so he decided that, after he refilled the decanter, he would head back to the ice house to make some notes. Sasha and

Nikki were scheduled to go on a ride with Michael and Edith that afternoon; maybe he'd see if Elise wanted to take Pansy on another walk.

He was still going over his afternoon options when he stepped into the kitchen but his mind skidded to a halt when he saw Cate. Leaning over a counter making a list, her elbows rested on the countertop as she gently twirled a pen back and forth between her fingers. The natural fold of her button-down shirt had caused it to gape open and the view it offered was nothing short of spectacular.

She glanced up and smiled, but didn't adjust her position. "Hi, Caleb, did you have a productive sojourn around the house?"

Knowing she had no idea how she looked in that moment, and that she'd most likely be mortified if she did, he forced himself to turn away. Moving past her, he headed toward the walk-in pantry where the whiskey he'd watched her fill the decanters with days earlier was kept.

"I did," he managed to say. Inside the pantry, he slid the stopper from the glass and tried not to think about what it was he really wanted to do—to her— at that moment, even though he didn't *really* want to do it, even though he did. He ran a hand through his hair and rested his forehead against the pantry shelving for a moment. God, Tommy would kill him. And he'd deserve it. He knew, intellectually, that time had passed and life had to go on, but it didn't, and shouldn't, have to go on like *this*. With him finding himself not just desiring his best friend's widow, but desiring her with a fierceness that left him feeling like he'd just finished a prize fight.

"Caleb? Is everything okay?"

He lifted his head from the shelf and turned to find Cate standing in the pantry doorway, her head cocked in concern. Her shirt was back in place but, even so, thoughts of pulling her into that small, secluded space, pressing her against the wall, and doing things he absolutely should not be thinking about surged through his head.

"Everything is fine. Just fine." He topped off the whiskey in the decanter and handed it to her. "Would you mind taking this back to the library? I need to go write a few things down and give Jay a call."

She frowned at him, but nodded and reached for the crystal.

"And I was wondering if Elise might want to go for another ride this afternoon. Michael, Edith, Sasha, and Nikki will be out there. I don't mean to use her as a foil, but . . ." His voice trailed off as he realized what a jerk he must sound like. He had thought taking Elise out would give him a good excuse to be outside, but now that he'd said it out loud, to the young girl's mother, it sounded like he just wanted to use her. "Never mind, I can go by myself. It will be fine."

Cate smiled. "It's fine Caleb. She'd love it."

He searched her eyes and saw nothing but honesty. "You sure?"

She let out a small laugh. "Definitely."

"Okay. Well, okay then. I guess I'll go back to my room and get my stuff done. I think those four are scheduled to go out within the hour, so maybe Elise can be ready in about forty minutes?"

"I'll let her know."

He mumbled a thanks and began to move past her in the pantry doorway. Her hand on his arm stopped him. "Are you sure you're okay? You look a little, I don't know, distressed, maybe."

He fought the urge to laugh. "Distressed" didn't even begin to cover how he felt—low, disloyal, and scummy hit a little closer to the mark. "I'm fine," he managed to say. He knew she wanted more from him, she wanted him to reassure her, but it wasn't in him at the moment. The only thing really "in him" at the moment, was the knowledge that he needed to get away from her. He needed to get far away from her before he did something that neither of them would ever forgive him for.

• • •

Cate pulled out her phone and texted Jana as she watched Caleb walk away. She preferred to watch him coming toward her, but the view from behind was pretty nice too. If only something hadn't been bothering him. He'd brushed it off, because of course he would, but she knew him well enough to know he was hiding something.

Jana's confirmation text saying she'd have Elise ready beeped through. In reply, Cate sent off a quick "Thanks," then leaned back against the counter and returned to her last thought. The idea that she knew Caleb well enough to know anything struck her as novel, even though she'd known him more than a decade.

But as she thought back to when Tommy had been alive, she realized that, while she'd *known* Caleb—known his sense of humor, been able to anticipate his reactions to certain things, and understood his relationship with Brooke—that knowledge seemed superficial now. She'd never known him well enough to find out what he'd actually *thought*—not unless he had volunteered it—and never what he'd truly felt.

Her eyes drifted to the ice house. There were any number of reasons why she should think that she knew him better now than she ever had before, even though he'd been back in her life less than a week. They no longer had Tommy as a buffer, for one, but probably more to the point was what Caleb had mentioned that night in front of the fire: they were both different people now—still the same in many ways, but also very changed by each of their experiences over the past five years.

And with this realization came the thought that seeing Caleb again was almost like meeting someone new. They were both changed enough that it they were almost two different people—different people with a shared past, to be sure, but still, different than before.

There was something reassuring in that realization. She didn't quite know what or why, only that it settled and quieted something deep inside her.

• • •

"Elise, Sasha, Nikki, do you want to come help me get all the horses ready?" Mirielle asked the three young girls. As Caleb had hoped they would, he and Elise had arrived at the same time as Michael, Edith, and the girls. He'd made a big show of waiting until the family was saddled up before he and Elise would ride, but Sasha and Nikki had intervened, as he'd suspected they might, and now all three girls were following Mirielle around like ducklings.

He stood with Michael and Edith as they watched the barn manager and her assistants do all the work. "Are you enjoying your stay?" he asked the couple.

Edith, a tall woman with an aristocratic bearing but a playful, mischievous glint in her eyes, flashed him a smile. "It's been amazing. We've taken some gorgeous hikes, ridden out a few times, had some food that's to die for, and, best of all, other than meals, we're not really on anyone else's schedule other than our own."

"And, while we're here, our *schedule* is to pretty much have no schedule. No meetings, no appointments—"

"Other than spa appointments," Edith interjected.

"No appointments that require us to do anything other than show up," Michael corrected with a grin.

"The best kind," Edith concurred, bumping Michael with her hip.

He responded by slipping an arm around her waist and pulling her flush against him. Edith spun into Michael's embrace and when she stood before him, her hands resting on his chest, he quirked his eyebrows at her as a silent suggestion passed between them. Edith's head fell back with laughter.

"Time away from the day-to-day can be really good for you," Caleb said, turning away from the intimate connection between the two.

Michael nodded, keeping his eyes on Edith. He was also tall and, somewhere in his late forties, his brown hair was graying slightly. Based on what Caleb had heard from the staff and the other family members about this particular cousin, he had been expecting him to be a big man, not necessarily in size, but in personality and presence. And he wasn't disappointed.

"Was it difficult to get away?" Caleb asked, his eyes on the girls and horses.

Edith stepped out of Michael's embrace, but kept her fingers entwined with his. "I teach International Relations at a university in Boston, but it's my sabbatical year, so, for me, no."

"I work in the family business and since Douglas, my cousin who runs the empire, doesn't come to these reunions anymore, he felt it was important that I did," Michael said.

"I suppose there are worse assignments," Caleb nodded to the giggling girls.

Both Michael and Edith smiled. "Yes, you're right, there are certainly worse things," Michael replied. "With all the activities here at the house, there's plenty to do. We've even made it into town a few nights to hear some local music and try the local beer. We're enjoying having the time to spend together, especially with the girls."

Caleb's turned his attention to Sasha and Nikki, who were acting as though it was their job to make sure Elise was okay—treating her not quite like a little sister, but something more special. Mirielle had given the three of them tasks to complete for each horse and they were going through the line-up. Elise had picked the horses' feet and brushed their tails and now stood ready with the saddle pads. Sasha had brushed their coats and now held their bridles. Nikki was helping Mirielle with the saddles. The barn manager had whipped her three young charges into shape better than any drill sergeant Caleb had ever known, all the while keeping them smiling and giggling.

"Do you see them often?" Caleb asked.

"Not as often as we'd like," Edith answered.

"Sabrina and Dominique—well, Dominique anyway—are always so busy that it's hard to find a time to meet up," Michael said. "And, to be honest, it's hard to be around Dominique. I think she's missing the forest for the trees when it comes to her kids. Then again, I can't put it all on her; there's no reason we can't just come by and take the girls every now and then," he added.

"Forest for the trees?" Caleb asked as Nikki and Mirielle began saddling the horses.

"Too busy for her own kids. Of course, it's easy for me to say that, not having any of my own," he said with a self-deprecating smile.

"Ready, Mr. Whatley? Ms. Barnard?" Mirielle asked, ending their conversation as she approached them carrying riding helmets.

Caleb studied the line of five horses. Nikki, Sasha, and Elise, each donning a helmet, stood holding the reins of their respective mounts.

"It was nice to meet you both, and please let me know if we can do anything to make your stay any more enjoyable," Caleb said, shaking hands with each of them. They offered him some last-minute trail advice then moved to meet Mirielle.

Heading toward Elise and Pansy, he glanced back at the couple. They were listening to the barn manager's directions to a new trail, gesturing with her hands.

There was a different kind of energy about those two than any of the other cousins he'd met so far. Livia seemed bored but had a spark to her; Dixie was all fun and games; Sabrina seemed nervous and fixated on avoiding conflict; Anthony, though friendly enough, seemed a bit shallow; and Erica, well, he imagined that Erica played up the bohemian-artist stereotype as a way to disengage from the rest of the group, except for maybe her father and brother.

But these two . . . Caleb watched them chat with the girls and lead their mounts out of the barn as he boosted Elise onto Pansy's back and responded to her question about which trail they'd take. No, he thought, those two seemed remarkably—well, he couldn't quite put his finger on it. "Settled" wasn't the right word; there was an energy between them that was too vibrant for that word. Perhaps "solid" was as close as he could get to the vibe he got when observing and talking to them. Solid in themselves and each other.

He watched all of them mount their horses using the mounting block outside the barn, then ride out of sight. Turning his attention back to his own charge, he had Elise urge her pony forward, even though he held the lead, and together they exited the barn, turning north rather than south, where the other four riders had gone.

Michael and Edith were definitely different. Whether that was good or bad remained to be seen.

. . .

"Here, I brought you some breakfast," Cate said, handing Caleb a plate as she stepped into his room.

He took the offering, lifted the cover, and eyed the blueberry pancakes, roasted potatoes, and link sausages—all locally sourced and made, no doubt. "You didn't need to do that." She really didn't, but that wasn't going to stop him from enjoying it. He cleared a spot at the table, set the plate down, grabbed some coffee for each of them, then gestured for her to sit beside him.

"There's local maple syrup in that little cup, too," she said. Real maple syrup was one of the few things he insisted on; he'd rather eat pancakes without any syrup than use fake syrup.

"Is the family gone yet?"

She shook her head and sipped her coffee. "No, they'll be gone in about forty-five minutes."

The night before, Cate had confirmed that the Whatley family had committed to an outing at a famous local resort. It was too chilly to play golf, but this resort had an indoor pool for the girls, trails for those who wished to hike, and good old-fashioned music and theater entertainment throughout the day. The plan was for the entire family to spend the afternoon there, have a late lunch followed by sunset cocktails, then return to The Washington House for a light evening meal. All of which would leave Caleb ample time to search through their guest rooms, especially since Cate had given most of the staff the afternoon off as well.

"Do you want any?" he asked, gesturing to his plate. "You're eyeing my pancakes, I can see it."

She grinned, snatched his fork, and took a bite. "Margaret

makes *the best* blueberry pancakes," she said after swallowing. He stared at the fork suddenly back in his hand. Damn, she was fast.

"What can I do to help today?" she asked, reaching back over to pick up one of his sausage links with her fingers and taking a bite.

"Didn't Margaret feed you?" He snatched the sausage back and popped the rest into his mouth.

"Of course," she smiled and licked her fingers, "but this is my favorite breakfast of all time. French toast, crepes, elaborate eggs Benedict—those are all good, but nothing beats pancakes and sausage. Okay, so, what can I do to help?"

He studied her for a moment to make sure she wasn't going to steal anymore of his food before he spoke. "You can be my watchman," he said when he decided his food was safe.

"Watchwoman," she corrected.

He rolled his eyes. "Right. Anyway, I know Margaret is staying behind to get the evening meal started and to help prepare for the arrival of the Italian cousins."

"Mirielle and Mark will be here too, but I doubt either of them will come inside the main house."

"Even so," he continued, mopping up syrup with the last of his pancake. "I don't want any surprises—people coming back early or deciding to go where they don't normally go."

"Fine. Watchwoman. I can manage that, although, to be honest, it sounds kind of boring. Can I at least hum the theme song to *Mission Impossible* while you work?"

He gave her his best scowl then shook his head. "Do it and I will toss you out the window."

She laughed, then sobered. "I know I shouldn't be so flip about all this, given what we think is going on."

"Sometimes humor is the only way to diffuse the tension."

"Though not a very tactful way," she said, rising and collecting his plate.

He rose too, reaching for the plate. "I can get that."

When she dodged his attempt, his hand skimmed her waist. Abruptly, he shoved it into his pocket.

"I'm headed back to the house to check in on things so I can just drop it off in the kitchen on my way in. Once the family is on their way to the resort, I'm going to quickly check in on Elise and Jana. They are headed back to that animal farm they went to the other day and I want to make sure Elise doesn't give Jana a hard time about wearing her jacket. That should only take a few minutes, then I'll be good to go."

He told her to come by when she was ready. After she left, he sat back down at the table and began culling through his notes again. Nothing new had come in from Jay and, though he was thinking that, given her connection to Summer Granger's death, Edith was his best lead as the potential victim, he wasn't ready to rule anything else out just yet.

After a while, he leaned back in his chair and listened to the commotion of everyday life outside. The sounds of car doors opening and closing signaled that the Whatley family had left and the staff was now taking advantage of the impromptu time off. Glancing out the window, he saw Cate leaving the main house through its kitchen door, her green hat covering her red hair and her hands shoved into the pockets of her winter vest. It wasn't an easy feat to get sixteen people transported and entertained for the day and, given that the plan hadn't been fully committed to until the night before, she'd more or less put everything in place in less than four hours. She'd also done it all without once showing a hint of stress at the request. In fact, as he thought back on the few days he'd been there, he hadn't seen her lose her cool once, not even when presented with a beheaded snake.

He didn't expect that she was always so cool and collected, but he admired her ability to be that way when it came to her job. And judging by the way her staff treated her, she obviously had their respect too. She expected a lot from them, and they seemed happy to live up to her expectations, but she also had a softer, fun side that helped keep them all in good spirits during their long days.

A knock at his door by, no doubt, the woman in his thoughts brought him out of his reflection. He called for her to enter.

"Ready?" she asked, popping her head inside.

He gathered up the papers he'd spread out and tucked them into a folder, then pulled a sweater on over his t-shirt and followed her out and up to the main house.

"Let's start in the north wing and make our way down the hall," he said once they were inside, steering her toward the servants' staircase that led from the kitchen to every floor in the house. She followed behind him with a set of keys and, when they reached the second floor, she let him into the first guest room, which happened to be Agnes's.

He wasn't sure what he had been expecting, but the mess that greeted him hadn't been it. In fact, it looked like the room had been tossed. "Cate?"

She poked her head in and scanned the space. "Agnes doesn't like Annie and Lucy to come in and clean on a daily basis. They only come in every other day to replace the towels and once a week to change to the linens."

He glanced around again. "Okay."

"At least she's not likely to notice if you make a mess."

"Do you really think Agnes wouldn't notice if one thing had been moved so much as an inch?"

He watched Cate's eyes travel around the room. Twisted slips and undergarments were strewn about the bed and chairs, a scrunched up jacket lay on the floor at the foot of the bed, and shoes appeared to have been tossed randomly throughout the room. Face and hair products seemed to have popped up like mushrooms everywhere—the bathroom, the vanity, the bedside tables, even the fireplace mantle.

"What does an eighty-five year old woman, who has approximately one hundred hairs—most of which are on her chin—need with so many hair products?"

"Caleb!" Cate remonstrated, though with little effect since she laughed as she said it. He shook his head then waved her off to get to work.

Twenty minutes later, he'd found exactly what he thought he'd find in her room—nothing. Cate locked up behind him but instead of moving onto the next room, which was Anthony's, Caleb opted for Sebastian's instead, simply because he wanted to get it out of the way. While he hadn't decided to strike anyone off his list just yet, Agnes and Sebastian were pretty low on it.

Ten minutes spent in the room of the fastidious professor confirmed Caleb's thinking. Agnes and Sebastian would be more or less stricken from his list of both potential suspects and victims. He'd keep his focus on the cousins and Edward.

Heading into Anthony's room, he paused at the doorway to get the lay of the land. On a back corner of the house, the room had large windows on two walls that let the sunlight stream in. The bed was made and the room, with the exception of a pair of muddy boots, was fairly tidy. Caleb started his search in the bathroom where, thanks to what he was now considering an inherited trait, he found a number of hair- and skin-care products. He examined each, but based on scent and weight, they appeared to be exactly what their labels said they were. The trash bin contained only a tissue and an empty travel-size shampoo bottle, and the towels hung neatly on the dowels.

In the bedroom, he went through each drawer, finding nothing that screamed either murderer or victim, then he scoured the shelves. Containing mostly books about the area, Caleb suspected that what he saw was simply standard reading stock provided by the owners of The Washington House. On the mantle was a decanter of port, two glasses, and a crystal candlestick holding a beeswax candle. Other than the muddy boots, which weren't exactly out of the ordinary, given the weather they'd been having, everything appeared tidy and harmless.

Leaving Anthony's room, he headed into the rooms of Erica and her brother Mark, which were remarkably similar to Anthony's in tidiness. The only interesting items he came across were a bag of marijuana in Erica's room and a Kama Sutra book in Mark's.

Moving into the south wing, he started with Edward's room, which he searched more thoroughly than he had Agnes and Sebastian's. The bathroom was filled with skin care products, something Caleb was beginning to expect by now. Edward also had his fair share of painkillers and anti-depressants, though all looked legally prescribed. Caleb *did* feel a spike of anticipation when he spotted a journal, but after spending a few moments flipping through it and finding only two entries, both biblical in nature, he set it back down, disappointed but in no way surprised. A pair of leather gloves provided another brief moment of excitement, but whether they were lambskin or not, he couldn't tell. Still, he managed to take a small sample from the inside seam which he planned to send to Vivi to find out if it was a match with the leather she'd found on the wire.

Edith and Michael's room was next. They were the only guests who'd left their window cracked open, which gave the room a distinct chill. Caleb noticed that they had nice stack of firewood in the bin beside the fireplace, however, along with their own decanter of whiskey and glasses. Other than the window, nothing seemed out of the ordinary.

In Sabrina's bedside table, he found a book on saving relationships. In Dominique's, he found one of her business cards with the name and number of someone named Steve scrawled on the back. Doing a reverse look up, he found that the number belonged to Steve Dunwoody, a partner in a Boston law firm that specialized in divorce cases. Caleb took that as a good sign, thinking it unlikely that Dominique would want to kill Sabrina if she was also trying to divorce her. Alternatively, a possible divorce could give Sabrina a motive to do the deed.

The room where Nikki and Sasha slept was in the condition he would have expected from a nine- and an eleven-year-old. Clothes lay in piles on the floor and the girls' riding boots, though *near* the stone hearth, lay tipped over and sprawled about like drunkards.

Still, he searched; he knew enough to know that someone plotting a murder wouldn't blink at hiding something in the room of two little girls. While he did find a stash of candy in the closet, there were no signs of adult occupancy or use.

Isiah and Livia's room looked well used, confirming his suspicion that the couple was very much in love and Livia was not having an affair. He still needed to find out why she spent so many nights away in hotels, but he viewed that task more as checking off a box than anything else. He did pause, however, when he came to a shelf full of prescription drugs.

"Cate," he called from the bathroom.

"Yeah?" she asked, joining him.

"Do Isiah or Livia have any medical conditions that you're aware of?"

She eyed the shelf and shook her head. "Not that I know of. Do you know what any of these are for?"

He picked up a bottle and read the label. "This is a low-grade antidepressant. And this one," he said, pointing to another, "is a blood thinner. Other than that, I don't know."

"Can we find out?"

He shot her a look. "Of course we can." He replaced the bottle he'd removed, took out his phone, and snapped a few photos. He'd send them off to Vivi later.

"Only one room left," Cate said as they headed out of Isiah and Livia's room and she locked the door behind them.

"Dixie and Luke."

She grinned. "I bet it will be the most interesting."

"Why do you say that?" he asked, following her across the hall.

Cate turned around and leaned against the guest room door. "Because Dixie likes sex," she said, blocking his entrance.

"Most adults do."

"I'm just saying, don't judge anything you might find."

He frowned. "I can assure you that nothing I might find in that room will be a surprise or cause for judgment. Assuming, of course, it's all consensual and legal."

"Of course it will be, Dixie is all about respecting your own and your partner's being."

He crossed his arms. "You seem to know an awful lot about Dixie's sex life."

"A few years ago, she and I had a bit too much to drink out on a private beach when the family reunion was in Key West. I lamented about how I wasn't getting any and she let me live vicariously through her for a night."

His brows dipped. "What does that mean?" The far off look of mischief he saw in her eyes made him think he shouldn't have asked.

"It means she spent a lot of time telling me about her personal life, the good, the bad, and the stuff that, when taken out of context, just makes you laugh. It was fun. Well, that's one word for it."

"What's another?" He shouldn't have asked.

"Arousing."

He *really* shouldn't have asked.

"Educational."

He needed her to stop.

"Inspiring."

"And on that note, may I?" he asked, gesturing toward the door. He needed to put a screeching halt to the images her words were evoking in his mind.

She smiled, turned around, and unlocked the door.

And he'd be damned if she wasn't right. He wasn't shocked, not by a long shot, but Dixie and Luke's room proved to be the only truly interesting one. Unfortunately, not for the reasons he'd hoped. They had a book on the Kama Sutra too, but also all sorts of adult toys to use as backup in case the ancient practices didn't work. Or so he presumed. Or maybe the toys were used in addition to the ancient practices. Or maybe they liked to try one after the other. Or maybe . . .

He glanced at the closed window. The room seemed unusually warm.

"Find anything?" Cate asked, leaning against the doorframe.

His eyes dropped down at the book on the bedside table, open to page eighty-six. A black-and-white image of a couple took up the top of the page. In it, a woman lay back on a bed with her legs draping over the side, one of them wrapping around a man, who stood between her thighs. Caleb knew just how deep a man could get in that position.

"Not anything that will help us figure out who our potential victim or murderer is," he answered, turning away from the book and walking toward the window. With his back to Cate and his eyes on *anything* less suggestive, he took a few deep breaths, trying to calm both his mind and body.

"What now?" she asked. "This is the last room."

"I'll take the few things I've noted that I have questions about and ask the right people for help."

"Help?"

"Contrary to what you may think, I don't know everything."

He nearly jumped out of his skin when he felt her come up behind him. Thankfully, she didn't put an arm around his waist or press against him, but she did rest her cheek against his bicep as she joined him at the window.

"It's pretty out there, isn't it?" she asked.

The wistful tone in her voice gave him pause, even as he let his eyes focus on the view and take in what she was seeing. "It is."

"This would be a nice place to come and stay when I'm not actually working."

Instantly, he envisioned staying there with her. Hiking through the woods, sharing a bottle of wine in front of the fire. Climbing into the big oak bed with her. Page eighty-six.

"Maybe they'll give you a few days off when this reunion is over and you can take advantage of being up here. You could go for rides with Elise." He needed to put some distance between them. Well, mostly, he needed to give himself some distance from her.

She sighed and pushed away from him and the window. "Yeah, maybe."

He turned at her tone, but she was already heading out the

door. "If you're done, I'll lock up and go see if Margaret needs any help prepping for the evening meal."

She had pulled away from him. They both knew that Margaret, who had planned to take a long walk that afternoon, wouldn't need a hand with the light meal. Caleb studied Cate's face, but she gave nothing away. Then he saw her rub the inside of her left ring finger with her thumb, as if she were searching for a ring that was no longer there. She'd been missing Tommy.

"Of course. I'll go follow up on what I've found. I'm sure you'll want to spend some time with Elise, so maybe we should just touch base tomorrow?" Her lips parted, but he spoke again before she could say anything. "I'll let you know if I hear anything, otherwise, we can talk tomorrow."

He didn't stick around to hear whether she had agreed or not.

CHAPTER 9

THE NEXT AFTERNOON CATE WELCOMED the Italian cousins, who arrived in a whirlwind of cheek kisses and bottles of wine for the family. Margaret had prepared an elaborate dinner and a number of the cousins had stayed up late into the night talking and drinking—which meant that Margaret would have to push back breakfast for the majority of the guests the next day.

Cate didn't mind any of the disruption or extra work, though. Nico, Alex, and Francesca brought with them a sense of fun and a zest for life that seemed to make the house, and family, come alive. Perhaps it was because they'd been raised outside the claws of the family patriarch, or maybe it was just their own style, but, in Cate's eyes, they were always a welcome addition to the Whatley family reunions.

"You should go to bed," Greg said. He was standing at the sink washing up some of the last remaining dinner dishes used by the staff. "Christine and I can stay up and wash the wine glasses once the last of them have gone to bed. Or Caleb can."

That caught Cate's attention. From her position at the kitchen table, she could only see Greg's back. "Caleb?"

"Yeah," Greg said, turning to look at her over his shoulder. "He's been coming over here at night. I don't always see him, but I've seen him a enough times to assume that he comes every night. You didn't know?" He finished with the last dish, dried his hands, and turned to face her.

"I knew he was keeping an eye on things. I didn't know he was doing a walk-through every night." Which was somewhat dismaying. Not that he was doing it, but that she hadn't known about it. She'd seen him briefly that morning, but ever since that strange moment the day before—that moment that had felt so incredibly intimate and then had just fallen apart—she hadn't really had a chance to talk to him.

"He's not really selling his business to ours, is he?"

Cate's eyes shot to Greg's. She studied his face. She'd worked with him for years and though he could be a gossip below the stairs, it was mostly, she believed, out of boredom. She didn't think there was a malicious bone in his body and, if she was honest, she rather suspected Greg was meant to be doing something else with his life. She could easily imagine him working as an EMT or a doctor, or any role that would put him in the position of taking care of people. That was Greg's biggest strength, knowing just what a person needed and when they needed it, and it was why he made such a great employee. It was also why she didn't hesitate to answer.

"No, he's not. I met him through my husband years ago. We were all really good friends—he and Tommy were the best of friends. He practically lived with us once Brooke was born. When he wasn't on assignment, that is."

"I hear a 'but' coming . . ."

"'But' we drifted apart after Tommy died. Neither of us is really sure why, but we did. I hadn't spoken to him since Tommy's funeral, not until the night he arrived here."

Greg's eyes widened. "That's a long time."

"It is. But when we found that wire and I knew, or suspected, what it was meant to do, I didn't know whom else I could turn to. The police would have been helpful, I'm sure, but they can't *be here*. They can't commit time and resources to something that *might* happen. And I couldn't just sit around and wait for the next thing to happen."

"That wire may have been there for a while. It might not have been meant for any of the Whatleys."

Cate shook her head. "No, Mark and I walked most of the

trails in the week before everyone arrived, and other people had been out there before that day."

"And then there was the snake."

"And then there was the snake," Cate repeated. "Something is definitely going on here, and Caleb was the only person I knew who might be able to help me figure it out and hopefully prevent anything bad from happening. The Whatleys may not be the most interesting of families, but I do like them and would hate for anything bad to happen to any of them."

Greg was thoughtful for a moment then pushed off the counter he'd been leaning on, and poured two glasses of red wine from a half full bottle that had been left on the counter. "Here," he said, sliding one in front of her and joining her at the table. "If you're not going to bed now, at least you can join me. And, for what it's worth, I think you did the right thing. Like I said, I know he's been checking on the house at night after everyone has gone to bed, and I'm sure he's been doing a lot of other things I don't need to know about. But, honestly, if there is anything any of us can do, Cate, all you have to do is ask."

She smiled. "Thank you, Greg. I appreciate it. At this point, with Christine being the snake killer she is, I think she's done enough. For the most part, just keep your eyes open. If you see anything, let either me or Caleb know."

"Of course," he responded instantly. "Now, I have a question."

She eyed him but said nothing.

"How was it seeing Caleb after five years? It couldn't have been easy seeing your husband's best friend."

Cate started to shrug then stopped. "It wasn't as awkward as I thought it would be. I mean, I think what was most awkward was the fact that we'd let five years slip away. Actually *being* with him again wasn't awkward at all."

Greg grinned. "I bet it wasn't."

"What does that mean?"

"It means you guys have chemistry."

"Greg."

"Should I not say that, since he was Tommy's best friend?"

Cate shook her head. "No, it's not that. I've moved on, and while Tommy will always hold a special place in my life, I have no intention of martyring myself to his memory."

"Then what's the problem?"

"What you saw was the two of us being awkward around each other."

"Which you just said wasn't really the case. In our business, we have to be good at reading people. You know that, Cate." He paused and took a sip of his drink even as he gave her a meaningful look. "I've seen the way he watches you. 'Awkward' is not the word I would use to describe it."

Cate wanted to ask what word he would use, but she knew better. "It's not that simple, Greg."

"I never thought it was. I'm not saying this is the case, but I could imagine all sorts of guilt and shame and denial if I found myself attracted to my deceased best friend's wife."

"Yes, well, it would also be quite shocking since you're gay."

"There's that too. But you know what I mean."

She took a sip of her wine before answering. "I do know what you mean and, yes, if what you think you see is true, he would be feeling all that. It's even deeper than that, though. He and Tommy saved each other's lives on more than one occasion. They were closer than brothers and more loyal than you could ever imagine."

"Loyal even in death?"

"Maybe even more so, if that's possible."

"So, even acknowledging he might be attracted to you would feel like he was betraying Tommy."

Cate nodded. "And he'd hate himself for it. And I'd hate myself for putting him in that position."

"And so?"

"And so, I do nothing. We'll get through this reunion, Caleb and I will keep our friendship, and I will move on with my life."

"That sounds rather boring," Greg sighed.

She smacked his hand. "That sounds like my *life*. Besides, I'm not convinced that you saw what you think you saw, anyway." And she wasn't. Only, now she *was* curious.

Good lord, she was going to hell. She'd just finished telling Greg why she and Caleb shouldn't travel down that path and not two seconds later she was acting like a teenage girl wondering if the boy in her class liked her.

"You don't have to be convinced, but I saw what I saw," Greg said, collecting their empty glasses as he rose from the table. "Now, on that note, why don't you head back to your room and tuck yourself into your nice cold bed—alone—and think about what I said."

"You are a heartless man," she said, rising as well and donning her vest and hat.

"Perhaps Dixie can lend you one of her toys," he grinned.

She smiled and shook her head, moving toward the door. "Perhaps I have some of my own," she called back. She could hear his laughter as she pulled the door shut behind her and headed into the, thankfully, brisk night air.

• • •

Caleb sat in the alcove of the small office opposite the library, where most of the cousins had gathered for port and chocolate; night having long ago fallen. With the arrival of the Italian family members the day before, the atmosphere had turned decidedly more jovial; the meals were longer, the laughter more frequent, and the wine even more plentiful than before.

Stretching his legs silently, he listened to their chatter. After rising late that morning, many of them had spent the day on a "fox hunt." He'd ridden alongside the hounds keeper to keep an eye on things. Thankfully, nothing out of the ordinary had happened on the drag hunt where hounds had followed a scent, rather than an actual fox. But it had been some time since he ridden English style and he was feeling a bit stiff now, even though the quality of the horse he had ridden far surpassed any he'd had the pleasure of riding through various deserts and mountains over the past five years.

From his position across the foyer, he heard Dixie's throaty laugh rise above the din of conversation. Leaning slightly forward to peer into the room, he could see feet flung out from chairs, an occasional hand passing into view, and, every now and then, a figure moving past the doorway. But even though he could see and hear quite a bit, unless someone stepped out of the room and looked closely, he'd remain unnoticed by those he observed.

They were currently discussing a gathering that had taken place years earlier, when they'd all been children, and apparently not very well-behaved. Caleb saw Nico, one of the Italian cousins, stand and pour some more port into Sabrina's glass. He found it interesting to see how relaxed Sabrina was around her cousins when Dominique wasn't around. She may have been trying to save her marriage, but Caleb had to wonder if she might be better off without her "better half."

He sighed softly and leaned back again. He hated this part of a mission. Not that this was really a mission, only it sort of was. Regardless, he was just playing the waiting game now. On one hand, he hoped he didn't have to wait long. On the other, if or when something happened, it would mean someone was in danger.

Hearing footsteps in the hall, he craned his head and watched Christine and Greg deliver two more decanters—one port, the other whiskey. He was glad the staff members were traveling in pairs. He didn't think the Whatleys would cause any problems, but too much alcohol had a way of facilitating unpredictable behavior.

Anthony and Sabrina stepped into view to relieve Greg and Christine of the delivery. When the staff members exited the room, they left the door opened just a little wider than it had been before. Caleb smiled. Cate had told Greg, Christine, and Margaret his true role there. He didn't know how it had come about, but she had and, overall, he thought it had been a good decision. They knew where he had stationed himself tonight and had been strategic in giving him a slightly better view.

Not that he'd seen anything of note yet. Still, he didn't plan on leaving his post until all the cousins had gone off to their respective rooms, even though he suspected this particular watch would yield very little. Like at many family gatherings, the cousins seemed more interested in talking about the past—childhood adventures and mishaps—than anything current or troubling.

Several hours later, Caleb hadn't changed his opinion; however, he did have a better sense of each of the cousins from having listened to the stories about them and, sometimes more telling, how those stories were told. Not surprisingly, Sabrina had always been the peacemaker. Anthony had been a hothead as a child and young man, something that didn't show now. Michael had been a bit of a daredevil, which didn't come as a surprise at all, given what Caleb had heard about the man. Nico seemed to always have been the ringleader when they were all together, and Alex, his twin brother, egged him on. Dixie, the youngest by quite a bit, had always tagged along and been taken care of by everyone else; despite the fact that they all seemed bent on trouble when they were together, they had always, or so it seemed, watched out for Dixie.

The first to leave the party were Anthony and Sabrina, followed by Erica and Mark. Michael and Edith said good night at the same time as Isiah and Livia; Caleb watched as both couples walked up the main stairs and turned toward their respective rooms. Alex, Nico, Francesca, Dixie, and Luke lingered. Knowing the remaining five could likely go all night, Caleb slipped out of the office and into one of the back corridors that led to the kitchen.

"Thanks for leaving the door open," he said to Greg and Christine as he passed through the kitchen.

"Anytime. Coffee or tea?" Christine asked.

Caleb shook his head and kept moving toward the back door. "I'll be back in a few hours," he said then stepped out into the night. Pausing to inhale the cool night air, he heard an owl hoot in the distance. His eyes strayed to the ice house, then the carriage house, where Cate was likely tucked up cozy with Elise, deep asleep, as she should be. He let his eyes adjust to the dark, then made his way to his own room. After changing into a sweatshirt and a more comfortable pair of pants, he put on his running shoes and a fleece hat. He had a couple of hours to kill and no interest in sitting around in his room letting his mind wander. It had been a long time since he'd gone on a night run and, tonight, it seemed like a particularly good idea.

• • •

"What's going on?" Caleb asked as he entered the main house's unusually quiet kitchen.

"Some folks had a bit too much to drink last night and are lying low this morning," Cate answered as she emptied out a vase of fading flowers and replaced them with fresh ones. Margaret was sitting at the kitchen table sipping a cup of coffee over a crossword puzzle; no one else was around.

"Who's down for the count?" he asked. His fingers brushed hers as he took the refreshed vase from Cate's hands and set it on the other side of the sink, making room for her to start on another one. He had intended to keep his distance from her, to the extent that he could. All her talk of sex when he'd searched Dixie's room had planted seeds in his imagination that he could keep mostly at bay when he wasn't around her. However, those seeds seemed to take deeper root and grow whenever she was close. Especially when she was smiling at him. And touching him.

"Nico, Alex, and Dixie seem to have it the worst." Her answer brought his mind back to the issue at hand.

"Makes sense. They were part of the group that stayed up the latest. What about the others?"

"Pretty much everyone that was up last night is sick, or at least feeling off. Margaret cooked a light breakfast for the siblings and the cousins who came down this morning. We sent some soothing things up to those who didn't—tea, crackers, those sorts of things."

"And Greg," Margaret added.

"Greg?" Caleb asked, taking another vase from Cate and setting it next to the first one. He'd help her place them around the house when she was done with the last two that sat beside her.

"He's not feeling well, either," Cate said.

Caleb frowned. "Did he drink last night?" He had a hard time believing that, even as fun loving as Greg was, he'd drink to excess on the job.

Margaret shook her head and answered, her eyes never leaving the crossword. "No, I think he's just come down with something. He was on a job before this one and has been working for more or less two months straight."

"That could wear a body down," Caleb said, as a thought filtered through his mind. He'd help Cate, but then he wanted to talk to Greg.

He made idle chitchat with the two women until Cate had arranged all the fresh flowers, then they each grabbed two vases and left the kitchen. He followed her around the house, leaving one in the downstairs library, one in the foyer, and two in the upstairs library.

"How are you?" he asked as she settled the last arrangement on the mantle.

She glanced at him over her shoulder as she moved a few stems around and smiled. "I'm fine. Greg and Christine sent me home last night, so I got a good night's sleep." A shadow of something passed through her eyes and suddenly her cheeks flushed. Her eyes darted away and she turned her attention back to the vase.

"Are you sure?"

"Yes, right as rain. What are your plans for the day?" She turned to face him, but leaned her back against the mantle. Away from him. He was fine with that. Sort of. But thought it unusual.

"I, uh, I was planning to go check on Greg, then maybe do a walk-through of the house and grounds." Great, he sounded like a green teenage boy talking to a girl he liked.

She tilted her head and her hair fell over her face a bit. "Greg might be asleep, but he's in his room if you really need him."

When she straightened, a strand of hair caught on her eyelashes. He raised a hand and brushed it back, tucking it behind her ear. It wasn't his fault if his fingers lingered a second or two longer than they should have.

He saw her eyes widen just a tiny bit as his skin made contact with hers. He stepped away. "I'll just go now."

She nodded.

"Are you good? Do you need help with anything?" he asked. "I won't be very long if you need anything else."

"No, I'm good. Thank you."

"Maybe I'll take Elise for a ride on Pansy today."

"She'd like that."

If they got any more formal, he'd be bowing and she'd be pouring tea for two. He gave her a clipped nod, turned, and strode away.

Jogging up the stairs to the third floor, he made his way toward Greg's room. When he stopped in front of the door, he paused and listened. Silence. Then the sound of someone vomiting. Taking some pity on the man, Caleb waited outside to give him some privacy, until he heard the toilet flush, the sink run, and the bed creak.

"Greg?" he said tentatively, knocking on the door.

A moan answered.

"Can I come in?" He took the garbled response as a yes and cautiously opened the door.

Greg had opened the window and lit a candle, lessening the stench of illness, but there was no doubt the man was in a bad way.

"Can I get you anything?" Caleb asked, approaching the bedside so Greg wouldn't have to move to talk to him. He got an eye roll in response. "Okay, maybe not. Does this feel like the flu?"

Greg managed a tiny shake of his head. "No fever."

"Did you drink too much last night after cleaning up?"

"Just a glass of whiskey."

"So, definitely not a hangover?"

Another tiny head shake. "Just worn down," Greg croaked.

"Just whiskey? Not port?"

Greg closed his eyes and nodded. The man wanted nothing more than to drift off to sleep.

"I'll have Margaret send up some tea and crackers in a few hours." Greg made a half-hearted effort to wave his hand in thanks. His palm made it about two inches from the mattress.

Stopping by the downstairs library on his way to the kitchen, Caleb paused to study the decanters. Three were empty and two still held a small amount of alcohol, whiskey in one and port in the other. Inspecting the empty decanters, he saw the remnants of whiskey in one and the telltale red rings left by port in the other two. He managed to pick up all five decanters then went to find Cate.

"Have these been touched since last night?" he asked, setting the decanters down on the kitchen counter. Cate was sitting at the table going over some lists, papers spread around her, but she looked up at his question.

"With everyone sick, including Greg, Christine hasn't made her rounds of the downstairs rooms yet, so no, I don't think so. Why?"

"Because I think it's weird that Greg is sick."

Her eyes studied him, then traveled to the empty decanters, before coming back to his. "Please tell me you don't think someone tampered with those."

He knew the implications, but he wouldn't lie. "I wish I could. I want to get these tested to confirm though."

Her gaze immediately swept the kitchen, taking everything in—all the food they would somehow have to prepare and keep safe.

"Do you think . . ."

"That other food or beverages might be contaminated? It's possible, but if someone was targeting the Whatleys in general, it seems like dinner would have been a better option than after-dinner drinks because not everyone joins in on that ritual." He leaned against the counter beside the decanters and watched her mind work out just how she and her team would need to adjust.

"So, you think the intended victim is someone who was there last night? How will you ever find out who, given that nearly all the cousins were there?"

"First things first. I want to get these tested. If we're lucky, only one was contaminated and at least some of the people there last night will have a preference for whichever one *wasn't* tampered with."

She tapped her pen on the table. "Meaning that if it was the port, if one of the cousins only drinks whiskey then we can rule that cousin out as the victim?"

"That's the thought. Of course, it rests on the assumptions that only one type of alcohol was tampered with and at least some of the cousins only prefer one alcohol over the other."

She bit the tip of the pen for a moment as she thought about what he'd said. "We may be out of luck there. I think all the cousins drink both port and whiskey, although some may have a stronger preference for one over the other."

He frowned and pushed off the counter. "I thought that might be the case. Are some of the cousins sicker than the others?"

"You want to try and rule them out by how much they might have had of each drink?" When he nodded she took a moment to think before answering. "Michael isn't sick at all. Anthony, Sabrina, and Edith are all uncomfortable and nauseated, but not praying to the porcelain god like Alex, Dixie, and Nico are."

"What about Luke?"

"He's somewhere in between Dixie and Edith, as are the rest."

"Where was Dominique last night? In her room?"

"She spent a good part of the evening playing pool by herself. She was in bed when I made my final rounds at around ten. Will any of this information help?"

"It all helps, but, like I said, first things first. I'll go start the process to get these tested, and if you could make a list of which cousins prefer which liquor, if you know, that would be great."

"Sure. Should I drop it by later?"

"Why don't I take Elise out for a ride in a little bit and you can just leave the list for me at the carriage house." He much preferred if she didn't set foot in his room or anywhere in the vicinity of his bed. Not that he'd need a bed, if it came down to it. "Will an hour be enough time?"

She tapped her pen again and seemed to be contemplating *him*. Finally, she nodded. "Sure, I'll leave it with Jana. You can pick it up when you drop Elise back."

He thanked her and made his exit. He was already dialing Vivi's number, when he unlocked the door to the ice house.

"Caleb, I'm glad you called," Vivi answered, surprising him by recognizing his number. He wasn't altogether sure how he felt about the idea of Vivi either knowing his number or having it in her contacts list.

"Why is that?" he asked, placing the decanters, which he'd carried over in a box Cate had given him, on the table and removing his jacket while juggling the phone.

"I found a bit of trace evidence on the wire when I was examining it again today. I was planning to call you tonight."

"Please tell me it's something useful." He dropped into a dining chair and sent up what was as close to a prayer as he got.

"Well, usefulness is always relative, but it was wax. A special kind of wax though; the kind used on waxed jackets."

Vivi was right; the news was relative. The Washington House was the type of facility that, he assumed, would have any number of waxed jackets available for staff and guests. Not to mention that employees such as Mirielle and Mark probably had their own. Even so, he knew Cate, with her attention to detail, would know if any had been worn by family members and, if so, when.

"Thank you, that could be useful."

"But that's not why you called, is it?"

"No, it's not." He eyed the box sitting in front of him. "What do you know about poisoning?"

She paused. "What kind of poisoning?"

"That, I don't know."

"Symptoms?"

"Vomiting, fatigue, intestinal discomfort."

She let out a little breath. "That could be about a thousand different things, depending on dose and delivery."

"I don't know about dose, but I think it was delivered in either port or whiskey."

He could hear her drumming her fingers on a table. "So an oral delivery that was diluted by alcohol."

"Is it possible that it could have interacted with the alcohol to make people sick?"

"A lot is possible with poisons and alcohol. How many people?"

"Twelve, but they have varying degrees of symptoms. The worst seem to have flu-like symptoms without fever."

"The severity of the symptoms could reflect the quantity consumed, a particular sensitivity, or some pre-existing condition, so it makes sense that some would be sicker than others."

"So, any ideas?" he asked.

"I'm sorry, not without testing the delivery mechanism or the blood of one the people who imbibed."

"What if I bring you the samples? I could leave tonight, stay at my sister's, and bring them to you at the lab tomorrow morning." He had intended to package up a sample and send it, but this seemed more efficient. He could drop the entire box with Vivi and be back before early afternoon the next day.

"That works for me."

He heard hesitation in her voice, so he asked.

"No, I'm not hesitating," she replied. "I'm just, well, I'm just wondering if you want to be away when whatever is going on is going on. Between the wire and a potential poisoning—"

"And the snake," he interjected.

"The snake?"

He smiled at the horror he heard in her voice then proceeded to tell her about the copperhead.

"Okay, well, that's a bit, I don't know, it just doesn't seem as well planned as the wire and the poison. Although, all three methods leave a great deal to chance and are, I suppose, interesting choices."

Her musing tone brought her psychology background to mind—a field he knew next to nothing about, at least not in the subtleties. Though he and Vivi weren't as close as he'd like, her suggestion that there was likely some sort of warped psychology at play reminded him that he needed her experience. Not to mention that she was right, he shouldn't be leaving the house unattended, especially not now.

"They are," he said, picking up on her train of thought. Why go to the trouble of trying to kill someone and yet leave so much to chance? "I want to bring you these samples rather than mail them, but you're right about leaving the house right now. Let me bring in someone else to stay here while I'm gone. I should be able to have someone here by mid-afternoon tomorrow, can we meet tomorrow night instead of in the morning? I'd like to pick your brain on what's going on here and leave you the port and whiskey bottles that I *think* are responsible for making everyone sick."

"Ian's on shift tomorrow night, do you mind coming by the house? I'll have Jeffery too. Maybe Kit and Garret can come so Garret can weigh in as well."

Her statement struck an odd chord. He'd worked with Garret for nearly seven years and was almost as close to him as he'd been to Tommy. But not once had he thought to bring Garret in on this. Not because he didn't trust his former partner or think he wouldn't have something to contribute, but because of Kit. He didn't want to pull Garret, the man his sister loved, back into their old world. Not even the tiniest bit.

"Garret doesn't need to be a part of this, but meeting at your house works for me. What time?"

They settled on a time and he was about to hang up when she stopped him. "You met Lucas at the wedding, right?"

He'd met Lucas Rancuso at the wedding, and few other times over the past year. He was a homicide detective in Boston and as close to Vivi as a brother. "Yes, I did."

"Well, he might not like me telling you this, but he quit his job last week. He hit twenty years last Thursday and more or less filed his paperwork and walked out that day." She paused, clearly hesitant to continue, though he knew she wanted to.

"He's kind of at loose ends," she started again. "He's too young to retire completely, but he doesn't want to be a detective anymore. I think he might be looking for something in the private industry, but he hasn't decided yet."

"And you think he might be a good person to come up here and keep an eye on things?"

"Well, he *is* a former detective. He's really good at *detecting* things."

Caleb smiled. She sounded just like a proud little sister. "That's actually a good idea, and I think he'd fit in well with the dynamics around here. Do you think he'd mind coming for a week or so?"

"Not if Vic could join him on the weekend," she said, referring to Lucas's husband, who was a police officer in a small town north of Boston.

"I'm sure that would be fine. Let me check with Cate. Can you text me his number?"

Vivi agreed and they ended the call.

He eyed the decanters for a moment and contemplated running an experiment on himself. But, accepting that he'd be better off staying healthy, taking Elise for a ride on Pansy, and then handing the poison detection responsibilities over to a professional the next day, he moved into the kitchen to find a safe method of storing the liquids. Ten minutes later, all the decanters were empty and the fluids he'd drained were safely deposited in two glass jars surrounded by dish towels. He placed all the containers in a cabinet over the refrigerator and cleaned up, being careful to wipe the few drops of liquid that had spilled onto the counter with a paper towel. By the time he'd finished, he still had fifteen minutes to kill before meeting Elise. He could lounge around his room or suck it up and head to the carriage house early, knowing he might run into Cate.

Two minutes passed before he grabbed his jacket, hat, and keys and made his way next door.

• • •

It seemed ridiculous to think the house felt any quieter than it had the day before, when most of its guests had been ill, especially considering that many of those who'd been sick were now up and about. They weren't running any marathons, but they *were* slowly and steadily going about their days. Still, with Caleb gone not even an hour, the house felt bigger, quieter, and emptier somehow.

Sitting at the kitchen table in the main house, Cate watched the rain that had moved in overnight fall in a steady stream. Through the window she could see leaves bent under the weight of raindrops and, though she was tucked inside the warm kitchen, she swore she smelled the scent of freshly dampened earth.

It would be a good day to cozy up in front of a fire. Of course, that thought flowed into thoughts of cozying up in front of a fire with Caleb. She waited for a pang of guilt, anticipated one even, but it never came. She recalled her realization a few days earlier, of what different people they were now than they'd been five or eight years ago. The idea had settled into her body and seemed to have taken root, because when she thought of being attracted to Caleb now, of wanting to be with him physically, there was no room left in her mind to give any credit to what she had once thought she *should* feel.

"How are the accounts?" Margaret asked, walking into the kitchen and nodding toward the paperwork spread before Cate on the table as she made her way to the coffee pot. Just in case whatever had made the guests sick hadn't come from the whiskey or port, they'd cleaned out all of the food and any open containers in the kitchen. They'd kept unopened wine, sealed foods, and those sorts of items, but anything that had been opened or didn't come packaged had been tossed. Consequently, they were restocking.

"We'll be okay. Thanks for being flexible on the menu.

Christine was able to pick up a lot of the fall greens from local farmers. She's on her way to the butchery to pick up some meats."

"We'll have to shop daily, now, won't we?" Margaret sat down across from her and took a sip of the coffee she'd poured. She also slid a cup in front of Cate, avoiding the piles of papers.

Smiling gratefully, Cate wrapped her hands around the warm mug. "Not daily, no, but more regularly. Before he left this morning Caleb added locks to the pantry. We can use the small refrigerator and freezer in there to hold some of the perishables, but we definitely won't have the kind of storage we had before."

"What about using the big freezer?"

"Probably fine, but I don't want to take any chances." So far, they'd been able to keep the suspicious incidents quiet. The Whatley family knew about the wire, of course, but not the snake. As to the poison, well, for now, the cousins remained under the impression that they'd simply had too much to drink. That said, she and Caleb had agreed that, if poison was discovered, they'd need to tell the family. It would be too dangerous not to.

"Speaking of not taking any chances . . ."

"Did you meet Lucas?" Cate asked with a smile. Caleb had introduced her to the former detective shortly before he'd left. Despite Lucas's intimidating height, he had kind eyes and she'd liked him immediately. She'd set him up in one of the bigger corner rooms on the third floor. Greg, who was feeling better, was currently giving him a tour.

"Yes, I did. He's a strapping lad, to say the least. It's a bit weird to be in this position, I mean, have you ever had something like this happen at one of your events before?"

"No, but this isn't the first event to have security, you know that. Think of Lucas like that. Friendlier than most security details we work with, but same idea."

Both Margaret and Cate turned their attention to the stairwell as two voices filtered down. Annie and Lucy, the live-in house-cleaners, joined them a few moments later.

"Coffee?" Annie asked, grabbing a cup and holding it up to Lucy in question as she moved toward the pot.

"Yes, please," Lucy answered. Both Cate and Margaret declined refills.

"Done with the rooms for the day, ladies?" Cate asked.

"Almost," Lucy said over her shoulder as added some sugar to her cup. "Most of the family are in one common room or the other, but Dominique shouted at us to leave her alone and Isiah and Livia, well, I think they were making the most of having the bad weather keep them in for the day. In fact, they've asked if they could have some wine and a cheese and charcuterie plate sent up later instead of attending dinner."

Cate glanced at Margaret.

"Assuming Christine is able to get back with the shopping, that shouldn't be a problem," the cook replied.

"And Edward," Annie said.

"Oh, yeah. Edward," Lucy repeated.

Cate frowned. The elderly man rarely caused any problems. He wasn't the friendliest member of the family—in fact, very few people seemed to actually like him—but he didn't usually give the staff a hard time. "What's wrong with Edward?"

"I don't know," Lucy said as she and Annie joined them at the table. "He was out somewhere in the house, but came back when we were in the middle of cleaning. We were almost done, mind you, and were just finishing up with the dusting and rearranging when he came in and told us to leave."

Annie frowned. "It was weird. He was quite harsh at first, but then just said he had a headache and wanted to lie down. When we offered to have something sent up, he shook his head and shooed us out."

"Though he thanked us as we left," Lucy added, which they all found unusual. Edward, though not overtly rude to the staff, was rarely gracious either.

"He seemed a bit confused, actually," Annie said thoughtfully.

Cate shared a look with Margaret. She'd only told *her* staff about the potential poison, neither Annie nor Lucy knew.

"Did he have anything to drink last night or the night before?" Cate asked Margaret.

"Not to my knowledge. It's my understanding that he doesn't drink much. At most, I've seen him have one glass of wine with dinner. Christine or Greg might know if he partakes otherwise."

Cate made a mental note to ask. "I'll have Christine check on him later this afternoon. At his age, if he's feeling at all unwell, I want to be sure we take care of him," she said.

The three women nodded.

"I'll check in on him before lunch, maybe bring him a cup of the tea he likes," Margaret said.

Cate murmured a thank you and wondered what Caleb might find when they tested the port and whiskey. As a precaution, they'd emptied every decanter in the house, refilling them with new liquor. Of course, if someone was truly intent on carrying out a poisoning, it wouldn't be difficult. Most of the time the decanters sat unsupervised throughout the house and would be easy enough to tamper with. But she'd checked with Caleb and, while he did see the risk, he thought that, even if someone wanted to use poison again, they'd be unlikely to use the same delivery method after having already failed. No, he seemed to think that if there were to be another attempt, it would be much more targeted. Which made her feel oddly relieved. It wasn't very kind of her, but if any of this resulted in death, she'd rather it be just one person that died than have a whole group go down as collateral damage.

"Did you meet Lucas while you were upstairs?" Cate asked the housecleaners.

Annie and Lucy shared a look.

"Yes, we did." Annie said.

"What's that look mean?"

Lucy laughed and shook her head. "Nothing. It means nothing. He seems like a nice guy and, given the threat your company received, I'm glad we have someone to keep an eye on things," she said.

With the mention of the threat, Lucy was repeating the fudging of the truth Cate had told the permanent Washington House staff. She trusted them to an extent, but, well, they weren't *her* staff, so she didn't trust them enough to tell them the whole truth.

"But he's rather striking, isn't he?" Lucy continued. "I'm mean, I'm not attracted to him, but he's hard to not to stare at, don't you think?"

Annie nodded vigorously, "He does have a rather commanding presence."

Cate couldn't help but laugh.

"And what are we telling the family? I mean, he's not likely to go unnoticed is he?" Lucy asked.

"We've told the family that we've seen quite a few people lingering at the gates to the property and, while we have no cause to be specifically concerned, we'd rather have someone on the premises who could manage a situation, should one of them decide trespass while the Whatleys are here." This was an extension of something Caleb had said to Agnes and Edward several days earlier, so the lie flowed easily. And, truth be told, while the family members weren't each billionaires on their own, collectively they were worth quite a lot, and so was the family business. Cate didn't like to think of it, but the reality was that a kidnapping wasn't out of the realm of possibility, and, given the way the family had accepted the explanation of Lucas's presence, she knew the possibility wasn't foreign to them either.

CHAPTER 10

Caleb pulled up Vivi's long driveway a little before seven o'clock. Light flooded from the house, though it quickly faded to black in the dark and rainy night. He knew most of the couple's friends used the back door as the main entrance, but he didn't feel comfortable being that familiar, so he grabbed the box of decanters and made his way to the front door instead.

"Caleb?" Vivi's voice called from somewhere in the house after he knocked.

"Yeah, it's me."

"Come in."

It felt strange to enter the house on his own and he felt a flash of uncertainty as he stepped over the threshold.

"I'm just putting Jeffery down for the night." Vivi appeared from the hallway to his right. She had the toddler perched on her hip. Six-months pregnant with her second child, she didn't look incredibly comfortable toting the boy around, but he didn't feel as though he knew her well enough to offer to help with the toddler. He'd probably scare the boy, who was staring at him with the same pastel-green eyes as his father's.

"Can I help with anything while you're putting him down?"

"No, go ahead and set that box on the kitchen counter, but if you could slide it to the back, that would be great," she said, turning back toward the hallway. "Just give me ten minutes."

She disappeared again and he heard murmurings of the mother and son having a quiet conversation. He moved into the kitchen and placed the box well out of toddler reach, then, at a loss, searched for something useful to do.

Caleb had worked with Ian, Vivi's husband, a time or two back when Ian had been an Army Ranger. A man didn't lead the kind of life Ian had led and then completely change habits, so Caleb wasn't at all surprised to find the house tidy. It looked lived in, for sure, but tidy.

Spying a basket of toys that had been dumped over in a corner of the living room, Caleb figured he'd make himself a little useful. He still wasn't all that comfortable with Vivi, so asking her for favors, any kind of favors, made him uncomfortable, especially since he had no idea whether or not she would ask for something in return. If she did, as intelligent and curious as she was, the world of what she might ask for was wide open. Maybe by picking up after Jeffery he could balance the scorecard a bit before they even began their discussion.

"You didn't have to do that," Vivi said as she came back into the room a few minutes later without her son. He shrugged, added the last toy to the righted basket, and waited for her to take a seat.

"Help yourself to something to drink—beer, wine, juice," she said, sinking down onto the sofa. A fire blazed in the fireplace and, when she put her feet up on the coffee table, he almost relaxed in the cozy room. "I'd get it for you, but I've been on my feet all day."

"We can do this another time."

She waved off his offer so he sat down. "I left the port and whiskey on your counter. I took the liquids out of the decanters and put them into jars, but I brought the crystal too, in case you need it."

"Thanks. From the sound of it, there won't be a shortage of fingerprints, but maybe we'll find something interesting. Now, what did you want to talk over with me?"

He hesitated again, owing someone a favor could turn around and bite him on the ass.

"Let me see if I can help you," she said, smiling at him like she could read his thoughts. "You have a potential murderer and a potential victim both staying in the same house, likely related, but you don't know who either is, or why any of them might want to kill any of the others. And you want the benefit of my keen intellect and years of training to help you think things through."

She had smiled as she'd said the last part and he couldn't help but smile back. "More or less," he replied with a shrug. "Except that I have about *a hundred* reasons why any one of them could be either the killer or the victim. Love and money being the two most prominent motives applicable to just about everyone in the house, with the exceptions of Sasha and Nikki, who are nine and eleven."

Vivi rested her head on the back of the couch. "That does sound like a puzzle. Give me a rundown on everyone staying there."

For the next few minutes he did just that. Spending time on each cousin and sharing what he'd learned from Jay and his contact in Boston about Dominique. The only people he glossed over were Nico, Alex, and Francesca, only because they'd just arrived. He didn't even spare Agnes, Edward, or Sebastian, despite their advanced ages.

She peppered him with questions along the way, most of which he could answer, some of which he could have used Cate's help with. When he'd pretty much exhausted everything he knew, he sat back.

"Would you mind getting me a glass of water?" Vivi asked.

"Of course," he said, springing up instantly.

She directed him to the glasses and he filled one from the sink. "Grab yourself a beer from the fridge, if you like," she added.

He debated for five seconds then opened the fridge and pulled one out. After handing the glass to her, he sat back down with his bottle.

"So, the bad news is, unless there is another attempt, it's going to be difficult to narrow down the intended victim. I'm sure you've mapped out who was both out riding the day the wire was found and who was drinking the night of the possible poisoning, but even so, like I said on the phone, all three methods leave a lot to chance. I think taking a closer look at who's on both lists is a place to start, but I wouldn't rule anyone else out yet."

He rested his bottle on his belly. "My thoughts too."

"So, since we may not be able to narrow down the list *that* way, how about looking at the methods used to try and commit this murder?"

"Meaning?"

"Meaning stringing the wire must have required someone with some strength to make it taut enough to do any damage. Whoever brought the snake into the house had to have some comfort with the animal, since not many people would willingly put themselves in the same room as a copperhead. As to the poison, well, they would have to be either stealthy enough or invisible enough to get it into the containers, not to mention smart enough to know what to use, assuming it's not something as run-of-the-mill as rat poison."

"None of those methods would rule out a woman, would they?"

Vivi shook her head. "No. The wire would require strength, but any relatively fit woman would be able to do it."

"What did you mean by stealthy *or* invisible? Are they not the same thing?"

"They can be, and often someone with stealth can *make* him- or herself invisible, but there are also people out there who are, just by their natures, relatively invisible—and usually not intentionally. It's just part of their makeup. Does that remind you of any members of the family?"

Caleb thought about it for a long moment, then tilted his head from side to side in indecision. "For a lot of them, I would say definitely not. They like being seen and heard and have at least some kind of engaging presence. There are a few I don't see as often, though. The only problem is that I don't know if that's because they are 'invisible,' as you're suggesting, or because they are just on vacation and spending some quiet downtime."

Vivi mulled this over. "Fair enough. One thing I will point

out, though, is that the methods this person has used are all very dramatic, don't you think?"

"Dramatic?"

"I mean, if someone gets shot or stabbed to death, it's horrible, but these methods—decapitation, snakebite, poison—they would all cause an additional kind of shock at the method, not just the death itself. I believe that, in the news, they'd refer to it as 'bizarre,' or 'unusual.' All the methods are a bit archaic and all are methods that would catch someone's attention."

He hadn't thought of it that way, but her statement had more than a ring of truth to it. Death by any of the means attempted so far would be talked about for many years to come.

"So, you think the killer might be someone who wants attention?"

"Or someone who has a macabre sense of entertainment."

"You think they might find murder entertaining?"

A half smile touched her lips. "I like how you feigned shock there, Caleb. You know as well as I do that there are too many people out there who view killing as entertainment."

He eyed her for a moment then let his own head fall back to rest against the back of his chair. "I try not to think about it too much."

"I know. Kind of makes you want to go take a shower, doesn't it? It's one of the more disturbing parts of my job, meeting people like that. I do like to catch them, though."

"Cheers to that," he said, lifting his bottle in her direction.

She joined him in the toast and took a sip of her water.

"So, what should I do now?" The ease with which the question slipped off his tongue surprised him.

"I'll take that stuff to the lab and test it tomorrow. If we're lucky it will be some rare form of toxin that's easily traced."

"Not holding my breath."

She laughed. "Me neither. It's always one foot in front of the other in situations like this. As for you, go spend some time with your sister. I think Garret is down in New York for the night. You can head back to the gothic murder mansion in the morning to keep an eye on things. I'll also look into whether or not I can predict what kind of attempt could come next. You have a pretty bizarre set of methods on your hands, and it's even weirder that none have been successful—not that I'm complaining. Still, it's a unique set, I'll do some digging to see if I can find a pattern or if there are other crimes using similar methods that have occurred."

"Thanks," he said, taking his cue and rising from his seat. He reached for her glass, which she handed over, then deposited his bottle in the recycling bin in the kitchen and placed her glass in the dishwasher. "You okay for the night?"

She rolled her head, which still lay against the back of her chair, and looked at him. "Yeah, I'll be fine. A little tired is all. If you can help me off this couch so I can waddle to bed, I'd appreciate it."

He held out a hand and she clasped it, pulling herself up. "I'm so much bigger this time around."

"But everything is okay? With you? And the baby?"

She smiled as she walked him to the door. "Yes, thank you for asking. Everything is fine. I'm just a little more uncomfortable this time. Now, go and see your sister. I assume she's expecting you?"

"I called her last night after I spoke to you, and then again just before I arrived here."

That earned him a big smile. "Maybe there's hope for you yet, Caleb Forrester." She went up on tiptoe and brushed a kiss across his cheek. "I'll call you tomorrow after I run the tests."

"Be careful with it," he said, suddenly questioning the wisdom of leaving the evidence with her and Jeffery.

"I'll be fine. Now, go on with you. Kit will be waiting."

He lingered for a moment, then nodded and headed back to his car.

Fifteen minutes later, he pulled into the parking area of Kit's house. She met him at her door wearing one of Garret's old Army sweatshirts, black yoga pants, and her hair pulled back, a sure sign she'd been writing all day. She followed him downstairs and plopped down on the couch in the family room while he dropped his bag on the bed in the room he usually claimed as his own when he visited. When he came back out, she was watching at him, an expectant expression on her face. She wanted to talk. He knew that look well. Whenever she was cooped up all day writing with no interaction, she turned into Chatty Cathy as soon as someone came into her orbit.

"I need a beer before you accost me."

She waved him upstairs, but called after him. "I'm not going to accost you, you know. I just want to hear what you are doing in New Hampshire. And bring me a glass of that wine on the counter."

With good reason, Kit didn't like not knowing what he was up to when he was off doing whatever it was he was doing. There were times when he legitimately couldn't tell her, but they'd reached a point in their relationship where, if he couldn't tell her, he'd say so and she'd accept it. So long as when he *could* tell her, and she asked, he did. Unfortunately, what he was doing in New Hampshire fell into the latter category, so he'd have to talk.

"So? Dish," she said when he returned to the lower level and took a seat at the opposite end of the couch from her.

He didn't love talking about Tommy and Cate and Brooke, but he did it. The events at The Washington House were much easier to cover, but that was to be expected since those events felt more professional than personal, unlike all the other stuff. Nevertheless, while he told his sister a lot, more than he ever had before, he held back just a little bit. He and Kit were still feeling out their relationship and he wasn't ready to bear his soul quite yet.

When he finished talking, she sat back and took a sip of her wine. "Wow," she said. "First, I want to say I'm sorry for your loss, for what happened to Brooke, that poor child, and to Tommy. I know it must have been beyond devastating to Cate, but you lost a best friend and a little girl that was probably closer to you than most other people were at that time."

Caleb looked away and blinked. No one had offered him condolences before. He didn't think he deserved it, not after what had happened to Tommy, but that didn't stop the sense of gratitude he felt for Kit's recognition of his loss. It unfurled in his chest then traveled to his heart and throughout his body. For the first time, he let himself truly feel his own loss. Not Cate's, not anyone else's, but his own.

God he missed them. Both of them.

He glanced down at the bottle in his hand, the local IPA suddenly losing its appeal. He futzed with the label and let the memories wash over him. "You know, she could have been mine. Biologically, that is."

Kit hesitated. "She? Who? Wait—your what?"

"Brooke." He looked up and prepared to say what he had never said to anyone before. Because he needed to. Because it was time.

"You're not saying . . ."

He appreciated the doubt he heard in Kit's voice as she tried to ask him if he'd slept with his best friend's wife. It gave him some confidence in himself and his character, knowing she didn't believe he would do such a thing.

He shook his head. "No, not in that sense. It was just that, well, when Cate was first trying to get pregnant, both she and Tommy had some tests done. Tommy was quite a bit older and he'd been adopted, so he knew nothing about his health history. Anyway, the tests came back that he had a low sperm count. Low enough that they questioned him ever being able to impregnate Cate naturally."

"Did they do in vitro?"

"No. His count was too low even for that. Not that they couldn't have tried, it just would have been really expensive and the chances of success weren't great." He paused and turned his gaze back to his fingers wrapped around the bottle, back to the past. "They asked me if I would be a donor. I didn't hesitate, not for one second. After everything Tommy had done for me, it was the least I could do for the two of them."

"But you weren't, were you?"

"Turned out, they didn't need me. Fate, or whatever, was

smiling down on them and, a week before I was scheduled to, uh, well, you know, Cate got pregnant. Brooke came along nine months later."

"They must have been thrilled."

"They were. They would have been thrilled with any child, but, yes, Brooke was a welcome surprise for all of us. She wasn't mine, but I doted on her as if she was. Or maybe more like a grandchild."

"But she could have been, yours. You were willing. And when she was taken from you . . ."

She let her voice trail off, because what she was thinking didn't need to be said out loud. When Brooke died, it had felt like he'd lost his own daughter. And the only reason he even inserted the word "like" was because he'd witnessed first-hand what her death had done to Tommy and Cate. He didn't feel as though he had the right to claim even a portion of what they had gone through.

Caleb and his sister sat in silence for a long time as he let what he'd finally spoken aloud settle around him. Taking the pain out of the shadows and into the light hadn't been as gut wrenching as he'd always imagined it would be. Then again, maybe that was because he was talking to Kit. His strong, vital survivor of a sister who he knew would *never* discount or mock the pain of another. She'd been through too much of her own to trivialize someone else's.

"I've never told anyone about that. Not even Garret," he said into the quiet of the room.

"I'm so sorry, Caleb. I'm sorry that it happened and I'm sorry you felt that you needed to keep it to yourself. I'm sorry you've carried it with you all these years. I know you didn't wallow in it, but that kind of pain doesn't go away. It may take a break or dull to a low roar, but it comes back, doesn't it? It always comes back."

He held his sister's gaze and eyes, so much like his, stared back at him, reflecting his own pain. "It does," he said quietly. "Sometimes, when I least expect it, it does." He thought of the night of Drew and Carly's wedding, when Emma had slipped her hand into his and pulled him onto the dance floor. Memories of

Brooke's small hands tugging him around had flooded his mind and he had felt like he was drowning.

"Have you and Cate talked about Brooke at all?" Her voice was soft and non-judgmental, though he heard her unasked question: Wasn't it time he and Cate talked about Brooke, and maybe even Tommy too?

He shook his head. "I don't know if I can. I know that, back then, I never would have been able to, and, even though I just talked to you about it, I don't know if I'm ready to do the same with her." He glanced up and the look of disappointment he'd anticipated from his sister wasn't there.

"It takes a long time to heal from what you and I went through, Caleb. All the lies, the betrayal, the guilt, the . . ." She paused, not knowing what other phrase to use to describe the horror of a man they had both had called their father. She took a deep breath. "I had a little more help than you did, emotionally, anyway, when I found out what kind of man he was, so I get it. I understand your hesitation. But I also know that, like me, you're a work in progress, and I hope that, when you feel up for the task, you'll talk to Cate. It's possible that you're the only person she really has who she can talk to about her first daughter. There might come a time when you two need each other for that reason alone."

Caleb hadn't thought about the situation that way. He'd always assumed that Cate had people to talk to, and she probably did. But that didn't mean she didn't want or need to talk to him—he'd been such a part of their lives then. Kit had a point, there probably wasn't anyone who understood Cate's loss more than he did. He knew Cate would try to take on some of his own pain if or when they talked, but she might also feel better knowing she wasn't alone in missing Brooke. She might want to know that her daughter had touched someone else's life nearly as deeply as Brooke had touched her own.

· · ·

Kit's suggestion still rolled around in Caleb's mind as he jogged up her driveway at the end of an early-morning run. He'd just reached the house and paused to catch his breath when his phone rang.

He glanced at the number, frowned, then answered. "Drew?"

"Yeah, it's me."

"Aren't you still on your honeymoon?"

"Yes, but I heard you were in town and I have a favor to ask."

"How could you possibly know I'm in Windsor?"

"It's a small town. The more time you spend there, the more you'll learn that the laws of communication are a little different. In this case, Marcus is housesitting for us and Carly called him to check in. Turns out that he'd just run into Ian, who had mentioned that you were coming up to see Vivi. Both being the men that they are, they were, of course, intensely curious about what you wanted to talk to Vivi about. As am I, although that's not why I called."

Caleb pulled the phone away from his ear and stared at it. The former CIA spy might be slowing down in his forties, but he was obviously never going to change. Putting the phone back to his ear, Caleb asked, "Okay, so why did you call?"

"The training facility."

It was all he said, but Caleb knew what the man was referring to—Drew's version of retirement. He wasn't going to work in the field or even run a team out of Langley anymore. Instead, he was setting up shop in Windsor, where the company would send agents to him for final training. It actually seemed like a pretty good gig to Caleb. Drew would no longer be in the game, but would get to continue putting his skills to good use. He could live in the town his new wife had no interest in leaving and still have time for other pursuits, like working with his brother on the family business. And Caleb wouldn't be at all surprised if a family was in the making for Drew and Carly, as well.

"What about it?" Caleb asked.

"There is some question about the layout of the shooting range in the basement. Can you go by and make sure it's getting done right?"

Caleb glanced at his watch. He had plenty of time to get back to New Hampshire. "Yes, of course. You'll let them know I'm coming?"

The design and building of the facility was a closely guarded secret—only people hired by the CIA had been given the clearance to even know of the plans, and only a handful of them had been allowed to see the complete architectural renderings. What would appear to be a charming stone home set in a valley to any accidental trespasser would actually hold four bedrooms, a training room, an arms room, a shooting range—despite the fact that the CIA was more about intelligence than gun fights—and a state-of-the-art intelligence gathering, analyzing, and planning system. From this location, Drew would train one or two agents at time in preparation for specific missions.

"I will. Ask for Lawton when you get there," Drew said.

"And there won't be any problems?"

Drew had read Caleb in when the project had first started, bringing him on as a consultant, but Caleb hadn't been by the facility in a few months.

"No. It's a new crew. Different from the one that was there last time, since they're working on all the interior stuff now, but I'll call Lawton and let him know you're coming."

"Want me to call you back when I'm done? Aren't you in Europe somewhere?"

Drew laughed. "Yes. I'm currently standing in the middle of nowhere in the Netherlands while my wife looks at a horse."

"A horse?"

"Yes, Carly thought it would be a good idea to combine our honeymoon with horse shopping." Carly was definitely a woman who had her opinions.

"Um, should I say 'have fun?'"

Again, Drew chuckled. "There are worse things than spending my days trekking around the countryside in France, Belgium, the Netherlands, and Germany, and then retiring to cozy inns with good food and even better company in the evenings." When put that way, Drew did have a point.

"I'll head out there in an hour or so and sort things out. I'll call you before those cozy evening hours."

"Thank you, I appreciate it. Oh, by the way, Carly asked me if you thought Emma would want to learn to ride."

"Emma?"

"Yes. Carly is thinking of bringing a pony back, kind of a school master for any or all of the kids that want to ride."

Caleb wasn't sure about Emma, but another little girl popped into his mind who would do just about anything for a pony. "Do it. It's a good idea. I don't know for sure if Emma will ride, but between her, Jeffery, Daphne, Charley, and anyone else who might come along, I'm sure the pony will be well loved, if not ridden," he said, referring to the kids within Kit and Carly's circle of friends. Drew also had a brother with kids, and there was Dani Fuller, a friend of both Kit's and Drew's, who had three kids and came down to visit a few times a year from Portland. There was definitely no shortage of kids to love a pony.

"Most women bring back clothes and jewelry from trips to Europe, we'll be returning with a cargo-load of horses. Just so you know."

Caleb smiled at the exasperated affection he heard in Drew's voice. "Don't pretend you don't like it that way."

"It is rather unique, I'll grant you that." Despite the fact that neither man had made much of an attempt to befriend the other, a friendship had grown between them just the same. They both knew the ins and outs of living lies, and somehow that had led them to trust each other more than most men. Still, that didn't mean they were going to discuss how Drew might *feel* about his new wife, not that it needed discussion. Caleb ended the call with another promise to touch base when he finished at the facility, then headed into Kit's house to shower.

He was still in the thick of it at Drew's facility three hours later, dealing with a problem concerning the wiring to the air-vac system that needed to be in place for the shooting range. The long and short of it was that Drew needed to rearrange the orientation of the enormous basement that lay hidden below the charming house. Or rather, since Drew was away, *Caleb* needed to rearrange the basement of Drew's facility. As soon as possible.

Another two hours passed before he and the lead contractor had arrived at a workable solution. Actually, it was more than workable. As Caleb eyed the updated plans, he actually thought they were better than the originals. He'd texted Drew the basics throughout the day, but now that they'd arrived at a final solution, Caleb asked Lawton to send the plans to Drew over a secure line for him to sign off on. While he waited for Drew's reply, Caleb stepped outside to call Cate. As he brought his phone to life, a call from Garret came through.

"You're back in town," Caleb's former partner said.

"Just overnight. I'm supposed to be leaving today."

"To go back to New Hampshire?"

"You've been talking to Kit."

"Of course I have. What she didn't tell me, though, was what is going on in New Hampshire."

"There's a good reason for that," Caleb said, staring off at the hillsides. The leaves were starting to lose their color and a few trees were already bare. "I didn't tell her everything that's going on there; she doesn't need to know. Neither do you." He had talked to his sister a lot the night before, more than probably any other single time, but he hadn't gone into the specifics of what might be happening at The Washington House. He hadn't wanted Kit to know because then Garret would end up knowing. And then Garret would want to get involved. Something Caleb didn't want to happen. His friend had very intentionally left his previous life behind, and Caleb wasn't about to drag him back into it.

"She said you were there helping Cate."

Sometimes Caleb hated how interconnected his life had become. He sighed. "Yes, I am. And yes, it was weird seeing her at first. But I'm glad I went, for both personal and, well, the other reason."

"Which you can tell me about tonight."

"Uh, no. I'm heading back to New Hampshire as soon as I can. I'm already about four hours behind schedule, thanks to Drew."

"Stay. I'll be home in two hours. We'll have a beer, maybe go to Anderson's for a flat iron steak."

It was the steak that almost persuaded him. Almost. "No, I want to get back to New Hampshire. Lucas Rancuso is there now, keeping an eye on things, but I don't like leaving Cate and Elise when so much is up in the air."

"Elise?"

Caleb clenched his jaw to keep from snapping at his friend; he just wanted to get on the road, or at least call Cate, and it wasn't Garret's fault he'd been so delayed. "Long story, Cate was pregnant when Tommy died. Elise is their daughter. Now, if you don't mind, I really need to call Cate and tell her I'll be late getting back tonight."

Silence met his statement. Followed by a very annoying chuckle. "Okay, but whenever it's all resolved, you'll have to fill me in."

"Maybe."

"Say hi to Cate for me."

"I will."

"Don't do anything dumb."

Caleb knew Garret wasn't just referring to what was going on at The Washington House.

"Good-bye, Garret." Caleb hung up before his friend could say anything else and promptly called Cate to let her know he wouldn't arrive until well after the house had gone to bed. She assured him that Lucas was doing a good job and, so far, nothing else murderous had happened. He spent another few minutes talking to Elise, telling her about the horse facility Carly was setting up, and ended the call by promising to bring her to meet the horses once they had all arrived from Europe. He hadn't given much thought to what it would mean to bring Cate and Elise to Windsor; all he'd been thinking about was how much Elise would love seeing the horses.

He was sliding the phone into his pocket when it rang again. This time, it was a call he'd been waiting for.

"Vivi?"

"Yes, hi. We've identified the toxin. It's duaricine, an alkaloid," she said without preamble.

"The source?"

"Well, it's being tested in some anticancer trials, but unless someone at the house is involved in those trials, it's unlikely that's where it would have come from."

"Isiah Whatley owns a pharmaceutical company, could he have access?"

"He could, but Caleb, so could just about anyone with a book on local flora and fauna."

"Local flora and fauna?"

"It's derived from the moonseed plant. A plant that grows all along the east coast and comes into fruit this time of year. The naturally occurring dose in just two seeds, each of which are about the size of a wild grape, is enough to kill a human."

Fuck. "And you said it grows all over the east coast."

"It grows everywhere that matters to you."

CHAPTER 11

HAVING ARRIVED BACK AT THE ice house late the night before, Caleb stood at the kitchen window attempting to replace lost sleep with coffee. In twenty minutes, he was scheduled to catch up with Lucas, but at the moment, he was watching Cate walk across the drive. Her red hair, covered with the same green hat he'd seen her wear every day since he'd arrived, flowed down her back, swinging gently as she strode toward him with purpose.

Not bothering to knock, she used her key to enter.

He leaned against the counter, greeting her with a shake of his head and a smile. She shut the door, crossed the room, and enclosed him in a hug. Caught off guard, he hastily uncrossed his arms and wrapped them around her instead of himself as he tried not to spill any of his hot coffee on her.

"I'm glad you're back," she said into his chest.

"Um, me, too."

She stepped back. "I talked to Lucas this morning. He said he's coming over here after he makes his morning rounds so you two can talk?"

"Yeah, I figured I'd let him finish up with that. In the meantime, I've been doing some research on moonseed."

"First things first, did you eat breakfast?"

He laughed. He didn't know why her question had made him laugh, only that it had.

"Seriously, Caleb. You got back late and didn't come to the main house to eat this morning."

"Yes, I ate," he answered, still smiling. "Greg brought a plate by before you were even over there." He gestured to the plate in the sink. "What about you?"

"I'm headed back to the carriage house after this to eat with Elise. Okay, so what were you saying about moonseed?"

With a gesture, he offered her some coffee, which she declined, so they moved to the table where he'd spread out the research he'd dug up. "This is the structure of the poison," he said, sliding a piece of paper in front of her. "Not that it matters, but I wanted to understand it better to see if it might be used in any of the drugs Isiah and Livia's pharmaceutical company either distributes or tests."

"And is it?"

"Possibly." He felt a frown forming on his lips. He wasn't a chemistry expert, so all he had was his best guess—a somewhat informed guess, but still a guess. "I dug up all the drugs that they distribute, and I'm pretty sure I also found all the ones currently in testing, but I can't be sure, so I'm going to put another call into Jay today to see if he can get a complete list of the drugs affiliated with their company. Once I have that, I'll run it by Vivi, or maybe Lila, and see what they have to say."

Cate examined the image of the molecular structure. "I know who Vivi is, but who's Lila?"

"Dr. Lila Rose. She works at the hospital my friend Jesse runs. She's a hospitalist, but she also has several degrees in chemistry."

Cate's eyes flicked to his then she reached for another image. "But this is the naturally occurring seed, isn't it?"

Caleb nodded.

"It looks a little like deadly nightshade."

"The berries do look a little alike, but moonseed berries look more like wild grapes when they're growing, whereas nightshade fruit tends to look more like shiny berries. Both can be fatal, of course."

"And we have this here?" She ran her finger along the image of the moonseed berry as she spoke.

"I assume so. It's on my agenda to take a walk and see what I can find later today. Maybe I can bring Elise?"

When she looked up at him, the absurdity of taking a four-year-old on a hunt for poison hit him. Then again, why not? It was important for kids to learn about what was safe to eat in the wild and what was not.

"That seems like one of those things that, as a parent, I should automatically say 'no' to, but I can't actually come up with a good reason why I should." A corner of her mouth lifted into a self-deprecating smile. "Just be careful—and I know you will," she said, holding up a hand to stop his protest. "Sometimes there are things that mothers just need to say, and people need to let us say them."

He grinned. "I can deal with that. How about if Elise is ready in an hour? We'll probably be out for a couple of hours."

"That's fine, I'm sure Jana will appreciate the break. Let me double-check with Mirielle to make sure that Pansy can go. I'll text you if there are any problems and, if not, Elise will meet you at the barn in an hour."

"Sounds good." Caleb eyed the kitchen window. Lucas was strolling across the gravel toward the ice house, his strides leisurely but confident.

"I'll let you get to it, then," Cate said, preparing to leave as Lucas knocked. She opened the door and let the tall man hold it for her as she stepped outside. With a wave good-bye, she turned and headed toward the carriage house.

As Lucas entered, Caleb went back to the kitchen and the coffee pot.

"You have a nice little setup here. Private."

At Lucas's comment, Caleb glanced back, looking for an implication about his relationship with Cate. All he found was the man scanning the space admiringly. It was funny what guilt could do to you. "Yeah, well, this whole place is nice. Is Vic going to be able to come up? Not that this is a vacation or anything."

Lucas shrugged. "Maybe. I think I've been driving him crazy

this past week since I quit. I'm not sure retirement suits me all that well, so he may be enjoying this little break from me."

There was something Caleb liked about what Lucas had just said. Well, not necessarily *what* he'd said, but how he'd said it. He didn't seem concerned about the fact that his spouse would want time away from him—about the possibility that it could be a negative reflection on the strength of their marriage. In fact, it sounded like it was just the opposite, as if acknowledging that his spouse was his own person with his own needs actually made their relationship stronger.

Caleb knew this in theory, but it hadn't been until recently, until spending time in Windsor, that he'd begun to understand that the theory wasn't just a theory and that there were people, couples, who lived it every day. Couples who knew that a relationship wasn't two halves making a whole, but two complete people making something entirely new.

"So, this is what I've got," Caleb said, getting his mind back on the subject at hand and gesturing to the table as he walked over with two mugs of coffee. He'd already given Lucas copies of all his files on the Whatley family. The only new information he had to share now was about the moonseed.

"And Vivi said it was added to the whiskey?" Lucas took a mug and picked up the same image Cate had been studying.

"Yes, and not the port."

"Which makes sense, since, according to this," Lucas held up one of the documents Caleb had printed out, "it tastes bitter. It would probably be more easily disguised in whiskey than port."

"Or, the intended target prefers whiskey."

"Unfortunately, Cate told me that most of the family members drink both."

"Here's the list she made me. You're right, she said they all drink both, which is why both are available throughout the house at all times, but she's noted the guests who have a *preference* for whiskey over port."

Lucas perused the list for a moment then looked up with a

sigh. "So what are you thinking? I have to say, as a former homicide detective, it's a little out of my element to investigate a homicide that hasn't already happened."

Caleb laughed at Lucas's overdramatized expression of dismay. "This isn't exactly within my wheelhouse either. There aren't any arms dealers or international traffickers involved, so far, but we do what we can," he shrugged.

Lucas smiled in commiseration and set the list down.

"So, what did you think of the family?' Caleb asked.

Lucas stood, then moved over to one of the chairs beside the fireplace. Caleb switched on the gas flame and joined him.

"They aren't as dysfunctional as they could be," the former detective started. "Dixie has attachment issues, as in, she doesn't want to be attached to anything. Makes me think mom and dad probably weren't the most attentive parents. Isiah and Livia, well, they're polite, but when the rest of the family gets to be too much, they are just as happy to hole up together—it's kind of sweet, actually. Michael and Edith seem to be pretty grounded in who they are, although I get the sense that wasn't always the case for Michael. And some of the other family members, primarily his brother, don't seem to be convinced that the change is real. Agnes is a terror, though I think I may have intimidated her just a tad, and Edward is a bitter man who's still angry that his wife died before he did. As for the Brandts, well, they're hardly around. Erica and Mark have been spending most of their time with their dad and, more or less, act like this is a vacation for the three of them rather than a reunion. The Italians are intentionally oblivious to any of the more unpleasant dynamics—they just seem to want to have a good time. Last but not least, there's Dominique and Sabrina and, well, there's a couple on a collision course with divorce court if I ever saw one."

"You think?" Caleb asked, referring to Sabrina and Dominique. Lucas's entire summary pretty much gelled with his, but he hadn't come to the conclusion Lucas had about Sabrina and Dominique, not yet, anyway.

"Definitely." Lucas stared into the fire. "As far as Dominique is concerned, it's already over. She left the marriage, mentally and emotionally, long ago."

"Then why stay together?"

Lucas snorted. "Money, the kids, comfort, laziness. There are any number of reasons why she hasn't left yet."

"Could the planning of her wife's murder to get the money be one of them?"

Lucas paused, giving the question some thought, then shrugged. "Could be, but that's not the read I get on her."

The former homicide detective had far more experience dealing with families than he did, so Caleb nodded and accepted Lucas's perspective.

"So, what are you going to do now?" Lucas asked.

"Take it one step at a time, which, to be honest, is killing me. More specifically, I'm going to take a hike around the trails in a bit to see if I can find moonseed growing nearby. I'd like to know if it's readily available here. If not, then we'll need to start looking into how it got into The Washington House."

"And who might have brought it."

"Well, that's the sixty-four-thousand-dollar question, isn't it?"

"And, in the meantime, I'll keep an eye on the goings-on at the house." Lucas pushed to his feet and Caleb followed. "Cate's worried about you, you know," Lucas said, pausing at the door.

Caleb frowned. "Why would she be worried?"

"Because you're not sleeping much, because this isn't in your wheelhouse, and because, if something happens that you can't stop, you might blame yourself. Also, because people worry about those they care about."

"She doesn't need to worry."

Lucas shrugged. "It doesn't matter if she *needs* to, she is."

"Am I going to be able to stop her from worrying?"

"Probably not, but you may want to talk to her a little more, not just about the details of what you are doing, but about what you think and, more importantly, any doubts you have."

That didn't sound so bad. "I can do that."

"And I don't mean doubts about what is going on with the Whatley family, I mean doubts about *yourself.*"

That sounded a lot worse. He opened his mouth, ready to point out that he didn't have any doubts about himself, but Lucas cut him off.

"You have doubts. We all do. If we think we don't, we're either lying to ourselves or not invested enough—in ourselves or the situation—to care about what happens. I don't think that's the case here." Lucas's dark eyes held Caleb's. He found himself shaking his head.

"Doubts aren't a weakness," Lucas continued. "If we don't question things, if we don't question *ourselves,* every now and then, we'll miss the answers we need to learn from." He paused for a moment, wrapping his scarf around his neck, then his lips quirked into a smile. "Now, on that sage note, I'm going to head back to the main house and to grab another one of Margaret's scones."

● ● ●

It didn't take long for Caleb to find what he was searching for. At the edge of a field less than a mile from the main house, a moonseed plant climbed more than twelve feet up the trunk of a tree. He knew the species could grow much taller, but even at the shorter height of this one, now that he knew what it was and what it could do, the otherwise charming vine took on a sinister air—like a witch beckoning him into her gingerbread house.

"Those look like grapes," Elise said as he studied the plant. "Can I have one?" She was perched on Pansy a good eight feet away and there was absolutely no danger of her getting her hands on a moonseed berry, but his heart still lurched at the thought.

He took a deep breath. "No, sweetheart. I know they look like grapes, but they are actually poisonous. *Very* poisonous."

She tilted her head and studied the bush, her curls showing

just below her riding helmet. "Well, that's not very nice of them to look like grapes. Someone could eat them by mistake."

Or use them to kill someone. "That's true, and that's why it's important to know what's growing in the wild and never eat anything that you aren't sure about." The comment launched them into a discussion of all things poisonous in the wild, a discussion that lasted nearly the rest of their hour-long walk along several trails. As they made their way, he pointed out a few other poisonous plants he'd learned about in the last twenty-four hours. They found some nightshade and came across a few yew trees as well. Realizing how little he knew about poisonous plants made Caleb want to study everything ever written so that he could teach Elise exactly what not to eat.

Thankfully, all the talk of poison didn't seem to bother her. In fact, she seemed much more interested in the science behind it all than the potential horrors, and when they finally returned to the barn she was chatting happily about learning to read so that she could discover more about poisons on her own.

After they'd taken care of Pansy, he returned Elise to Jana and headed back to his room. Not only were his boots covered in mud, but he'd managed to get mud on his jeans too, as well as horsehair on his jacket. Shucking his dirty clothes and shoes, he pulled on a button-down shirt, black pants, and black formal shoes and made his way to the main house. Rather than enter through the kitchen, he circled around the house, looking for any moonseed in the immediate vicinity, then came in through a door at the opposite side of the house from the kitchen.

He made his way to the heart of the house, but stopped in the downstairs library on the way. On the mantle stood two new decanters. He approached to get a closer look; something appeared off about them, different somehow. He realized that, though they were similar to the ones he'd taken to Vivi, the designs in the crystal were different. The two on the mantle matched each other. But the five he'd taken were all different from each other, not part of matching sets like what he saw now. He hadn't thought anything of it at the time, but he made a mental note to ask Cate about the decanters' designs.

Cate. He knew he'd likely find her in the kitchen this time of day, going through the accounts and schedules in the lull between the end of the lunch cleanup and the beginning of the dinner prep.

He slowed as he approached the kitchen doorway, hearing the murmur of voices. The conversation sounded subdued and intimate; he didn't want to interrupt if there was something serious being discussed. When he paused outside the door, he recognized Cate and Lucas's voices.

"You know what it's like to lose a loved one, then," Cate said.

"I do. Not a child, but a partner. That was bad enough."

Caleb heard the sound of a mug being set down on the table.

"It was the worst time of my life. Although I almost hate to say that, since it feels like I'm tempting fate," Cate said.

"I know what you mean. You try to pretend like your world hasn't fallen apart because, if you believe it has, fate might decide do something worse just to prove you wrong."

Cate gave a soft laugh. "Exactly."

"So tell me about Tommy."

Cate let out a breath. "He was a great guy, a good man and a good father. He was a lot older than me, but we were what each other needed. He helped me feel more settled when I had to leave the surfing circuit after my knee surgery. He gave me a home and a reason to laugh. He *became* my home, if you know what I mean."

"He sounds like a great guy."

Again, Cate laughed, only this time it was tinged with sadness. "I don't want you to think it was all wine and roses. We had our moments, that's for sure. But yeah, he was a great guy and I still miss him. All the time."

Caleb heard a mug slide across the tabletop. He imagined that Lucas had moved it out of the way in order to reach for Cate's hand.

"There won't ever be anyone like him again," she said.

Caleb heard the pain, and maybe even the tears, in her voice. Feeling ashamed of his own feelings toward Cate, ashamed to the point of being angry with himself, he turned and stalked away. She was still mourning Tommy and here he'd been, imagining what it would be like to take her to bed. He shouldn't have been thinking those things. Even if he didn't intend to do anything about them, he shouldn't have been thinking about her like that. Instead, he should have been focusing on helping her grieve, because clearly she still was.

He hadn't been there for her five years ago, he couldn't change that. But he could be there for her now.

• • •

"Caleb?" Cate called as she entered his room without knocking. She thought perhaps she should stop doing that, but she'd also noticed that Caleb had stopped locking his door.

"Yeah, in here," he said, stepping out of the bathroom. He had obviously just showered and, just as obviously, hadn't expected a guest, so he stood before her with just a towel wrapped around his waist. Again.

The urge to walk toward him, slip her hands behind his neck, and pull him to her, feeling his skin against her as she kissed him, left her speechless.

"Did, uh," she dragged her eyes away, struggling to find something to say. "I haven't seen you since this morning, did you go for a run too, even after your hike?"

She hazarded a glance and saw him nod as he moved toward the dresser. Having unpacked his clothes from his bag, he began rummaging for something in the drawer, maybe boxers. Maybe a condom.

Where had *that* thought come from? "I'll, um, make us some coffee while you dress." She spun toward his kitchen.

"I had a question I meant to ask you earlier," he said once her back was turned. "I noticed that the two decanters you put in the library to replace the ones I took were a matching set."

"The ones in the libraries and the common areas are all matching sets."

"And the ones in the bedrooms?"

She heard the rustle of pants being pulled on. "Those may be different. They are smaller sized depending on the occupants' preferences."

"So if Dixie likes whiskey better, her whiskey decanter will be larger than her port decanter?"

Cate turned around, figuring it would be safe to face him now that he was wearing pants. She caught him just as he was putting on a t-shirt. "Yes, but not hugely bigger, just a little bit bigger."

"And the design?"

She had to think about that. "The designs may be different. I'd have to check with Annie and Lucy on that, they'd be more familiar with that kind of detail. Why?"

"Because none of the five I took to Vivi matched and I wonder if that might mean something."

She moved to turn the coffee machine on but he stopped her with a gesture. "I'm going to have a beer, want one?"

His suggestion felt more inviting than he'd been recently, so she nodded.

He grabbed two bottles, popped the tops, and handed one to her. "Let's sit," he said, turning the fire on.

"You think someone might have brought decanters from their room, replacing the ones normally in the library?"

"Or supplementing them. You said they are usually set up in pairs in the common rooms. I took five from the library, so the extra three decanters had to come from somewhere. They could have been brought in by the staff, I did see Greg and Christine provide two refills, but I wonder if they were brought down from one of the rooms."

She curled up in the chair across from him and searched her memory for anything unusual regarding decanters, other than the poisoned one, of course.

"If one of the guests brought a decanter from their room,

it would have been easier to add the poison to the whiskey in private," he continued. "But, of course, they'd have had to walk around carrying a decanter. Wouldn't someone have noticed?"

Cate shrugged. "Sure, assuming we saw them. But it's possible that it happened late at night or when the staff were busy doing other things." She watched Caleb study the fire as she spoke. "Over the years, we've noticed that when the Italian cousins arrive, there tends to be much more partying. When the common areas run out of alcohol, people bring it from their owns rooms to share—usually late at night, when they don't want to bother the staff for refills."

He remained silent for a moment, thinking. He was always thinking. Finally, he let his head fall back against the chair. "So the long and short of it is, it's possible that someone put poison into the decanter in their own room, then took it to the library, and possibly even brought one back from the library to their own room, so as not to appear to be missing one. In that case, we may never figure out who, unless someone on staff has eagle eyes and an elephant memory."

"Were you hoping that identifying where the tainted container was originally located would give you some direction?"

He gave a wry laugh, his head still resting against the chair. "It would be nice to have *some* way to narrow things down."

Her heart lurched at the frustration she heard in his voice. "I'll ask the staff, particularly Lucy and Annie, to find out if they know which decanters were where. I'm not sure it will yield anything, but I'll ask. What about the poison itself? Weren't you going to call someone?"

"Lila Rose. She called me back and said that the type of poison Vivi found was the naturally occurring kind and not the kind they'd synthesize for a drug."

"So that rules out Isiah and Livia."

He shook his head. "No, it just means we can't rule anyone else out. If they'd been the only people with access to a synthetic form, we'd know where to focus. Since it's natural, though, and Elise and I confirmed today that moonseed is everywhere—"

"It could still be anyone." She finished his thought.

He nodded.

"You hate this, don't you?"

He raised his head, searching her face with his golden eyes. "I hate that I can't figure this out. I don't hate that I'm here trying." He looked so earnest, so sincere, like having her believe him *meant* something to him.

"I'm glad you're here trying, Caleb," she said, knowing he'd hear the sincerity in her voice. "I know I could have called the police, but they wouldn't have been able to focus on it like you have, and that's assuming they believed me in the first place. I'm also just glad you're here. After the last five years, I'm glad you're here."

• • •

There was something different in her tone that caught Caleb's attention. He studied her expression, but he couldn't place what emotion had infused her words. Perhaps a little wistfulness? Maybe a little regret? Or was it something else altogether? He wasn't sure what to make of it, so, in true cowardly fashion, he changed the subject. "Have you had dinner yet?"

"No, I was going to join Elise and Jana, but they're going to some Halloween festival in town tonight."

"What do you say we clear our heads of this place and head into town to eat tonight? That is, if you can get away?"

Cate smiled. "I'm pretty sure I can manage that. Give me an hour to wrap things up with the staff for the night?" She rose from her seat and he followed.

"Of course. I'll check in with Lucas and make sure he's set too. Meet back here in an hour?"

She nodded and was quickly out the door and making her way to the carriage house to check in with Elise before she left for the festival. He was on the phone with Lucas thirty minutes later when he glanced out the window and saw her returning to the main house to touch base with the staff. She'd changed into a pair of fitted jeans and heeled boots and, rather than a sweater and her winter vest, she wore a beige pea coat tied at the waist. Her long hair flowed loosely down her back with no green hat topping it.

He had intended to talk to her about Tommy over dinner. To tell her how sorry he was that he'd all but abandoned her after the funeral. He wanted her to know that he would never do that again and that, if she ever wanted to talk about Tommy, he would always be there to listen.

But those thoughts fled from his mind as he watched her stride across the back parking area. He didn't want to dredge up the past tonight. He didn't want to talk about Tommy or Brooke or even The Washington house. No, he wanted to talk about things unrelated to death and murder. He wanted to see her smile, hear her laugh. He wanted to know what she planned to do about her job once Elise started school, and he wanted to know about her life outside of work.

She disappeared into the house and he realized that inviting her out to dinner might not have been his most brilliant idea.

• • •

They were driving home from a big meal at a local pub when his cell rang and Vivi's name popped up on its screen. The evening had unfolded more as he'd hoped than as he'd originally planned and, for the moment, he wasn't going to feel guilty about it. Cate had talked a lot about how she might change her job once Elise started school, he'd talked more about the friends he'd made in Windsor, and they'd laughed. They'd *both* laughed. He'd wanted Cate to have a good time, to have a true night off, but he'd forgotten how good it felt to let go and laugh himself, to be lighthearted, to joke around, and have fun.

However, the tone of the evening faded a bit when he hit the hands-free wireless and answered the call.

"Hey, Vivi."

"Caleb, I was just doing some reading and chatting with a few of my friends at the FBI about the methods of murder you're encountering—"

"I have Cate Thomson in the car with me," he cut her off. He wasn't sure what Vivi was going to say next, but just in case any of it was classified he wanted her to know someone else was listening in.

Vivi paused and in the glare of the oncoming headlights Cate cast him a concerned look.

"Hi Cate, I'm Vivi DeMarco, a friend of Caleb's."

Caleb's brow furrowed a touch at Vivi's use of the word "friend;" he wasn't quite sure they were there yet, but maybe it was just easier to explain things that way.

"It's nice to meet you, Vivi. Caleb mentioned that you're helping out, so thank you for that."

"I'm happy to do it. Anytime any of his sister's friends can do something to beholden him to Windsor, we're all in. For her sake, we'd like him to stick around more."

"Vivi," Caleb warned.

Cate, still looking his way, raised an eyebrow, which he pretended not to notice as he glanced over his shoulder to change lanes.

"But on to the reason I called," Vivi continued, as if he hadn't spoken. "One of my colleagues at the bureau forwarded some interesting research and a few case files to me that may give us, if not a lead, at least something to think about."

"And?" Caleb prompted.

"So, the snake method of killing has only been recorded two or three times in the past two decades, so that one alone doesn't give us much. However, as for the other two methods, the research points to them being deeply personal. With a few exceptions here and there, people who kill by beheading or poisoning do so because they want to watch their victim die. And people who want to watch a specific person die tend to crave that because they view it as vindication for something, some deep, personal slight the victim has perpetrated against them."

"But we're talking about a family here," Cate jumped in, surprising him. "You could find slights and, no doubt, decades-long grudges within any family if you dug deep enough."

"You're probably right, and that is exactly where I was headed next. Given that three different methods, all with the same type of psychology behind them, have been used, I think you need to be looking for someone with a deep, long-lasting grudge. Not a slight, not a petty grudge, but either a long series of perceived wrongs or one massive one that has been simmering for years."

"Edward Whatley," Caleb said.

"He's definitely the one I'd put at the top of my list," Vivi agreed.

"Edward?" Cate asked.

"Remember?" Caleb glanced back over at Cate for a moment. "Edith Barnard killed his foster daughter in a car accident twenty years ago."

"And with the fairly recent death of his wife," Vivi added, "his daughter's tragic death might be growing in intensity in his mind."

"Festering," Cate said.

"Exactly," Vivi concurred.

"But I've never sensed any tension between them, even when they're in the same room," Cate pondered aloud.

"I don't know that Edith knows who he is. She was seventeen years old when it happened and Summer had a different last name than Edward," Caleb pointed out.

"Not to mention that, based on the files, it looks like Summer had distanced herself from Edward and his wife at the time she was killed, so they may not have been a part of any of the post-accident investigation," Vivi said.

"But is Edward strong enough to string that wire I found?" Cate asked him.

"He is. It would take some strength, but he's pretty fit for an eighty-two-year-old man. I understand he walks a few miles nearly every day."

Cate bobbed her head. "Yeah, and if he was out walking, it would have been easy enough for him to pick moonseed."

"Also, his wife was on the board of the Bronx Zoo," Vivi chimed in. "I hope you don't mind, but when I couldn't reach you earlier, I went ahead and called Jay and asked him to look into Edward's past a bit more. He found the connection to the zoo and even a picture of Edward and his wife handling various snakes in the reptile habitat during a fundraiser."

"Ugh," Cate said.

At the same time, Caleb spoke. "When couldn't you reach me?" He slowed to make a left turn onto the two-lane road that would take them back to The Washington House.

"About an hour and a half ago. I called your phone and it went to voice mail, so I just called Jay."

"We were out to dinner," Cate explained before he could stop her.

A beat of silence passed. "Really."

Caleb could all but hear the gears turning in Vivi's head. Her intelligence was definitely a double-edged sword.

"Yes, not to change the subject, but it was this great pub with an excellent selection of local beer. I'd highly recommend it, of you ever make it up this way," Cate added.

"So, Edward has the motive, means, and the opportunity," Caleb said, bringing the conversation back from where he didn't want it to go. "What do you recommend we do, talk to him? Watch him?"

In the dark of the car, Cate slid him a curious look but said nothing.

Vivi didn't miss a beat. "*Talk* to Edith and *watch* him. Edith may deny she's a target at first, believe me, no one wants to believe someone wants them dead. But if you give her something to think about, she seems like a reasonable person, at least from her files, and if she is, she'll eventually give it some thought and allow for the possibility."

"And then?" Caleb asked. This was completely out of the realm of his expertise.

"If she opens herself up to the possibility, she should be able to reflect on her interactions with Edward and sense if anything was off. Maybe it was something small he said to her that she brushed off, or maybe a rude interaction she wrote off that she may rethink. If, upon reflection, she acknowledges that what we are suggesting could be a possibility, then you should talk to him."

"And if she doesn't?" Cate asked.

"Is she an intuitive person? Is she someone who you think has a pretty reliable instinct?"

"Absolutely," Cate said at the same time that Caleb answered, "Yes."

"Then there you have it. If she truly hasn't sensed anything, I still wouldn't write him off, I'd keep an eye on him, but it would probably be worth going back and digging a little deeper into all the others too."

Caleb let out a frustrated grunt. He knew he needed to keep all options open, but he'd didn't have to like it. He hoped Vivi was right and that Edward would be their man.

After he'd promised to keep in touch and Vivi and Cate had exchanged pleasantries and nice-to-meet-yous, he hung up just as they pulled into the drive. The Washington House loomed against the dark sky, most of the lights doused for the night.

"Tomorrow?" Caleb asked.

Cate pursed her lips, no doubt wondering how they would broach the subject of someone possibly trying to kill Edith with Edith herself, but she nodded.

"Tomorrow, then."

CHAPTER 12

CATE WATCHED CALEB LEAN FORWARD as he spoke to Edith. The four of them sat in the office off the foyer, Edith and Michael on the dark leather couch, and she and Caleb in the two wingback chairs. He had never seemed to have much time for the softer side of things before. Not that he had been hard or cold, he just hadn't been one to express, or encourage others to express, a lot of emotion. Then again, that was the Caleb she'd known five years ago. This Caleb, who'd grown and changed over the years, was different. It was time she stopped being surprised by that.

So, instead of lingering on her own revelation at finding him to be so empathetic and gentle, she made a conscious decision to sit back, figuratively, and watch the scene unfold.

"You think Edward Whatley is trying to *kill me*?" Edith said.

Michael shook his head. "My uncle may be bitter, but he isn't a killer."

"I know this is a lot to take in, but the evidence we have suggests that Edward is being driven by the death of his daughter, Summer Granger, at your hands, Edith. I know it was twenty years ago, but that's a long time for a grudge to fester." Caleb's gaze stayed on Edith and, with that, Cate knew he was trying to convey the seriousness of the situation.

"Summer Granger was Edward's daughter?" Edith asked.

Caleb nodded. "His foster daughter, to begin with, but he and his wife adopted her when she was eleven."

"And just *how* do you think he is going about trying to kill Edith?" Michael asked. "I know we found that wire across the trail one of the first days we were here, but you can't possibly be coming to this conclusion based on that."

Caleb looked to Cate and she nodded, agreeing that he should tell them everything.

"There was the wire, and then, about a week later, one of the staff came across a poisonous snake in the south wing of the house," Caleb stated.

Edith drew back. "A snake? There aren't any poisonous snakes in New Hampshire."

Caleb ran a hand through his hair. "Actually, there are. One is an endangered species and the other is also quite rare. The copperhead we found is the latter of the two."

"It's a rare enough species that the odds of one finding its way into the house and up to the second floor are, well, they aren't likely," Cate explained.

"But a snake?" Michael asked. "Who kills someone with a snake? It doesn't sound any *more* likely to me that someone would bring a snake into the house then let it loose, hoping that it might bite the right person."

"All of the methods attempted have been extremely chancy," Caleb agreed. "But let me ask you this: did either of you get up extremely early last Wednesday and leave your room door open for a bit? We found the snake just before sunrise, so I'd be curious to know if you left your room at any time in the night or early hours of the morning."

Michael and Edith shared a look and, by the way Edith's eyes widened and Michael's narrowed, Cate already knew the answer.

"Yes, we did. At around two in the morning, Edith woke up because the room was unusually warm. She got up to open the window and, well . . ."

"Well, the night was a beautiful one, Mr. Forrester," Edith continued as Michael took her hand. "I woke Michael up and we stepped outside for a bit to watch the stars."

Cate expected Caleb to drill home the point that this was when the snake, that had been placed there earlier, could have escaped their room; instead, a look of sympathy flashed in his eyes. He knew what lay ahead for Edith—the knowledge that someone wanted her dead wouldn't be easy to shoulder.

"Was there something else?" Michael still held Edith's hand gently in his, but his voice had become stiff. Knowing someone in *his* family was trying to kill someone he loved wouldn't sit easy with him, either. Having known Michael for some time, Cate suspected anger, more than fear, would dictate his response.

Caleb seemed to sense it too and determined that straightforward honesty was the best option. "The morning that everyone got sick after drinking late into the night."

"The night after the hunt?" Edith clarified.

Caleb nodded. "The reason people got sick wasn't because they overindulged, it was because the whiskey was tainted. Poisoned, to be exact."

Cate heard Edith suck in a breath.

Michael went still. "Poisoned with what?"

"Moonseed," Caleb answered. "A few berries can be fatal for an adult. It was delivered via the whiskey to better hide the rather pungent taste."

"But we all drank whiskey that night," Edith pointed out.

"My god, he could have killed us all," Michael said.

"I don't think that was his intent." Again, Caleb leaned forward and shared with them what they'd deduced based on conversations with Annie and Lucy concerning the decanters and also what they'd confirmed with Vivi. "Of the two decanters that held whiskey, only one tested positive for the poison, the smaller of the two. The staff distributes the decanters throughout the house and places the smaller decanters in the guest rooms and the larger ones in the public rooms. Based on that, we know that the decanter containing the poisoned whiskey came from someone's room. My guess is that one of you went to your room to grab yours that evening?"

Michael's hand tightened on Edith's and for the first time, Cate saw real fear in in Edith's eyes as she glanced at Michael.

"I did," she said, going white. "Over dinner, Nico had been talking about how much he enjoyed whiskey, and, while I enjoy it as well, we just don't drink that much in general. I knew how the night was going to unfold, so even before everything got started in the library that night, I brought ours down to share with the rest of the family."

Caleb shot Cate a look. At least they had confirmation on the decanters. "Thankfully, port ended up being the drink of the evening and not much of what was in your decanter was consumed, judging by how full I found it the next day," he said.

"But if we *had* consumed it?" Michael pressed.

"I didn't ask that specific question of the person who tested it, but my guess is that maybe two or three glasses could have been enough to kill a healthy person," Caleb answered.

Again, Edith looked at Michael. "An amount that wouldn't be unusual for most people to consume in one evening."

Michael squeezed Edith's hand. "All this has been happening under our noses and you haven't said a thing."

Cate felt that the glare Michael shot in her direction wasn't undeserved, but Caleb responded, keeping his tone measured and reasonable. "Everyone wrote the wire off as a practical joke, maybe something someone would catch on their helmet and get knocked off. A good laugh. But Cate's instinct told her something else. I've worked for various government agencies for nearly two decades and I'm a good friend of hers. When she suspected something, she knew the police wouldn't be able to do anything without more evidence, so she called me."

"And a lot of good that's done, since both the snake and poison incidents happened *after* you arrived. You should have called Douglas and had him send additional security," Michael said with an accusing glare at Cate.

"We've also brought in Lucas Rancuso, a retired Boston homicide detective. As to why we didn't call in additional security until after the poison, what would we have said? With a wire that could have been a practical joke and a snake that, even though rare, technically *could* have gotten into the house, what would we tell the security detail to look for? Family members doing anything that looks sketchy, but we can't say who it might be or who they might be targeting?"

Caleb paused to let his point sink in. Until the poison, which was the first attempt that couldn't be mistaken for anything but an intentional attempt on someone's life, they hadn't had much to go on other than instinct and a few odd occurrences.

After a few beats, Michael's eyes relaxed a touch. He was still angry, and Cate thought he had a right to be, but he seemed less interested in blaming them now. "And after the poison?"

"We wanted to talk to you about that," Caleb said. "We can call Douglas and have him send security from the company, or we can keep on as we have been and, if you give what we've said some thought and agree that our theory is a possibility, we'd like to speak to Edward about it."

"I wouldn't think you'd need our permission," Edith said.

"You're right, we don't *need* your permission, but the reasons behind Edward's possible actions are deeply personal and painful, to *both* of you, and we want to be sensitive to that, and we want you to be prepared for any repercussions that might come from dredging up the past."

Edith turned her gaze toward the window. For several moments she simply sat and stared. When she started to speak, she kept her eyes turned away. "It was so long ago, but some days it feels so close. In an instant, Summer Granger's life was gone and mine was forever changed, in ways I think I'm still discovering."

Michael reached out and rubbed Edith's arm. Another beat passed, then she turned to offer her partner a sad smile. "Let me think about this, if you don't mind. I understand what you've said and I take the information you've told me very seriously, but I still need time—time to really think about whether or not I can truly believe it. Not the facts you've given me, but the implications of them."

Caleb nodded and began to rise from his seat, but Michael

halted him, asking, "Why Edith? There were so many of us out riding that day, and so many of us in the family drink whiskey, why did you narrow it down to Edith?"

Caleb sat down again and glanced at Cate before answering, then told them everything Vivi had shared with them the night before as they'd driven home from dinner—a dinner that felt miles away from where they were now.

Doubt still lingered in Michael's eyes when Caleb finished. "What you say makes sense, but is there no one else it could apply to? I was riding with Edith, it was my whiskey too, as well as my room the snake may have been in."

Caleb inclined his head, acknowledging the truth of Michael's assessment. "That is also one of the reasons it's taken longer than we'd have liked to narrow down the intended victim and killer. Your family has a lot of skeletons, which makes for a lot of potential victims and killers. Is there someone in the family you think would want to kill you, something that makes you think you might be the intended victim instead of Edith?"

Cate expected him to dismiss the question but Michael gave it some thought before answering. "In the family, no, no one I can think of. Outside the family, there are possibilities."

"You're talking about the family of your friend who was killed on the trek, aren't you?" Caleb asked.

Michael looked slightly startled. "Yes, actually, I am. They've never believed that what happened was an accident. They think the other friend on the trip and I made it all up to cover up for our negligence or, worse, to cover up for killing him."

"His brothers live less than an hour from here, did you know that?" Caleb asked.

Michael drew back. "No, I didn't know that. Surely, one of them could be behind this?"

Caleb shook his head. "There hasn't been anyone at the House who wasn't supposed to be here. We looked into that. And, yes, while it's possible one of them could have been responsible for the wire, it's not likely that either of them could have put the snake in your room or poisoned the whiskey."

Michael deflated a little at that and Cate thought it was sweet that he'd much rather a killer be coming after him than Edith. "And there's no one else in the family?" Michael all but pleaded.

"Like I said, your family has a lot of skeletons, and motives of money and love are pretty much everywhere when I look at the Whatley family tree. Edward's grievance is the only one we could find that would make sense with the kinds of attempts we're seeing."

Michael sighed and leaned back against the couch, finally accepting that he and Edith had to at least contemplate what they'd just been told. "Do you want to leave the reunion, Edith?"

The question didn't surprise Cate, but she wished it hadn't been asked just the same. If someone was intent on killing Edith, she'd much rather solve the mystery, and hopefully avert the crime, than just delay it.

It appeared that Edith agreed when she shook her head. "If it turns out to be true, we need to resolve the situation, not run away from it. Still, I'm not entirely comfortable with the idea, so why don't we just think on it a little bit? We can see how we feel tomorrow." She held Michael's gaze for a moment then, finally, Michael nodded and rose, pulling Edith up alongside him.

"I trust you are taking precautions now?" Michael asked Cate.

Prepared for the question, she detailed the litany of security measures they'd put in place, from locking up the food, serving liquor from sealed bottles only, and having the staff take extra turns around the house. In the end, though, Caleb warned them to stay alert. Security could be breached and having them aware of the situation was as good a defense as all the other precautions in place.

Michael didn't look entirely convinced by that statement, but Edith, who seemed to be built of stern stuff, nodded and promised to stay diligent. The two said their good-byes and Cate was left with Caleb in the quiet of the office.

"Well, that was fun," she said, turning to find him staring off in the direction the couple had gone.

"It happened to my sister, you know," he said.

Cate's heart stuttered. "What happened to your sister?"

"Last year, she saw something she wasn't supposed to see and someone came after her. My sister is one of the best people I know. She's strong and tough and smart, and has more empathy than I ever thought a person could have, and still, someone wanted her dead."

Cate walked over to him and wrapped her arms around him. He didn't hug her back, but that's not why she'd done what she'd done. She'd only wanted to offer him support, she didn't need anything in return.

"My sister, she, well, she had some stuff happen to her when she was a teenager, stuff that could really turn a person against the world, but she didn't let that happen, at least not in the long run. But when she found out that someone wanted her dead, it was just another reminder of how frail life and love and joy can be—there she'd been, living a good life, laughing with her friends, falling in love with Garret, and because of one minute of something she'd seen by accident, someone wanted to take it all away."

Cate leaned back and studied Caleb's face, though he was still staring off to where Edith had gone. "But you didn't let that happen, did you?"

His eyes dropped to hers. "It wasn't just me. It was me, Garret, Drew, and few others, not to mention Kit herself."

"But, together, you didn't let that happen, did you?"

"No, but I still remember the look of hopelessness in her eyes when she realized what was actually happening."

"And you saw that again in Edith today?"

He nodded and then, much to her surprise, wrapped his arms around her and rested his cheek on the top of her head. "I did, and I hated it. I know Edith was involved in the death of Summer Granger, but I read the report and she wasn't at fault. She wasn't even speeding when Summer darted in front of her. Edith is a good person, and I hate that she just learned how sometimes that just isn't good enough."

CHAPTER 13

THE NEXT DAY CALEB WAS washing a mug in the ice house kitchen when he saw Margaret open the back door of the main house and point Edith across the drive in his direction. He glanced over his shoulder to where Elise and Cate were sitting in front of the fire, a game of snakes and ladders on the floor between them. Cate had given Jana the morning off and they'd both joined him for breakfast.

"Edith is coming to visit," he called over his shoulder.

He heard Cate murmur something to Elise, then felt her presence beside him. "What do you think she'll say?" she asked.

He didn't know, but he had a guess. "She's coming alone. I don't take that as a good sign." Before he could elaborate, they heard knocking on his door.

"Good morning. I hope you don't mind me coming by," Edith said as Caleb opened the door to invite her in. She didn't look the least bit surprised to see Cate in his room so early in the morning; however, her eyes did linger on Elise, who sat by the game board in her pajamas intently studying their visitor.

"This is my daughter, Elise. Elise, this is Ms. Barnard," Cate made the introductions.

Elise offered a shy smile and a wave.

Edith offered a bigger smile and a wave back. "Hi, sweetie."

"Can I get you some coffee?" Caleb offered.

Edith's eyes danced to Elise then came back to his in question.

He turned to Cate and gave a little nod in Elise's direction.

"Let me text Christine and have her come get Elise for a little bit," Cate said. No one was interested in talking murder in front of the child.

The three adults chatted about inconsequential things like the weather, the architecture of the main house, and the vast trail system in the area until Christine popped by and swept a giggling Elise away to get dressed for a morning of helping in the kitchen.

When the door closed behind the two, Caleb turned to Edith. "Would you like some coffee now?"

She nodded, and when he looked to Cate, she accepted as well. He filled three mugs and they settled at the small kitchen table. He was glad he'd cleared it of all his files before breakfast. There were things about the Whatley family Edith didn't need to learn from him, or even know that he knew.

Edith fiddled with the handle of her mug and stared down at the near-black liquid. Caleb and Cate let her have a moment to gather her thoughts. Finally, she raised her eyes, took a breath, and spoke. "I believe everything you told me yesterday about the wire, the snake, and the poison, but I'm still having a hard time believing any of it was meant for me."

"It's not something anyone really wants to believe," Caleb said.

Edith shook her head. "It's not that. After we talked yesterday, I went over in my head all the interactions I've had with Edward since I arrived. There haven't been many, he keeps mostly to himself and, to be honest, he's not Michael's favorite uncle, so we don't tend to go out of our way to spend time with him. Even so, he's been nothing but kind to me. Unusually so."

"What does that mean?" Cate asked, taking a sip of her coffee.

Edith lifted a shoulder. "You know how he is. Crotchety, cranky, not a very pleasant man. He always seems to be quoting some piece of scripture or another, especially around some of the more rowdy cousins, like Nico and Dixie. Strangely though, he's pleasant to me, more so than he is to his own nieces and nephews."

Caleb glanced at Cate to see if she was thinking the same thing he was. "Do you think—"

"That his kindness is all a ruse?" Edith finished.

Caleb nodded.

"No, I don't. Well," Edith paused, "it doesn't *feel* insincere, but then, I'm aware enough to know that, if someone was truly capable of the kind of planning and long-term hatred you've been describing to me, they might also be very good at hiding it." Her eyes dropped back down to her coffee and she lifted it with both hands to take sip. Once she'd set it back down on the wooden surface, she glanced at each of them.

"I'm concerned about what's going on, who wouldn't be? But is there *anyone* else in the family that could be the potential target? What about Sabrina?"

"Why do you say that?" Caleb asked.

Edith treated them to a small eye roll and a you-know-why look before she spoke. "Because she and Dominique are definitely not doing well as a couple. Sabrina was out riding with me that day. She spends more nights with the girls than she does with Dominique—often changing rooms in the middle of the night so that the rest of the family doesn't see her avoiding her spouse. She could have let the snake out then. And as to the whiskey, she prefers port over whiskey, but I've noticed that, for some reason, she switches to whiskey when she drinks with Nico, Alex, and Dixie. I don't really know why, maybe because they prefer it and, at heart, Sabrina is a people pleaser. To her detriment, in my opinion."

"Could you see Dominique doing any of the things we've discussed?" Cate asked.

Edith opened her mouth then shut it. She pursed her lips for a moment then finally shook her head. "The poison, yes. I could definitely see that. But the snake? Or going out into the woods to string the wire?" She shook her head again. "I don't think she'd even come up with something like the wire. It would take someone with at least a rudimentary knowledge of horses and riding to think that one through." Edith let out a big sigh. "But even if it wasn't Dominique targeting Sabrina, there are other options. What if it was Isiah? He'd benefit financially from his sister's death and he definitely could have done all the things we've talked about. Or maybe Dixie is the target. She was present all of those times, too."

Caleb met Cate's silent gaze. Denial was part of the process, and Cate seemed to recognize it as well, so they both said nothing, giving Edith the time to absorb what she fought against. Their guest went quiet for a few moments, no doubt reflecting on what she didn't want to reflect on. But when Edith met his gaze again, Caleb didn't see the acceptance he had anticipated; he saw fear.

"What if the target really *is* Michael?" Edith asked. Her voice was quiet, as if saying it out loud would make it so. "What if those brothers *have* found a way to get to him? You don't know what it was like when he came back from that trek."

"You two were together then?" Caleb asked, surprised. His intel had the couple meeting about a year after the incident.

She shook her head. "No, I met him later. It changed him, though. Hugely. What happened up on that mountain was the embodiment of the classic moral dilemma. Do you cut the rope, killing one man to save many others? Only it wasn't theoretical for them. In doing what he did, Michael saved his own life as well as the lives of his friend and the two Sherpas traveling with them. But he actually had to look into the eyes of one of his best friends as he cut that rope. With every slice of the blade, he knew he was delivering his friend to certain death. "

Yes, Caleb could see how that would change a man.

"His friend insisted that he do it," Edith continued. "Wouldn't you? Wouldn't you sacrifice yourself to save four others? Well, I suppose not everyone would, but Brett did. As it was, when the survivors finally made it down the mountain, they were all barely alive. And that was something Brett's family couldn't forgive Michael or the others for. Mostly, they blamed Michael," she added quietly.

"Why's that?"

"Because he was the one who'd convinced all of them to go, he had even paid for it. Brett didn't have the kind of money Michael has, so Michael bankrolled the whole trip."

"And because he paid for it, he was at fault," Cate said.

Edith nodded. "So, is it possible it's one of them?"

Just like Michael, Caleb knew Edith would rather someone be after her than the person she loved. Despite her reticence to believe that Edward could be an attempted murderer, her bigger fear was that Michael was the true target.

Caleb took a deep breath. "No one has seen anyone on the grounds that shouldn't be here, but we will continue to investigate it. I'll double-check to make sure they have no ties to the house or anyone who works here. If needed, I'll also send someone to check on their whereabouts."

Edith met his gaze for a beat, then blinked and turned away. "Thank you. I know you're fairly certain I'm the target, more than fairly certain actually, but I appreciate your help in looking into that for me."

"We *are* fairly certain that you are the target, but being 'fairly certain' isn't the same as being positive. Dr. DeMarco even cautioned us against becoming singularly focused when we first talked to her. She said that if you didn't truly sense anything off about your interactions with Edward, we should go back and widen our search again."

"So, will you?"

"Yes, we will. But I'm not ready to give up on our theory just yet. You seem a remarkably instinctive person, at least that's what *my* instinct says," he said, making her smile a bit. "And if you don't think he's harboring any malicious intent toward you, that's something I'll take into consideration."

"But?" Edith inquired.

"But I'm not ready to rule him out. You just learned about all this yesterday. It's a lot to take in and process. We'll be keeping an eye on him, *and* we'll also go back and comb through everything we know to see if there is anything we might have missed."

"Thank you," Edith said, quietly. The room stayed silent as she took the last sip of her coffee, stood, then walked her mug to the sink. "I know what I said about not feeling any insincerity from him, but again, I'm not sure I would feel it if he's really good at covering up something like that. It's just not something I have any experience with, so I appreciate you staying vigilant about all of this. With all of this." She made a vague gesture to where they'd been seated talking. "So, what do you do now? Or, more specifically, what should *I* do now?"

Caleb stood and placed his and Cate's mugs in the sink as well. "Now, you stay vigilant. We won't talk to Edward yet, not until we do another pass through all of the information we have and check into Brett's family. But if we don't find anything, then . . ."

"Then you'll talk to him?"

He nodded.

She stared at him for a beat, then took a fortifying breath. "Fair enough. Now, I should get back. I left Michael playing chess with Agnes. I'm not sure either of them will be left standing when I get back," she said with a wan smile.

Cate laughed. "I'll walk you back. I want to make sure Elise isn't disrupting Margaret's lunch preparations. I'll talk to you later?" she asked, turning to Caleb. He inclined his head in agreement and ushered the two women out. Once he'd shut the door, he turned to study his stack of files piled at least two-feet high. It was going to be a long morning.

• • •

Cate found Elise upstairs with Margaret arranging flowers. The two looked to be having a good time, and since she wanted to talk to Caleb about the conversation they'd just had with Edith, she asked if Margaret wouldn't mind keeping Elise a bit longer. The older woman, who was usually missing her grandchildren this late into a job, readily agreed, so Cate made her way back down the servants' staircase to the kitchen.

She paused on the landing halfway down the staircase as the murmur of voices rose and she heard someone utter Caleb's name. She wasn't naïve enough to think that the staff didn't gossip, but she wasn't happy to overhear them gossiping about Caleb. She took a few steps down to hear better.

"Yeah right, I wish I had a *friend* like that," Greg said.

"You have *friends* like that visit you all the time," Christine replied. "Let's see, there was Ken from San Francisco, Sam from DC . . . shall I go on?"

"Not even close," Greg laughed. "They're hardly the same as Caleb and Catherine. Have you *seen* the way he looks at her? His eyes are so hot, I'm surprised we need the heat on in the house when he's around her."

Cate frowned.

"They do have chemistry," Christine agreed.

"Like, off-the-charts chemistry."

"Do you think either of them will ever do anything about it?"

In her mind's eye, Cate imagined Greg shaking his head. "I doubt it, at least not without a push. Catherine's been out of the scene for so long, she probably can't even recognize his interest, even if she could bring herself to acknowledge her own. And then even if she did acknowledge her own, I'm not sure she'd want to put the friendship at risk by initiating anything. She told me they'd been estranged for several years before she asked him to come here and I'm betting she's too afraid to lose him again."

"How could she *not* recognize his interest? His eyes hardly leave her and he's always getting her coffee and offering to help out and things like that. It's kind of sweet."

"Kind of? That's the thing, their chemistry is off the charts, but it's *also* really sweet to watch them together, don't you think?" Greg asked. "They look out for each other, take care of each other. They seem to have all the right stuff for a real relationship: attraction, for sure, but they also genuinely *care* about each other. Really, what more could you ask for?"

"But even so . . ."

"Even so," Greg continued, "I'm not sure Catherine has the guts to see what we all see, let alone act on it. Like I said, she's afraid she'll lose him again."

Cate listened to the voices fade as the two moved out of the kitchen, the topic moving to something more benign. She leaned against the wall of the stairwell and closed her eyes. How much of what she'd heard was true? Yes, she and Caleb did tend to take care of each other, but the rest? Did he really watch her? Was there really so much chemistry between them that even the *staff* had noticed?

She knew how *she* felt when she was with Caleb, but did he feel the same? Did she even *want* to know if he felt the same? Because, if he did, what then? The answer came swiftly as images of kissing Caleb, feeling his skin beneath her fingertips, wrapping herself up in bed with him for hours on end flashed into her mind. But then what?

Could they have a relationship? She lived in Florida and Caleb, well, he didn't actually seem to live anywhere, though she knew he liked being close to his sister and had been spending a lot of time in the town where she lived. Cate pushed away from the wall and made her way down the last few steps into the kitchen. She wondered what Kit's town, Windsor, was like. Was it a small Northeast town filled with clapboard houses and bucolic fields? Or was it a suburb of Albany, the capital that she knew wasn't far away?

She paused near the sink and eyed the ice house through the window. She had intended to go talk to Caleb about Edith, but after what she'd just overheard, and what she'd just imagined, she wasn't sure she was ready to see him. The images that had flashed through her mind of her and Caleb together were still so vivid, she knew she wouldn't be able to hide her thoughts from him.

A rueful smile touched her lips. In fact, until she figured out how to process what she'd just overheard, she had a sneaking suspicion that she was going to end up acting like a flustered teenage girl every time she saw him. It was a humbling thought. In her mid-thirties, she should be able to handle being attracted to someone by now. And it wasn't as though she hadn't been attracted to other people since Tommy's death, she'd even been out on a few dates. But the way she felt about Caleb, almost as if she were compelled to be near him, craving his touch, his smile, and his presence, was undeniably different than simple attraction. And that truth was what she didn't know what to do with.

"Mommy, are you still here?" Elise called, skipping into the kitchen with Margaret following. Elise carried a small vase and Margaret two much larger ones, all three filled with flowers needing replacement.

"Margaret said I could pick out some flowers and make my own bouquet," Elise continued once she'd laid eyes on her mother.

Cate smiled at the pair. "That sounds lovely," she said. And like a perfect distraction, she thought. "How about I help you two?"

• • •

Caleb set down the last of the family folders that he'd read and re-read that day. He'd taken notes along the way and had jotted down a few questions as well, questions he needed answers to. Pulling out his laptop, he organized his thoughts, and sent an e-mail to Jay, who could help him dig into them.

Of particular interest was why Livia Whatley took so many trips to inns around North Carolina. He also wanted more information about the owner of one of the clubs Dominique frequented, a man whose business connections were more than just a little shady. The club itself seemed above board, but Roger Jardo had been involved in all sorts of suspicious dealings, including two fires that occurred at constructions sites owned by developers who hadn't hire Jardo's unionized crew.

And then there was Luke. So far, he'd been mostly on the sidelines of the investigation. Yes, he'd been named in the wrongful-death suit of Dominique's sister's mother-in-law, but since he hadn't been the primary physician involved, Caleb hadn't pursued that line of inquiry. However, he did want Jay to look into the deaths of three other residents at the facility where Luke worked. It was an assisted-care facility, so it wasn't so much the deaths themselves that had caught his attention, but the fact that, in the last five years, there had been numerous complaints about the facility.

The families of those three patients, in particular, had been the most vocal, which had brought attention to the situation, and Caleb wanted to find out whether or not there was any truth to their allegations of neglect.

After hitting send on his email, he decided to call Vivi and talk through the situation again. The conversation didn't yield much other than to emphasize what he already knew, that there wasn't a better place to find a long simmering grudge than within a family.

That was the rub.

He needed to talk to the family members because, if it *wasn't* Edward, he was pretty certain that whatever had happened to start and fuel this grudge—whatever it was—wasn't going to be found in his files. No, it was going to be found in the recollections of each of the family members. He just hoped he had the skill to identify it and drag it out into the light. That was definitely something Vivi would be better suited to, but he wasn't about to ask her to come for a visit and risk the wrath of her husband, a man who did not look kindly on people taking advantage of his wife's time, expertise, and generosity.

Caleb's eyes went to the main house. It was getting dark and he knew the family would be sitting down to dinner in a few hours. He hadn't seen Cate since she'd left with Edith that morning.

He caught movement in one of the third floor windows. Lucas. His height and build made him easy to recognize. Caleb realized that, even though he didn't have Vivi, he might have a pretty good substitute. He grabbed his phone and sent a quick text asking Lucas to stop by after dinner.

Once he'd received an affirmative reply, Caleb leaned back in his chair and let the quiet of the evening wash over him. He could see the glow of the kitchen lights from the main house and knew that Margaret was in full dinner-prep mode. Cate might be helping her, or maybe she was doing the accounts, or helping Greg and Christine get the table ready. Thinking of her, of how much she liked her job and how good she was at it, made him smile. He didn't doubt that she missed Tommy and Brooke, probably every day, but she hadn't let the pain and loss destroy her. Like Kit, Cate had put her life back together and moved on. She'd found something that she enjoyed doing and, in doing so, allowed—no, invited—joy and laughter back into her life.

Feeling the need to be close to Cate but not wanting to disturb her, Caleb shot off a text to Jana. A few minutes later, Elise was on his doorstep wearing a bear-shaped hat and a smile.

"Are you sure?" Jana asked him as she stood beside the child.

Caleb leaned down and swept Elise up into his arms. He could tell he'd startled her—there probably weren't a lot of people who picked her up, much less swept her up like he just had—but then she let out a little squeal and tucked her head against his shoulder.

"Yes, I'm sure. She thinks she can beat me at Snakes and Ladders. It's about time I proved her wrong."

• • •

The family had just been served dessert when Cate slipped out of the main house. She wanted to get to her place before Elise had her bath and went to bed. Her steps faltered, however, when she passed in front of the one of Caleb's well-lit windows. She hadn't seen him all day and, truth be told, she'd been avoiding him, but, suddenly, she didn't want to anymore.

Pausing to glance inside, she was startled to see Caleb and Elise sitting at his kitchen table, each of them with a bowl of ice cream. They were clearly having a serious discussion; Caleb was leaning forward with a spoon dangling from his fingers, nodding. Elise had her I-have-something-important-to-say expression on her face, and her eyes were fixed on Caleb. Then Caleb must have said something funny because slowly, ever so slowly, a smile spread across Elise's face, then she threw her head back, laughing.

Cate's heart squeezed and, without much thought, she took the few steps remaining to his front door and let herself in.

"Mommy!" Elise slid from her seat and ran toward Cate. "Caleb and I are having ice cream for dessert, do you want some?"

she asked as she enclosed her mom in a hug. "We played Snakes and Ladders and I won—"

"I won too," Caleb said, standing with a smile as Cate approached, Elise pulling her along. "You want some ice cream?"

She glanced down at the nearly empty bowls and shook her head. "No, thank you. I haven't had dinner yet, but I may take a rain check?"

"You know where to find me," he said.

"And you? Did you eat dinner?" she asked, turning toward her daughter, who was back at the table spooning the last of her ice cream into her mouth.

Elise nodded. "We had pizza. Jana brought it for us."

Cate glanced at Caleb. How long had he been hanging out with Elise? And he still had a smile on his face. It's not that she was *in love* with him, but it was hard not to fall just a little in love with a man who clearly enjoyed her daughter's company almost, or as much, as she did.

"Jana brought her by a few hours ago, then came back to see about fetching her home for dinner. We were in the thick of a Snakes and Ladders tournament, so she just brought us some pizza instead."

"Sausage and olive and mushroom," Elise added, not bothering to look up from licking her bowl.

"Your favorite," Cate said. Elise grinned.

"You tired?' she asked Caleb. Time spent with kids wasn't always physically exhausting, but it could often be mentally exhausting.

"No. I spent a good chunk of the day going through the files and digging into information. It was nice to have some down time. I'll get back to it tonight, but a few hours away from it was good."

Unable to think of anything to say and unsure why the idea of Elise and Caleb becoming friends had suddenly made her feel so emotional, she turned her attention back to her daughter. "You ready to go home? It's almost time for your bath."

"Jana said she'd pop by and get her," Caleb said. "We weren't sure what time you'd be done, so I think she was planning on taking care of the nighttime routine. She should be here any minute, actually." Cate turned to look out the window and spotted Jana making her way toward the ice house, just as he'd predicted. The temperature had plummeted once the sun had gone down, so she was bundled in a long coat and carrying another smaller one for Elise.

Cate moved to open the door for her and, a few minutes later, after more than a few hugs, Elise was ensconced in her coat and ready to head home to a warm bath and bed.

"Would you mind taking her for a few minutes?" Cate asked Jana. Asking had been an impulse, but a strong enough one that she couldn't ignore it. When Jana readily agreed, Cate gave her daughter a kiss and saw them out.

"What's up?" Caleb asked, leaning against the kitchen counter once the child and nanny had left.

She hesitated then took a few steps closer, bringing her to a spot in front of him.

He frowned. "You okay?"

Her heart beat against her rib cage and she was certain that the blood rushing through her system was turning her face red. Telling herself that it was now or never, she didn't give herself any more time to think about what she wanted to ask. "Are you attracted to me?"

She swore Caleb had stopped breathing, the narrowing of his eyes his only movement. Then he crossed his arms over his chest. "This isn't a conversation we need to be having, Cate."

"Why not?"

"Because we're friends."

"I would think being friends with someone you're attracted to would be a good thing."

"Don't be obtuse." He looked away. But he didn't *move* away. He sounded angry about the topic of conversation, but he hadn't moved away from her.

She took a deep breath. "Okay, then how's this? I consider you a friend *and* I find that I'm attracted to you. *Very* attracted to you. I understand what you meant, that there is always a risk of losing a friend if you cross a line and things don't work out. But my question to you wasn't 'do you want a relationship beyond friendship,' it was just whether you are attracted to me or not."

"If you weren't interested in a relationship, or something else, why would you ask?" His eyes were turned toward the window.

She paused and, when his gaze came back to hers, she answered. "I know what I want, Caleb. But I'm not so dense that I wouldn't realize what you might be feeling if, in fact, you are attracted to me. You loved Tommy like a brother. I'm Tommy's widow and you are a very loyal person. Which is why I'm not asking if you want a relationship, not yet anyway. I just want the answer to the most basic question, because, if you are, I think we should talk about it."

"There's nothing to talk about, Cate. Whether I'm attracted to you or not doesn't matter."

"Why not?"

She could see the pulse in his throat beating wildly. He wasn't as unaffected as he'd like her to think. As she stared at that spot, watching his skin jump, she saw it quicken at the same time as she heard him take a deep breath. Nervous anticipation had her breath catching in her throat. Her eyes shot to his.

"It doesn't matter because I'm not Tommy. I can't be him. I can't be what you truly want."

Cate drew back. Of all the things Caleb could have said, she hadn't anticipated that. "Why would you think I'd want you to be like Tommy?"

She saw the muscles in his jaw tense before he spoke. "Because he was a good man, because he was the person you vowed to spend the rest of your life with, because you loved him."

Her brow furrowed. "He was a good man and he was the man I loved and promised myself to—"

"And you'll never meet another man like him," Caleb finished.

The words sounded oddly familiar and gave Cate pause. Then it clicked. He must have overheard the conversation she'd had with Lucas a few days earlier. If that was the case, though, hadn't he heard the rest, the part where she and Lucas talked about her moving on and finding someone else? Lucas had done that with Vic. His love for Vic didn't diminish his love for Jeffery, his first partner who had died while serving his country, nor did his love for Jeffery make Vic a second choice. Knowing he'd lost a loved one and moved on to find another was the reason Cate had struck up that particular conversation. She'd needed someone to tell her what she'd already known: that it was okay to love again and that loving again wasn't a betrayal of Tommy.

"You're right, Caleb. I won't ever meet anyone like Tommy again and won't ever have that kind of relationship with anyone else again. But that kind of relationship isn't something I'd want now, either. Tommy's death changed me, just as it changed you. We're both different people now than we were when we first met, and I'm a different person than I was when I first met and fell in love with Tommy. I loved him deeply and, had he not died, we would probably still be muddling our way through our marriage. But he did die and because he did, I became a different person. Maybe not different at my core, but different, nonetheless. And this person here now, this woman standing in front of you, doesn't want to recreate a relationship that started when she was twenty. She doesn't want the same things from life that she wanted then and, more importantly, she doesn't *need* the same things from life that she needed then." She paused, staring into his golden eyes.

His expression gave nothing away, but his gaze was steady on hers.

She inhaled. "I don't want you to be like Tommy. I *need* you to be you."

Seconds ticked by as he said nothing, simply watched her watching him. She didn't know what more she could say, but she needed him to understand, to believe, what she'd told him. She opened her mouth to say something else when a knock at the door startled them both. She spun around as Caleb pushed off the counter.

Lucas's head came into view around the door. His eyes bounced between the two. "Did I interrupt something?"

She glanced over at Caleb, his look told her it was up to her to decide what to say. Lucas knew very well he'd interrupted, but maybe it was a good thing he had. It gave her an opportunity to make an exit and give Caleb some time to think about what she'd said.

"No." She shook her head. "We're done talking. I hope what I said makes some sense to you," she said to Caleb. He didn't say anything, but did tip his head in acknowledgement.

"I hope you'll let me know what you think." Once again, he said nothing, just watched her with his piercing golden eyes. On impulse, she leaned forward and brushed a kiss against his cheek. "Please, think about what I said," she whispered in his ear. She felt, more than saw, his nearly imperceptible nod.

"I'll let you two get to it, then." She stepped away and Lucas held the door open for her. A few seconds later, she was out in the bracing cold. She slowed her steps, not yet ready to have her mind occupied by Elise and the chaos of the carriage house at bedtime, then turned toward the barn.

Caleb's comment, something he so obviously believed, had stunned her. It had never, not once, crossed her mind that he would be a *replacement* for Tommy. All the reasons she'd given him as to why that wouldn't be the case had been true, but what really struck her was that, in thinking she might want him because he reminded her of Tommy, he'd given himself no credit. He seemed to place no value on all the qualities he possessed that had attracted her to him. He didn't seem to understand that she enjoyed being with him, that his sense of humor made her smile and laugh, and that his loyalty, intelligence, and strength all made her feel stronger and freer than she had in years. There were dozens of reasons why she liked Caleb for who *he* was. She liked that when they were together they were just as comfortable talking as being silent. She liked that he was always conscientious about her and thoughtful with Elise. But if he didn't see those things about himself, or if he didn't understand that she valued who he was, then thinking that to be with her he would have to live in Tommy's shadow made some sense.

She paused when she made it to the barn, its doors closed tight for the night, and turned her gaze to the stars. Wisps of clouds moved through the dark night, obscuring the points of light for moments at a time. Looking up at the vastness of the sky, the same sense of calm she had once felt when looking out at the ocean settled over her and she knew what she needed to do. She was a tiny speck in the universe—not even that, really. Her problems and challenges were real, but not insurmountable. And she could either let time, as it marched steadily forward, make the problem go away, or she could step up to the challenge and use what relatively little time she had on this planet to make her life what she wanted it to be. It wasn't really a question that needed an answer.

CHAPTER 14

ARM TUCKED UNDER HIS HEAD, eyes open in the dark, Caleb lay in bed listening to the silence. He'd closed the shades on the window facing the main house, blocking out most of the already gentle security lights that illuminated the back of the house, but it still wasn't dark enough. Not black enough for him to fall asleep.

His ears, tuned into the steady rhythm of the night, recognized an owl hooting in the distance. In his mind, he tried to follow the flight of the night hunter, but another sound, a sound he both dreaded and desired, shot through his system. His heart constricted sharply as he heard the quiet sound of a door being shut followed by the shuffle of feet on gravel. Under normal circumstances, he'd be up and out of bed, investigating. "Now" wasn't normal, though. Not after what Cate had said to him earlier that evening.

He heard a key turn in the lock of his front door and felt a small gust of cold night air sweep through the room as Cate paused then stepped in. She shut the door behind her and still he didn't move.

"Go home, Cate."

He heard keys being set down on the countertop and the sound of her toeing off the fuzzy slipper-boots she wore. He had to stay focused on the details. If he didn't, his mind and body would react in ways he didn't want them to. He listened as she removed her jacket, the sound of the zipper echoing in the room.

And then she was there, standing at his bedside. In the dim light he noted that she wore nothing but a tank top and a pair of thin cotton pajama bottoms. His stomach tightened.

"Move over, Caleb. It's cold."

"Then maybe you should go home."

She sighed and then rather than take his advice she drew the blankets back and lay nearly on top of him. "If you're not going to scoot over, then this will have to do."

He shot to the other side of the bed. It wasn't far enough. Especially when she sidled over close enough to touch him. At least she wasn't on top of him anymore. That was a good thing, right? Lying on his back, he stared at the ceiling.

She lifted a finger and traced it down his chest, making him both pleased by the fact that he tended to sleep nude, and dismayed by the fact that that he tended to sleep nude. Moving her hand back up, she laid her palm flat on his chest. "I like spending time with you, Caleb," she said.

He didn't answer, couldn't, because her leg was inching up over his.

"You make me laugh, you make me think. You ask me questions rather than tell me answers." She leaned forward and brushed her lips across his bare shoulder, pressing her body against his. "You let me work when I'm working and, when I'm doubting myself, you support me and value me. You came when I needed you. After five years, you came. You didn't hold a grudge, just welcomed me back into your life, just as I've done the same."

He went rigid—in every way—when she moved over him and straddled his hips with her thighs. There was no way to hide his reaction to her now, although she didn't seem focused on that. With her hands placed on either side of face, she leaned down and kissed him. Just a gentle touch.

"You're smart, you're capable, you're loyal, Caleb. You love your sister enough be a better person for her. You have so many people in your life now that you speak about with fondness and respect, and that says something to me about who you are as a person, what you value, and how you want to live in this world." She hadn't moved as she'd spoken and her lips had brushed against his with nearly every word. When she paused, though, she closed the small gap and let her lips linger on his. "You've not only welcomed me back into your life, but my daughter too. She adores you and she's a surprisingly good judge of character." Her lips pressed down, again.

He was trying to take deep breaths through his nose to calm the storm raging inside him, but each time he did, his body pressed against hers. The desire, the want, and, yes, the need to be with her had risen in him so fiercely that he wanted to cry out. He wanted to release it, he wanted to bury himself inside her and beg for her forgiveness.

She sat up, walking her hands down his chest. She stared at him for a long moment, then raised her arms and swept her shirt off.

His body jerked under his leashed craving.

"It's you I want, Caleb. You. Everything about you. And, tonight, it's just you and me." She leaned down, her skin on his. "Please, Caleb."

The chain broke.

He reached up and fisted one hand in her hair as other slid to the back of her neck, drawing her into the kiss he'd been fantasizing about for days. She kissed him back with a hunger he couldn't have dreamed about and, dropping her hands back to his chest, she moved them as if touching *him* was something *she* needed as much as he.

Leaving one hand on the back of her neck as he tasted her, he slid the other down along her side and under the waistband of her pajama bottoms. Gripping her bare hip, he pulled her against him harder. A moan of pleasure escaped her and with it came another frenzy of need.

He rolled them over so that he was on top, then moved down her body and quickly stripped off her pants. Once they were both naked, he sat on his haunches for a moment to drink her in. He hadn't begun to touch her in the way he wanted to, but, even so, he knew what they both needed first.

He reached out and touched her, running a single fingertip

down between her breasts, over her belly, then lower. She closed her eyes in pleasure and raised her knees, inviting him. "Caleb," she whispered. "Please."

"Protection?" he managed to ask.

"It's taken care of. Now. Please, Caleb."

That wasn't an answer he usually accepted, preferring to use condoms—something he could control—but the thought of sliding into Cate, of feeling her with nothing between them, had him rising over her. She wrapped a leg around his waist, urging him in. He was more than happy to comply and, slowly, ever so slowly, they joined.

And it was Caleb's name on her lips every time she came apart that night.

• • •

Cate stirred in bed and slowly realized she was alone. Not that this was unusual; with the exception of the nights Elise crawled into bed with her, she'd been waking up alone for the past five years, but still, she was surprised that Caleb wasn't there. She opened her eyes to confirm that the space beside her was empty and her gaze caught on the fire burning low in the fireplace.

Raising herself up on one arm, she glanced around. The back door was cracked open just a hair, causing a slow but steady influx of cool air to flow into the room. Which would explain why Caleb had turned the fire on. It did not explain, however, why Caleb had opened the door in the first place.

Swinging her legs off the bed, she picked up one of his sweatshirts lying on the dresser and pulled it on. She also grabbed a throw blanket that was hanging on the back of one of the chairs and made her way to the door. Pushing it open farther, she poked her head out and glanced around and then, not seeing Caleb, she looked down.

Wearing nothing but a pair of sweatpants, he sat on the floor of the porch with his back against the house and his knees pulled up.

"Caleb, it's cold out here."

"You should go back inside, then." Except for his lips, he didn't move.

She sighed softly. She'd known this would come. She hadn't fooled herself into thinking that just because they'd done what they'd done—which, to be clear, was something she planned to continue doing—Caleb wouldn't struggle with it. What she'd said to Greg about how difficult it would be for Caleb to not feel as if he'd betrayed Tommy still held true. Even if he'd enjoyed what they'd done. Perhaps even more so *because* he'd enjoyed it.

She'd known they'd have to talk about it at some point, she just hadn't anticipated doing it in thirty-degree weather at three in the morning. She slid down beside him and arranged the blanket around the both of them. His skin was freezing, but she knew he'd warm up quickly.

Slipping her arm through his, she leaned her head on his shoulder. "Talk to me."

He hesitated. "I'm not sure I can."

"I'm sure you can. You may not want to, but you can."

He didn't answer right away so she snuggled closer to him, not only to enjoy the warmth, but also hoping that her closeness might encourage him.

He let his head fall back against the side of the house. "Tommy's death was my fault, Cate. I didn't . . . I can't . . ." He paused, struggling to find the right words. "It just was. He's dead because of a stupid decision I made. I regret it like you wouldn't believe, but what's that when measured against what you and Elise lost? I hate myself for what happened that day and I can't imagine why you wouldn't hate me too. And now I've made it even worse, because, well," he raised his hand and gestured back toward his bedroom. "Because I never told you the truth and, after tonight, I'll understand if you hate me. I'd ask for your forgiveness—for Tommy *and* for tonight—but it seems too big a thing to hope for."

Hearing his words, Cate realized that while she'd known they'd have to talk about Tommy, she hadn't expected to hear what had just come out of Caleb's mouth. She no more believed Caleb was responsible for Tommy's death than she was, but it wasn't what she believed that mattered.

"Tell me what happened that day," she said. She knew Tommy had been shot while on a mission in Russia, but hadn't ever heard, or asked about the details.

Caleb hesitated, then began. "We were in Russia tracking a drug trafficker, only it turned out drugs weren't the only thing he trafficked in. He was into kids too and, later, we learned women as well." Cate felt his pulse kick up under the hand she had wrapped around his wrist.

"My dad was into all that. He was an arms dealer, a trafficker in people, all sorts of things," he continued.

That piece of information, of Caleb's history, was something she hadn't known.

"It was why I got into the business I did. I found out about it when I was nineteen and he wanted to bring me into the 'family business.' Instead, I took a chunk of the trust fund my mom left me and vowed to ruin the empire he'd built."

"That's when you met Tommy?"

He nodded. "Yeah, he took a kid, whose idea of roughing it was staying at a four-star hotel, under his wing and turned him into the man I am today. He saw something in me that I didn't even know existed. He could have taken advantage of me. There were so many opportunities, so many times that he could have laughed and taken off with my money or my equipment or my life. But he never did. He stuck by me. He trained this spoiled, rich kid and taught me how to survive in that world so that I could bring my father down."

"And you did, didn't you? Destroy your father?"

"We did. I had a little help from my sister that I didn't know about at the time, but between the three of us, we orchestrated his destruction."

"And what happened to him?"

She felt Caleb tense under her cheek that rested against his bicep. "He died in a car accident. Rolled his Porsche down a hill."

"And neither you nor your sister mourned, did you?"

"Not for him, no."

She wondered whom they *had* mourned for, perhaps their lost childhoods, but that was a conversation for another day. "So what does your father have to do with what you and Tommy were doing in Russia?"

"When we found out he was trafficking in kids, well, that's always been a hot button of mine. So much of what we saw in the work we did just sucked, but when it came to trafficking kids, that was the one thing that always set me off."

"And so?" She pulled back just enough to place a soft kiss on his bare shoulder then tucked her head back against him.

"So, I wanted to do everything in my power to bring the man down and make sure his operations were completely dismantled. We started by taking out his inner circle, the people who would take over if something happened to him. Some we, well, *took care of*, others we scared off or were able to get into custody with authorities who couldn't ever be bribed to let them go again."

"Destroying the body of the snake before getting to the head."

"Exactly. It didn't take too long, a few days. The main guy we were after, we called him Vlad the Bad, was young, so his operation wasn't too big or too entrenched yet."

"And then?"

"And then it was time to go after Vlad himself." He paused then took a deep breath. "It was my plan that Tommy, Garret, and I implemented that day. Garret was responsible for the front of the compound, I was going to take the rear, and Tommy was going to plant the diversionary explosives—explosives that would go off and drive Vlad and the few men with him out of the house."

By the way Caleb's words slowed, she knew that what she was about to hear was the part he replayed in his head over and over.

"Tommy set the first explosive according to the plan, but when he went to set the second, he discovered an easy way into the house—a door that had been left unlocked. We debated whether to go ahead with the original plan or make a modification. Getting into the house unnoticed would make things cleaner, but we all knew that a gift like that unlocked door was, well, the possibility that it was a trap or decoy most definitely crossed our minds.

"In the end, though, we decided to try it. Of course, not surprisingly, it *was* a trap. Vlad had upped his security once his inner circle had started dwindling and we got caught in a close-range fire fight with twelve of his men."

"The three of you against twelve of them?"

She felt his muscles tense as he continued. "The end was in sight when Tommy died. He was shot by the last of Vlad's men still alive. Tommy took the man down with him, but that was little consolation when we saw Tommy go down." Hearing this, she was glad she hadn't asked for the details immediately after Tommy died. She didn't think she would have been strong enough to handle the emotions conjured by the imagery of Caleb's words.

He stopped talking and she stayed snuggled up to him as he took several deep breaths in the quiet of the night. "And there you have it, Cate. It was my idea to go for the whole organization and not just Vlad. It was me who okayed the alternate the plan. I *knew* Tommy wasn't ready to come back into the field and, not only did I agree to bring him along when I shouldn't have, but I put him in one of the most stressful situations we could have come across. It was me and *my actions* that got Tommy killed."

She could feel him sitting rigid against her, waiting for her rejection, her anger. Well, he wasn't going to get either of them. "Did you know I was the one who told him to go?" She let the question hang and, a few beats later, he drew back to look at her. She turned her head up to meet his gaze. "I did. I'm the one who told him to call you."

His brows shot down. "Why?"

She sighed and let her head fall back against his shoulder so she was gazing out into the night. "Because he wasn't handling Brooke's death very well. Neither was I, really. We were both so angry, feeling so hollow and empty. Then, when I started going to therapy, Tommy just got mad. And mean. I tried to get him to go with me. Don't get me wrong, I wasn't crazy about the idea of therapy either, but I knew enough about grieving to understand that if I had any chance of making it through Brooke's death, I would need help. Tommy didn't agree. I know people grieve differently, so I didn't begrudge him not going with me, but I did begrudge the fact that he *wasn't* dealing with his loss. Or rather, he was, but his way of dealing with it was to get angry at every little thing. And he was just plain mean."

"Mean?"

It was her turn to hesitate. She didn't like to speak ill of the dead and, in her heart of hearts, she knew Tommy's behavior was born of the loss of their daughter, but while that might make it understandable, it hadn't made it any easier to live with.

"Yes, mean. He yelled at me all the time. And I mean *all the time*. He criticized me for going back to work, then, if I came home early to make dinner for him, he called me lazy and said the company should fire me. But, if I came home late, I was a bitch who would rather spend time working than with him."

Caleb's head spun toward her. "He called you that?"

She nodded. "That and many other things. Honestly, he probably wasn't wrong on that last point. By then, I did prefer to be at work than to be at home with him. Not only did I not want to subject myself to his abuse, I was also angry that he got to wallow in it when I was working my ass off to deal with things in a healthy way, in a way that didn't hurt the person I loved." She paused and thought back on that period of her life. She'd felt as though she hadn't just lost her daughter, but her husband too.

"I didn't hate him really, but I hated what he'd become, and I *was* angry. I was angry that he couldn't see that I was hurting too. I was angry that he was lashing out at me in his pain. *Me*, as if I wasn't suffering too. Finally, it got to the point where I didn't know what to do, and I thought that maybe if he went away he'd come back the man I knew he could be. So I told him to call you."

Caleb's hand met hers and their fingers intertwined. "I had no idea, Cate. I'm so sorry you went through that."

She shrugged against his body. "You asked for my forgiveness, but you aren't going to get it. There is nothing to forgive, Caleb. You no more killed Tommy than I did. Yes, I understand that it was your plan, but how many times did I hear you guys talk about getting lucky? About getting out of a sticky situation by the skin of your teeth? I blamed myself for Tommy's death too. But after a few years of therapy and some tough love for myself, I know that the only person truly responsible for his death was the man who shot him. Tommy was just a man whose luck had run out."

She squeezed Caleb's hand and rubbed her cheek against the skin of his shoulder, enjoying the feel of it. "I know what I've said won't change what you think or how you feel right away—like I said, it took me years to accept that Tommy's death wasn't my fault. I hope you'll think about it, though. I hope you'll come to understand and believe that I don't blame you. Even in my darkest hours, I never blamed you."

They sat in silence for a few minutes, then Caleb slid his arm around her shoulder and pulled her closer, placing a kiss on the top of her head. As he did so, the blanket opened a bit and a shiver traveled through her body.

"I'm glad we talked about this, Caleb. I'm glad it's out between us and, hopefully, it's something we can keep out in the open. I don't want to feel uncomfortable talking about Tommy. He was a good man, a good husband, and he's Elise's father. I want to be able to recognize and celebrate that with you. It may not come right away, but that's what I hope, for both of us." Caleb didn't exactly nod in agreement but he did seem willing to consider what she'd said.

"In the meantime," she said, detaching her hand from his and spreading it across his belly. "I only have about two hours before I need to sneak back home." She slid her hand lower and raised her lips to his ear. "Why don't we get back into bed and get warm?"

• • •

Caleb stood at the kitchen sink and rinsed his coffee mug. Cate had left hours earlier and, at her request, Greg had brought breakfast by the ice house a short while ago. The shades were now up and light flooded into the suite. As he placed the mug on the drying rack he watched a dust mote dance in front of him.

He didn't have any interest in dissecting what had happened the night before. He didn't regret it, but he also knew that if he thought too much about it he could make himself, if not regret it, at least feel as if he'd done something he shouldn't have. But Cate's words, her feelings of guilt over Tommy's death and then her subsequent acceptance that she had nothing to do with it, had made a tiny crack in the wall of Caleb's own guilt. If he let her words, her truth, sink in and grow roots, the guilt and shame and self-loathing he'd been carrying with him for years might actually break up and fall away. He wanted that. He didn't want to give it so much power any more. And so he wasn't going to dissect what had happened the night before; he wasn't going to look for reasons why he might have fucked up. He was just going to let it be and hope that the thoughts Cate had seeded took root within him and grew.

He turned away from the window, away from the view of the main house, and pulled out his phone. Checking the weather, he opted to pull on only a thick sweatshirt over his long-sleeved shirt before taking a turn around the property. He also tugged on a black knit hat. It was supposed to be pleasant, but not *that* pleasant.

"We might have a problem." A text beeped through from Lucas.

"??" Caleb typed back.

"I think you need to come over here."

Caleb glanced around his room to make sure everything that should be hidden was. "Be right there."

"Meet me in the office."

Caleb slid the phone back into his pocket and, after locking his door, jogged across the parking area and entered the kitchen. The warm room smelled like coffee and blueberry muffins; Margaret and a few of the staff sat at the table enjoying both. He paused and inhaled deeply.

"Have you heard?" Cate asked, entering through the hall doorway and walking straight toward him. Like a teenager, he hesitated, unsure how to act around her in public after their night together.

Apparently, she had no such qualms. She went up on her toes and kissed him. On the lips. "Good morning, by the way. So, Lucas texted you?"

He cast a glance at the staff, all of whose eyes were all riveted on the two of them. He glared back at each of them and, after a brief moment, they went back to their coffee and muffins, though not without a few grins and raised eyebrows.

"Caleb?"

"Good morning to you too. And yes, Lucas texted me, but I don't know what's going on. He just said I needed to come over."

She nodded, distracted. "He's in the office with Mark, the groundskeeper, not Mark Brandt," she clarified. "Come on." She grabbed his hand and pulled him out of the kitchen.

"I'm more than happy to cancel the shoot if you can think of a good reason why," Caleb heard Mark saying as they approached the office.

"Because having these people around guns right now is a terrible idea," Lucas responded.

"You're going to have to give me more than that."

Once she and Caleb had entered the room, Cate made sure to close the door behind them.

"What's going on here?" Caleb asked.

Mark looked to Lucas and Cate to answer.

"The family has asked to go hunting today—" Cate started.

"Hell no," Caleb cut in before she'd even finished.

Cate rolled her eyes at his tone. "Thank you for your helpful input, Caleb. I think we're all on the same page about that, but the question is how we should handle it with the family."

"I can't just tell them 'no,'" Mark said. Caleb had chatted with the groundskeeper a few times during his time at The Washington House. Though he looked to be almost a caricature of himself, with his heavy flannel button-down shirt, work boots, and lumberjack beard, Caleb had found him to be knowledgeable, dedicated to his job, and in possession of a rather sharp sense of humor on occassion.

"Can you tell them the guns are being cleaned?" Caleb suggested. They'd only told The Washington House staff the bare facts about the wire, the snake, and the poison, and hadn't discussed any of the implications. If he could, Caleb would rather avoid broadcasting their concerns beyond Cate's staff.

Mark shook his head. "That might work for some, but several of the family members have their own."

That gave Caleb reason for concern. "Who has their own gun and where are they kept?"

"Michael, Anthony, Edward, Dixie, even Sebastian has his own," Cate answered.

"Pretty much everyone but Sabrina and Dominique," Mark added.

Caleb cast a you-gotta-be-kidding-me look at Lucas who clearly commiserated with him, but was leaving the decision about what to do with the information in Caleb's hands.

"Any chance you can check for permits?" Caleb asked Lucas.

Shaking his head, Lucas replied, "Not my jurisdiction anymore, but with this family, I'd bet they're all legal."

Caleb thought they probably were too. "What if we said it was too late in the season? *Is* this even the season? Even if they have gun permits, do they have hunting permits? Could we use that as an excuse?"

Mark shook his head and answered the first question. "Just about everything but deer are in season right now. Hell, even deer are, if you want to hunt with a crossbow."

The Cate chimed in to answer the rest. "When we planned this trip, we asked specifically about hunting so that we could obtain those permits before they arrived," Cate said. "Anyone who was interested had to send us a copy of their gun license and proof that they'd taken a safety course. We registered them all for permits and licenses, as needed, to hunt while they were here."

Caleb ran a hand through his hair, dislodging his hat. There was no way they could let the family go out into the woods with guns. Even if Edith wasn't one of them. Which begged the question. "Is Edith planning on going?"

Mark nodded. "Yes, she doesn't really want to shoot, but she wants to go with the group."

Fuck. "Is there *any* way we can dissuade them or give them something else to focus on? Something that we could hype up as a true family affair, since, I assume Agnes isn't going to go out hunting? Another trip off the property, maybe?"

"Another trip would take too much time to plan," Cate said.

"What if I set up the trap shooting box?" Mark asked, seeming to suddenly remember an option none of the rest of them had known they had. "It wouldn't get them away from the guns altogether, but we could set it up on the front lawn and turn it into a friendly family competition, or something like that. Several of the family prefer rifles over shotguns, but we're far enough out in the country that using a rifle won't be unsafe. We could make it work," he said, clearly warming to the idea.

Lucas looked thoughtful at the idea and Cate seemed to have already begun working out the logistics of how she could pull it together in her head. No doubt also contemplating the chances of successfully shifting the family's focus from hunting to a friendly skeet-shooting contest.

"I think that could work," she said slowly. "We could make it a garden-party type thing, bring tables and heaters out. I think we even have some fire pits we can move to the front lawn and veranda. We could serve lunch and cocktails out there for the entire family."

"We could take that big chalkboard Margaret uses for scheduling and shopping lists in the kitchen and turn it into a scoreboard," Lucas chimed in.

"What do you think?" Cate asked Caleb.

He still didn't like that there would be so many guns in the hands of so many family members, but at least this way, they could keep an eye on everyone.

"Any chance Vic was thinking of coming up today?" he asked Lucas. Cate and the staff would be busy running the event and, even though he and Lucas would be able to stand watch, having one more person there wouldn't hurt.

Lucas smiled. "Actually, yes, he has two days off and decided to visit me. Apparently, he's not completely bored of me yet. He left a little over an hour ago so, with the way he drives, he'll be here in about two hours."

"It's a four-hour drive from Boston," Cate said.

"Don't ever drive with Vic if given the chance," Lucas responded with a smile.

Cate laughed.

Caleb felt the tension drain from his chest. At least they'd be in a position where they had a little more control. "Will everyone be using their own guns?" he asked Mark.

Mark shrugged. "Some of them have rifles that are better suited to hunting than trap shooting, so we should have some of our own shotguns available."

"And where are those kept?" Lucas asked repeating the question Caleb has asked earlier.

"All the guns are in gun safes in a locked room in an out building that is also locked when I'm not there. There are two safes; one for the house guns and one for the guests'."

"And who has the keys?" Caleb asked.

"Normally, I keep the keys to the guest safe, but since this is a family gathering, each family member also has a key to that safe so they can access their gun whenever they want. The general manager and I have keys to the house safe."

"The general manager was given the month off while the family's here and I have essentially taken on the role. I believe she was going to take the time to visit her family in Florida," Cate said.

"Georgia, actually, but yes, I just talked to her yesterday. They were headed out to the coast for the last few days of her vacation," Mark said.

"And I know I probably don't need to ask," Caleb said to Mark, "but I need to ask, do you take care of those guns?"

Mark's eyes narrowed at the implication of possible negligence in his duties. "Yes, I take them apart and clean them every week, whether they are used or not. If they've been used, they are cleaned thoroughly and checked before they are put back. Minor repairs are done by a man in town, but if there is anything major wrong, we stop using that piece and replace it with a new one."

"And when was the last time you cleaned them?" Lucas asked.

"Yesterday, actually."

Still not in love with the skeet-shooting party idea, Caleb decided it was better than the alternative. And he knew Cate could make it work for the family in a way that wouldn't appear that they'd been denied anything they thought they deserved.

"Okay, Lucas, I want you and Mark to be the only ones who handle the guns—all guns—unless someone is actively using them."

Both men nodded.

"Cate, can you be sure to get as much of the social stuff set up on the veranda as possible, so we'll have fewer people on the lawn where the shooting will take place?"

"Yes, I'll put one fire pit on the lawn, but leave all the refreshments and food on the patio. We also have some chairs that are usually out in the summer, big chairs with cushions, that we can put out to help keep people up there. Heating lamps can be put out too, of course."

He took a deep breath. "Okay, let's do this. Cate, let me know if you need any help handling the Whatleys."

She smiled. "Thanks, but I just need to get Agnes, Nico, and Michael on my side, then everyone else will fall in line. I'll tempt Agnes with hot toddies and the opportunity to mock her nieces and nephews. Nico doesn't particularly like tromping through the woods alone, so the idea of a garden party will be more up his alley anyway. And Michael, well, given the circumstances, I don't think Michael will object at all."

He loved her confidence and her ability to plan and strategize on the spot. "Good then," he said with a smile. "Let's get to it."

• • •

Caleb stood guard watching over the guns not far from where Isiah was shooting. He'd asked each family member to let Vic and Lucas know if they wanted to shoot their own and for those who did, the two men had personally carried those guns from the outbuilding to the shooting area. Under the guise of maintaining order, Caleb had taken each firearm and placed it alongside the house guns on one of the two racks Mark had brought out. This way, people were at least kept from wandering around with weapons. He still didn't like it, but with Vic and Lucas keeping an eye on things from the veranda, Mark monitoring the ammunition, and him watching the racks and shooters, it was better than the original hunting plan.

Dixie's laughter brought his head around. She was warming up her hands over one of the fire pits Cate and her staff had set up on the stone veranda. No one was allowed to drink and shoot, but Dixie didn't really need to drink to find a lot to laugh about. Ensconced in chairs on the other side of the fire from Dixie were Agnes, Sebastian, and Edward—the elders. Agnes was the only one partaking in the refreshments Greg had offered around; she sat bundled up in a blanket, sipping a hot toddy, and scowling at whatever had made Dixie laugh. Even seeing that that scowl, Caleb was relatively sure that the wayward niece was actually her favorite.

Beside his sister, Edward sat upright in his chair with a wool blanket folded over his lap and a tweed flat cap on his head. He didn't appear to be enjoying himself, but that came as no surprise. Sebastian, on the other hand, looked relaxed as he smiled at something said to him by his daughter, Erica, who stood beside him.

At the sound of the trap launching the pigeon, Caleb turned back to watch Isiah raise his rifle and fired. The clay disk shattered. Livia cheered and drew a little mark on the chalkboard beside Isiah's name. The family had agreed that they'd each have the chance to shoot twelve clay pigeons in a row and that for each one hit, they'd get a mark. The top four shooters would then have a second round, then the top two from that group would have a shoot-off to determine the best shot.

So far, with Sabrina, Anthony, Dixie, Alex, and now Isiah finished shooting, Isiah was in the lead with a score of eleven. With a smile on his face, Isiah handed the rifle back to Caleb, who checked it then returned it to the rack.

Nico, their next shooter, moved toward Caleb. Having traveled from Italy, he hadn't brought his own gun, so needed to borrow one of the house's shotguns. As he'd been doing all morning, Caleb checked the barrel and the essential parts before passing it to Mark, who loaded two cartridges into the chamber and handed the weapon to Nico. He happily acted the part of negligent playboy, but Nico could certainly shoot straight, managing to hit all twelve. In true playboy form, he laughed it off, complaining that now he would have to wait another round before being allowed to drink.

Edith approached Caleb next, Michael at her side.

"She needs to use that one," Michael said, pointing to one the two guns he'd brought. "She's only been shooting a few times and that's the only one she's ever handled."

Caleb pulled out the bolt-action rifle and examined it as he had the others. As he handed it over to Mark he felt a tug in his gut at not being able to do a more thorough examination before letting her shoot it, but the look Michael gave him told him it wasn't an option.

"Are you sure she shouldn't try one of the ones that's already been fired?" Caleb asked. Then at least they'd know she'd be shooting a gun that had already been proven safe.

"No," Michael said firmly. "It's been locked in in the safe since we arrived and, given it's the only one she has experience with, it's the best option."

Caleb wasn't so sure, but he inclined his head, acknowledging Michael's preference, then nodded to Mark, who handed the loaded rifle to Edith. After watching closely as she checked the weapon and flipped the safety off, Caleb's eyes swung to Lucas and Vic, standing on the veranda keeping an eye on the rest of the family, watching for any odd behavior. As Edith stepped into position, Caleb scanned the veranda. Anthony and Alex stood with their backs to the rest of the family, talking to Christine, who stood just inside the house. The rest of the Whatleys were either sitting in the chairs Cate had brought out or were warming their hands by one of the fires.

Edith called for the trap to launch the clay pigeon and Caleb's gut tightened. This wasn't a good idea. His skin began to crawl as he watched Edith raise the gun, following the pigeon's climb into the sky.

Only a shot didn't follow.

Edith lowered the gun and paused. Caleb's watched her closely, hoping she'd change her mind about shooting that day and he could relax just a touch.

But no, she just laughed. "It surprised me, I couldn't get an eye on it."

Michael smiled and touched her shoulder in support. "Remember to track ahead of the disk as it rises, and don't forget to tuck the butt of the gun against your shoulder to help steady it."

She nodded, looked at the boxes, then took her position again. "Pull!"

The second pigeon flew into the air and Caleb watched as Edith raised the gun again. This time a shot rang out, echoing across the small valley.

And Edith fell.

CHAPTER 15

CALEB WAS AT HER SIDE almost before she hit the ground. He could hear the screams of other family members and knew they were swarming toward Edith, even with his attention focused on her as she lie prone on the cold October ground, blood pouring from a gaping head wound.

He whipped his sweatshirt off and pressed it against her head. He had no idea how bad the injury was, but Michael, now kneeling on her other side and crying out her name, did not need to see it.

Caleb felt for a pulse and, thankfully, found one—faint, but there. He scanned the crowd growing around him. "Greg!" he barked. "Call 9-1-1, now!" The young man froze for a moment, then pulled out his cell phone, even as he ran into the house, presumably toward a land line, should he need it.

"Lucas?"

"Here," Lucas answered, appearing at his side.

"The gun." He didn't need to say more than that. Lucas would know what to do.

"Got it."

"Vic? Mark?" They were both there. "Take the rest of the guns and lock them up with the ammunition. Go over all of it. Thoroughly."

"Caleb." Cate was beside him holding towels. He gave a pointed look at the stack of clean towels, then one toward Michael.

She seemed to understand his meaning and turned toward Michael with calm, compassionate eyes. "Michael, the ambulance will be here any minute. She's still with us and we're going to keep it that way. There's an excellent hospital just a short distance from here."

Caleb wasn't at all sure Edith was going to "stay with them," but Cate's attempt to distract Michael's attention from his girlfriend while Caleb switched out his now blood-soaked sweatshirt for the towels worked.

"Oh my god, it's all my fault," Michael said, turning back to Edith, gripping her hand, and bringing it to his lips.

"It's not your fault," Cate said soothingly.

"It is. Caleb didn't want her to use the gun. I insisted. I thought it would be safer, I thought it would be better. It's the only gun she's ever shot with." His words ran together, spurred on by grief, fear, and adrenaline. Caleb could sympathize. Michael had already watched one friend die. What was happening to him in this moment wasn't something Caleb would wish on anyone.

"I hear the sirens, Michael. They'll be here in just a few seconds," Caleb said, trying to keep his voice as calm as possible, even as he felt Edith's blood soaking through the towel and covering his fingers. He knew head wounds bled a lot and hoped that was the extent of it, that there wasn't anything more than blood seeping out.

The ambulance came into sight and, as Greg directed them to drive over the lawn, Cate moved to Michael's side. "We need to move out of the way, Michael. We need to let the paramedics do their job."

Michael's frenzied, panicked eyes shot to back Cate, but the confidence and surety he heard in her voice must have sunk in. He gave Edith's hand one more kiss then moved away as the paramedics jumped out of the ambulance.

Caleb watched as family members moved back to make room, but he didn't relinquish his position until an EMT was at his side and ready to take over. As soon as that was the case, Caleb moved away, grabbing one of the extra towels Cate had left on the ground. His hand was covered in blood. He didn't want to look at it and he doubted anyone else did either.

They all watched in silence as the EMTs went to work. Cate stayed by Michael's side until they loaded Edith onto a stretcher and moved to put her into the ambulance.

"I have to go with her," he said, moving toward the vehicle.

"They need to keep working on her," Cate said.

"I'll take you," Anthony said, stepping to his brother's side. Anthony was sheet white.

Then again, as Caleb scanned the group, they all looked, understandably, shaken. Even Agnes seemed without an opinion to share.

"I have my keys here already," Anthony said, taking his brother's arm. Michael nodded and began to follow Anthony, even as he tried to keep an eye on the ambulance as it maneuvered its way off the lawn.

"We'll follow you," Dixie said. "Luke is a doctor, he can help us understand anything the doctors tell us." Neither Dixie nor Luke waited for a response before they too headed to their car. Within a few minutes, all three vehicles were exiting the gates.

"Cate?" Caleb turned to find her beside him. There were so many people there, he wasn't sure what to do. He'd seen his fair share of gun wounds, but never in this kind of setting, a setting that was supposed to be safe and happy, and especially not with so many family members present.

"We'll take care of it," Cate said to him, sensing his discomfort. "You'll take care of the rest?" She gestured with her head to where Lucas stood, holding the remains of Michael's gun, the others having been taken away by Vic and Mark.

"Yes."

"Okay then." She stepped away and started directing her staff to help the family.

They jumped into action at her words and as Caleb and Lucas made their way to the ice house, the staff began ushering the elders inside and offering rides to anyone who wanted to head to the hospital.

"It's been tampered with," Lucas said, holding up the bolt

component of the gun as they came around to the back of the house. Under normal circumstances, it would be attached to the gun and would have teeth that, when properly loaded and locked, would lock the bullets in place before firing. This gun, however, didn't have any teeth. Or rather, it had two of the five it was supposed to have. The others appeared to have been seared off.

"Someone filed through the teeth just enough so that, when the she pulled the trigger, the locking mechanism failed and sent the bolt piece straight backward."

"Into her head," Lucas said grimly.

"I examined the gun before she fired it, how could I have missed that?"

They'd arrived at the ice house and as they entered Vic came from the direction of the outbuilding where the gun safes were located and joined them.

Lucas placed the rifle on the table, along with the remains the teeth that had detached from the gun when Edith had fired, and the three men stared at the mess.

"The mechanism is black," Lucas pointed out. Then he reached forward and rubbed a fingertip over where one of the teeth should have been. He pulled it away and rubbed it against his thumb. "Grease," he said, holding his finger up to show them the black substance. "Whoever did this probably filed most of the way through the teeth then filled the gap with grease. Unless you'd had the opportunity to take the gun apart, you probably never would have noticed."

Caleb wasn't so sure about that. There was some truth to Lucas's statement, but he couldn't help feeling that if he'd run his fingers over the teeth, he would have felt the ridge where it had been filed. "We need to call the police," he said.

"They'll be here without you calling them if you want to buy yourself some time with that," Vic said with a nod to the gun. Caleb glanced up in question. "The hospital is required to report gunshot wounds to the police. They'll report it, then the police will come to check into it. I'm not saying you *shouldn't* report it, just that the police will get involved one way or another."

Caleb turned to Lucas for his opinion. Vic was the chief of police in the small town the couple now lived in, but Lucas, as a former homicide detective, had the most experience.

"I think you should call them. With everything else going on, this," Lucas said, indicating the gun and its parts that lay on the table before them, "needs to get bagged as evidence and taken in for processing as soon as possible. If you think Edward is involved, they need to know that too. I no longer have jurisdiction and though Vic might be able to pull a brotherhood type of card, if it's time to start arresting people, or at least begin an official investigation, we need to bring the local team in."

"I agree," Vic said.

"Okay then, let's do it." Caleb made the phone call himself, answered as many questions as he could succinctly as he could, and, after he'd hung up, texted Cate to let her know the police would be arriving shortly.

Once she'd texted back that she'd received his message, he slipped the phone back into his pocket and eyed all the files he'd collected. "Well, gentlemen, how do you feel about helping me sort through some of this stuff before they get here?"

• • •

Caleb sat in one of the upholstered chairs and stared into the flames. It was nearing ten p.m. and he hadn't seen Cate since the accident that morning. The police had come and gone long ago. They'd been none too pleased that they hadn't been called in sooner, though the lead detective's hostility had wavered for a moment when she'd discovered that Vivi had done the processing and testing of the evidence Caleb had collected so far. Vivi was the kind of resource the local police never would have had access to without Lucas, Vic, and Caleb, so while she had glared at each of them every chance she'd gotten, she had stopped haranguing them once they'd handed over Vivi's reports.

And as soon as he'd handed over everything else—all the background checks, all the histories, all his own notes—she and the two other officers who'd accompanied her had promptly departed the ice house and spent the rest of the afternoon in the main house. Caleb had been told to stay put and, deciding that obedience would serve him better under the circumstances, he'd spent the rest of the afternoon combing through the copies he'd made of everything he'd just turned over to the detective.

Cate had kept him in the loop as to what was going on in the main house, as had Lucas and Vic, both of whom the local detective had allowed to accompany her, so long as they didn't speak. But as the afternoon had worn on, Cate's texts had shifted from updating him on the investigation to updating him on how the staff were coping with the family, and he had decided that he didn't need to 'stay put' any longer. Wanting to avoid adding to the chaos of the main house, he'd gone to the carriage house and joined Elise and Jana for dinner, then, after Elise had had her bath and he'd cleaned up the kitchen, he'd spent some time reading to her before she'd gone to bed.

But now he was back in his room, alone with nothing but his thoughts, and wondering if Cate was going to join him. Her most recent text had said that she was just locking up for the night, but she hadn't indicated if she was coming to see him or not. He set the now empty glass of port he'd been drinking on the side table and let out a long exhale. Twenty-four hours earlier, he wouldn't have let himself even consider the possibility that she'd show up for the night. Now, he more than considered it, he craved it.

Running a hand through his hair, he rose, deciding to prepare for bed. Cate had Elise to think of; just because she'd been able to sneak away once didn't mean she could, or would, do it again. Having turned off all the lights but one of the bedside lamps, he pulled the blinds at the front of the room, brushed his teeth, and he pulled his shirt off. He was just unbuttoning his jeans when the front door opened.

His hands stilled as Cate's eyes caught his.

She shut the door behind her and set her keys down on the kitchen counter.

"How are you?" he asked. It had been one hell of a day for her.

"I'll be fine." She stepped into the bedroom area, stopping at the foot of the bed, not quite close enough for him to reach her.

"Any news on Edith?" He wondered if Cate had any idea what it did to him to have her looking at him the way she was looking at him.

"Still in ICU, but upgraded from critical to stable."

"That's good." The conversation was starting to get tedious, but he didn't want to assume she'd come for the reasons that he hoped she'd come.

"I heard you spent the evening with Elise?" She removed her jacket and a wave of anticipation crashed through him. She was dressed, but wearing the same tank top she'd worn the night before, the one she seemed to like to wear to bed.

"I did. I figured you'd been so busy all day that she might like to see another friendly face. Especially given all the chaos."

"Thank you, that was very thoughtful."

He frowned, he hadn't really thought of it as being thoughtful. It was just something he'd wanted to do. Both for him and Elise. "How did you know? Jana told you?"

She smiled and held her phone up in answer. At his questioning look, she punched in her security code, hit a few more buttons, then took the last few steps that brought her to his side. She held up the device for him to see. On the screen was an image of him sitting on Elise's bed with Elise curled up under his arm. He held a book on his lap as Elise, wearing her characteristic serious expression, was pointing to something on one of the pages. Caleb remembered that she'd been explaining how elephant families live together as they looked at a picture of a mother and daughter elephant pair.

"She's pretty damned cute," he said, smiling at the photo.

Cate's lips quirked. "I think this *photo* is pretty damned cute." She shut the phone off and reached behind him to put it on the bedside table. When she straightened their eyes locked and he studied her.

"Are you tired?"

She held his gaze for a long moment before a small, impish smile hinted on her lips. "Not really, no. You?"

"Not in the least," he said, sliding his arms around her and bringing his mouth down to hers.

An hour and a half later, they lay in the dark of the room, naked and sated. The flames from the fire caused shadows to dance on the walls and ceiling and in the light, Caleb lay on his side, tracing the line of Cate's bare back. By her breathing, he could tell she was in that space between sleep and wakefulness. Although he wanted her to drift off into her dreams, he had every intention of enjoying the night himself.

"Can't sleep?" Cate murmured, turning her head against the pillow to look at him.

"Just enjoying the view." He ran a fingertip down her spine as she smiled, eyes closed. "You should go to sleep, though. I know you're tired."

He bent down and brushed his lips across her shoulder blades. "It's rather hard to go to sleep when you're giving my body all sort of ideas."

"Just your body?"

"I'll admit, my mind is a bit too tired to get very creative right now."

He ran his hand over her curves, down the back of her thigh, and slid his palm between her legs. "Why don't you let me take care of your body, then?"

Cate's eyes opened slowly, even as she raised her hips to give him better access. "You'll just take care of me?"

He nodded and, to prove his sincerity, stroked her gently.

"And what about you?" she said on a sigh.

"There's plenty of time for me when you're less tired."

Her eyes closed and a quiet moan of anticipation escaped her as she lifted her hips again. "I'll most certainly give you a rain check."

"I'll hold you to it," he said, leaning over her, making it more difficult for her to move. "Just let me," he whispered in her ear. And as she acquiesced, he showed just how it good it could be if she let him, at least on occasion, control and worship her body.

• • •

Caleb walked Cate to the carriage house in the early hours of the morning, after she'd made good on her rain check and then some. Once he'd seen her safely inside, he hit the trails. Like the day before, there was very little for him to do, so starting the day with some physical activity—followed by a run—seemed like the most productive way to burn off his energy. His feet pounded the frost-frozen trail as he wound through the forest. It was the darkest hour before dawn when he'd started, but thirty minutes into his run, sunlight was starting to filter through the trees and light the trails, allowing him to pick up his pace and push himself.

As his body fell into a new rhythm, he tried to keep his mind focused on his breathing. Only his mind wasn't cooperating. The police would undoubtedly arrest Edward in the next day or two, and then his reason for being at The Washington House would disappear. Even if he decided to stay the rest of the reunion, there was only less than a week left. What would he do next?

He could always go to Florida—at least for a little while, or maybe every now and then. He didn't want to assume that Cate would want him around too much and, if he was being honest with himself, he had to admit that what she'd said to him the other night out in the cold about Tommy did need some time to sink in. Yes, he knew he wanted to be with Cate, but that didn't mean that everything he'd felt, everything he'd believed about himself over past five years suddenly went away with her magic words. No, he needed time to truly come to terms with it. Which didn't mean *not* seeing Cate, just maybe not jumping in headfirst.

He slowed his gait to a jog then, a half mile later, moved into a walk. He was approaching the trees where the wire had been strung and, like a moth to a flame, wanted to take another look.

The scarring caused by the thick metal was still visible on the trunks of both trees and probably would be for several years to come. Caleb reached up to touch it. It wouldn't tell him any secrets, but he felt the need, regardless. With his arm raised, he realized just how high the wire had been strung, at least eight feet off the ground. His brow furrowed as he circled around the tree where the ladder to the deer blind was nailed to the trunk. He tested the rungs and took a few steps up. He hadn't been able to do that the day he'd been out with Elise, but now that he was up he realized how hard it actually would have been to string the wire.

Edward would have had to reach both arms around the trunk to wrap the wire around enough times to keep it in place upon impact, not to mention what he would have had to do to the ends to keep them anchored. All in all, it was no small feat and, as Vivi said, rather dramatic.

Feeling a niggling sense that he was missing something, Caleb climbed down the ladder and continued to make his way back to the house at a pace slow enough to let his mind think things through better. But by the time he reached the main grounds he was no more enlightened than he had been fifteen minutes earlier. Feeling frustrated with himself, he jumped into the shower and decided to head to the main house for the day to let Cate put him to work.

• • •

As he'd predicted, the police did indeed show up. Agnes remained with him in the upstairs library as he tried to figure out new and inventive ways to lose to the elderly woman at chess, but the other family members gathered downstairs. How the news of the police's arrival had spread so quickly he hadn't a clue, but as he listened to their murmured voices and footsteps on the parquet floor, it was easy for him to imagine the scene downstairs as the lead detective and her two officers were besieged by Whatleys.

"It's all a bunch of poppycock, I tell you," Agnes said, moving one of her knights into a particularly vulnerable position.

"What? Finding out who tampered with that gun and tried to kill Edith?" He flicked his gaze up to the older woman's face, curious to see her reaction.

She only pursed her lips. "It was Michael's gun, and he was just as present as Edith for all those horrible events you so willfully kept us ignorant of."

Caleb dropped his eyes back to the board. "Yes, but there is someone with a strong motive to want Edith dead."

"Edward? That's nonsense. He wouldn't hurt a fly. Much too soft, that brother of mine. That's why he was never chosen to run the family business. Get me a glass of whiskey."

He looked back up at her from under his brows.

She scowled. "Please."

He rose, leaving the chessboard behind. He was nearly certain that when he returned it would look nothing like it had when he'd gotten up. He poured her a glass, smelled it, then walked it back. The staff had been keeping an eye on all the liquor, but now that he knew what moonseed smelled like, he couldn't help but check it himself before passing it to the old lady.

"It was my understanding that the reason he didn't join the family business was because he didn't want to."

"Didn't have the chops," Agnes corrected raising her glass.

"He's hardly a slouch. He was a tenured professor in humanities at one of the best colleges in the world."

"A pussy job."

Caleb blinked. By now he'd come to expect just about anything and everything from Agnes, but that word had thrown him off. He cleared his throat and refocused on the board. Funny, she was missing another pawn now.

"So, if you don't think your brother is responsible or that Edith is the target, what *do* you think?" The one good thing about everything coming out into the open was that it was easier to talk to the family about all the skeletons in their closets. In fact, they'd all been more than happy to waylay him at various times throughout the day to air dirty laundry.

The only thing he'd heard that had actually given him pause concerned Livia Whatley's weekend trips. It turned out that the trips he had originally thought could be evidence of her infidelity were actually weekend getaways she had planned with her husband. It was their *thing*. Once a month, Livia found a new place for them to visit together and she managed all the details. The reason the information had given Caleb pause was not because he'd found it suspect, but rather because he'd found it fairly sweet. Especially when he'd commented to Livia how nice it must be for them to enjoy the time together and she'd replied that sometimes the most valuable trips she and Isiah had were ones where they weren't so much enjoying each other, but were committed to trying.

"You're not listening, boy," Agnes chided. "You may have a pretty face and look like the statue of David, but your brain seems to have gotten the shaft."

Caleb took a deep breath.

"You think Michael is the target."

"Give the boy a medal."

"And why do you think Michael is the target?" he asked, trying to hide his impatience by sounding overly patient.

Her eyes narrow at him. "Have you even *looked* into his life? There are probably dozens of ex-husbands, ex-girlfriends, former friends . . . that he's screwed over."

"Do you like *any* of your nieces or nephews?"

She opened her mouth then snapped it shut. With a sniff, she drew herself up. "I rather like Dixie. The only one with spirit, really. Gets it from her father, of course."

"Of course she does." Because she couldn't possibly get a good trait from anyone without Whatley blood.

"But that's not the point. I'm just saying, and you mark my words, Michael is a trouble maker. Always has been and always will be. Oh, he's charming as a snake and never seems to get into trouble, always talking his way out of things. That kind of behavior over a long period of time can create some nasty karma."

Caleb made a move on the board that he hoped would cost him the game then turned his attention back to Agnes. "You believe in karma?" Over his dead body.

Once again, her eyes narrowed. "No, of course I don't believe in karma. A man makes or breaks his own future. But *Michael* seems to be believing in that poppycock these past few years. Always going on about making up for past sins and seeking forgiveness. It's all rather dull, really."

Yes, he imagined someone trying to live a good life would be boring to Agnes. He was about to reply when Cate announced her presence with a knock on the doorframe, then entered. "Everything okay?" he asked her with a subtle gesture of his head to the foyer.

"They are questioning Edward again in the downstairs office and have asked if you would like to join them."

"Yes, he would," Agnes interjected.

He shot her a scowl. "I'm capable of answering myself, Agnes."

"That's Ms. Whatley, to you."

"Then, Ms. Whatley, I'm capable of answering on my own, thank you. Now, if you'll excuse me. And, by the way, you just won." He gestured toward the board with his head. She whipped hers down and then, after a quick scan, let out a small gasp.

"You cheated," she said as he moved toward Cate.

"I followed the rules you set."

"What rules? I didn't set any rules."

"Exactly," he called back over his shoulder, making Cate laugh.

"Does she honestly try to prove how good she is by trying to get you to win?" Cate asked as they made their way down the stairs.

"I'm not sure 'honestly' is the word I'd use, but knowing how to maneuver your enemy into any position is a show of skill. There might also be some warped psychology in this circumstance, too."

"So, really, you're showing a better mastery of the board by being able to outmaneuver her maneuvers, even if you lose?"

They hit the foyer where a few family members still lingered about, casting glances at the closed office door. "It's not really losing, is it? Agnes and I redefined the game we chose to play. So, in losing, I'm actually winning."

"And what would happen if you just decided to *win* win, the traditional way?" she asked, pausing outside the door to the office.

"I'd be changing the game on her. She might feel momentarily triumphant, but once she realized that I'd changed the game and her 'loss' wasn't really a 'win,' I imagine, with Agnes, it would be all out war."

Cate let out a huff of a laugh. "Yes, I can see that. It's a good thing she's so old, because her mind is definitely diabolical enough to be behind everything that's been going on, even if her body isn't. Ready?"

He nodded as she knocked on the door then opened it. She gave his arm a gentle squeeze as he entered the room, then he heard the door shut behind him. Lucas, Vic, the lead detective, and her two officers all sat on one side of the room. And a very nervous Edward sat alone on the other.

CHAPTER 16

"HE SAYS HE'LL ONLY TALK to you," Cara Hanley, the lead detective, said.

"Didn't you all talk yesterday?" Caleb asked, directing his question to both the detective and the man sitting on the leather sofa by himself. Edward stared out the window, but the way his head was cocked told Caleb he was listening.

"Yes, but something has changed his mind," Detective Hanley replied.

"Mr. Whatley, I'm happy to talk to you, but I don't really understand why it's me you want to talk to. This is a police matter," Caleb said, walking over the window and into Edward's line of sight.

Edward, with his legs crossed and his hands folded in his lap, studied Caleb the way someone might study a piece of art if unsure whether it was true genius or complete junk. After a few beats, Edward leaned forward. "I'll speak to you because, despite the fact that you're engaging in a rather sinful relationship with Ms. Thomson, certain members of my family seem to like you."

Caleb glanced at Lucas, who raised an eyebrow in return. It seemed the Whatley siblings were quite something. Caleb wondered what dear old mom and dad had been like to produce children like Agnes and Edward.

"I barely know your family."

Edward inclined his head, as if to say, "Of course you don't, you're a servant." Instead, he said, "Be that as it may, Livia believes you're trustworthy."

"You don't even like Livia," Caleb pointed out.

The old man responded with a disappointed look that Caleb was quite certain any number of Edward's students had witnessed over the years. "Whether I like her or not has nothing to do with whether or not she's a good judge of character. Her ability is a fact, my disposition toward her is nothing but my opinion."

Yes, Caleb would have loved to have met mama and papa Whatley. "So, what do you want to talk about, Edward?"

"How should I know? These people," Edward gestured toward Detective Hanley and her officers, "brought me in here. I suspect it has to do with what's been happening to Edith." At the mention of her name, Edward's eyes raised slightly and he blinked. Remorse maybe? Perhaps he was preparing to lie?

"Are you trying to kill Edith?" The tactic had its risks, but with that tiny chink in Edward's armor exposed, Caleb had to take advantage of the opportunity.

Edward inhaled swiftly and drew back in his seat. "Is that what this is about? Do you really think I'm trying to kill Edith?"

"Are you?" Caleb pushed.

Edward's gaze and stance hardened. "No, I am not. I'm not sure anyone is trying to kill Edith, but I think I'd like my lawyer here before I say any more."

Caleb felt the energy in the room shift. The police, including Vic and Lucas, smelled blood. Caleb studied Edward's face and wasn't so sure. His blue eyes were as hard and cold as ice. But they were open. Not just physically, but emotionally. No, Caleb would bet that Edward wasn't going to hide anything he knew, but it was anyone's guess as to when he'd decide to reveal whatever knowledge he held.

• • •

Much later that night, Caleb stood in the kitchen as Greg handed him a pot to dry. The house had been thrown into a frenzy for a second time that day when Detective Hanley had arrested Edward

Whatley for suspicion of attempted murder. After the chaos had died down, Caleb had offered to stay in the main house for the rest of the day to help the staff, giving Cate a chance to spend time with Elise.

Edward still wasn't talking and didn't seem to mind too much that he'd be spending the night in a jail until his lawyer arrived. Agnes had offered to bail her brother out, but Edward had told her not to bother, adding that he wouldn't mind a night away from the family.

Edward's certainty and lack of drama had frustrated the police and they hadn't formally arrested him until several hours after the conversation in the office. Caleb had found Edward's response interesting as well, although he wasn't sure he agreed with Detective Hanley's assessment that Edward's calm acceptance of the situation was due to the fact that he believed his lawyer would be able to get the charges dismissed. It wasn't an altogether unfounded thought. Most of the evidence was circumstantial and any good lawyer would be able to poke more holes in it than a sieve. Still, Detective Hanley had seemed to think arresting him now was worth the risk in the hopes that the elderly man might have a visit from his conscience after spending a night in jail.

Caleb wasn't so sure the night in jail would be anything more than Edward had said, a night away from his family. So he was glad he'd spent the day moving around the house, helping the staff, and taking every chance he'd had to talk to any family member who showed interest.

He hadn't learned much about Edward other than that his late wife had been adored by everyone and no one had any idea how Edward had landed her. He heard, during more than one conversation, how bitter Edward had become since she'd died. The general consensus was that Edward was a truly unlikeable man; however, no one believed he had it in him to kill Edith, even *after* they heard about the death of Summer Granger.

Caleb dried the pot and hung it on the rack as he mulled over the family's response. Could so many people be wrong about

Edward? He knew the answer was a resounding yes. Well, to be more precise, he knew people could be fooled by others very easily, especially when the truth wasn't something they wanted to see. And who wanted to admit to having a murderer in the family?

No, it wasn't unusual that Edward's nearest and dearest, such as they were, didn't believe him to be guilty. Still, something about their response to his arrest was niggling at Caleb and it was making him crazy that he couldn't put a finger on it.

"I think it's strange, don't you?" Greg interrupted Caleb's thoughts with the question as he handed him the last pot to dry.

"What's that?"

"That he would pick all those weird ways to try to kill someone. Have you *seen* his medicine cabinet?"

Caleb stared at Greg. "Maybe the medication he uses wouldn't do the job." In his mind, Caleb ran through the bottles he'd seen in Edward's bathroom, recalling the names, and uses, of each.

Greg snorted. "Take a look yourself. If you haven't already. I'm not an expert, but it's filled with pain killers and anti-depressants and a whole bunch of other things I didn't recognize. It just seems like some combination of those would have done the job better than a snake. Or a beheading."

"Why were you in his cabinet in the first place?" Although of course he'd done the same, Caleb didn't like the idea of Cate's staff snooping. It wasn't really any of his concern, but he thought she might like to know if they were. But there was something to be said for Greg's theory. Individually, the medicines Caleb had seen hadn't raised any alarm bells, but collectively? Well, that was something he'd ask Vivi about.

"It wasn't what you think," Greg said, leaning against the counter. "I was in the room one day, changing out the flowers for Christine, when he came in. He'd been on a walk and had fallen or slipped or something like that. I offered to call a doctor, but he just asked me to grab his bottle of painkillers from the bathroom. I watched him take one then he stripped to his boxers and climbed into bed. We didn't see him again until dinner."

"When was that? Do you remember?"

Greg thought as he turned to wipe down the counter. "I'm pretty sure it was the day the Italian cousins arrived. No, it was definitely that day." He finished with the counter, folded the dish towel, and hung it on the oven. "I remember now, because he didn't come downstairs to greet them the way everyone else did. Even Agnes came down."

So, Edward had been out tromping the grounds the day before the whiskey had been poisoned. The police had gone through his room with a fine-toothed comb that afternoon, looking for evidence. Caleb wondered if they'd found any trace of moonseed—not that they'd tell him. Maybe they'd told Vic, though.

Caleb glanced at the clock on the wall. It was after ten o'clock, his question for Vic could wait. "You good here?" he asked Greg with a vague gesture toward the rest of the house. They could hear the rumble of a few voices coming from one of the game rooms, but Caleb thought most of the family members were in their rooms by now.

Greg waved him off as he knelt down to check on the alcohol Cate had locked in the cupboard—with only two keys, one for Cate and one for Greg, one or the other of them was always on duty when it came to making sure the house stayed well stocked.

"Yeah, go on. I'm just going to check the situation in the pool room, then I'll head upstairs. When the house is quiet, I'll do my final rounds. Vic and Lucas came with me last night. I wouldn't be surprised if they joined me again."

Caleb thanked him, then promised to be back to help in the morning, as he pulled on his hat and stepped out into the cold. The porch light was on at the carriage house, but it had been a long day for Cate. If she was sleeping, he didn't want to wake her. So he made his way, with measured steps, toward the ice house, breathing in the sharp air. He liked the way it felt flowing in and out of his lungs, clearing his head and stinging his face. It made him feel alive and grateful to be so.

Of course, there were a few other things that made him feel

grateful to be alive, and finding Cate in his bed when he returned his room definitely topped that list.

• • •

Late the next morning, Caleb stepped into the local police department and glanced around for Detective Hanley.

"Can I help you?" a young man at the reception desk asked.

"He's with me," the detective said, coming from a room to Caleb's left. The department's building was surprisingly big, considering the relatively rural area. She led him up a set of stairs, down a couple of hallways, then stopped in front of a closed door. "Thank you for coming."

Caleb almost smiled. He'd bet that she hadn't wanted him there at all. He'd bet that when Edward had continued to refuse to speak to anyone but him, her superior officer had "suggested" that she comply. He'd also bet that Edward's desire to speak only to Caleb was more a matter of power than anything else—he would take every opportunity he could to showcase the dominance of the Whatley family.

"Is he in there?" Caleb nodded to the closed door.

"Yes, as is his lawyer. Who came from Boston this morning bearing several books."

"Books?"

"Books. What kind, I don't know. He won't show them to anyone but you."

Books were a strange thing to bring to an attempted-murder investigation, but then again, this entire investigation was strange, so maybe Edward was just keeping up.

"Shall I?" He gave the door a meaningful look.

Detective Hanley's jaw clenched as she glared at him then, after a long pause, stepped aside.

"We'll be watching from the observation room, and I'll have an officer posted outside the door as well."

"In case Edward lunges across the table at me?" He didn't stop the twitch of his lips from growing into an actual smile.

"It's just protocol," she bit out.

He laughed. "Fine. Now, may I?"

She eyed him one last time, then stepped aside. As he turned the knob and opened the door, he heard her calling for an officer to stay posted by the door. When it closed behind him the two men in the room looked up. Edward sat at the table with his lawyer, a man so thin as to be gaunt—so thin that Caleb was certain he could see the man's bones as he held a pen in his left hand to jot something down.

"Mr. Forrester," Edward said.

"Mr. Whatley." Caleb took a seat at the table opposite Edward and his lawyer.

"This is my attorney, Rupert Hardgreaves."

The man gave a jerk of his head, which Caleb assumed was supposed to be some sort of acknowledgement, then started to stack some of the books Detective Hanley had mentioned. Hardgreaves placed four leather-bound volumes on top of each other, each about two inches thick, and slid them in front of Caleb.

"What are these?"

"These are my journals, Mr. Forrester." Edward reached across the table, picked one up, and handed it to Caleb as he spoke. "I'm a prolific journal writer. I always have been."

"And what are these journals for?"

"Open that one to the page I've marked."

Caleb's gaze dropped down to the book in his hand as he opened the front cover. The handwritten date indicated that the content of the journal covered a nearly eighteen-month period twenty years earlier. As directed, he flipped to the page Edward had dog-eared and began to read.

"Two children. Gone. Today our Summer was taken from us and writing these words is the way to make it real. Because it doesn't feel real. I don't believe she won't ever walk through our door again. I don't

believe we won't ever hear her laugh again. I don't believe that all those little hopes we had for her future won't ever happen.

"She was not in the best condition when she was killed. The friend who brought the news tried to be delicate about it, tried not to tarnish her death with anything more ugly than it already was. But the truth came out. She'd been trying so hard to stay sober, but she'd fallen. Fallen so far that her friend was fairly certain, had the incident never happened, had Summer walked home instead of into the middle of a street, that the day would have been lost in a haze of blackout for her anyway. Only now, her blackout is permanent, and in her descent she has no doubt scarred another young soul. Seventeen. That's how old the driver was. A young girl, obeying the rules of traffic, doing everything she was supposed to be doing.

"And yet she has played a part in another's death. I think it's possible the world might have lost two young souls today. I only hope that poor girl does not take this tragedy upon herself. It was not her fault. She was yet another victim of Summer's addictions."

Caleb looked up from the page.

Edward sat so still across from him, as if the raw pain the journal carried might crawl from its pages and drag him back to those few days after the death of Summer Granger.

Rupert Hardgreaves gestured to the next book in the stack. It lay open to a page, but Caleb flipped to the cover to see the dates. This book covered a two-year period about nine years earlier. Turning back to the page, Caleb proceeded to read about Edward and his wife's pleasure when they'd heard about the success of a local therapeutic riding program just west of Boston. Run primarily by a PhD student, the program helped teens and returning veterans who had been diagnosed with PTSD. The trust of the animals, and the responsibility of their care, had been helping those involved in the program work through some of their trauma. The PhD student who ran it was named Edith Barnard. Caleb read how Edward and his wife had not only been pleased that Edith had found a way to manage the trauma Summer's death had no doubt caused her, but also impressed that she had then opened her arms and offered help to others.

"And then there's this," Hardgreaves said.

Caleb set the journal down and reached for the small stack of documents offered to him. But as his hand closed around them, Edward's hand came down on them, halting the transfer.

"These are confidential, Mr. Forrester," Edward said.

"I can't promise that. This is an investigation."

Edward's blue eyes held his. "Hardgreaves has already succeeded in having the charges dropped against me. Their evidence is circumstantial, at best, and I think we both know there won't be any physical evidence."

"Then why bother bringing me in? Why not just walk out?"

"Because, as much as my family, such as they are, may not be my cup of tea, I have no interest in having them dance around me thinking I'm a murderer with a good lawyer. I want them to know I had nothing to do with it. I also want to keep these," he said with a wave to the books and materials on the table between them, "private. My thoughts and feelings and actions are not for them to know, unless I decide otherwise. Telling you, convincing you, is my way of indirectly providing them the reassurances I have no interest in providing directly."

"You think that if you convince me that you're innocent, I'll be able to convince them?"

"I have no doubt that will be the case."

"I think you're giving me too much credit when it comes to your family's perceptions."

"I think you're giving them too much credit when it comes to their ability to care. You see, most of them don't actually *care* if I'm guilty or innocent, or at least not enough to examine the evidence or the situation thoroughly. They just want to be *told* I'm innocent, then they will happily get on with their lives. The police won't do that. You will."

Caleb drew back at the certainty of the statement—not because of what it implied about the family, but because of what it implied about Edward. No, the family didn't care whether Edward was guilty or not, but the heart of the matter was that they didn't particularly care *about Edward*.

And though Caleb knew that, in large part, the situation was Edward's own doing, he couldn't help but feel some sympathy for the man. Possibly because a small part of Caleb knew how he felt. He knew the solitary, gaping loneliness that came after having pushed everything and everyone out of your life, the feelings of insignificance and unworthiness that were a part of that, and the darkness that hovered constantly on the edge of everything. It was a darkness so black and deep that only the sheer power of denial, denial of its very existence, could keep it at bay.

"I see."

"So, can I trust you to keep this confidential?"

Caleb knew Edward didn't just mean the documents he was about to see, but all of it—the pain, the doubt, the loss, and even the sympathy and concern for the young girl Edith had once been.

It wasn't his story to tell, so he nodded.

Edward lifted his hand from the documents and Caleb held them up to read. Slowly, he flipped through each of the four sheets. In just over ten years, Edward and, before she'd died, his wife, had donated more than five million dollars to Edith's therapeutic riding program. She no longer ran it, given that she now taught full time, but she was still an active board member for the thriving program that served hundreds of teens and vets each year. Thanks, in no small part, to the Whatleys' donations.

"There's an endowment set aside for the program, too."

Caleb raised his eyes from the documents, silently encouraging the man to continue.

"In my will. I have no children and my nieces and nephews have no need for my money. I've made donations to other organizations as well, of course, but there is a twenty-million-dollar bequeast in my will to be set up as an endowment for the program. They manage their finances well and the money we've donated in the past has helped them secure other funders. With the endowment, they shouldn't have to be concerned about their finances for a long while."

Edward may have been cold, and even harsh, but Caleb did not doubt, not even for a second, his sincerity in wanting to support not just Edith, but the way in which she'd turned such a tragic set of events into something that benefited so many others. Edward admired Edith, and in his way he was honoring her and protecting her through his support of a program that obviously meant so much to her.

"I see," Caleb said again.

"Do you?"

Caleb dipped his head in acknowledgement. He understood more than Edward would ever know.

"Then we're agreed? I did not try to kill Edith, nor do I have any intention remotely close to that?"

"Yes, we're agreed."

"And you'll let it be known?"

"Yes."

"Good, then I think we're done here?" Edward said, turning to his lawyer, who remained silent but began to gather all the journals and documents.

"Will you be returning to The Washington House?" Caleb asked as he rose from his seat.

"Yes." Edward also rose and donned his coat that had been hanging on the back of his chair. "Despite what you might think, I put a great deal of stock in my family relations and we still have several days remaining."

"And if you return to Boston, you likely won't receive any updates on Edith," Caleb said. A gentle tease to see if he could get the man to lighten up a little.

Edward glared at him then rolled his eyes slightly in an exasperated gesture. "My family is like a bunch of frightened hens—running around clucking at the rain, always talking but rarely saying anything of worth. Whatever chance I might have of getting even the tiniest bit of *useful* information out of them will drop to nil if I return to Boston."

Caleb smiled. "You heard she's out of ICU, then?"

Edward paused with his hand on the door and let out a grateful sigh. "Yes, I had heard that. Out of ICU and in stable condition. I'm having Hardgreaves take me to the hospital now that we're done here. I assume that she knows who I am now, and I believe the time has come to properly introduce myself."

Caleb watched as Edward and his lawyer exited the room. Edward wasn't quite the man he put himself out there to be, and a small part of Caleb hoped that when Edith talked to him, maybe, just maybe, she would be the one to break him from his shell by offering him some warmth and comfort. Of all the guests at The Washington House, if any of them could convince Edward to melt a little bit of his icy self, it would be Edith.

"What did he show you?" Detective Hanley demanded as she entered the room.

Caleb took a moment to study her. Focused, intense, and pissed that Edward had slipped through her fingers. He also suspected that she was fairly shallow in her ability to assess potential suspects and having one walk away now meant that she had to go back to the drawing board—an extremely inconvenient proposition. Of course, it meant *he* had to go back to the drawing board too.

"Well?" she barked.

"I'm not at liberty to say," he said as he headed down the hallway.

"What do you mean you're not at liberty to say? This is an attempted murder investigation," she said, catching up to him.

"And you heard me give my word that what I saw would remain private." He reached the stairs and started jogging down.

"I could arrest you for accessory after the fact."

He laughed. "You'd have to arrest him first to peg me as an accessory, and by all accounts, I hear your case fell apart." He didn't actually know if it had fallen apart, but it sounded better than saying Hardgreaves had poked holes in it.

"Then obstruction of justice," she said as he reached the front door.

"Or maybe I could file a complaint for harassment. Look, I know you're pissed he isn't your guy, and I don't like the idea that an attempted murderer is still out there, either. But *he isn't your guy*, and the longer you stand around arguing with me, the more time you're giving this other person to plan their next move."

She looked ready to throttle him, but rather than wait around to see what she might say or do next, he turned and left. He needed to get back to the house and uphold his end of the bargain he'd made with Edward.

• • •

When Cate passed by the door to the downstairs library, she saw Caleb talking with Livia and Dixie. His voice was pitched too low to hear what he was saying, but both women were listening intently. Her attention was so focused on the library that she all but jumped out of her skin when the house's front door opened. With her hand pressed against her heart, she watched Michael walk in, followed by Anthony. Both men paused when they saw her, then their eyes traveled to the library doorway.

"Is he telling them?" Michael asked.

Cate's brows dropped. "Telling them?"

"About Edward?"

Her eyes darted back to the library. Caleb had texted her that he had something to tell her, but she hadn't had a chance to talk to him since he'd returned. She had no idea what had happened or what he was telling Dixie and Livia. "I don't know."

As Michael let out a big sigh, his shoulders sagged and he seemed to deflate in on himself. He hadn't left Edith's side since the accident and the circles under his eyes, stark against his pale complexion, attested to his exhaustion.

"Can I get you anything?" Cate asked, walking over to take both men's coats. Christine, appearing just then, took the coats from Cate and hung them in the coat closet.

"Coffee? Something to eat?" Christine chimed in over her shoulder.

Michael, too tired to answer, looked to Anthony, who stepped forward and put a hand on his brother's shoulder. "Why don't you have some coffee and eat something, then you can shower and have a rest. It's been a long few days."

Michael nodded just as Caleb and the two women exited the library. Immediately, Dixie and Livia came to comfort Michael.

"Why don't you take him into the breakfast room? We'll have some food brought in," Cate said to Anthony. When he agreed and began to usher the three out of the foyer, she glanced at Christine, who gave her a quick little salute and headed to the kitchen to talk to Margaret

"What was that about? Something about Edward?" Cate asked Caleb, who had walked over to stand before her. It had been rather presumptuous of her to show up in his bed the night before, but she felt that if she didn't remind him of what it felt like to be together—sexually or not—he'd have the opportunity to draw back and reflect on what they were doing. And, coward that she was, she wasn't prepared to face any explanation other than what they were doing was right or good. She didn't want to hear regrets or doubts.

She knew that eventually they'd both need to truly accept what they were doing together, given their past. She just wanted to give their future, whatever it may be, a better chance, and she knew the only way to do that was to keep those doubts and questions from gaining a hold of either of them for too long. They needed to be stronger before they tackled those. She just hoped Caleb felt the same way. Or if not exactly the same, that he was at least willing to travel the path she was setting for them.

"Let's talk in the office." He didn't wait for her response, moving past her and into the room on the other side of foyer.

Her heart stuttered for a moment, wondering if this was going to be "the talk," but just as quickly, reason told her not to jump to conclusions. Just because she had been thinking about their relationship didn't mean he had been doing the same. With so many things going on, it was likely he would just want to catch her up on the investigation.

Or, as she discovered, he didn't really want to talk at all. The moment she entered the room, he grabbed hold of her arm, locked the door behind her, and sank his hands into her hair as his mouth descended on hers. She knew it wasn't a prelude to sex—it was simply a kiss, a connection, a primal touch—and she wrapped her arms around his neck to pull him closer. He dropped one hand from her hair, ran it down her spine, and splayed it across her lower back, pressing her into him.

After several intense moments, she felt him draw back slowly until, finally, her head rested against his chest and his cheek on her head. He kept one hand in her hair, massaging her neck, and the other on her lower back, but hers had dropped from his shoulders to wrap around his waist.

"I know I probably shouldn't do things like that while you're working, but, well," he paused. "Well, I just needed to."

Cate smiled against his chest. "I think I might have needed it too." They stayed like that a while longer, enjoying the feel of each other, until voices in the hall brought them back.

"So, what is this about Edward?" she asked, stepping out of his arms. His hand slid from her neck and down her arm before he lost contact all together. The kind of regret she saw in his eyes was the kind she was okay with. But he gathered himself in, took a breath and told her what Edward had shown him at the police station. They sank down onto the sofa together as he talked and though he made it clear that no one else was to know about the journals or the donations, or really anything other than that Edward was unquestioningly *not* involved in the attempts on Edith's life, she listened in astonishment at the depth of character Edward kept hidden.

When Caleb finished talking, she stared, speechless. "I had no idea," she said, finally. "I mean, it doesn't really change the fact that he's a bit of a curmudgeon—"

"A bit?"

"Okay, *a lot* of a curmudgeon. Especially since his wife died. But to think of the man who views a night in jail as a nice night away from his family and to juxtapose him against the man who had, and has, such empathy for Edith is, well, it's a lot to take in."

At opposite ends of the small couch, they had each draped an arm over its back as they faced each other talking. "I suspect it has something to do with the first Mr. Whatley, Agnes and Edward's father." Caleb traced a finger down the back of her hand as he spoke.

It wasn't just the touch that she liked about that gesture, but also the fact that Caleb didn't even seem to notice he was doing it; the subtle comfort in that unconscious movement made her heart warm to him even more.

"And Mrs. Whatley, I suppose," he added, hooking one of his fingers under hers. "I have no idea what they were like as parents, but judging by how Agnes and Edward turned out, I'm guessing there was something not quite warm and safe in that household."

Cate believed that there was truth in that statement, even though no one had ever spoken about it. The cousins often made vague comments about their parents' upbringings, however, no one discussed the topic openly. "Yes, I suspect you're right." She pulled his hand toward her and placed a kiss on the tips of his fingers before she released him and stood. "So, what now? In terms of finding out who is trying to kill Edith?" She moved to the window where she'd seen some movement and caught sight of Dixie and Luke heading out for a hike.

"Agnes is convinced it's Michael we should be looking at as the potential victim."

Cate bobbed her head in thought. "Our focus was on Edith primarily because Edward made such a strong suspect, now that that's no longer the case, perhaps Agnes is on to something. Did she have any ideas as to who or why?"

He gave her a wry smile. "She said it was karma. Probably an ex-girlfriend or the husband of some woman he'd chased and conquered at some point."

"As if we're mountains to be climbed and claimed," she said with a shake of her head. She'd always hated it when people spoke of men "conquering" women, like the enemy or, as Agnes had said, like a major feat to be accomplished and bragged about at dinner parties.

"Her words, not mine," Caleb replied with a grin.

Cate rolled her eyes, finding it easy to believe that Agnes had made such a comment. "Word choice aside, do you think there's anything to it?"

Caleb shrugged. "Detective Hanley will have to broaden her investigation and I'm going to go back and review some of my notes tonight to see if I can have another conversation with Livia. She's just far enough outside the family that she isn't often noticed, but she's close enough that she hears things."

"Not to mention, she's incredibly observant."

"I agree, but what makes you say that?"

"She was the first person to notice I was pregnant with Elise. The reunion that year was about three months after Tommy died. The company had told me to take as much time off as I needed but I'd gone back to work pretty quickly afterward because, well, I didn't have much else to do, and staying home didn't appeal to me much. I hadn't been feeling well, but I thought it was just stress. The first day of the reunion, she asked me when I was due. Shocked the hell out of me, but, of course, she was right."

Caleb shifted in his seat, not meeting her eyes.

"Caleb, it's funny. You can laugh. I was four months pregnant and had no idea, and here was someone who saw me *once a year* pointing it out to me. It was a hell of a way to find out."

"You shouldn't have had to go back to work so soon."

She held back the sigh that wanted to escape her. "I didn't *have* to, I chose to. Looking back on it all now, yes, you could have stuck around more, and, yes, I could have reached out to you. But neither of us did and we've both come out on the other side of that little hiccup in our relationship just fine."

He eyed her as she approached him then drew back in surprise when she took a seat on his lap and wrapped her arms around his neck. "Repeat after me," she said.

His eyes narrowed.

"We are okay."

His eyes got narrower.

"It's not hard, Caleb. Just say it. We're okay."

"But—"

"That's not what I told you to say. No 'buts,' no 'what ifs.' No 'could haves,' 'should haves,' or 'would haves.' I just want to hear you say 'We're okay.'"

His jaw twitched. "Cate."

She leaned her forehead against his and looked into his eyes. "Caleb."

His eyes searched hers. Finally, he took a breath. "We're okay."

She smiled and leaned forward, brushing her lips against his. "Yes, we are. Now, if you wouldn't mind figuring out who is trying to kill whom, I would greatly appreciate it," she said, moving back, but not off his lap. "My company has never had a guest die during one of our events, and I'd prefer to keep it that way."

"That and you kind of like this family, despite their eccentricities."

"Maybe," she said with a soft laugh as she rose. "There could be some truth to that. Even if Agnes did call you man candy."

As she exited the office and headed down the hall to check on Margaret, his laughter followed her. She liked the sound. She liked it a lot. She just hoped that if she got out of his way and stopped distracting him, he might be able to dig something up to help put this whole situation to bed. And once that was done, she planned on making him laugh as often as possible.

CHAPTER 17

"WHO WOULD HAVE THOUGHT HAVING too many suspects would be as much of a pain in the ass as having none?" Caleb grumbled.

Vivi, on speakerphone, laughed. "It doesn't seem like that should be the case, but, you're right, it can be a total P-I-T-A."

They'd been on the phone for forty minutes, giving each member of the family a meticulous going-over. For the third time. Caleb hoped his problem was just that he was missing something, but he was beginning to suspect that what he needed just wasn't there.

"Where do I go from here, Vivi?"

There was a long pause before she answered. "I think we need to take a step back and think more about the pure psychology of the crimes."

"We've *been* talking motive. For almost an hour." He sounded whiny. He hated it when he sounded whiny. "What do you mean if not motive?"

God, he wanted this over. He wanted it all to go away so he could spend time with Cate and Elise.

Even though it came completely out of left field, the thought had come on so powerfully and swiftly it nearly took his breath away. It wasn't such a surprise that he wanted to be with them, but the feeling of wanting to gather them in and take them home, like his own family, sent him off-kilter. They weren't his family and, hell, he didn't even *have* a home. But logic often failed to sway emotions.

"Caleb?"

He rubbed a hand over his face. Vivi. "Yes, sorry, Vivi. I spaced out for a minute there."

A beat of silence. "Everything okay?"

"As okay as it can be right now. What were you saying?" In his mind's eye, he saw her drumming her finger on her desk, debating whether or not to press him. Thankfully, she opted not to.

"What I was saying was that looking at motive, means, and opportunity aren't getting us anywhere. For each attempt made so far, there are several family members that may have had motive and opportunity, but not means."

"Or means and opportunity, but not motive," he said, catching on.

"Exactly. So we need to take a more dispassionate look at the psychology of these kinds of crimes."

"You said it was likely someone with a long-held grudge."

"Or flare for the dramatic."

"The only dramatic person at this reunion is an eighty-five-year-old woman who dislikes her family and uses social media."

Vivi chuckled. "Okay, so maybe we focus on the long-held grudge. Only, I will say that I've done some digging on the type of clubs Dominique has been visiting. They aren't your usual kinds of sex clubs."

"There are 'usual' kinds of sex clubs?"

"You know what I mean."

He could almost hear her roll her eyes. And, yes, he did know what she meant. "And?"

"Your contact told you they are BDSM clubs and, well, I asked around and a few of my Boston colleagues told me that while they do focus on facilitating those particular sexual desires, two of the three clubs fall out of the spectrum that even people in that world generally feel comfortable with."

"I'm not even going to pretend I know what that means." He was all for sexual adventurousness but had no concept of what fell within the boundaries of acceptable versus unacceptable in the world Dominique was exploring.

"There's a lot of role-play, which, in and of itself, doesn't pose any questions, but one club has extreme role-play. Of the violent sort."

"Beating and such that gets out of hand?"

"Beatings can be part of the relationship when done in a certain way, but I think what you're asking is whether or not the role-play is always consensual, and that's where they start to fall out of the spectrum. A few people I talked to alluded to events frequently getting out of hand and consent being somewhat questionable."

"But what does this have to do with what's going on here?"

"Maybe nothing. I'm not sure we can rule Dominique out, though, if we're looking for someone with a flare for the dramatic and a rather loose relationship with ethics. However, I say that without knowing if she participated in any of the events that raised those concerns or, if she did, whether she was one of the perpetrators or a potential victim."

"So we focus on the grudge angle, but keep an open mind on the drama?"

"Exactly."

"Okay, so as far as grudges go, where do we start?"

And, true to Vivi form, they started with the psychology of it all. After another thirty minutes on the phone, during which Ian arrived home from work and popped into the conversation for a few minutes as well, Caleb had confirmed what he'd suggested to Cate earlier that day—that he needed to talk more with Livia. Hopefully, she'd give him more insight into all the familial slights and perceived slights. Then he could start tallying them up to see if, at the end of the day, any of them added up to murder.

• • •

By the time he made it back to the main house, the kitchen was in full dinner-prep mode. He'd thought to sneak through and see if he could find Livia before night fell and the wine began to flow, but Cate waylaid him at the door leading into the main part of the house.

"The police are here," she said, a hand on his chest.

A wave of annoyance flowed through him. He doubted Detective Hanley had the insight to even think of, let alone do, anything outside the box, and what he and Vivi had been discussing was definitely outside the box. But he'd have to stand aside and let her do her thing before he could do his.

"Are they talking to the whole family or just certain members?" he asked, hoping that maybe he could catch at least one or two of them on their own.

"Everyone but Edward, who has decided to take his dinner in his room tonight, and Michael, who is still sleeping."

Caleb bit back a growl of frustration. He'd just have to wait until morning. With one last look toward the main part of the house, he took a deep breath and exhaled.

"Okay, what can I do to help, then?"

Four and a half hours later—the police long gone—he was back at the sink with Greg drying the last of the dinner pots. He could hear laughter, mostly Dixie's and Nico's, coming from one of the game rooms where many of the family members had retreated after dinner. Edward had appeared at the dining table to join the family for dessert and, other than what seemed like an obligatory comment from Sabrina about how she was glad to have him back and that it had been ridiculous of the police to think he was capable of such a thing to begin with, the topic of his recent arrest wasn't mentioned.

Having been stationed, at his own request, in the butler's pantry between the kitchen and the dining room throughout dinner, Caleb knew that, in addition to the bare minimum of recognition given to Edward, the family seemed to be mostly ignoring what was happening in general. Edith was not mentioned once, and only one inquiry was made, again by Sabrina, about Michael, who'd remained asleep in his room throughout the meal. Caleb did hear quite a few snipes and cutting remarks, though. Every time

Sabrina tried to say something pleasant about someone, Dominique cut her off, telling her that her Pollyanna outlook came across as more clueless than kind. Anthony snapped at Livia when she asked for red wine with her bass and, in response, Isiah snipped back, pointing out that Anthony had always been more flash than substance when it came to class. Agnes jumped in a few times with her charming criticisms—telling Sabrina her hair looked atrocious and she should really wear it up for dinner, and barking at Dixie and Luke to keep their hands to themselves, amongst other comments.

All in all, while the fact that there was most likely an attempted murderer sitting at their table and they were all refusing to acknowledge it, Caleb sensed tempers were definitely fraying. Then again, maybe it had nothing to do with the attempted murders. Maybe four weeks was just too long for a family reunion.

He was revisiting that thought as he placed a dried pan on the counter when Cate walked into the kitchen, put a hand on his back, and examined the work he and Greg had completed.

"Nice job, gentlemen."

"Thank you, *Cate*," Greg replied with a cheeky grin.

Caleb had given up on calling her Catherine a while back; she would always be Cate to him. And while the staff would never be so disrespectful as to question the affection they saw between their boss and Caleb, every now and then, they couldn't help but tease.

"Good night, Greg," Cate said with a shake of her head.

"Trying to get rid of me?"

"Good night, Greg," Caleb echoed, causing the younger man to laugh as he moved away from the sink and dried his hands.

"I'll just do one more liquor check then head up to my room for a few hours. I'll do the same walk through I've been doing with Lucas and Vic again tonight."

Both Caleb and Cate had turned to lean against the counter, but Cate was leaning into Caleb as well, her head resting on his arm. "Thank you," she said to Greg. "That sounds good. Call or text if there are any problems."

Greg agreed and moved toward the servants' staircase, but he paused before heading up. "In all seriousness, are you guys okay for the night? Is there anything I can do? I feel a little useless just washing dishes and organizing outings for the family. Is there anything more I could be doing?"

Cate laced her fingers in Caleb's. "Thank you, Greg. I appreciate the offer, I really do. But the best thing you can do, the best thing all of you can do, is your jobs, which will then let the police—"

"And me," Caleb interjected.

"And Caleb, do theirs."

Greg studied them both for a moment. "But if you need anything . . ."

"We'll let you know," Caleb finished.

Greg gave a sharp nod then turned and headed up the stairs, leaving them alone. For a few moments they stood in the silence, hands laced together, her head leaning against his arm.

"You okay?" he asked, brushing a kiss across the top of her head.

She sighed. "Yes, just worried that the reunion is almost over and we're still not sure what is going on. Did you talk to Vivi?"

"I did. We had an interesting conversation," he said, then told her about what he and the good doctor had discussed.

"Is that why you wanted to be in the butler's pantry tonight? So you could hear how they interacted now that the pressure is building? See if you heard any patterns that might be as old as the cousins themselves?"

"It is. Since I didn't have a chance to talk to them directly today, I figured I could at least listen to see if I heard any evidence of a long-term annoyance, or hatred, that was deep enough to warrant killing someone."

"Well, did you?"

At her question, he turned and looped his arms around her. Hers came around him as well and she dropped her head against his chest. He could feel her fatigue against his body. "A lot of bickering and general criticisms, but without knowing some of the background that I hope to get tomorrow, it's hard to say if any of it means anything."

She took in a deep breath and leaned into him more. "Maybe we should go to bed, then. Sleep on it, so you can start with the family tomorrow?"

He wanted her in his bed, but he wasn't sure that was what she'd meant by her comment, and he didn't know how to ask without sounding like an eager teenager. "Sounds good. Shall we?" he asked, pulling away and gesturing toward their coats.

A few moments later, as Cate rifled on her keychain for the correct key to lock up the back door to the main house, he stepped out into the night and surveyed the vast building, hoping it might reveal something.

His eyes scanned the roofline and turrets, outlined against the moonlit sky that loomed overhead. Light flooded from the third floor, where the staff members were likely still awake. From the second floor, however, only filtered light shone through some of the window hangings. Agnes was the outlier, of course, and her window glowed brightly; no doubt, the woman had left both the light on and the curtains open when she'd headed to bed.

"Is it whispering any secrets to you?" Cate asked as she took his hand in hers.

"I wish it would. I really do," he said with one last scan.

"You and me both, but since it appears to be holding its secrets close to the vest tonight, let's go light a fire and curl up in bed."

Distracted from his perusal of the house by her comment, he dropped his gaze to hers. When she gave him a sheepish smile, he couldn't help but offer one in return.

"That's the best plan I've heard all day." He tightened his hold on her hand and started to tug her along to his lodgings. She was snuggled up against him as they made their way to his room, but when they reached the porch of the ice house and he looked at his kitchen window, which was open just a crack, he paused.

"Caleb?" Her eyes tracked his line of sight then came back to him. "Did you leave that open? Please tell me you left that open."

"I did," came his sharp reply as he spun around to look back at the main house.

"Good, then let's go in. It's freezing out here."

He felt her pull on his hand, but he was fixated, his eyes searching in the dark night. He took a step off the porch and then another, releasing Cate.

"Caleb?"

And then he found it. What hadn't felt right to him when he'd first looked up at the back of the main house. When he'd first felt that the house was trying to tell him something.

"Michael and Edith always sleep with their window open, don't they?" His eyes were locked on the closed window of their room.

"Yes, almost always. Although the other night, they closed it." Cate came up beside him and, in the corner of his eye, he saw her head up turn to the window in question.

"It's so uncommon for them to close it that you remember when they do," he pointed out.

She hesitated. "Yes, I suppose so. Edith mentioned once that she likes to hear the night sounds here. We chatted about how different being in the country is to living in the city. The conversation stuck in my mind so when I pass by the house at night, I tend to look to see if it's open. It sounds kind of strange but when it's open, I take it as a sign that she and Michael are still enjoying their stay."

"And do you remember when you saw it closed?" In his gut he knew the answer. He'd worked it out himself, but he needed her to confirm.

"It was about two weeks ago, I think. The day you first took Elise for a ride on Pansy."

"You mean the night before Christine found the snake in the house?"

He could feel her go tense beside him as they both stared at the closed window.

"Oh god, Caleb. No one has seen Michael since he went up to shower and rest this afternoon."

He didn't wait to think about it any longer before he grabbed the keys Cate held out to him and rushed back into the house.

CHAPTER 18

"Get Lucas and Vic," Caleb called as he ran through the kitchen toward the servants' staircase.

"Get us for what?"

He paused long enough to see both men sitting at the table having a piece of the cake Margaret had served for dessert that evening.

"Michael," was all he said.

He heard their feet, and Cate's, on the stairs behind him as he took them two at a time to the second floor. Passing through the north wing, he finally came to a halt outside Michael and Edith's door. Their locked door.

He glanced at the keys on the key chain and knew there was a master key there somewhere, but not knowing which one it was, he dropped them on the ground, glanced at Lucas and Vic, who nodded at his unspoken decision, and then to Cate.

"Stand back, everyone. Cate."

Lucas reached out and pulled Cate behind him.

Caleb knew the locks on these doors, he'd examined them well the day he'd searched the rooms, and he knew it would only take one swift, strong, ram for the door to open. He just didn't know what they'd find on the other side.

Counting to three in his mind, he rammed his shoulder against the door and, as he'd anticipated, it gave way easily. Less than two seconds passed before he realized what had happened.

Michael lay on his bed, his color ashen. Caleb couldn't tell if he was still breathing, but he didn't have time to stop and check, not yet, it was too dangerous.

"Cate stay outside and call the police and an ambulance. Lucas get Michael out. Vic, the fireplace."

Both men voiced their assent as Caleb moved to the four windows and opened each of them as wide as they could go. Moving to the bathroom, he opened the two windows there as well. When he rushed back out of the bathroom, Lucas had Michael in his arms.

"Vic?"

"The gas line was open, not fully, but enough. I think we need to get out of here."

Caleb agreed and they all exited the room, closing the battered door as best they could behind them. With the gas line off and the windows open, the room would air out relatively quickly, and with that particular danger was under control, Michael was their priority.

The commotion had brought people into the hallway from their rooms or the game room, and Caleb had to bark orders to get them to move back as Lucas carried Michael to the upstairs library where he laid the unconscious man on settee.

"Does he have a pulse?" Caleb asked as Vic and Lucas, both trained in basic emergency care, began to examine him.

"Yes, but faint," Vic said, his fingers on Michael's neck.

"Cate?"

She appeared beside him. "Police and the EMTs are on their way."

"The family?" Can you get them out of here, was left unsaid.

"I'll take them downstairs."

His attention was drawn to Michael, but, at the same time, he tried to keep an eye on who went with Cate and how they each seemed to be reacting to what was happening. Agnes lagged behind, the first genuine look of concern he'd ever seen her express etched onto her face. Anthony appeared shaken and Dominique annoyed. Sabrina and Dixie had their arms linked and their heads together as they listened to Cate's orders.

"How is he?" Caleb asked once the family had left the room.

"He's still unconscious, but his pupils are responsive and he's breathing on his own," Vic answered.

"Is there any more we can do?"

"Not until the paramedics show up," Lucas said.

As if on cue, they heard the sirens coming up the drive. A few minutes later, two EMTs came up the stairs with Greg. Lucas, Vic, and Caleb all stepped back. None of them needed to say much of anything. It was clear now that Michael had always been the target, and the attempt that had been made that night could have not only killed him, but possibly many others as well had someone entered that room and flicked on the light switch. If that had happened, Caleb suspected half of the south wing would have been blown to pieces.

But, the hell of it was, they still didn't have a motive. Agnes was right, there probably *were* people out there who wanted Michael dead, but none of them were anywhere near The Washington House, and certainly not near enough for such intimate crimes. Caleb knew he needed to look at everyone again through the lens of what he and Vivi had talked about earlier that day, but as he started to do that in his head, Detective Hanley and her two trusty officers arrived.

"What the hell happened?" she barked, as if it was his fault.

"Exposure to gas," one of the EMTs answered. "He's starting to come out of it. We won't know if there are any long-term effects, but the good news is, he's becoming more responsive. Nausea might follow though, so if there is a container or bucket around . . ." She let the question hang.

"I'll bring something," Greg offered then disappeared down the hall.

Caleb, Lucas, Vic, Detective Hanley, and her people all stood silently as the EMTs kept an eye on Michael's vitals and adjusted and monitored his oxygen mask. A few minutes later, Greg arrived and placed a bucket by his side. Greg's timing was impeccable; within three minutes, Michael's eyes were opening and he'd started to cough. When he got a panicked look on his face, the EMTs soothed him, removed the oxygen mask, and let him vomit into the bucket.

"Water," Michael croaked when he'd finished.

When one of the EMTs nodded to Greg, he walked to a cabinet and brought back a fresh bottle of water. Twisting the cap off, he offered it to Michael, who now sat upright, but kept his head resting against the back of the small couch. Giving a small wave of thanks with one hand, Michael tried to take the bottle in his other. Unable to lift it himself, he let an EMT guide it to his lips, taking a few sips before the oxygen mask had to go back on.

The switching off between water and oxygen lasted another fifteen minutes until Michael asked for some tea and indicated that he felt well enough to talk. Unfortunately, his talking added very little color to the picture. He remembered Anthony accompanying him to his room after they'd had a snack. He'd asked his brother to give him one of the sleeping pills the doctor had prescribed and then, once Anthony had left, Michael had laid down and not woken up until just now.

Detective Hanley was clearly pissed that Michael remembered nothing more, and when one of her officers suggested they go interview the family she gave a snort before grudgingly agreeing.

"Bring them here," Michael said, halting their exodus from the upstairs library to the one downstairs.

"I beg your pardon?" Detective Hanley said.

"I want to hear what they have to say and if someone is trying to kill me, I want to be there when you question them."

Caleb thought the idea was actually quite brilliant. It was one thing to try to kill someone and not see it happen, but quite another to look that person in the eye and lie about it. Of course, he had known plenty of people who could do that, people who could raise a toast in your honor then slit your throat, but he didn't think the Whatley clan was that practiced, or sociopathic.

To his surprise, the detective agreed and sent her officers to bring the family up. Sabrina and Dixie immediately rushed to

Michael's side while his brother hovered nearby. Agnes and Edward, for the first time, looked to be deep in conversation as they took seats at the chess table and cast concerned glances at their nephew. The others, with the exception of Nikki and Sasha, who had been moved to an empty room in the north wing, filed into the room, filling the chairs and window seats.

Caleb scanned each of their faces with Vivi's insights playing like a soundtrack in his mind. Was it Isiah, who'd lost several businesses early in his career because of Michael's carelessness? Or maybe Anthony, who would stand to inherit his brother's portion of the family money? Or maybe Livia, tired of so many years of slights?

Agnes moved a piece on the chessboard as she spoke to her brother, then moved another. Her actions were thoughtless, but something in them triggered a thought. Swiftly, Caleb latched onto it and filtered through everything he remembered reading in the files and hearing from the family and staff. He sorted the details in his mind and created a timeline. Then slowly, everything fell into place.

"I'd like to get started." As Detective Hanley spoke, the room fell silent.

Caleb felt Cate come up beside him and, though she didn't take his hand in hers, she brushed her fingers against his.

"As I'm sure you are all aware, an attempt was made on Michael Whatley's life tonight. Whoever intended to kill him did so by opening the gas line to the fireplace and poisoning him." Her announcement was met with dead silence. "As soon as the fire department clears the room, we'll be searching it for evidence, but in the meantime, I'm going to need to question each of you about your whereabouts this afternoon and evening."

"I don't think you need to bother." At Caleb's pronouncement, he felt all eyes fall on him, including a glare from Detective Hanley.

"If you don't mind, Mr. Forrester, this is my investigation."

"Then you need to arrest Anthony Whatley for the attempted murder of both Edith Barnard and Michael Whatley."

That got the room talking. Everyone burst out in denials, questions, and confusion. Everyone, Caleb noted, except Michael who was studying his brother closely.

"I've done no such thing," Anthony protested hotly. "That's ridiculous. Why on earth would I want to kill my own brother?"

Everyone fell silent again, waiting for the answer.

Caleb took a few steps toward the chess table and moved one of the pieces Agnes had shifted earlier. He watched her study the board and knew, when she looked up at him with wide eyes, that she understood. He saw a flash of sorrow in her eyes, but she gave him a small nod of encouragement.

"Because he changed the game on you, Anthony," Caleb said.

"What game? What the hell are you talking about?"

"The game in which he plays the self-centered, fun loving, spoiled brat without a care—or much of a brain—in his head, and you get to be the dutiful, smart, well-respected brother."

Anthony blinked. "I have no idea what you're talking about."

"You don't? I'm pretty sure you do. I'm pretty sure it served your purposes when he stole your high school girlfriend and married her and you could label him a self-centered prick and the rest of the family was hard pressed to disagree, especially when they divorced less than two years later. But my guess is that your mission to make your brother useless—charming, but useless—probably started long before that."

"You're making no sense, Mr. Forrester."

"I think you know exactly what I'm talking about. It served your purposes to have a brother who showed no interest in the family business and really no head for business at all. Those few companies he started with Isiah? You were involved too, weren't you?"

"Yes, I was. All three of us ran them. Or tried to, anyway. Michael missed one too many investor and customer meetings for them to get any traction."

"And why was that?"

"Why was what?"

"Why did he miss so many meetings?"

Anthony shrugged. "Out too late the night before, not interested in talking business, busy with someone else's wife. Who knows?"

"I think *you* do. I think you know exactly what your brother was doing because you needed him to keep doing it. You needed him to stay self-absorbed, you needed him to prefer jetting off on spontaneous trips to Saint Tropez or the Alps for a bit of fun with a private plane full of like-minded friends, and you probably encouraged him to do just that."

"And what reason would I have to do that?"

"Because you knew the one thing that no one else did. No one except maybe Douglas Whately."

"What is that, Mr. Forrester?" Michael asked.

"That you're smarter than Anthony," Caleb said, turning to speak to Michael. "By leaps and bounds, would be my guess. You're smarter, better at business, and considerably better with people. And if anyone else found out, your brother knew he'd be moved down the chain of succession and maybe out of the family business altogether. In fact, that's happening already, isn't it? Douglas is starting to minimize Anthony's role already, isn't he?"

"I have enough money to live comfortably for the rest of my life, Mr. Forrester," Anthony interjected. "Losing a job isn't worth my brother's life."

"But it's not really about the money, is it?" Caleb asked swinging his attention back to Anthony. "For a while, I think we all assumed it was about money, given how much net worth is represented in this room. But it's about more than that. It's about your own pathetic self-worth, it's about constantly wanting to be better than your little brother. Your little brother whom everyone likes, with whom everyone wants to spend time, who you know is better than you in just about every way."

"If this is true, Mr. Forrester," Michael spoke, sounding stronger by the minute. "Why now? My god, I'm in my forties, surely he would have had plenty of opportunity before now."

Caleb glanced at the chessboard again. He picked up a pawn and rolled it between his fingers, before setting it down in a different position. "Because you changed the game on him, Michael."

"Again with the game," Anthony threw up his hands, but Michael raised a finger to silence the objection.

"In what way?" Michael asked.

"After the incident on the trek, you changed."

"Well, yes, watching a man die to save you can do that to a person."

"I agree, it can, and it did. You came back a different person. You were no longer content to play the role you'd always played in the family. People *mean* something to you now. Loyalty means something and, at the risk of sounding old fashioned, so does honor. Can I ask how it came about, how Douglas Whatley brought you back into the fold of the family business?"

Michael furrowed his brow in thought as he thought back. "I approached him and asked if there was a small division somewhere that I could have a hand in. I acknowledged my past behavior and didn't expect his trust right away, so I only asked for a chance to slowly prove my worth and my value. The family businesses employ a lot of people and we treat them well, I started to see the responsibility in that and I wanted to become a part of it."

"But the thing is," Caleb said, "Douglas has always known what your brother has always tried to keep hidden—that you were better positioned to run the company than anyone else in the family, including Anthony."

"And he'd just been waiting for me to see the same thing," Michael said, his voice tinged with a little bit of wonder that someone could have thought such things about him when he himself would never had contemplated them.

Caleb nodded. "And when you did, you changed the game your brother had been playing with you for years."

"And so he wanted to kill me. To take back the throne, so to speak." Michael's voice, bewildered, but not disbelieving, had dropped. He turned to his brother. "Anthony?"

"You don't really believe him, do you?"

Caleb could see the conflict in Michael's eyes. Of course, he didn't *want* to believe that his brother was trying to kill him, but deep down, or maybe even not so deep, Michael seemed to see a hint of truth in the tale Caleb had told. Judging by the way everyone had begun shuffling away from Anthony, it appeared that everyone else did too.

Caleb looked at Detective Hanley. With her arms crossed across her chest, she seemed to be glaring at nothing in particular. "I don't have enough evidence to arrest him," she said.

"You don't," Lucas agreed. "But you do have enough to hold him. He was the last person in Michael's room and could have easily turned on the gas line. It's enough to hold him and enough for a warrant to search his room again. I imagine, now that you know where to focus, you'll find evidence of moonseed and maybe even metal shavings from when he tampered with Michael's gun. How or when he accessed the gun, you'll have to figure out, but concentrating your efforts in his room might give you what you need to bring formal charges."

The detective tapped her foot several times, then gave a curt nod. "Hold him on suspicion of attempted murder. You," she said, pointing to the taller of her two officers, "get on the phone with the judge and get another warrant to search the house."

She paused and her eyes scanned the room before landing on Cate. "I don't want anyone going anywhere tonight, so I'll be posting officers around the house. We'll also have the evidence collection team here as soon as the warrant comes through. I assume you have no problems with that?"

Cate shook her head.

"You've got to be kidding me," Anthony said as the officers approached him. "Are you really going to let this happen, Michael?"

"If you're innocent, it will prove that too," his brother answered.

"Will you at least call my lawyer?" Anthony shook off one of the officers to indicate that he wasn't going to fight them and they didn't need to cuff him.

Michael nodded. "Of course, Anthony. We'll be sure he's there tomorrow morning."

Anthony cast one last glare around the room, not that anyone in the family other than Michael and Agnes met his scathing look, before he preceded the officers out of the room. As soon as they heard the front door close, the room seemed to erupt with activity. He heard Cate issuing directions to have another room made up for Michael even though the fire department had given the all clear. Nico and Dixie poured some drinks and, for once, Dominique seemed at least a little concerned about Sabrina.

Caleb was about to turn from the room when Michael waved him over.

"Thank you," he said holding out a hand.

Caleb took it in his own and shook it. "I'm not sure 'thank you' is the quite the right phrase. I was sorry to be the one to point the finger."

Michael shrugged. "If it turns out to be true, you're nothing but the messenger, but a messenger who saved my life, nonetheless, so again, thank you."

He wanted to ask if Michael thought he was correct, but Caleb had no right to push the man on his thoughts regarding his brother's guilt or innocence. "If there is anything I can do, just let me know."

Michael gave a small wave of gratitude and Caleb turned to go, but the man called him back.

"Yes?"

"I hope you won't think less of us for hiring him a good attorney," Michael said.

Caleb thought about his own sister, about everything she'd been through and everything he'd do to protect her. "No, sir, I won't." Why his opinion mattered to Michael, he didn't know, but Caleb didn't miss the look of understanding that flashed across Michael's face as he turned to leave.

He was just saying good night to Lucas and Vic in the hall when Cate, who'd left to get Agnes settled, stepped out of the room and into his sight. He nodded to the couple, who were headed to their room, as she came to a stop in front of him. He knew she had a few more things she needed to do before she could retire for the night, but that didn't stop him from looping his arms around her and leaning down for a kiss.

"Need any help?" he asked pulling back.

She shook her head. "No, we're almost done. How did you know all that? How did you know it was Anthony?"

He lifted a shoulder. "He's still innocent until proven guilty, but the long and short of it is, if someone was trying to kill Michael and it wasn't an outsider, the only person with the psychological make up Vivi and I talked about was Anthony. He's the only one close enough to Michael to have had the chance to form the kind of grudges Vivi had talked about. When I realized that—that it wasn't the big things, but the little things—I started to remember what some of those little things that I'd heard about from the family."

"The girlfriend, the failed businesses? Michael's personality change?"

"Exactly. Then when Agnes started playing with the chess-board, it reminded me of the conversation you and I had."

"About changing the game. And that, if you changed the game without redefining the rules, Agnes would probably launch world war three."

He had to smile just a little at that, but it quickly faded. "Michael and Anthony's fraternal relationship isn't quite the same as mine and Agnes's over the chess board, but yeah, the principle is the same. Michael changed the rules and left his brother out in the cold. I don't think Michael gave his brother any thought when he changed; he was just focused on becoming a good man, the kind of man who could shoulder the responsibilities of the family business. But as Michael worked to become a better person, Anthony knew that not only would his brother's talents push him out of the line of succession, they'd also highlight just how barely competent he is."

Cate mulled this over for a moment then let out a deep sigh. "As much as I hate to think of someone I know as a murderer, I do hope the evidence team finds what they need so that the family gets the closure they deserve."

Caleb thought about the high-powered attorney the family would no doubt hire for Anthony. They might get the closure, but it may not be what Anthony deserved. "I feel the need to talk to my sister," he said, out of the blue. It was late and she was likely asleep, but still he wanted to talk to her.

Cate smiled. "Why don't you go back to your place and give her a ring. I'll come down as soon as I'm done."

"To my place?' he clarified.

She went up on her toes and kissed him. "Yes. As tragic as all of this has been, I have to say, I'm feeling a little relieved that we at least have some answers. In fact, it's making me feel just a little bit giddy, which may be totally inappropriate, but there you have it. I feel like we need to celebrate a little."

"Celebrate?" He leaned down and nipped her earlobe. "So, you're saying I should start thinking of ways to 'celebrate?'"

She gave a throaty chuckle. "Well, I do do most of the event planning around here. If you took it over, just this once, mind you, you would be doing me a huge favor."

He laughed. "You can ask for that kind of favor anytime."

CHAPTER 19

CALEB STOOD ON THE FRONT veranda and watched Cate wave off the last of the Whatley family—with the exception of Miachel, who'd checked into a hotel closer to the hospital, they were all headed home. Anna and Lucy were already cleaning the place, getting ready for the house to reopen as a bed and breakfast, and Greg and Christine were helping Margaret pack up. He, Cate, and Elise would stay one more day to make sure everything was ready to be handed back to the regular manager, then they were headed to Windsor for a few days.

The events of the reunion and the depth of Anthony's hatred toward his own brother had left the family quiet and subdued, and Caleb wondered if they would have a reunion at all the following year. If they did, Anthony would be conspicuously absent. The family had hired a lawyer for him, a very good one at that, but Detective Hanley's team had found enough evidence in his room, including remnants of moonseed, metal shavings, the file used to tamper with Michael's gun, and a pair of gloves with a tiny scratch that aligned to the fragment Vivi had identified, that the prosecution was in the process of building a very solid case against him.

While Caleb had empathy for Michael, who had a long road ahead of him as he worked to come to terms with his brother's betrayal, after being with the Whatley family for nearly three weeks, he'd be glad to head back to Windsor. He smiled as Cate jogged up the steps and stopped in front of him.

"That's the last of them."

He tucked a strand of her hair behind her ear. "Shall we go inside and check on everyone?"

"No, why don't I do that and, if you don't mind, maybe you could take Elise out? Jana is packing and leaving tonight, I'm sure she'd love to have a hand watching her."

"Of course." He took her hand in his and they headed back into the main house. "Mirielle is still here, maybe I'll take her out on Pansy one more time. Carly was going to pick up a pony on her honeymoon, but I'm not sure if it will have made it to the states yet."

Cate pulled him to a stop. "Very little of what you just said made sense."

He chuckled. He supposed it didn't, if she didn't know Carly. "Carly and Drew, the couple that just got married?"

She nodded.

"Drew took Carly on a horse-hunting trip for their honeymoon. They spent several weeks traveling around Europe looking for a few for Carly to bring back to the stables she's starting. I talked to Drew while I was in Windsor and he told me that Carly was thinking about picking up a pony since there are so many kids in our circle of friends in Windsor, not to mention in Drew's family. I told him they should. I figured, at the very least, Elise would love it."

Cate blinked and, in her astonishment, he realized not really what he'd just said, but what it had meant. His heart started to thud in his chest. He thought about taking it back, well, not really taking it back, but soft-pedaling a little bit. The truth was, though, he didn't want to. He didn't know where he and Cate were going from here on out, but he wanted them to be together, or at least to try. And if they were going to try, then it meant she and Elise would spend some time in Windsor, since that's where Kit was. There was still so much up in the air, but if she wanted to stay involved with him at all, Windsor would become part of her future.

Finally, Cate nodded. "Um, okay. That sounds good. A walk

with Pansy sounds good. Will Carly and Drew be back from their honeymoon when we get to Windsor?"

They resumed their walk toward the kitchen. "Yes, everyone will be there. It might be kind of overwhelming, but we don't have to participate in anything. We can do, or not do, whatever we want." He didn't exactly feel great about her reaction. Now that it was out there, he realized he'd hoped for a much more positive response. But he also recognized that they had some navigating to do, they still had some bumps and hurdles to get through before either of them would be in a position to make decisions about the future.

"I'd like to meet your sister and see Garret again. Maybe meet Vivi too, she seemed interesting."

Caleb thought there were many words to describe Vivi, and "interesting" was certainly one of them.

"And if Carly has horses, well, we know whom Elise's favorite will be. But I think we should just figure it out when we get there. In the meantime, let's get everything wrapped up here, and then we can, well, we can sort the rest out."

Again, not the enthusiastic response he'd hoped for, but he'd take it. "I'll get out of your hair then, and Elise and I will see you when you're done." He let go of her hand, but she pulled him back and down into a kiss.

"I'm looking forward to not being here," she whispered against his lips.

He didn't quite know what her enigmatic statement meant. Instead of answering, he kissed her again then walked away. They'd figure it out—whatever "it" was, they'd figure it out. He had to.

• • •

"So, I invited a few people over for dessert and after-dinner drinks," Kit said, passing a plate of roasted vegetables to Cate.

"Kit." Caleb's warning voice. His sister just rolled her eyes at him while Garret tried to hide a smile.

"What's for dessert?" Elise asked.

"Elise," Cate admonished. They'd just sat down to dinner, the five of them, and this was Cate and Elise's first time meeting Caleb's sister. Cate was more nervous than she'd thought she'd be, but Kit, a stunning woman who did indeed have the exact same eyes as her brother, had been nothing but welcoming and warm.

"Now, there's a girl after my own heart," Garret said, sending a smile in Elise's direction.

Cate turned her attention to the man across the table. Garret had changed quite a bit in the five years since she'd last seen him. She suspected he'd probably changed the most since meeting Kit and leaving behind the world in which he'd been immersed when she'd first met him. He certainly smiled a lot more now.

"Kit made little individual chocolate cakes that she'll put in the oven just before we want to eat them so they're gooey and warm," Garret said. "And she got ice cream and caramel sauce too." Elise's eyes widened at the thought before she turned toward her mom with a hopeful look.

"That sounds pretty amazing," Cate said, "but you need to eat dinner first."

"Okay," Elise said before casting a forlorn glance back at Garret, her new partner in crime, who responded with a look of commiseration.

"Caleb has told me about some of the people who live here, some of your friends. Will we meet them tonight?" Cate asked, feeling as though she and Elise were about to be put on show.

She didn't know what Caleb had told Kit about them, but even if he hadn't said a word, she knew him well enough to know that, just by bringing her and Elise there, he was making a statement. Not to mention the fact that he had also opted to stay with them at the bed and breakfast where Drew and Carly's reception had been held, instead of in his sister's guest room where he usually stayed.

She was grateful that he'd been mindful of Elise's impressions and had booked two rooms. She was also grateful, however, that the rooms adjoined. When they'd arrived the night before, she'd been able to put Elise down and then join him in his room. They hadn't done anything but sleep, but she'd liked being close to him.

"You will," Kit said. "My friends Jesse and David are going to stop by with their daughter, Emma. She's your age, Elise," Kit said, directing the second part of her sentence to the four-year-old at the table. Turning back to Cate, Kit added, "And another couple, Matty and Dash, are coming too."

"With the twins?" Caleb asked.

Kit shook her head. "No, Dash's parents have them for the night. Their twins, Charley and Daphne, are around eighteen months old," she explained to Cate. "And, of course, Vivi and Ian and Drew and Carly, two more couples. Marcus, Carly's brother, might stop by, but well, Caleb, you know Marcus. Oh, and Trudy and Wyatt are planning to drop by as well, I think."

Cate's eyes sought Caleb's. There were so many names and though she'd heard some of them before, she wasn't sure what Caleb's relationships were like with most of them. He gave her an apologetic look that said they'd talk about it later. No doubt, he'd get them out of Dodge if she wanted, but he wasn't going to say anything now that would put her in the hot seat.

She thanked him with a small smile, passing the roast over to him after placing a few slices on Elise's plate. The rest of the meal's conversation flowed easily from topic to topic and she learned about Kit's writing and how she came to be in Windsor. She heard how Kit and Garret had first met and about Garret's new job. Elise told them everything she'd recently learned about the goddess Athena, making Kit and Garret smile. Cate talked about her work, life in Florida, and the upcoming events she'd already planned. And she didn't miss the not-so-subtle hints from Kit about how great a place Windsor was to raise kids.

She was just helping Caleb load the last of the dishes into the dishwasher, something they'd both insisted on doing, more to give each other a little time together than for any other reason, when people started arriving.

"We don't have to stay long," Caleb said, drying his hands on a dish towel.

She'd enjoyed getting to know Kit and wasn't feeling quite as anxious as she'd expected, so she gave him a shrug. "Let's see how things go."

He was studying her face closely, making sure she was really okay, when a woman said his name and he looked away. Cate turned to see a petite blonde bearing a remarkable resemblance to Marilyn Monroe standing a few feet away.

"Jesse," Caleb said, stepping forward and brushing the woman's cheek with a kiss before giving her a hug and turning back to Cate with a smile. "This is Cate. Cate, this is Jesse Hathaway. Jesse, be nice."

Jesse hit Caleb on the arm. "I'm always nice. Now, Cate. I understand you've known Caleb for a long time?" The tiny woman looped her arm through Cate's and started pulling her away from Caleb. "And is this your daughter?" Jesse asked, pointing to Elise.

Cate bobbed her head to both answers. "Her name is Elise."

"Emma, did you meet Elise?" Jesse called over her shoulder.

"Yes, I just introduced them," a man with cropped brown hair and deep brown eyes said, joining them, a little girl at his side. Elise, who'd been talking to Garret, joined her mother.

"I'm David Hathaway. Jesse's husband," he said, holding out his hand.

Jesse released Cate's arm so that she could shake David's hand. She did so and then smiled at the couple. They seemed nice enough.

"And he's my daddy," Emma said, resting her head on his leg.

"I don't have a daddy," Elise said.

Cate couldn't help the reaction that came over her. Her body tensed and her heart rate kicked up. Instantly, Caleb was at her side. She didn't know how to handle the situation—was this one of those times when she should comfort her daughter, or just let it blow over?

Caleb saw her distress and brushed a reassuring hand down

her back. As he opened his mouth to step in, Emma cut him off. "I didn't have a daddy either, but I have one now."

All four adults cast startled looks at each.

"My daddy died before I was born," Elise said.

Emma's eyes widened. "I'm sorry. My grandma died. But then I got a new mommy and daddy. You have a mommy, don't you?"

"Hi Emma, it's nice to meet you. I'm Cate, Elise's mommy."

Emma smiled. "You have a mommy, now maybe you can get a new daddy too!"

Elise giggled and soon both girls were laughing and Emma was dragging Elise to the toys and play area she knew well from the time she spent at Kit and Garret's house.

Cate looked at Caleb who had gone an interesting shade of pink.

Jesse was the first to laugh. "Out of the mouths of babes," she said. "Now, let me introduce you to everyone." She hooked her arm in Cate's again and they were off.

And hour and a half later, with dessert long gone and few more bottle of wine opened, Cate stood in the living room with Vivi, watching Elise and Emma play with Jeffery.

"He's doing well for it being so late in the evening," Cate said.

"He's like Ian that way. If we're home, he's out like a light by seven, but if we're out and he's entertained, he'll happily stay up until all hours of the night."

At the mention of Ian's name, both women looked over toward the kitchen where Ian stood talking to Caleb and Drew. All three men were smiling and chuckling. Carly, who'd spent a great deal of time telling Elise about the stables she was building and the pony she'd just bought, was deep in conversation with Dash, who, in addition to being Matty's husband, was the town vet. Matty and Jesse were talking with their heads bent together and intense looks in their eyes; Cate couldn't help but wonder if she should be worried about the topic under discussion.

Then Caleb laughed loudly and her eyes went back to him. She knew he'd been nervous about bringing her there, not because of her, but because he knew that everyone would be wondering about them. He was relaxed now, however, surrounded by family and friends, and it was a side of him she had never even dreamed of.

Yes, when he'd come to stay with her and Tommy and Brooke, he'd been like family, but there had always been a little bit of hero worship in his relationship with Tommy. After hearing him talk about how he and Tommy had met, she understood better why he'd always acted as if he'd owed Tommy something, because he had. Only the more she thought about it, and the more she saw Caleb interacting with his new friends, the more apparent it was to her that Tommy could have done a better job of making it clear that no one had owed anyone anything.

Here, in Windsor, Caleb was an equal, he was a friend and he had friends, and it was clear as a bell to her that he was more relaxed, more *himself*, because of that.

"I find that when it comes to social situations it's better to surprise Caleb. If you give him too much warning, he'll find a way to get out of it." While Cate had been lost in thought, Kit had joined her and Vivi unnoticed. "It probably wasn't fair to do that to you, though," Kit continued, looking at Cate, "but I figured I would just get it all out of the way in one night."

"All what out of the way?"

"Meeting you," Vivi said, then took a sip of the tea she held. "Kit's right. Caleb is a good man," she continued, "but the way he lived, and the length of time he lived that way, has made it difficult for him to adjust to what some of us would call a normal life. Yes, I know 'normal' is relative, but there you have it."

"What Vivi means is that if everyone had waited for him to introduce you and Elise to each of them, it could have taken a year. He's incredibly decisive when it comes to his work, and Garret says he has one of the most strategic minds he's ever worked with, but socially, he's well . . ."

"He's a bit of a beast, at times," Jesse said, joining them along with Carly and Matty. "A beast I adore, but still a beast."

Cate didn't like the way this conversation was going. "Don't worry," Carly jumped in. "They mean well. Believe me, we'd all like to see more of Caleb around here. But he isn't the easiest guy to get to know. Although, I will say he and Drew have hit it off."

"But they hated each other when they first met," Kit pointed out. "And, honestly, I think part of his hesitancy with people stems from his guilt about me."

Vivi reached out and squeezed Kit's arm.

"I don't know how much he told you about our upbringing," Kit said to Cate, "but we were both, well, let's just say we had the rug pulled out from beneath us when we were teenagers."

"I know," Cate said. "He didn't tell me everything, of course; he said some of it wasn't his story to tell, but he did tell me a lot, and I know he still feels like he let you down."

Kit's eyes flicked to her brother. "I know he feels that way, and he'll probably continue to until he works through it all, but that's why I think he can be so difficult to get to know. He feels guilty."

"And, in his guilt, he's ashamed, so he keeps people, keeps *you all*, at a distance?" Cate asked. That had not been her experience with Caleb, but she could see how it might have been the experience of these women.

"Which is why we don't let him," Jesse said.

"It's why I pop social events on him," Kit said.

"And why I have Emma call him Uncle Caleb," Jesse added.

"And why I bug him all the time to read pieces of the books I write to verify that they are reasonably accurate," Matty said.

Cate laughed. These women were doing more or less the same thing she'd done to him: taken away his opportunity to stew and build a bigger, stronger walls to keep people out. Faced with a subtle but constant barrage, eventually the wall would crumble and something new could be built.

"And you, what do you do?" Cate asked Carly.

"I don't do anything myself, but my husband, who knows a lot more about the kind of work Caleb does than I do, engages him in projects of one sort or another all the time."

"And you?" Cate turned to Vivi.

Vivi shook her head. "I'll admit, I've probably been the last to warm up to him, but that's been my issue, not his."

Cate raised her brows, which prompted Vivi to continue. "I lost my brother a few years back, so I don't have as much empathy or compassion for people who don't value their siblings as I used to."

Knowing the pain of loss, Cate couldn't help but reach out and offer what comfort she could. "I'm so sorry. I know what's it's like to lose someone."

"Unfortunately, a lot of us do," Carly said. "But we also know what it's like to find someone. Whether it's a partner or friend or new family." She added the last bit when Emma let out a huge laugh that made Jeffery giggle.

"So, while I may not have been as engaged as the others so far," Vivi continued, "I do admit he's growing on me."

"Well, if it makes you feel any better, it took him a while to grow on me, too," Kit said and they all laughed. "But, seriously," Kit's voice dropped to match her comment and she focused on Cate. "I'm not going to presume to know anything about your relationship with my brother, but I will ask that—and he'd kill me for saying this, but too bad—if you care for him at all, please don't give him any more reasons to keep people out. I know you can't promise anything, and I don't expect you to, but I hope that you will treat him well and, if you can, you'll help us help him realize that this world of friends and family isn't such a scary place."

Cate's heart hurt at hearing such sincere words spoken by a sister who obviously loved her brother very much. As much as she didn't want to dwell on it, she knew every word Kit had spoken was true. Caleb was afraid. He was afraid he would let someone down again, the way he'd thought he'd let her and Tommy down when Brooke died, the way he thought he'd let his sister down, the way he'd thought he'd let her down when Tommy died.

That guilt, that shame, was enough to pull a man down into the darkest of places.

But, like the women who surrounded her now, Cate wasn't

going to let that happen. She knew they couldn't keep the darkness at bay all the time, but she believed, that day by day, with each dinner, each gathering of friends, each smile and friendly touch, they could bring enough light into his life to sustain him until his own fire sparked enough to drive the darkness away on his own.

Cate cleared her throat and looked at Elise playing with Emma and Jeffery. "The scariest thing he'll get from us is Elise getting *hangry* enough to start world war three over a drop of spilled milk."

It was the right thing to say, bringing levity and Cate's own truth to the moment. All of the women laughed and Kit even leaned forward to give her a hug, whispering, "I'm glad you're here."

Cate closed her eyes in the embrace. "Me too."

CHAPTER 20

THE NEXT WEEK FLEW BY faster than Cate had anticipated. They hadn't made any plans but, somehow, they always had something to do. The three of them had hiked a few trails, Cate and Kit had gone to lunch several times, they'd all spent some time at Carly's new barn, and Cate and Elise had spent even more time there when Caleb had headed out to meet with Drew.

Carly's promised pony wasn't due to arrive for another ten days, so she'd also taken them down to meet Trudy and her daughter Mara—neither of whom had been able to stop by that first night at Kit's. Given that it was a relatively slow time for Trudy until the thoroughbreds in her barn started foaling in January and February, Cate and the trainer spent more than a few hours chatting and drinking coffee while Mara showed Elise all sort of things around the stables. Even though she was a few years older than Elise, Mara had taken to the young girl and had Elise trotting on a lead line by the end of the week.

Cate and Elise, and sometimes Kit, had also spent time just driving around the lovely Hudson Valley, poking around in shops, and exploring new parks while Caleb did some work. Since Elise and Emma had become fast friends, Emma had accompanied them on a few of these ambling outings as well.

One thing Cate and Caleb hadn't done during that week in Windsor was make a decision as to what they would do next. She'd thought about bringing it up, of asking him what would come next once the week was over, but couldn't bring herself to do it. She didn't want questions and doubts and long conversations. She just wanted to *be* with Caleb, and to give this thing between them, this really good thing, a solid try. And because she believed that it would be more than just something they'd "try," she was slowly gathering the courage to take Kit's advice.

When, on their second to last day there, Cate and Elise returned to the bed and breakfast from a walk in the woods with Matty and Kit, each of whom had carted one of the twins, and she saw a new sign posted at the gate, she knew it was time to take the bull by the horns.

• • •

Caleb pulled into the parking lot of the bed and breakfast and switched off his Range Rover's engine. He stared into the darkness for a long moment, thinking about what he was about to do. If it was a mistake, he could fix it, he could change it, but it had been a long time since he'd put as much hope into a plan as he had in this one.

Pulling on his hat and scarf, he exited the car and made his way to his guest room. Sliding the key into the lock, he opened the door to silence. An unusual silence. At this time in the evening, Elise was usually chattering away, getting ready for dinner.

"Cate? Elise?" he called, his heart climbing even farther into his throat. What if they'd left? He hadn't given Cate any real reason to stay, not yet. What if she'd just left? He knew, intellectually, that she wasn't the type of person to just up and go, but, when it came to Cate, he was quickly learning to get comfortable with the occasional dissonance between his emotions and logic.

"I'm here," Cate said, coming toward him through the open doorway between the two rooms.

"Is everything okay? Where's Elise?" He didn't like how pale she looked. "Cate?"

She smiled, took is hand, and pulled him over to the small sofa in front of the fireplace. "She's fine. I asked Jesse and David to take her for the night."

He didn't quite know what to make of that.

"We need to talk," she said.

As they sat down, his eyes shot to hers. He hated the nervous look he saw. His heart started to pound against his ribs and he felt something like panic begin to course through his system. In an effort to stop her from taking things where he was sure she was taking them, he began speaking without giving her a chance.

"I know we haven't talked about what happens now or what happens next. Honestly, Cate, I don't know the answer to that. I've never really had a relationship before. Not one like this. But even though I don't have a crystal ball, I don't want to be without you. Drew has offered me a job at the training facility he's building. When it's active and he has trainees there, the hours will probably be irregular, but I'll have lots of days where I won't work at all, and I won't travel as much or really do the kind of work I used to do at all. I can come live down in Florida, if you're okay with that, and we can see where things go. Then, when Drew needs me, I can just fly up here, work a week or two, then come back to you and Elise. I want to make this work, Cate. More than anything I want to make this work."

His last sentence felt more like an admission to himself than anything he had intended to say to her, but everything he had said was the truth. She wasn't responding, though. She just sat there, staring at him, and the doubts and questions and even fears he'd put aside came clawing back. "Unless, of course, that's not what you want," he somehow managed to say.

"No," she said, shaking her head. "No, no, no."

His heart pretty much stopped. "No, it's not what you want?"

She drew back and looked at him. Then smiled and launched herself into his arms. He caught her, barely, and, still confused, held on as she buried her face in his neck.

"Uh, Cate?"

Her grip around his neck loosened but she barely moved. "No, I don't want you to come to Florida for me and Elise."

She *sounded* happy, but those words did not sound like happy words to him. "Okay, I won't visit you in Florida. Does that mean you want me to visit you somewhere else?"

"Yes. No. I mean, yes."

He pulled her off his chest and set her just far enough back on his lap to look into her eyes. "You're killing me here, Cate. What do you want?"

She was still smiling. "I just bought this bed and breakfast, Caleb."

One breath, two breaths. "You what?"

"I came back today and it had a for-sale sign up. It just went on the market today and I bought it. I want to be with you, Caleb, and your family is here. Not just your sister, but Garret and all the others, too. Elise starts kindergarten next year and I wanted to find a way to keep doing what I love to do, planning events, but not have to travel so much. So, when I saw the sign, I just took it as, well, a sign." She rolled her eyes, still smiling brightly. "I've already talked to Margaret, who was planning to retire from the company within the year, and she agreed to come be our cook, and there is a house on the property where we can live. I mean, it's probably too early for us to live together, but Elise and I can live there until, well, until you and I feel like it's the right time, and if we get to that time, then there will be plenty of room for all of us—"

He stopped her babbling by covering her mouth with his. Never had he felt so grateful to have someone like her in his life, and he intended to never let either of them forget it.

When kissing her wasn't enough, he pulled back and rested his forehead against hers and held her gaze. "Thank you."

She gave him an impish little smile.

"So, just to be clear: you're going to move here and run this bed and breakfast and host all sorts of fancy events and Elise will go to school with Emma next fall and I'll work with Drew on his projects and we'll see where things go?"

She bit her lip and nodded.

"And this feels good to you? Like the right decision for you and Elise?"

Again, she nodded.

A strong sense of calm washed through his body. This decisions that they'd each made to be together were the right ones. The certainty he felt swept away any lingering doubts. He smiled at her as he slipped a hand under the back of her shirt and pressed her against him. "You have no idea how glad I am to hear that."

She smiled against his lips, even as he kissed her. "Is that right?"

"Hmm." He trailed kisses down her neck, and as her throaty chuckle vibrated against his lips, he felt it all the way to his soul.

"I think you should show me, then."

She shrieked in surprise when he lunged to his feet, swooping her up and taking her with him.

He walked to the bed and very gently laid her down, following her with his own body. "It would be my great pleasure."

ACKNOWLEDGMENTS

A LOT HAS HAPPENED SINCE my last book was published, including obtaining a new publishing partner. Thank you to EverAfter Romance for entering into this partnership and I'm looking forward to working with you to bring my readers more of the Windsor Series. Though some things have changed, other haven't; thank you to Sarah C and Angeli, your constancy in my life gives me more joy and strength than you know and I'm looking forward to our next getaway. And of course, my books wouldn't be the same without my editor, Julie Molinari.

I also want to thank Michael Angiulo for walking me through the differences between rifles and shotguns and handguns and all the other myriad weapons we discussed—Edith's injury wouldn't have been the same without your input (and to be clear, any mistakes are mine and mine alone). I also hope you like your namesake character—like you, he's a family man, committed to his partner, to being a good man, and to having some (or a lot) of fun along the way.

Last I'd like to thank Cate Takemori who encouraged me to write Caleb's story (and by "encouraged," I mean "demanded." There might have been a bribe of wine in there too). In all seriousness, Cate, I couldn't have picked a better namesake; the grace you show through your humor and intelligence is truly humbling

CPSIA information can be obtained
at www.ICGtesting.com
Printed in the USA
BVOW03s2111170917
494990BV00035B/94/P